SPRING CLEANING

ALSO BY ANTONIO MANZINI

Black Run

Adam's Rib

Out of Season

SPRING CLEANING

A Novel

Translated from the Italian
by Antony Shugaar

ANTONIO MANZINI

HARPER

NEW YORK • LONDON • TORONTO • SYDNEY

HARPER

Originally published as *Era di maggio* in Italy, in 2015, by Sellerio Editore, Palermo.

FIRST U.S. EDITION PUBLISHED 2019.

Library of Congress Cataloging-in-Publication Data has been applied for.

ISBN 978-0-06-269652-6 (pbk.)

19 20 21 22 23 LSC 10 9 8 7 6 5 4 3 2 1

To Mamma and Papà

A man alone,
In the privacy of his room.
With all his reasons why.
All his mistakes.
Alone in an empty room,
talking. To the dead.

—GIORGIO CAPRONI

CONTENTS

MONDAY

AOSTA, THE SHADOW OF THE 'NDRANGHETA LOOMS BEHIND THE LOAN SHARKS

They lent money to businessmen and private individuals at dizzying interest rates, only to move in later to seize ownership of property and bank accounts. That was the business model of Domenico "Mimmo" Cuntrera, a native of Soverato with a long criminal record, arrested by the police in the aftermath of an investigation into the murder of Cristiano Cerruti, right-hand man of local builder Pietro Berguet, the owner of Edil.ber.

In the course of a press conference, Police Chief Andrea Costa declared: "We went straight to the core of the organization, thanks to the wide-ranging and thorough investigations carried out by my men, but I can't add anything more because we're certain that this is only the tip of the iceberg."

"There can be no question that Mafia-related organizations have been sinking their roots for years into the territory of the Valle d'Aosta, and I believe that this latest episode brought to light by the police of Aosta simply offers further evidence of that fact," commented Carabinieri General Gabriele Tosti, of the Turin Anti-Mafia Investigation Directorate.

"We're faced with a direct attack against the decent people of this country. We must redouble our determination not to abandon the businesses of this region to the malicious intent of these Mafia-related organizations," thundered Judge Baldi from the prosecutor's office.

Domenico Cuntrera, being held on suspicion of the murder of Cristiano Cerruti, was arrested at the Swiss border after hastily fleeing the Posillipo pizzeria he owns here in Aosta. In the murder suspect's possession were numerous documents now being examined by investigators. It is thought that Cuntrera is probably associated with an organized crime 'ndrina. The arrest of this man might mark the first real success of law enforcement against the forces of organized crime currently infiltrating our territory.

—GIAMPAOLO GAGLIARDI

Rocco felt a vague surge of satisfaction as he noticed that his name hadn't appeared once in that article. Still, it wasn't enough to alleviate his state of prostration. He hadn't left his residential hotel room for three days. In the past three days he hadn't once turned on his cell phone, he hadn't laid eyes on the office or his colleagues, he hadn't gone for his usual breakfast in Piazza Chanoux, he hadn't smoked a joint, he hadn't seen Anna. Aside from taking Lupa out for a walk and a pee, he remained behind closed doors in his apartment in the Vieux Aosta Residence, staring at, variously, the television set and the ceiling, as often as not finding the latter far more interesting. Lupa seemed to love this new life, which consisted of long naps on the bed next to her master, ravenous meals, and romps through the historic center of town to help digest meals. It was understandable. She'd been abandoned in the snow, where she'd wandered for days on end through forests and across fields, narrowly avoiding death countless times. To be able to curl up in the warmth of a safe haven now, on a soft and cozy goose-down blanket, without anxieties or fear of tribulation or the risk of being hit by a truck? Well, it seemed to her like a dream come true. And she luxuriated in that toasty comfort, relishing every second of that newfound safety.

Newspaper in hand, Rocco turned the page.

STILL NAMELESS: THE MURDERER OF RUE PIAVE

Still unidentified is the man who broke into the apartment of Deputy Chief Rocco Schiavone on Rue Piave on Thursday night, where he fired eight bullets from a handgun, putting an end to the life of Adele Talamonti, age 39, from Rome, a friend and confidante of the deputy police chief. According to recent revelations, she was in Aosta paying her friend the deputy chief a visit, and now the victim's body has been transferred to the capital, where it has found interment in Montecompatri, the victim's family's hometown, not far from Rome. Many unanswered questions remain, however, concerning this murder. Was she really the murderer's chosen target, or was it Dottor Schiavone, who wasn't home the night of the murder? At police headquarters, everyone's lips are sealed; at the prosecutor's office, the silence is deafening. There is a sensation in the air that in the city's offices, executive and otherwise, the wagons are being circled to protect the deputy chief, who has been stationed in Aosta since September last year. An effective policeman, he has already solved a number of important cases, not least his successful cracking of a loan-sharking ring run by organized crime. We wonder, however: Is this an investigation that warrants a wall of secrecy to keep from tipping off the culprits, or is it more of a delaying action being run by law enforcement now that one of their members is at the eye of the hurricane? If the latter were the case, we might rightly point to a corruption of the rule of law. Instead, we choose to rely on the guardians of the law, and we await further developments with our trust in the institutions of democracy unshaken.

——SANDRA BUCCELLATO

"Oh, go fuck yourself!" Rocco hurled the newspaper to the floor. "Wall of secrecy, my ass!" he shouted at the pages of newsprint scattered across the room. Who was this Sandra Buccellato? And what was she insinuating?

This was the second article that the reporter had written about the murder with that acid tone. "Adele Talamonti, age 39, from Rome" was the girlfriend of Sebastiano, his oldest and closest friend from Rome. The victim was a dear old friend who now lay buried in the cemetery of Montecompatri. What the fuck was the venom that this journalist was spreading with that article?

Here's what Sandra Buccellato ought to have written in the newspaper instead: "Dottor Schiavone! They murdered a friend of yours in your home, and for days now, instead of investigating, you've been lying around shut up indoors like a hibernating bear? What are you waiting for? Get your ass in gear and try to figure out what happened. While you're licking your wounds, that bastard is walking the streets, a free man, doing as he pleases. Get busy, Schiavone!"

The truth was that Adele had died in place of Rocco. Those eight 6.35 mm bullets that someone had fired into her body as she lay sleeping peacefully in his bed on Rue Piave had actually been meant for him. For him and him alone. Adele had been his responsibility, and now she was dead. Yet another case.

Just like Marina.

He watched as the day wilted like a flower clipped from its stem.

Someone knocked at the door. Lupa, sprawled on the unmade bed, cocked an ear. Rocco didn't move. He waited. Whoever it was knocked again.

Now they'll leave, he decided.

He heard his visitor's footsteps move off down the hallway. He drew a sigh of relief.

That pain in the ass had left, too.

He slowly sank back onto the bed, settling into the down quilt. Lupa snuggled into his armpit. Man and dog fell asleep, like a pair of shipwrecked passengers clinging together for safety.

"Caffè macchiato and a decaf!" Tatiana shouted. Corrado Pizzuti didn't move, his eyes blank as he stared at the dishwasher tray loaded with demitasse cups and cappuccino mugs waiting to be run.

"Corrado, wake up, it's seven in the evening! Caffè macchiato and a decaf!" Corrado snapped to and turned his gaze to the two customers at the counter. They were Ciro and Luca, two constables of Francavilla al Mare.

"What, did you fall asleep?" asked Ciro.

"Why don't you make an espresso for yourself? You could use it!" chimed in Luca.

Corrado busied himself at the espresso machine.

"It was a beautiful day, wasn't it, Tatiana? Bright and sunny. Why don't we go get a nice seafood dinner together this evening?" Luca had been flirting with Corrado's business partner, Tatiana, for three years now, getting nowhere. And he still hadn't figured out that the Russian woman had been married to the CPA De Lullo, a childless widower, for the past two years. "Why don't you take your wife out for a seafood dinner!" Tatiana retorted, with a courteous smile.

Corrado smiled faintly. Tatiana was always courteous. Always smiling. Always positive. Maybe that's why he had invited her to become his partner three years ago. Not because she'd invested any money: Tatiana didn't have any and couldn't raise any. But Corrado needed someone to work alongside, someone honest, someone he could trust, someone he could leave in charge of the bar if he had to go away for whatever reason. As he had the week before, when Enzo had shown up in the middle of the night to take Corrado against his will and force him to drive him all the way to Aosta. Who had given that bastard his address in Francavilla? How had Enzo found him? He was being blackmailed by that murderer, and now there was nothing he could do but obey his orders and hope and pray that Enzo would soon vanish from his life.

"What's wrong?" Tatiana whispered. Corrado smiled at her. "You seem worried."

What could he say to her? That lately every day was an endless nightmare? That he would gladly board the next flight for anywhere, anyplace at all, on the far side of the planet? Instead, all he said was "This is for you, Luca!" as he handed the espresso to the town constable.

"Well, Tatiana? Are we going to go have this seafood dinner or not?"

"Here's what you can do, Luca. Finish your espresso, take Ciro with you, and just continue your rounds. Maybe you'll be lucky and manage to write a few tickets before your shift ends!"

Ciro burst out laughing and slapped Luca on the back. "Come on, Luca, you don't have a chance!" And the two constables left the bar. Outside they crossed paths with Barbara as she strode into the Bar Derby with a thirty-two-tooth smile.

"Corrado, could you make me two pots of tea? I'll take them with me to the shop!"

"At your service!" Corrado replied with alacrity. The two proprietresses of the bookshop next door to the café intimidated him. Not because they were stern or authoritarian. Barbara and Simona sold books, and for that reason, in his eyes, they were wreathed in an aura of mystery. After all, everyone orders espressos and panini, but books? And yet the shop seemed to be thriving. As if they were two priestesses of a cult he understood nothing about, he respected them and granted their every whim. "With a lemon, like always?"

"With a lemon, like always!"

"Corrado, as soon as you're done making those teas, turn on the lights outside, it's time . . ." said Tatiana; then she gestured to the bookseller, who followed her out of the café. Tatiana wanted a word.

On the sidewalk outdoors, she lit a cigarette. She offered one to Barbara, who thanked her but declined.

"What's wrong, Tatià?"

"Corrado's acting very strange. Four days ago, he shuttered the café. He was gone for two nights. He didn't tell me why, he didn't even tell me where he had gone. Ever since he returned he's been . . . I don't know, pale and uneasy, with his head in the clouds, and he jumps at the slightest noise."

"What do you think it is?"

"I don't know. But I don't like it one bit."

They looked at the man busy heating an aluminum pitcher full of water. "Corrado had a pretty rough past in Rome. One time he told me that he can't go back there."

Barbara's eyes lit up. "What kind of past?" An inveterate reader of John le Carré and P. D. James, she glimpsed conspiracies and mysteries around every corner.

"Rough stuff, like I told you." Then she added, in an undertone: "He's even been in prison . . ."

"So what are you saying?"

"I don't know. There's something that's eating at him."

"The tea is ready!" shouted Corrado. Barbara squeezed Tatiana's arm in solidarity and went inside. The Russian woman remained outside to finish her cigarette, staring up at the sky. The sea went on driving its breakers against the beach and the rocks. Soon it would be dark. The bookseller walked past Tatiana with her two teas. "We'll talk more later," she whispered as she passed by, and then headed out toward her own shop. The Russian woman discarded her cigarette and went back into the café. Leaning against the espresso machine, Corrado was staring at the crate of fruit juices. "Here, Corrado, why don't you just go home. I can close up tonight."

"What?"

"I told you, go home. Get in bed, or lie down on a sofa and watch TV. Get some rest. After all, the day is done."

Corrado nodded. "Yes . . . yes, all right. I'm going home, then."

The woman went behind the bar. "Are you sure that you don't have a fever?"

"Huh?"

"Do you have a fever?"

"No. No, what fever are you talking about?" Corrado replied. "So, can you close up?"

"I already told you that I'd take care of it."

The man pulled his head down into his shoulders, grabbed his windbreaker off the coatrack, pulled his woolen cap out of his pocket and yanked it down on his head. "All right, see you tomorrow."

"See you tomorrow."

Tatiana stood there and watched him walk off.

THE LIGHT WAS DYING. SOON THE SEA WOULD BE NOTHING but a patch of darkness spangled with the lights of the fishing boats. He decided to go home along the beachfront esplanade so he could get some fresh air. He crossed paths with two young men jogging and a woman who was returning home from a walk with her dog. Only two cars and a ramshackle rattling scooter went past. Francavilla al Mare was a vacation town. Especially along the beachfront, most of the houses and apartments were shuttered, locked up until their rightful owners came back in the summer months. Corrado lived on a street not far off the beach, and besides him, only three families lived in his apartment house, with its two stairwells and twelve apartments.

Things just couldn't go on like this. An endless torture. He only slept a few hours a night, and they were weary, agitated, gray, dreamless hours.

All things have a start and a finish, he told himself over and over again. Why won't it ever end for me?

How much longer would he have to pay for the error of his ways? It was worse than serving a life sentence without parole. Maybe it really would be better to land in prison, he told himself. Why hadn't that policeman, six years earlier, killed him along with his accomplice? Now he found himself chained to the spot, helpless, frightened, and in the hands of a killer.

"This thing has to end!" he said to himself all in a rush, as he inserted his key into the lock of the metal gate that led into the courtyard. He went to the left, toward Staircase A. He opened the ground-floor door. His apartment was half a floor up, on the mezzanine. He turned the key just once and walked through the door. He turned on the light. He took off his hat and heavy jacket and hung them on the hooks next to the door. He drew a deep breath and walked into the kitchen. Enzo Baiocchi was sitting at the table. He was watching TV and smoking a cigarette. The windows were closed, as well as the shutters, and the room reeked of stale smoke and old coffee. He felt a tightening in the pit of his stomach.

"Welcome home," Enzo said to him.

Corrado said nothing. He opened the refrigerator, pulled out a bottle of water.

"You didn't buy any fucking groceries."

Corrado glanced briefly at Enzo out of the corner of his eye as he went to the dish rack for a glass. It would have required only a good sharp blow with that glass bottle to the back of his head, powerful and determined, and his nightmare would have been over.

"No, I didn't."

"So what am I supposed to eat tonight?"

Enzo's bleached-blond hair, stiff and dry, looked like frayed rope. The man put out his cigarette in his espresso cup.

"You could have brought a couple of panini from the bar . . . a sweet bun . . . goddamn you!"

"It didn't occur to me."

"I'm going to go out to dinner in Pescara tonight. Give me a fifty-euro bill."

Corrado finished pouring the water in his glass. He drank. He set the glass down in the sink. "No," he said.

"No what?"

"I'm not giving you a penny, Enzo. I'm fucking sick and tired of this."

Baiocchi turned slowly to look at him. "What are you saying?"

"I'm saying that you've been here for three days. You wanted me to take you to Aosta, I did, now each of us can go his own way." Even he had no idea where he had scraped up the gumption. But he'd said it. "How much longer do you need to stay here?"

Enzo rose slowly from the chair. "As long as I want. Don't you think of busting my balls. And you know why?"

Corrado shook his head. Enzo stuck his hand in his pocket. He pulled out a receipt. "Take a look at what I found in the pocket of your jacket. You're an asshole!" And he held it out in front of his eyes. "You see that? You know what it is? It's got your full name on it, first and last, and the name of the hotel in Pont-Saint-Martin where you slept, and you even gave them your ID." He smiled, baring his yellow teeth. "Asshole! This is all anyone needs, more than enough. Just remember, Corrà, if I go down, you're coming down with me."

Corrado darted away from the sink. "Why don't you go back to Rome and leave me in peace?"

"I'll go back, don't worry, I'll go back. Once things have calmed down. Why, what do you know about it?"

"What do I know about it? Hell, what do *you* know about it!" Corrado shouted. "You even fucked up. Instead of shooting that cop, you shot some poor girl who had nothing to do with it! You're blind as a bat!"

Enzo didn't move. He stared at Corrado, expressionless.

"It must be a problem with your family, Enzo! You and your brother, Luigi, both always seem to miss the target!"

Enzo lunged and was on him in a flash. He slammed Corrado against the wall. A knife had suddenly materialized in his hands. He pointed it at Corrado's throat. "Watch what you say, you piece of shit! Don't you dare mention my brother, ever!" The tip of the knife carved into the flesh of Corrado's neck. Corrado opened his mouth and shut his eyes. A drop of blood rolled down the steel blade. "Just remember! If I go down, you're coming down with me." The bandit released his grip and rapidly put the knife away in his pocket. "Shave and take a shower, you reek of grease."

TUESDAY

At police headquarters, things went on as usual, even without Rocco. Officer Casella was on duty at the front entrance, Deruta and D'Intino were struggling to deal with a lost ID or two, Deputy Inspector Caterina Rispoli was on the telephone in the little ground-floor office, Antonio Scipioni was busy taking crime reports. Italo Pierron seemed to be the only one who missed his boss. Standing in the doorway, he was looking into Rocco's empty office. The desk, the locked window, the bookshelf with the books of law that had never been cracked, the crucifix on the wall, the photo of the president of Italy, and the calendar. He only happened to notice it for the first time on that sunshiny spring day. The calendar was stuck at the eighth of September of the year before, the day that Rocco had first begun duty at Aosta police headquarters. The deputy chief had never so much as looked at the calendar. Many were the times that he'd told Italo that as far as he was concerned, each day had been like any other for years now. And aside from whether it was hot or cold, he couldn't detect any other substantial differences.

"What do you have under your arm?"

Italo whipped around. Standing in the middle of the hallway was Caterina.

"Nothing, I was just taking a look at the office." He glanced down at the construction paper that he had rolled up in a tube. "Oh, you mean this? It's just something I wanted to hang up. Sort of a joke."

Caterina pointed at the roll, her curiosity piqued. "Well, what is it?"

"You'll see in just a minute." He walked over to the wall next to the deputy chief's office door. He unrolled the construction paper; then he pulled a pack of colorful thumbtacks out of his shirt pocket. He had a hammer tucked into his belt. He tapped the tacks into the construction paper on the wall. Then he stepped back to admire his work. "What do you say, is it straight?"

Caterina studied it. "Yes. I think it is. But what is it?" And she stepped closer and started reading.

Italo had divided the sheet of construction paper into five large rectangles that represented a ranking of Rocco Schiavone's multiple pains in the ass, from sixth to tenth degree. By now everyone in the office was familiar with that list. It rose from sixth ranking, an array of milder annoyances, all the way to the top, tenth degree, where the very worst pain in the ass of them all perched solitary and cruel: an open case.

Caterina broke out laughing. "So you know them all?"

"The ones I know I wrote down here. Then, as we go along, we'll come up with others, and we can keep adding them until we've devised a complete overall view of the matter."

"Have you tried calling him?"

"He won't answer my calls. He won't answer anybody's calls."

"Did you try swinging by his apartment on Rue Piave?"

"They've removed the seals," said Italo. "Among other things, I left him a note from the chief of police. He says that he's found him an apartment on Via Laurent Cerise. Only Rocco would at least have to go take a look at the place."

"Don't worry. Lately, it's not as if apartments have been going like fresh bread," Caterina replied. "Speaking of bread, Deruta is asking if he can have time off, because apparently he needs to help his wife out at her bakery." Caterina headed off down the hallway.

"Caterina? You do remember that tomorrow night we're going to my aunt's house for dinner, right?"

Without turning around, Caterina replied, "Tomorrow night I have yoga!" and rolled her eyes. She thought back to the deputy chief's list of pains in the ass. Maybe she should draw up a list of her own, and she would definitely put dinners with relatives at the ninth degree.

SPRAWLED IN HIS BED, ROCCO WAS LOOKING AT THE FACING wall. He had fixated on a stain in the uppermost corner. A gray patch. It looked like Great Britain. Or the silhouette of a bearded man laughing. Lupa's tail swished through the air. The dog pricked up her ears and raised her muzzle. Three seconds later someone knocked at the door.

"Dottore? Dottore? Everything okay?"

It was the voice of the doorman in the residential hotel.

"Dottore, there's a visitor to see you. Could you please open the door? Answer me!"

He had to answer now. He got up and dragged himself over to the door. He turned the key and opened it.

The doorman was accompanied by an enormous man. Rocco recognized him: the deputy chief of the Turin mobile squad, Carlo Pietra, deployed to Aosta since Rocco had shut himself up in that residential hotel room.

The deputy chief threw the door open wide. "Come on in . . ." he said. Pietra barely cracked a smile, stepped past the concierge, and walked into the room.

"Do you need anything?"

Schiavone said nothing. He limited himself to shutting the door.

"How's it going?"

"Well, it's going."

Carlo Pietra was like a human sphere who seemed to fill up the 325 square feet of the room all by himself. He had cheerful, light-blue eyes; he wore a sparse beard and long hair. "May I?" he asked Rocco, pointing to the only armchair in the one-room studio.

"Why of course, make yourself comfortable."

He sat down, making the armchair creak. He looked at the deputy chief, his growth of whiskers from the last several days, his unkempt hair. Then he opened the binder that he had been holding on his knees and stuck his face into it. "Certainly, it's depressing in here," he observed as he leafed through the various documents.

"It's not as if things are that much nicer at my old place." Rocco opened the little fridge. "Want anything to drink? Let's see . . . I've got a Coke, some fruit juices, and three mini bottles of some brand of whiskey I've never heard of."

"No, thanks."

"Otherwise, I can make you a cup of coffee with a filter pack. It's better than you'd think."

"No, no, nothing for me. I'm going out to dinner at a trattoria and I want to have plenty of room." And he smacked himself three times on his ample belly.

Rocco went over to the galley kitchen in the corner. Actually, he felt like a coffee. "Well then, Dottor Pietra, tell me everything."

Pietra pulled out a handkerchief and blew his nose. "Listen, let's do one thing before we start getting tangled up with formalities?"

"Certainly."

"Can we use the informal? Be on a first-name basis?"

"That would be better." The deputy chief pressed a button, and the espresso immediately began tumbling out of the coffee maker and into the porcelain demitasse cup.

"So, in that case, Rocco, do you feel like going over the situation quickly?"

"Let's go." Rocco picked up the espresso and went back to sit on the bed. Lupa had fallen asleep again.

"First of all, do you have any idea of who might have entered your apartment on Thursday, May 10, and shot . . ." Pietra hesitated as he leafed through the pages in the binder.

"Adele Talamonti," said Rocco. "That's right. Adele Talamonti was at my home. She was the girlfriend of a close friend of mine, Sebastiano. She'd come up here to lie low, a maneuver that was meant to force Sebastiano to lose his mind trying to find her. Yes, I know . . ." Rocco said, anticipating Pietra's skeptical glance, "complete bullshit, but what she was hoping to do was rekindle her boyfriend's passion and interest. Anyway, the killer assumed that the shape in that bed was me, and he shot her."

Pietra nodded. "So that means you don't have the foggiest idea who it could have been?"

"Not the foggiest."

Carlo scratched his head. "Listen, Rocco, I've read a few things about you. And let's just say that . . . at first glance, I'd say that you have a pretty messed-up past."

"'Messed-up' is a euphemism, Carlo."

"Which means that, even if it's no easy matter to go dig into it, you must have some suspicions."

Rocco shook his head. "No. I really don't. All I know is that whoever tried to kill me is bound to try again."

Carlo Pietra looked around the room. "And you're waiting for them here?"

"No. I'm here because I don't have a place to live anymore. As soon as I find a new place, I'll move. Especially for her"—and he pointed at Lupa. "She's a little cramped in here."

Pietra seemed to notice the dog for the first time. "I don't know about that. I prefer cats." The deputy chief of the mobile squad hoisted his oversized body off the chair. "All right, then, I'm going to call on the police chief. I'll hand over all the documentation I have, and then I'm heading back to Turin. There's nothing else for me to do here. When are you returning to active duty?"

"I still have some vacation time to use up."

"And you're going to use it up here?"

"I don't feel like going anywhere."

"It's been a pleasure." Pietra extended his hand and shook Rocco's. "How do you like being in Aosta?"

The deputy chief thought it over for a few seconds. "Have a safe trip."

IT WAS MASSIMO, HIS FRIEND FROM VITERBO, WHO HAD given him a recommendation of the best dog food for Lupa. You could rely on Massimo. He bred Lagotto Romagnolo dogs for truffle hunting and he trained them like soldiers. So Rocco had taken a picture of his puppy and texted it to his friend. Massimo replied: "My good friend Rocco, it's hard to tell the breed. At a glance, I see three: setter, Brittany, and a shepherd of some kind. Anyway, she's a beauty, hold on to her." He picked up the dog food bowl, all the food eaten now, and placed it in the sink of the galley kitchen. Then he picked the newspaper up off the floor to crumple it up and throw it away. His eye landed on the article by Buccellato:

> We wonder, however: Is this an investigation that warrants a wall of secrecy to keep from tipping off the culprits, or is it more of a delaying action being run by law enforcement now that one of their members is at the eye of the hurricane?

He crushed the newsprint into a ball and hurled it into the trash can.

"I HAVE 7 DOWN, 'AIMLESS, MEANINGLESS,' ELEVEN LETTERS."

Marina is sitting on the bed, next to Lupa. She's petting the puppy with her right hand. In her left hand, she's holding La Settimana Enigmistica, *the weekly puzzler magazine.*

"'Vague'?"

"Hold on, it starts with p *and ends with* s.*"*

"'Pointless'?"

"Rocco, I said it has eleven letters."

Eleven letters . . .

"It's pretty ugly in here . . ."

"Yes, it is."

"Oh, Lord, it's not like Rue Piave was much to look at, either."

"True enough," I answer her.

"You need to find yourself a place."

"It's useless." Then I stop to think. "'Useless'?"

"What?"

"The answer for the crossword puzzle. Is 'useless' the answer?"

"Rocco, that's seven letters and it starts with u. *I said eleven letters and it starts with* p. *Hold on, let me solve 12 across . . . 'Receive an offering' . . . That's easy, 'accept' . . . 'The fictional grimoire by Abdul Alhazred' . . ."*

"By who?"

"The Necronomicon.*"*

"How on earth do you know these things?"

"I just do. And that means that 7 down was . . . 'purposeless'!"

"'Purposeless'?"

"Exactly."

I look at her. "Are you mad at me?" Obviously, she's mad at me. One thing is certain. My wife always reels off strings of words as big as Saturn's rings, but by now I'm used to that. "Are you mad at me? Then why don't you just go ahead and tell me so, directly?"

She sets down the magazine, gives Lupa a kiss on the muzzle, and heads off to the bathroom. She stops in the doorway. She looks back at me with her enormous eyes—"Do something, for Christ's sake!"—and vanishes through the door.

THERE THEY WERE, MILLING ABOUT, MUTTERING UNDER THEIR breath. Donkeys. Only donkeys walk in circles and turn millstones. These tattered remnants of men did nothing but wear out shoe leather and the grass in the courtyard.

"All done, everyone inside!" shouted a young guard with a wispy beard and his skin still speckled with acne. Agostino, a.k.a. the Professor, stood up, followed by Oluwafeme, the Nigerian giant, and Erik the Red. Another fucked-up day, the umpteenth fucked-up day. He slowly walked through the door that led into the staircase of Wing 2 of the house of detention of Varallo. He greeted the bald prison guard with a grin and started up the steps. He didn't even notice the glances of respect from the other convicts. Or the requests for summary justice brought to him with trembling hands during social interaction hour, when the cell doors were left open and you could wander around the prison wing, collecting cigarettes and debts. Those prison walls were starting to nauseate him. He needed a change; he needed a transfer. Fresh air, new surroundings, a new life, new people to subjugate. Two convicts he'd like to take with him were Oluwafeme and Erik, competent, loyal, and, above all, dangerous. Plus, Erik was a fabulous cook. "What are we having for dinner?" he asked him as they filed through the last door before the corridor of the prison wing.

"Tonight, I'll make you pasta alla carbonara. And chicken breast with lemon."

Agostino nodded. "Will there be olives in the chicken?"

"Of course there will, Professor!"

He exchanged handshakes with a couple of convicts who'd extended their arms to him, and then, finally, he walked into his cell. The only bed that wasn't part of a bunk bed was his. He immediately noticed that someone had moved his pillow. The sheet was folded wrong. He slipped his hand under the blankets and pulled out a note, a sheet of paper torn from a graph paper notebook.

"Tomorrow!" it read.

Agostino looked at Erik and the Nigerian. Then he popped the piece of paper into his mouth and began chewing.

"What's that?" Erik asked him.

"The antipasto . . ."

"Colombo Police Station, go ahead."

"Put me through to De Silvestri."

"Who's speaking?"

"Deputy Chief Schiavone."

He held the line. His old police station in Rome, where he'd worked for years and where De Silvestri was still on duty, the senior officer who had watched him enter the police force, a man with the memory of a computer and the intelligence of a Nobel laureate. With the receiver of his cordless phone in one hand, he looked out the window. Gray and damp. It was threatening to rain from one moment to the next. But the glass of the windowpanes wasn't fogged over, a sign that the outdoor temperature was finally catching up with the spring.

"Dottore? What's happened?" De Silvestri began in his rheumy voice.

"You heard about it?"

"By pure chance, on the regional news broadcast. Someone had it in for you, didn't they?"

"Yes. I need some help, Alfredo."

"Anything I can do."

"Anyone who's been released recently?"

"What do you mean by 'anyone'?"

"Anyone I might have put behind bars. I don't know, anyone who might have it in for me?"

He heard the officer breathing. "Dottor Schiavone, are you asking me to reprint the yellow pages?"

"Okay, but forget about the little stuff. Misdemeanor thefts, cases of fraud, that kind of bullshit. Focus on the heavy stuff."

"How long do I have?"

"As long as you need."

"I'll call you back."

Rocco ended the call. He'd suddenly felt a pang of hunger. He woke up Lupa.

"Shall we go out?"

"Can I go up and see Chiara?" asked Max.

"All right, but don't stay long, all right? She's still very tired," said Giuliana Berguet.

Max smiled with his perfect teeth, swept back his head of long blond hair, and climbed the stairs that led from the living room to the bedrooms. He hadn't seen his girlfriend in days. He'd never once gone to the hospital to see her. Hospitals freaked Max out. All it took was a glance from a sick person and he started to feel each and every malady afflicting him. An amputated leg, a heart attack, appendicitis, there wasn't a single pathology that would fail to infect the young man like a bad smell wafting into his nostrils.

He had texted her dozens of times, but Chiara had always replied with brief phrases and broken words: "I'm fine," "we'll see each other soon," "don't come to the hospital," "say hi to everyone at school." Then there was that thing with Filippa. It hadn't been his fault—she'd practically thrown a half nelson on him—but he was dating Chiara. He'd tried talking to his father about it—Dr. Turrini, the head physician at the hospital. But his father had just given him a grin and said: "Max, you're twenty years old, you're handsome, you're healthy. Fuck her and don't give it a second thought. You can think about more serious things when the time comes." Sure, more serious things. But he couldn't pull a dirty move like that on Chiara after everything she'd been through. Kidnapped! Max couldn't bring himself to think about it. She'd languished for days, her head in a hood, in a freezing garage, abandoned in the mountains, without food or water. The two guys who had taken her and then had been killed in a crash? He'd even met them. He'd also sold them an entire package of Stilnox that he'd stolen from his father's medicine cabinet. And he knew exactly what Stilnox was good for: making someone helpless. A rape drug. You give it to a girl and then you can fuck her—she won't even remember. Is that what they'd done to Chiara? Had they raped her? And did that make him responsible? Was it his fault? But if he hadn't sold the pharmaceuticals to those two sons of bitches, someone else would have done it instead.

Before knocking on the bedroom door, he focused on a single thought: Careful what you say, Max! Don't fuck up!

He knocked. There was no answer. He slowly opened the door. "Chiara? Chiara, it's me, Max . . ."

The girl was stretched out on the bed, fully clothed. She had a blanket over her and was looking out the window. Her feet were tucked into a pair of colorful thick woolen socks, and they poked out from under the blanket. Slowly she turned her head. As soon as she saw the boy, a smile flickered onto her face and then faded out immediately. "Ciao."

"Ciao." Max shut the door and went to sit at the foot of the bed. "How's it going?"

Chiara shrugged. "Fine. How about you?"

"Fine." He looked at her.

Her hair was messy; there were circles under her eyes. "I missed you," he told her. "How do you feel?"

"Tired."

"When are you coming back to school?"

"I don't know. For now, I can't think of it."

Max sighed. "Can you get some sleep, at least?"

"No."

"How's your leg?"

During her imprisonment in the cellar at an elevation of three thousand feet above sea level, Chiara had injured her leg, and the wound had become infected. She needed a crutch to walk, but the doctor was optimistic. "Listen, would you stop peppering me with questions the way the journalists do?"

Max lowered his head. He was just trying to inquire about his girlfriend's state of health. Chiara turned back to look out the window. "I don't think I'll ever be better."

"Why do you say that? They stitched up the wound!"

God, what an idiot, Chiara thought to herself. A handsome cretin. "I'm not talking about the leg, Max. I relive it in my dreams every night. Every night I'm tied to that chair, with the hood over my head. All alone. And outside it's raining, it's snowing, and I'm all alone. Without water to drink . . ."

"But the two guys that kidnapped you are dead now, Chiara. Now no one can hurt you again, you know that?"

The girl whipped her head around and looked Max in the eyes. "How do you know? Are you certain?" She furrowed her brow. "Have you noticed? I turned nineteen and didn't even have a party. Because I don't want to have anyone else looking at me the way you're looking at me now." A tear streamed down from her eye; both eyes were shut tight. "That poor girl who was kidnapped and . . . who knows what else they did to her!"

"Chiara, I don't—"

"Are they talking about me at school? And what are they saying?"

"That they want to see you again."

Chiara softened her tone. "How are you, Max?"

"Okay, I guess. Things are horrible at home."

"How so?"

Max looked down at his hands. He continued rubbing them against each other. "Lots of things aren't going well, Papà and Mamma are . . . I don't know what. I can't take it at home anymore."

Chiara heaved a sigh of annoyance. "Then just leave. You have plenty of money."

"You think it hasn't occurred to me? But until I finish school, I don't get a penny . . ."

At last Chiara smiled. "I love you, Max. I really do. But you have to promise me something."

"Of course."

"Don't come back to see me again."

Max opened his eyes wide. "But . . ."

"Go to school, go with your friends, but don't think about me again. Chiara Berguet no longer exists."

"Why not?"

"If I knew, I'd tell you. But I don't know. I really don't know . . ."

"Won't you even give me a kiss?"

"I'm sorry, Max, just let me sleep. I'm so tired . . ."

DOWNSTAIRS, JUDGE BALDI, SITTING IN THE EXCEEDINGLY luxurious living room in the Berguet home, was stirring his espresso, tiny spoon tinkling against the porcelain of the demitasse cup that the housekeeper, Dolores, had just brought him from the kitchen. Pietro and Giuliana were eyeing him.

"I'm happy to see you looking well, Signora Berguet," said Baldi.

"Yes, thanks, at last I'm getting some sleep."

Then the judge turned to look at Pietro. Unlike his wife, he was pale, he couldn't seem to keep his hands still, and he was lighting one cigarette after another.

"All right, then, I'm here to get something straight. Your company was in the running for a contract with the regional government. Right?"

The judge had touched a nerve. Pietro's face had gone from pale to bright red. "They eliminated us!" he exploded. "They kicked us out of the competition! Mafia infiltration, they say. Do you understand, Dottor Baldi? My daughter kidnapped by that . . . that bastard

Cuntrera and then *I'm* the Mafioso? I tried to explain it to the commission. Those pieces of shit blackmailed us!"

"Pietro!" his wife exclaimed. But Pietro wasn't listening to her. "And now Edil.ber is a 'company at risk of Mafia infiltration'!?"

"And what did they say to you?"

"They told me: 'Don't forget about Cerruti, your right-hand man . . . he was a member of that organization' . . ." Pietro Berguet lunged to his feet from the sofa where he'd been sitting. "And they have a point, Dottor Baldi. They have a thousand points! Cristiano was in it up to his neck, my own right-hand man, and what could I say? There *was* Mafia infiltration, and how."

Baldi sipped his espresso. "I understand that the company that won the competition is called—"

Pietro beat him to it: "Architettura Futura. They're young, they only went into business a couple of years ago." He went to the window. "They've never won a contract this size before, though."

"Do you mind if I ask what's involved?"

"A new wing of a hospital and two medical clinics, in Cervinia and in Saint-Vincent."

"How much money are we talking about?"

"A lot, Dottore. A lot."

"Now what are you going to do?"

"I'll try to file an appeal. But I'm sure I'll just waste a lot of money on lawyers."

"This Architettura Futura . . . who's the owner?"

"Luca Grange."

"Of Aosta?"

"Of Pont-Saint-Martin."

The door to the living room swung open and Max appeared. The boy had a sad demeanor, like a dog that's been beaten.

"Hi . . ." he said, as if under his breath.

Giuliana smiled at him. "Dottor Baldi, this is Max . . . Chiara's boyfriend."

"Yes, yes, I know him. And I know his mother very well, too. How's it going, Max?"

"Just so-so . . ."

"Did you say hello to Chiara?" asked Giuliana.

"Yes. Well, thanks and excuse me. See you soon."

"Actually, if you make sure we don't ever see you again, you'd be doing me a favor!" Dottor Berguet suddenly shouted.

"Pietro!" Giuliana scolded her husband, eyes wide-open in shock.

"Go back to your mother, Max, and to that asshole father of yours! And please convey to them all my very worst wishes!"

"Dottor Berguet?!"

"You know what, Baldi? The fact that it's all come to this? Well, I can thank the mother of that boy, right there . . . Go on, Max, get out of here, beat it!"

"I'm sorry . . . excuse me," the young man managed to stammer out, his eyes downcast. "I never—"

"And thank your mother for me!"

Max lowered his head and slunk out of the room with his tail between his legs. Giuliana stood up, red-faced. "Pietro, what did that poor boy have to do with anything—"

"Do you want to know who suggested I get in touch with Cuntrera in the first place? To borrow money from that piece-of-shit Mafioso? Do you want to know? That poor boy's mother! Laura Turrini, from the Vallée Savings Bank! And I'm supposed to tolerate the presence of that little shitface in my own home!" And with the arteries in his neck swelling, he turned to Baldi. "That's where you'll find the rot, Dottore. Right there, in those houses, among the Turrinis, their friends, in the elegant drawing rooms of this city."

"Dottore, please, calm down . . ."

"My ass, I'll calm down. And what do all of you do? All you're good for is . . . is coming around here, sitting on the sofa, making sad faces and saying how sorry you are?" By this point, Pietro Berguet was a river flooding over its banks. His rage had broken the levees of his good manners, and now there was no stopping him. "If you care to know, where you'll find them is at the Lions Club, or the Rotary Club, or else at the Ristorante Santalmasso, outside of Aosta, where dinner costs two hundred euros! That's where you ought to cast your lines, out there! Not sitting on my sofa, in my home, drinking my coffee and saying how sorry you are!"

"Pietro!"

"Oh, go fuck yourself!" And after giving the sofa a swift kick, he stormed out of the living room.

Giuliana and Baldi sat in silence. The woman was the first to speak: "Please excuse him, Dottor Baldi. He didn't mean to insult you."

"Don't worry . . . these things happen. But rather, tell me," the judge went on, changing the subject, "do Chiara's friends come to see her?"

Someone in the house slammed a door.

Giuliana sat down again. "To tell the truth, she receives more phone calls from journalists than from her classmates."

Baldi set down his demitasse on the glass coffee table. "Have you considered psychological counseling?"

"She won't hear of it."

"You ought to insist."

"We'll try. Listen, my husband and I have never had a chance to thank you and the people at police headquarters for everything you did for us . . ."

With a brisk wave of the hand, the judge put a halt to Giuliana Berguet's saccharine serenade. "Please. I'm not here to get thank-yous. And in any case the only person you ought to thank is Dottor Schiavone. If it hadn't been for him, there's a good chance that Chiara would no longer be among the living."

"We wish we could, but we can't get in touch with him at police headquarters. Nobody seems to know how to find him."

"You don't have to tell me!"

THE DEPUTY CHIEF WAS WATCHING A POLITICAL TALK SHOW. With the sound off. The guests on the panel looked like so many fish in an aquarium. Their mouths were opening and closing. Their teeth were almost constantly bared. But the thing that interested him most was the eyes. Totally dystonic with respect to the mouths. The wider open the mouths, the deader the eyes. He watched, cataloguing the fish in that aquarium: The woman with her legs crossed and her face ravaged by the efforts of some plastic surgeon was a moray eel. The little fat man with a triple chin and thinning hair was a puffer fish. The bespectacled member of parliament was a clown fish. Then a sudden rustling noise interrupted his string of fantasies. Someone was slipping a piece of paper underneath his door. Rocco got up from the bed, bent down, and picked it up. The doorman of the residential hotel was informing him that Anna had tried to get in touch with him six separate times, and asking him please to call her back.

Calling Anna back was out of the question. He didn't have the energy to spend an evening with her, eating culinary concoctions and spouting bullshit. He didn't even feel any yearning for her lips, no urge to sleep with her. He'd never been able to fall asleep with his arms around any woman but Marina. With her, he could easily spend the whole night tangled up with her limbs, never once shifting position, moving arms or legs, lulled by her respiration into a sleep where he would chase after her in his dreams.

His phone rang.

"What the fuck!" He picked up the receiver without thinking. "Schiavone here . . ."

"A call for you from Rome," said the chilly voice of the receptionist downstairs. "By the way, I didn't want to bother you, but I did slide a message under the door."

"Yes, I saw that, thanks. Please go ahead and put the call through . . ." A few moments later, the voice of his old friend Officer Alfredo De Silvestri rang out from the phone.

"Dottore, it's De Silvestri."

"Do you already have something for me?"

"Yes . . ."

"Then let me put you on speaker, that way I can take notes while we talk. If I try to use my shoulder to press the receiver against my ear, I get a crick in my neck." Rocco pushed the button and went over to sit at the little desk facing the window. There he had a notepad and a couple of pens. "Go right ahead, Alfredo. I'm ready."

"All right, then, let's get started." De Silvestri's voice filled the room in the residential hotel. "I skipped everyone who, as you instructed me, sir, had anything to do with small-time capers, thefts, fraud, and other two-bit offenses. I'd start with Antonio Biga. Do you recall the name?"

"Vaguely."

"Back in 2004. He did eight years for armed robbery and—"

"Oh, yes, right, right, of course. Antonio Biga . . ."

"Antonio got out three months ago. Last known address is Viale Massaia 85. At the Garbatella."

"Anything else?"

"Certainly. Number two. Stefania Zaccaria. You put her behind bars for pandering in 2006. She got out last year."

"Stefania Zaccaria. A little short thing?"

"Yes, it says here she's five foot two."

"It could very well have been her. She's half a lunatic. She might not have come all the way up here herself, but she could easily have found some loser willing to do a piece-of-shit job like that. I'm making a note. Stefania Zaccaria. And then, what do you think about Fabio Zuccari?"

"Yes, of course, he's the first one I thought of myself. He's in the hospital. He's got cancer and it's eating him alive. Then there are the two Gentili brothers and of course Walter Cremonesi."

The Gentili brothers held the current record for burglary, having ransacked seven apartments in a single day. Walter Cremonesi, on the other hand, was a diehard. He first entered Italy's prison system in 1976 for membership in an armed gang, a renegade militant of the extreme right. Armed robberies, murders—he treated Rebibbia prison as if it were a revolving door to a supermarket. The last time, Rocco had nailed him for armed robbery and murder. "Where are the Gentili brothers?"

"Apparently in Costa Rica. They've opened a restaurant. I'd rule them out, Dottore."

"And Walter Cremonesi? Why isn't he still behind bars?"

"You're asking me? Good conduct. It seems as if, once they're in prison, these people are magically transformed into lay sisters who go to church every Sunday to say confession."

"He seems like a good candidate. How old is he now?"

De Silvestri did some quick calculations. "He'll be fifty-eight next month."

"Let's not forget to wish him happy birthday."

"Nobody's heard anything from him in years. They thought he was in Paris. In any case, no one else occurs to me for now."

"Call me the minute you hear anything new."

"You can count on it."

He looked down at his notepad. He'd only marked down two names: Antonio Biga and Stefania Zaccaria. He underlined them three times.

The time had come to catch a plane to the capital.

"Caterina? It's me, Rocco . . ."

"Dottore! How nice to hear your voice, sir. We've been missing you!"

"Don't tell lies. You're no good at it. Listen, I need a favor . . ."

"I imagine it has something to do with Lupa, am I right?"

"Exactly. Will you keep her for me?"

"I'll swing by to pick her up tomorrow morning."

Too bad, thought Rocco. He would have preferred that same evening.

"Thanks, Caterì. Till tomorrow."

"See you tomorrow, Dottore."

"Caterì, help me remember something. Weren't we on a first-name basis now?"

There was a brief pause. Then Caterina smiled, or at least that's what Rocco imagined. "Till tomorrow, Rocco."

The deputy chief felt a stirring in his loins.

Maybe he was coming back to life.

WEDNESDAY

"Taxi . . . taxi . . . do you need a taxi?"

At the arrivals level at Fiumicino Airport, there was a crowd of men with prominent bellies approaching passengers and whispering that magic word: "Taxi . . ."

Rocco said nothing. He was striding briskly toward the parking lot for medallion taxis. It wasn't the act of a law-abiding citizen. It was just that the medallion cabbies had paid more than the price of an apartment for that permit, and it seemed offensive to rely on these unlicensed interlopers.

"Taxi, Dotto'? Can I take you into the city?"

"What taxi are you talking about!" snapped the deputy chief.

"Then how are you going to get home?"

Rocco planted both feet on the ground and surveyed the illegal driver. "I'm going home in my department-issued car. I'm a deputy chief of police. Now are you going to get the fuck out from underfoot, or do I have to lose my temper?"

The unlicensed interloper took two steps back, shooting glances at his colleagues, who all looked down at the ground and stopped pestering passengers for a moment. "Now you don't have to snarl at us, strictly speaking, Dotto' . . . We need to make a living, too, you know!"

"That's a matter of opinion!"

The sun was shining, but the exhaust fumes stripped away all poetry from that blue and cloudless sky. Rocco climbed into the first cab available.

"Via Poerio, please . . . number 12."

"On my way," said the cabbie, switching on his meter. "Beautiful day, eh?"

"Right. But now, all the way to Monteverde, I'd appreciate a little silence. Nothing about soccer, A.S. Roma, S.S. Lazio, thieving politicians, the collapse of the city, it's all the Communists' fault, and all that bullshit. Thank you!"

"You don't have to add the vinegar, Dotto'. I'll be silent as a graveyard."

Getting a meeting with Antonio Biga and tracking down Stefania Zaccaria. No simple matter, either one. And most likely he would come up empty-handed. But he had to try, at least, look those people in the eye and get a whiff of their stench. Rocco felt things directly on his skin, first and foremost, and then he processed them in his *res cogitans*. There are vibrations and waves between people that are sometimes worth more than a hundred thoughts. It reminded him of his uncle's unfailing advice whenever they played cards together: "Rocco, never forget Signor Chitarrella's rule: a glance with your own eyes is always better than a hundred thoughts in your mind!"

The road from Fiumicino to Rome was jammed solid. The driver took a shortcut that would run through the Magliana quarter and take them to the Via Portuense. Filth everywhere. And colossal potholes that made the taxi lurch and jolt. It felt as if they were driving through a neighborhood in Beirut during the Lebanese civil war. He was reminded of a song by a Roman singer-songwriter who compared Rome to a bitch surrounded by swine.

"DOTTOR SCHIAVONE!" THE SHOUT OF SURPRISE ECHOED IN the stairwell. "How nice to see you again!"

"How's it going?"

"Fine. And you?"

"How do you think it's going? Tell me, though, has anyone come to see me in the past few days?"

The concierge on Via Poerio furrowed her brow and gave it a moment's thought. "No, Dottore. Aside from the usual bills, and I just always send those up to you in Aosta."

"Thanks."

"You'll find the apartment a little dirtier than usual. This week the cleaning lady didn't come. Her daughter's having a baby."

"Not a problem."

He stepped into the elevator and rode up to the top floor. To the penthouse. His home.

There was a stale, shut-up smell in the air, as he'd expected, and the furniture was draped in plastic sheeting. He didn't even glance at his apartment. He went straight to the bathroom, took a quick rinse, changed his shirt, and went back out.

BRIZIO WAS WAITING FOR HIM AT THE USUAL BAR, ON PIAZZA Santa Maria in Trastevere. They hadn't laid eyes on each other in nine months. Brizio had shaved his mustache and combed his hair with a part on one side. He could still turn women's heads, and just as reliably, Brizio turned his own head to look at them. Since he'd turned sixteen, this was the only pursuit that Brizio had ever undertaken with even a modicum of serious intent. Then he'd met Stella, and he'd calmed down somewhat.

"You've aged, Rocco."

"So have you . . ."

They hugged. "How much time do you have?"

"As much as it takes."

"How is Seba?"

"We'll see him later, with Furio. Shall we take a walk?"

"So let's take this walk."

In May, Trastevere was full of tourists and the Piazza Trilussa steps were already teeming with young people sipping beers and licking gelati. They crossed Ponte Sisto and headed for Via dei Giubbonari. The Tiber was a slow-flowing stream of liquid sewage. Seagulls glided between plane trees and the roofs of the apartment buildings. Two kids raced after each other on bicycles.

"Rocco, from the names you gave me . . . I hear Walter Cremonesi is supposed to be in Paris."

"So?"

"I say 'supposed to be' because they've lost trace of him. But why would you think he has it in for you?"

"Don't you remember? The armed robbery on Piazza Bologna?"

"Fuck, though, Rocco, that dates back to 1999!"

"True, but I still sent him to prison."

"Do you really think that thirteen years later . . . No, I'd rule that out. And after all, Cremonesi isn't a psychotic. He's a piece of shit, but what good is a vendetta to him? He's always been connected with major hitters."

Rocco nodded, none too convinced. "What do you know about Zaccaria?"

"Stefania Zaccaria? Two days ago she had a head-on collision on the Rome beltway. Now she's at Santo Spirito hospital. She has more plaster on her than skin. If she comes out of there alive, she'll go make a pilgrimage to Medjugorje."

"Two days ago . . . isn't an alibi. What's more, she could always have sent someone up to do the job. What about Antonio Biga? What's he up to?"

"I don't know. He hasn't been seen around much. People say that he'd teamed up with the Casamonica clan. But I don't know about that. He's too much of an asshole."

"Does he live in Garbatella?"

"No. His mother's there. He lives right around the corner from Piazza della Chiesa Nuova."

"Is that where you're taking me?"

"All right with you?"

In the little piazza surrounded by the narrow lanes, there was an enormous fig tree, twisted and gnarly. Rocco and Brizio walked into the café across from the building where Biga lived. The deputy chief smiled at the sight of trays of tramezzini under damp cloths. "Bring me two. Tuna and baby artichokes for one and, let's see, chicken salad for the other. And a mineral water," he said cheerfully to the young woman serving at the counter.

Then they went and sat down at the open-air tables outside.

"Are you sure he's not home?"

"For sure," Brizio replied. "The neighbor told me that he's gone out. But he'll be back soon."

The tramezzini came, along with an espresso for Brizio. Rocco bit into one of the tramezzini immediately. "Ahhh. That's right . . . This is what I've been missing."

"Why, what are you saying, don't they have tramezzini in Aosta?"

"No."

"That's crazy . . ." said Brizio, sipping his espresso.

"It sure is, but they make plenty of good things up there, though."

"Like for instance?"

Rocco thought it over. "Panini with mocetta."

"What the hell's that?"

"Next time I'll take you. You can't really describe it."

THEY WERE CROWDING IN ON HIM, ALL THREE OF THEM, EACH double his weight and a good foot taller. Their heads blocked out the sun, suffocating him and erasing the walls and the guard tower.

"Abdul, how long do we have to wait?" the blond threatened him, the one with one eye sealed half shut by a scar and a tattooed snake writhing up his neck. Erik the Red, they called him there in prison. "Well, Abdul?"

It didn't strike Omar as wise to correct him on the name. "I don't know. Like I told you, there are certain things I don't do."

"I say bullshit!" snarled the Nigerian. The biggest guy there, the one who trained in the gym every day. In the outside world, he'd been a boxer; in here, he was a killer. "This morning, you piece-of-shit Moroccan, you were supposed to take a delivery of drugs!"

Omar wasn't a Moroccan. He was from Tunis. But he decided to turn a blind eye to that minor inaccuracy as well. The Nigerian's enormous hand crushed Omar to his chest. "You want to die at age twenty?" The Nigerian vomited the words onto him, flashing his set of white teeth, marked here and there by patches of tartar. The big black man's breath might even have been worse than his fists. "Eh? Do you want to die at age twenty, you piece of shit?"

Another minor inaccuracy. Omar had been born in Tunis on May 18, 1988. If he were to die today, as Oluwafeme was threatening, it would happen just a few days short of his twenty-fourth birthday. But he chose to say nothing, especially now that the African's enormous hand was clutching his Adam's apple.

"Listen carefully." Now the third member of the trio, the Professor, was speaking. The one with glasses. An NGO, Never Get Out. Two life sentences without parole, plus other judicial kibble he'd piled up in years of honored service. Behind the lenses, what he had weren't eyes, actually. They were two pieces of soulless glass. Two things he used to look through, to spy on the world, to observe but not to transmit emotions. "You see, Omar, my friends and I know all about the fucked-up things you do in here. That you have your friends from the outside bring you little presents, and that you peddle that shit around and save up money for when you get out. Because you're getting out, right?"

Omar nodded. He only had six months to go.

"Let me correct myself, because you'd *like* to get out, right?" The Professor gazed at him seriously. "And according to us, this morning your friends on the outside were supposed to bring you some presents. Where are they?"

"Today they didn't bring me anything, I swear it. Marini was in the visiting room. And when Marini's around . . . you know it yourself, not a fucking thing gets through! I'm not lying, Professor. I'm not—"

Oluwafeme was rapid and precise. A cross delivered with all the mass of his shoulder, connecting to both nose and lip. A sharp blow, practically invisible given the sheer speed of execution—that is if it hadn't been for the blood that gushed out of Omar's lips and nose. The young man's hands flew up to his face. In his eyes hundreds of lights flashed and popped, and a dull pain drilled into his skull. His legs gave way beneath him, but it was impossible to drop to the ground. Oluwafeme's other hand held him up, on his feet, pinned to the wall.

"But we don't believe you! And when we don't believe someone, what happens?"

Four-Eyes, the brains of the group, shook his head. "I don't know what happens to us. But the person we don't believe generally dies." He grabbed Omar's chin and glared into the eyes that Omar could barely keep open. "Do you understand what I just said? You'll die. Let me ask you one more time: Where is the shit?"

Omar couldn't breathe. He bowed his head and spat a clump of blood to the ground; then he looked up again. "Maybe I didn't make myself clear . . ." And he shot a glance over the right shoulder of the black man, who had his fist poised for another punch; now he could see his friend Tarek in the courtyard trying to find him. He needed to let himself be seen, or else he was a dead man. "Professo', which part of what I said didn't you understand? I don't have a fucking thing!"

The Nigerian ex-boxer let fly with another right to the temple. Omar let his head loll forward, but then Erik stepped in and raised it for him with an uppercut to the chin that crushed at least a couple of his teeth and opened a cut on the tip of his tongue. That punch was followed almost instantly by yet another roundhouse fist to the belly from Oluwafeme, a left this time, just to keep his other hand in if nothing else. Omar vomited his breakfast onto his shoes. But at that point the beating could no longer remain a private affair, and convicts began picking up on it all over the playing field in the courtyard of the Varallo house of detention. Tarek and Karim,

Omar's two close friends, noticed the brawl and came lunging at Erik and the Nigerian.

Tarek went sailing through the air a couple of feet off the ground and slammed a solid kick into the back of Oluwafeme's head; the Nigerian fell forward and slammed into the courtyard wall. Karim, on the other hand, had lunged onto Erik's back and was now hanging from his shoulders, a deadweight, clinging like a koala to a eucalyptus tree, digging his fingertips into Erik's eyes. The fair-haired man with the scar on his face writhed frantically, trying to toss him off, unsuccessfully. Omar had let himself slide to the ground, his mouth full of blood and snot. The Professor let fly with a kick at Karim, who was clinging to Erik's back, and hit Karim in the kidneys. The young man yelled out in pain but kept his fingers firmly planted in the Viking look-alike's eyes, as Erik tried to free himself from this wildcat that had landed on his back. In the meantime, the Nigerian, shaking his head, had stumbled back up on his feet. Warily, Tarek was waiting for him. Oluwafeme charged at him. Tarek tried to hold him at bay with what rudiments of karate he'd been able to pick up in a flea-bitten gymnasium back in Hammamet. But he was unable to do anything more than to annoy the giant Nigerian boxer. The other inmates of the house of detention stood watching the brawl that was now raging between the three Tunisians and the Professor's gang, but no one dreamed of interfering. The younger convicts broke off their soccer match; the older ones interrupted their game of cards. Aziz stepped away from the group that was milling around and chatting next to the woodworking shed and hurried over to help his fellow Tunisians. He ran straight toward Erik, who still had Karim fiercely wrapped around his back. In the meantime, Oluwafeme, former boxer that he was, had punched Tarek in the face and knocked him headlong to the ground. Omar, his face bloodied and his eyes swollen almost completely shut, was still trying to get back on his feet, but the Professor slammed his foot down on the young man's neck, pinning him down to the ground. With a jerk to one side, Erik finally managed to get Karim off his back, and now he darted toward him and seized him by the throat. He started squeezing, bringing greater and greater pressure to bear. Karim's eyes were already bulging out, and he clearly was unable to breathe. But just then Aziz waded into the fray, smashing his fist into Erik's head, right behind his ear; Erik released his grip, dropping Karim to the ground, where he coughed his heart out, desperately trying to suck air back into his lungs. Aziz shouted, trying to work up his courage, and then launched himself straight at the fair-haired scarface. He was windmilling his fists with all his strength and fear. Those punches, however, weren't finding their mark. Aziz was a shopkeeper, and brawls weren't exactly his forte, which Erik understood very well. He hung back and bided his time, until he finally let loose with a seemingly endless series of punches that ravaged Aziz's face. Jets of blood and saliva sailed through the air in all directions. At that point, the other convicts decided that the time had come to weigh in. They all surged forward to bring a halt to the massacre. From the main gate, at last, two correctional officers hurried up to put down the brawl. There were shouts and fists and kicks continued to fly. A third correctional officer, Federico Tolotta, standing guard in Wing 3, came rushing over at a dead run, in spite of his enormous bulk. He bent down to pick up the bunch of keys to the armored doors from the ground, clenched them in his fist, and hit the Nigerian hard with them in the back of the head, causing him to stagger. More armed guards swarmed into the courtyard. They took custody of Oluwafeme, Erik, and Agostino, a.k.a. the Professor, swinging their billy clubs freely. The brawl subsided. Omar and Aziz were beaten black and blue. Karim had gotten off with some difficulty breathing but nothing much more, whereas Tarek, after the punch from Oluwafeme, had gotten back to his feet and, aside from the jaw that creaked every time he bit down, seemed to be in reasonably good shape.

Two prison guards took custody of the North Africans and hustled them off to the infirmary. Erik, the Nigerian, and the Professor were taken to solitary confinement as they awaited further disciplinary actions.

Six guards under the command of Mauro Marini, the senior officer, were doing their best to restore calm among the other convicts. A convict on the other side of the courtyard, far from the brawl, was still lying on the ground, near the door that led to Wing 3. Officer Marini approached him. "Hey! On your feet!"

The convict didn't move. Marini kneeled down to turn him over. "Hey! You getting up?" He gave him a shake as he turned him. The man had both eyes open, pupils rolled up out of sight, mouth wide-open, a streamer of drool hanging from his lips.

"Oh, fuck . . ." Marini murmured, looking around as he tried to catch a colleague's eye.

"What's going on?" Daniele Abela, a new recruit, on staff for just a few months, shouted at him.

"Hurry, for fuck's sake!" Marini replied, placing two fingers on the neck of the man stretched out on the pavement. Abela and Tolotta, the gigantic guard from Wing 3, joined him.

"This guy's dead!" Marini opined.

"Oh, fuck . . . call the warden!"

ROCCO HAD ALREADY GULPED DOWN FOUR TRAMEZZINI AND two espressos. The afternoon was advancing solemnly, and the light was starting to shift from yellow to orange. He kept an eye on the street and the narrow lanes around Biga's apartment house. Brizio, continually distracted by the women passing in front of him, couldn't seem to concentrate.

"I'm starting to get sick and tired of waiting, Brizio. When is that asshole Biga going to get home?"

"Beats me . . . but I was just thinking something," said his friend. "If it really was him, then we're not likely to find him around. He shot Adele instead of you, and if I were him, I'd dive down some hole and pull it in after me."

"Who can say? Antonio is a member of the old guard."

Brizio nodded. They knew that the Roman underworld had always had this shortcoming: its arrogance. Roman wiseguys keep their chins up and proudly strut when the smart thing would be to duck and cover, but then they scurry into hiding the one day they could go around boasting of their exploits. Biga had to have reached age seventy by now, and after all the years he'd spent in the shadows, he felt protected and untouchable. At least in Rome.

Biga emerged from Vicolo delle Vacche. He was alone, and in spite of the fact that the evening was mild and springlike, he was walking with an umbrella in his hand. He wedged it down between the distinctive Roman sampietrini cobblestones at every step, leaning his weight on it. Rocco elbowed Brizio in the ribs, and Brizio immediately abandoned his scrutiny of a magnificent Teutonic maiden in short-shorts who happened to be passing at the moment.

"There he is now," said Rocco. And he got to his feet. As he drew closer, Rocco realized that what Antonio Biga had in his hand wasn't an umbrella at all. It was a peculiar walking stick with a bulge at the center that ended just under the hooked handle. When Antonio spotted the deputy chief, he was neither startled nor indecisive. He just kept hobbling along toward the policeman, with a smile on his face. To any outsider, it would have looked like a meeting of two longtime friends.

"Well, take a look at who's here. None other than Rocco Schiavone. Why are you around these parts? Did they call you back to Rome?"

"I've been looking for you."

Antonio took a deep breath. With a quick gesture of his hand, he pushed a button and the walking stick was magically transformed into a stool. "You mind? I just had my femur rebuilt. They replaced the tip of it with some material they use at NASA. But I'm still not all the way recovered." And he lowered himself down onto that little handheld perch that was undoubtedly of Chinese manufacture. "Nice, eh? People use it to go fishing."

Rocco was still on his feet. He gazed down upon him from above. "And do you go?"

"Where?"

"Fishing."

"I've never given a shit about fishing." And he broke out in a laugh that soon changed into a convulsive hacking cough. He'd turned red in the face, he was choking, but Rocco didn't move a muscle to help him.

"You aren't going to kick on me, are you? Not right here and now, Antò?"

The man recovered his breath. He dried his lips. "All right, then, tell me what you want, cop. After you ruined my life, I've heard that yours hasn't gone all that much better."

"They told it to you straight. By the way, best regards from the parents of Dottoressa Semplici. Do you remember her? The one you killed in the bank."

"I never killed anyone. You know it, I'm an innocent man."

"Of course you are. So, aside from hobbling around like a cripple, what have you been up to lately?"

"What can I tell you? You know what? I'm finally getting my pension in just two months."

"You're getting a pension?"

"Yeah. This is a great country!"

"You can say that again, if they're helping a piece of shit like you to survive." Rocco lit a cigarette. "Have you been doing any traveling?"

"When?"

"Lately?"

"Aside from Frascati? No. I haven't been anywhere." Antonio noticed that at the mouth of the alley another figure was leaning against the wall of the building. "Who's that? You go around with a bodyguard?"

"It's a friend of mine."

Antonio focused. "Well, would you take a look at that . . . it's Brizio! He's aged. The two of you, to come look for a relic like me?"

"Do you know where I live now?"

"I was hoping that you'd gone to stay with your wife in the boneyard. But instead, here you are, hale and healthy and going around busting people's balls, as usual."

"Are you sorry to see that?"

"Very sorry, my friend. Very sorry." The aged criminal sneezed. "I spent the first two years behind bars thinking about how to send you underground in a box to stay with the tree roots. Then I said to myself: Antò, what do you care? Get out of this cell and enjoy your life."

Rocco flicked the cigarette far away.

"Schiavò, did I ever send you my condolences for your wife?"

Rocco lashed out with the instep of his foot and knocked the three-legged stool out from under the man, spilling Antonio to the ground in the blink of an eye.

"You bastard!"

Rocco bent down and grabbed him by the lapels. "I'm letting

you talk because you're an old gimp and your words don't count for shit. But watch out, Antonio, don't overdo it."

The two men stared each other in the eye.

"Let me get up, give me a hand . . ." said Antonio.

"My ass," Rocco hissed. He leaned in closer, bringing his own face right up against the bandit's. "What do you know?"

"Let me understand one thing, cop. Did I ever say a thing to you? Never. So now why are you asking me all these questions? What are you hoping to find out?"

"Who took a trip to Aosta lately?"

Antonio smiled. His teeth were black, and he was missing a couple of incisors. "You're shitting yourself, aren't you?"

"Who?"

"I'm just sorry for Seba's woman, because she had nothing to do with any of it. Too bad. A nice piece of ass—"

Rocco gave him a straight-armed smack. "Don't you dare mention her name. Well?" And he grabbed the old bandit's jacket even tighter.

"I don't know. Consider the people who have it in for you. There's a lot of us, Schiavone . . . Time to get busy!"

"Antò, if I find out you have anything to do with this, I'll come back and break both your femurs for you." Rocco released his grip. He stood up and looked down at the old man with contempt. "All these years in prison haven't changed you a bit. You're just the same old dickhead as ever, only now with a broken femur. I hope I never see you again, Biga!"

He turned and walked over to Brizio, who hadn't moved from the street corner.

Antonio Biga was struggling to get up off the cobblestones. His legs were waving frantically like those of a cockroach on its back. "Schiavò, these things have nothing to do with me anymore. It wasn't me. And you want to know why? Because I wouldn't have missed, I wouldn't have shot the wrong person. I wouldn't have killed Sebastiano's girlfriend. I would have killed you!" The old man's voice echoed down the deserted alley. "If I've broken my femur, I'll file a criminal complaint!"

"Why don't you just complain to NASA!" Schiavone shouted at him. Then, with a nod to Brizio, "Let's go. It's not him. He knows, but he's not talking."

"Maybe a car will come by and run him over," Brizio said and pointed at Biga, who was crawling along the cobblestones, trying to use the stool to get back on his feet.

"No such luck, this is a pedestrian zone." Then Rocco looked up at the sky above. "There's still plenty of daylight. Shall we go pay a call on Zaccaria?"

"WE'RE SORRY, BUT THE NUMBER YOU'VE DIALED IS MOMENtarily unreachable . . ." Judge Baldi slammed down the receiver. "Where is he?" he shouted at his office. Then he stuck his forefinger into his ear and scratched. "Where is that mental defective?" he yelled at the walls of his office, empty but for him. He picked up the phone again.

"Aosta police headquarters, go ahead."

"This is Judge Baldi. Where is Schiavone?"

"We haven't seen him in a while, Dottore."

"Who am I speaking with?"

"Officer Deruta."

"Could you put me through to . . . Who else is there?"

"I couldn't say. Do you want the whole list?"

"No, who is there in Schiavone's place?"

"Ah . . . well, Pietra, from the Turin mobile squad *was* here. I don't know if he's in the office now. Did you want to speak with him?"

"No, I want to invite him out to dinner. *Of course* I want to speak with him!"

He detected noises in the background. A subdued buzz of conversation. Baldi rolled his eyes. Someone else took the receiver. "Dottore, this is Officer Italo Pierron speaking, how can I help you?"

"Where is Carlo Pietra?"

"You want the truth? I couldn't say . . . I haven't seen him since yesterday."

"Goddamn it to fucking hell! There's no time. You come straight over to the court building."

"What's happening?"

"We need to rush straight over to Varallo prison. Is there any hope of tracking down Schiavone?"

"I'll do everything I can. At the very outside, I can deliver him to you tomorrow."

"You're on your way up, Pierron."

"Dottore, why are we going to Varallo prison?"

"Someone murdered Mimmo Cuntrera!"

STEFANIA ZACCARIA WAS A PATIENT IN THE TRAUMATOLOGY ward at Rome's Santo Spirito hospital. She was resting on a bed in a single room, her right leg elevated in traction, one arm in a plaster cast, the other leg in a brace, and a bandage covering her left eye. Her lips, reconstructed by some completely incompetent plastic surgeon, were swollen and covered with scabs. At the foot of the bed was an elderly woman intent at her crocheting. Sunlight poured in through the window, brightening the bureaucratic pistachio-green paint on the walls, a hue that always seemed to give its utmost in settings like hospitals or prisons. Stefania Zaccaria had built up a small prostitution empire all her own. She'd bought dozens of one-room basement apartments in a variety of Roman neighborhoods and had parked Slavic and South American girls in them. A nice little revenue stream that, even in a year when business was lean, still brought in several hundred thousand euros. Rocco had put her behind bars not once but twice, and yet she'd always managed to wriggle out and back onto the streets somehow. The power of money and skilled lawyers, many of whom were also happy customers of her ring of girls. When Rocco entered the room, the old woman who kept Zaccaria company put down her crocheting and lifted her index finger to the tip of her nose. "Shhh . . ." she told Rocco. "She's sleeping."

The deputy chief walked over to the bed. Stefania Zaccaria had her one good eye closed. But her eyelid was quivering just a little too much. Rocco decided to go along with the game. "How is she?"

"So-so," the old woman replied. "And who are you? A friend?"

"A close friend. How did she get hurt so badly?"

"She crashed her car in Casalotti. She slammed right into a highway-department cement truck."

"It's just a lucky thing she's alive," said Rocco. Then he edged closer. Stefania was covered with scratches on her forehead and cheekbones. "How long has she been like this?"

"Counting today, it's been three days."

"What do her doctors say? Can I take her with me down to police headquarters?"

"To police headquarters?" the woman repeated, dropping her crochet hook on the bed cover.

"No, huh? Well then, I can always come in with the judge. Stefà, here we go again. I'm pretty sure you're going to have to come in and spend some time behind bars."

Stefania continued to keep her unbandaged eye closed.

"What on earth are you talking about? Can't you see what kind of shape she's in?"

"Oh, I can see. But six days ago, Stefania put her foot in it big time. And now that we've caught her red-handed, it's time to pay the piper. Am I right?"

"My ass, you are!" Stefania Zaccaria replied, opening her one good eye. "My ass, that you or anyone is putting me behind bars, Schiavone! All right then, what are you claiming I did six days ago?"

"Ah, so you're awake after all?" said the deputy chief in fake surprise. He noticed that she was also missing a couple of teeth. "You know better than I do, Stefania. It's more of the same!"

"Schiavò, I'm not coming with you to any police station. Go ahead and send a judge to see me, send whoever you like. You're going to have to talk to my lawyers!" And she accompanied the threat by hoisting herself up slightly, a movement that caused her a stabbing pang of pain at the base of her neck.

"Take it easy . . ." suggested the elderly woman.

"Shut up, you idiot!" Stefania shouted at her.

"That's no way to talk to a mother . . ."

"Commissa', this isn't my mother."

"And I'm not a commissario. I'm a deputy chief of police. In that case, just who is this lady, your aunt?"

"Not even. This miserable wretch does my housekeeping for me."

The little old lady nodded and smiled. "I keep house!" she proudly confirmed.

"Come on, Deputy Chief, tell me. What is it you think I did six days ago?"

Rocco pulled out a formica chair and dragged it closer to the bed. He looked at the little old lady. "Listen, Signora, could you do me a favor?"

"Certainly," she said with a smile.

"Could you leave us alone for just two minutes?"

The old woman looked over at Stefania. "Can I?"

"You don't need to ask her. You need to just stand up and leave the room for two minutes. Will you do that for me?"

The woman set her crocheting down on the mattress. "All right then, I'm going to go get a drop of water, if you don't mind." She stood up, smoothed her skirt, and with an off-kilter smile, she left the room.

"Excellent, Stefania. Now that we can talk eye to eye—well, at least one of your eyes, anyway," he said, pointing to the bandage across the side of her face. "Shall we have a serious conversation?"

"I'm always serious."

"Can you tell me where you were six days ago?"

Stefania rolled her good eye to the ceiling. She was thinking. "Six days ago . . . six days ago . . . so you mean Thursday evening?"

"Exactly."

"Let me think . . . You know, I don't remember. I think at home. Nothing special. But why?"

"Make an effort."

Stefania tried. "Nothing, I'm not getting anything. But why do you want to know?"

"You know why."

"No, I don't."

"Everyone in Rome knows."

"Not me, though. You busted my balls long enough."

Rocco extended a hand. He laid it on the young woman's good arm.

"Let go of my arm."

Rocco maintained his grip. "You know why I'm here. And you were expecting me. Was it you?"

"Who did what?"

Rocco clenched down on the arm. Stefania grimaced from the pain. “I told you we need to be serious. I’ll break your good arm, too.”

“I don’t know, I don’t know . . .”

Rocco tightened his grip. “You don’t know?”

“Yes, that is, I know . . . I know what happened to you . . . Let go of me, you’re hurting me!”

“That was the plan. So?”

“Ouch, that hurts . . . don’t squeeze so tight . . .”

“If you don’t open up about this, I’ll move on to the broken leg.”

“I didn’t have anything to do with it. I would have loved to, let me assure you. But I haven’t been thinking about you, I didn’t even know where you were.”

“So who told you that someone had come and paid a visit on me?”

“Let go of me, let go of me and I’ll tell you.”

Rocco let go of her wrist. He looked down at Stefania. “I’m waiting . . .”

Stefania Zaccaria gulped down a gob of saliva. “This one guy was talking about it . . .”

“This one guy whose name is?”

“What’s-his-face . . . I don’t remember the name . . .”

Rocco reached out his hand toward the leg in the brace. Stefania practically levitated off the bed. “Paoletto Buglioni!”

Rocco smiled. He stroked the arm that he’d just been crushing and stood up from the chair.

“You’re a piece of shit, Schiavone, you know that? Why don’t you go back to wherever you crawled out of?” While she was shouting, Rocco put the chair back and walked to the door. With his back to her, he waved good-bye to Stefania as she went on bellowing, making the bed and her leg traction creak: “There you go, good! Get the hell out from underfoot! Now I’m going to call my lawyers, Commissa’, don't kid yourself. You can't just come in here and threaten me, you know? If I make up my mind, I can . . ."

Schiavone didn't hear any of the rest of it. He was already out in the hallway. He crossed paths with a male nurse. "Listen, the patient in Room 209 is flipping out."

"What the fuck do I care! As far as I care she can flip right out the window!" And the nurse continued on his way.

ALESSANDRO MARTINELLI, AFTER A LONG CAREER IN LAW enforcement administration, had arrived at age fifty-four as the warden of the house of detention of Varallo, and he was sitting with both arms folded across his chest. In his office, as spartan as his attire, his only indulgence was the photographs of his three children, framed and enjoying pride of place on his desk. That aside, the room might as well have been a monk's cell. "I don't know," he was saying as he shook his head. "I can't say anything for sure . . . I'd prefer to have you talk to the doctor first . . ."

Sitting across from him was Judge Baldi in an elegant leather jacket, and Officer Italo Pierron stood next to the door.

"What's the doctor's name?" asked Baldi.

"He's the health-services director. His name is Crocitti," the warden replied.

THEY WALKED DOWN A DOZEN OR SO CORRIDORS, STRIDING past iron doors that opened and closed behind them in a symphony of screeches, squeals, and metallic thumps. The walls were painted the usual drab bureaucratic green. At last, they reached the courtyard. There were actually two courtyards, separated by a high masonry wall. "The roofed yard is for the prisoners in solitary confinement.

This larger, open-air yard is for the other prisoners." The warden was leading his visitors on a tour. Next to a small recess in the wall, not far from the entrance to Wing 3, were two prison guards and the prison doctor, Crocitti, bending over a white sheet from beneath which extended a pair of legs.

"A pleasure, I'm Baldi, from the Aosta prosecutor's office."

Crocitti stood up. Six feet and two inches of skinniness and gray hair, and a lifeless gaze behind his eyeglasses. "Crocitti's the name . . ."

Baldi looked at the corpse without a flicker of emotion in his gaze. "What do we have here?"

"Myocardial infarction," the doctor replied. "Fulminating heart attack killed him instantly. He must just have overexerted himself in the brawl."

"Domenico Cuntrera didn't die of a heart attack!" shouted Judge Baldi, so loudly that the doctor and both prison guards jumped in fright. Italo remained dutifully motionless while the prison warden gazed in embarrassment in the opposite direction. "I issued the warrant for this Cuntrera's arrest. He's a Mafioso who was running a loan-sharking operation, involved up to his elbows in the kidnapping of a young woman . . . Someone like that doesn't die of a heart attack. I want an autopsy."

"Yes, Dottore, and in fact an autopsy is automatic and mandatory. We'll take him to Vercelli and—"

"You can go to Vercelli on your summer vacation! This body is coming back to Aosta!" the judge shouted again.

"But . . ." the prison warden tried objecting. "We report to the Vercelli court and—"

"Listen carefully, Martinelli. This man belongs to me. I'll talk to the prosecuting magistrate in Vercelli. Italo! Alert Fumagalli. I want him to do the autopsy."

"Right away!" Italo stepped away from the little group.

"I don't think this is at all standard operating procedure," the warden complained.

"Martinelli, let me just say this, I don't give a merry fuck!"

"So you're certain that this isn't a heart attack?" asked Dr. Crocitti.

The judge looked him right in the eye. "I'll bet both my testicles that this was a murder."

IT WAS ALMOST MIDNIGHT, BUT IN THE STREET IN THE TRIESTE neighborhood, you'd say it was five in the afternoon from the traffic and the hustle and bustle. Paoletto Buglioni was standing in front of Hysteria, keeping an eye on the line of young people waiting to gain admission to the discotheque. Arms crossed, dressed in black, not a hair on his head, with a ferocious glare and several days' growth of whiskers on his face, he stood a good foot taller than any of the would-be clientele. His biceps looked as if they were about to rip the sleeves of his jacket asunder any second. As soon as the young people shouting and brandishing plastic cups brimming over with who knows what alcoholic potion reached the double doors and caught sight of that brooding giant, they fell silent and waited, suddenly docile and well behaved, for the bouncer to accord them entrance to the club. Rocco and Brizio stood leaning against the metal roller shutters of an antiques dealer, watching Buglioni from a distance of thirty feet or so. Paoletto looked up and noticed them. He nodded to Brizio, and Brizio nodded back. "He'll be right over," Brizio muttered to Rocco. Not two minutes later, another bouncer emerged from inside the discotheque, shorter but even more muscular than Paoletto. This bouncer was black, with dyed-blond hair and a pair of sunglasses. Buglioni leaned down and spoke into his ear, the other bouncer nodded, and then the giant stepped away from the line of impatient young people and strode decisively over to the deputy chief and his friend.

"Hey, Brizio!" At the sound of Paoletto's voice, Rocco barely managed to keep himself from bursting into laughter. It was a good octave higher than La Callas's voice, but it was also faint and weak. It seemed like the voice of a particularly innocent young girl.

"Ciao, Paolè . . . So do you know Rocco?" Brizio said.

Paoletto nodded but didn't extend his hand to the deputy chief. "So does someone have it in for you?" he asked.

"Who told you that?" Rocco asked.

The bouncer looked off to one side, pulled a pack of cigarettes out of his pocket, and lit one with a movement that he'd surely seen some actor or other use once. "It's just that people are talking about it . . ."

"You're the one who told Stefania . . . but who told you? What else do you know?" Brizio asked him.

"Beats me. You know how it is, Brizio."

"No, how is it?" Brizio retorted.

"Rumors going around. I'm sorry about Adele. How's Seba?"

"How do you think he is?" Rocco broke in. "He's fucking furious."

"If I could do anything for Seba, I would. But for real, guys, I don't know anything at all." And he took a puff on his cigarette, holding it between his thumb and his index finger. He narrowed his eyes and looked at Rocco. "How did she die?"

"Eight shots, 6.35 mm, small caliber."

More silence. Two young women walked out of an apartment house door, momentarily snagging Brizio's attention. Paoletto flicked away his cigarette. The neon sign of the antiques shop, reflected off his bald head, gave it a pale blue cast.

"How's your brother?" asked Rocco.

"I don't know."

"Did he tell you?"

"Tell me what?"

"About what happened up north?"

"I haven't seen Flavio for a while. You know that, right? He lives with Mamma, poor old thing, she's eighty-five, deaf, and not in the best of health. Anyway, now that I think of it, it was Antonio Biga who told me. You know him, right?"

Brizio nodded. He ran his hand through his hair. "Listen up a second, Paolè . . . If you hear anything, will you tell us? Either me or Seba?"

"Of course I will. You can count on it."

Brizio stretched out his hand. The bouncer clasped it. Then he shook Rocco's hand, too. "I'm sorry, Rocco."

The deputy chief and his friend walked away. Paoletto went back toward the discotheque. As soon as he saw the two men vanish around the corner, he stuck his hand in his pocket and pulled out his cell phone. "Flavio . . . yeah, it's me . . ."

His brother's voice answered sleepily: "What is it?"

"How is Mamma?"

"Wait, you're calling me at one in the morning to find out how Mamma is?"

"No, listen to me. Did you sell a gat, a 6.35 mm, a while ago?"

"So, what if I did?"

"Fuck, Flavio. You weren't supposed to sell that one, and you know it. Who did you sell it to?"

"Hey, why don't you mind your own fucking business?"

"This *is* my own fucking business, you asshole! Who did you sell it to?"

"Why do you want to know?"

"Because whoever it was, they used it . . . probably to shoot Adele up north in Aosta. Well?"

"Oh, fuck . . . and I thought he just wanted it for an armed robbery."

"Who?"

Flavio took a deep breath. "Enzo. Enzo Baiocchi!"

Paoletto rolled his eyes heavenward. "The cop is looking for him. Don't say a thing. Keep cool. And if it ever turns up again, throw it into the Tiber."

"You think they can trace it back to me?"

"I don't know. But you don't know a fucking thing and I never told you a fucking thing. To Enzo Baiocchi you had to go and sell it . . . Couldn't you think of anything stupider to do with it?"

ROCCO FELL ASLEEP DIRECTLY ATOP THE PLASTIC SLIPCOVER that enfolded the bed. And it was a sleepless night, with ghosts popping up relentlessly every time he shut his eyelids. From time to time he had the sensation that there was one sitting at the foot of the bed, gazing at him as he lay there with his eyes shut. And he was thirsty all night long.

THURSDAY

He got up at the first light of dawn, happy that his dreamless night was over. He hoped he'd never have to spend another night like it as long as he lived.

At 6:15 a.m. Rocco was on the terrace smoking the first cigarette of the day, sitting facing the rising sun as it painted the city orange and red.

"THERE'S NO ARGUING WITH HOW PRETTY IT IS, IS THERE?"

Marina holds her coffee cup with both hands and shivers a little from the cold. "That's why we bought this apartment, isn't it?"

"Actually, it was because it was close to your folks' place."

"Come on, let's have a contest. All right, you point and I'll describe."

After all, she gets every one of them. "Let's start with an easy one. That cluster of roofs down there?"

"The Basilica of Sant'Anastasia at the Circus Maximus."

"Good job. And that other roof over there, behind the Altare della Patria?"

"Torre delle Milizie! Come on, now, can't you come up with anything a little harder?"

"All right, that stand of cypress trees . . . you see it? Over Testaccio?"

"Santa Sabina! I'd like to remind you that that's where we got married!"

She's right. With the cypresses of the Aventine Hill and the Orange Garden right next to it. "Marì, do you know why they plant cypresses around cemeteries?"

She takes a sip of coffee. "Because of the roots. They're narrow and they sink down straight, they don't spread out horizontally, which means they don't bother the graves or tickle the dead." She looks at me and smiles.

"You sure know a lot of things."

"Right?"

I look at her. She turns her eyes to the city and narrows them slightly.

"Are those wrinkles I see around your eyes?"

"No. They're just folds. I didn't have time to get wrinkles." She turns to look at me. "Want to know the truth? You've forgotten my defects. It always happens with the departed, doesn't it? The first thing you forget about us is our defects."

"You didn't have any."

"Baboom!" And she breaks out laughing. "Admit it, Rocco. You're starting to see a mist, I'm starting to blur . . ."

"Wrong you are!"

"THIS ISN'T SOMETHING WE CAN CRACK IN TWO SECONDS . . ." said Furio, lighting a cigarette. Sebastiano was busy making sure that the cocoa powder didn't sink into the foamed milk. As always, Brizio was looking around. Piazza Santa Maria in Trastevere at that hour of the morning was already full of people, young women for the most part.

Rocco grabbed the demitasse of espresso. "Antonio Biga won't talk. Zaccaria has nothing to do with it. And Paoletto is just a megaphone."

"So much so that here in Rome everybody knows about it," Furio threw in.

"That's what I told you," said Brizio. "Huh, beats me, I've got to say. No one else comes to mind for the moment."

"What about this Walter Cremonesi?" asked Furio.

Rocco finished his espresso and slumped against the backrest of his chair. "I don't know. It's an old thing . . . so why now? He could have done it a long time ago, when I was still in Rome."

"He was just waiting for the right time?"

Brizio turned to look at his friends. "No. Cremonesi is a guy who works at the highest levels. He was up to his elbows in government-issued contracts, public works, zoning and regulations. Why take a risk when you're riding high like that? And after all, Rocco didn't put him behind bars all by himself."

"That's true," Furio agreed. "He'd have to have taken down that deputy inspector of the special task force . . . what's-his-name . . . I can't quite . . ."

"Nardella," Rocco said.

"Exactly. No, Walter Cremonesi doesn't have anything to do with this."

"I go over it and over it again, but I just can't figure out who it could be. And I don't like that," Rocco replied.

"This is a rat that's come back out of its rat hole," decreed Sebastiano, without once taking his eyes off his cappuccino and the pastry that he still hadn't touched. "Someone who hasn't been out on the streets for some time." He finally looked up, turning his glistening eyes from one friend to the other.

"I agree," said Rocco. "I was thinking the same thing. We need to go find someone who was doing time and just got out."

"Right!" Sebastiano added. "I'd bet my life that the guy who shot Adele is a prison rat, and now he's hiding out somewhere."

At the sound of the dead woman's name the other three looked down at the café table. But instead, Sebastiano smiled. "No, that's not right. Let's do this, anytime we hear Adele's name, why don't we just smile?"

And that's what they did. The only problem was that Sebastiano was forced to brush away a tear. "Jesus fucking . . ." he muttered, and with his hairy oversized hand he reached out and grabbed the pastry, bit into it, and tore off half, sprinkling his beard and his jacket with flaky crumbs. Then the sounds from Piazza Santa Maria in Trastevere broke into their reverie. They looked around at the Sinhalese street vendors peddling trinkets, the young people sitting on the steps and smoking. Rocco was reminded of that afternoon so many years earlier when he had spotted Marina for the very first time, on those very same steps, and decided, as the sun kissed the golden mosaics on the facade of the Basilica of Santa Maria in Trastevere, that he was going to make her his wife.

THE JOURNEY BACK FROM ROME WAS A NIGHTMARE. MORE than an hour's delay at Fiumicino. And when he landed at Turin he discovered that someone had locked his car in the parking lot. He'd had to call a tow truck to get his Volvo and leave Caselle Airport. Only when he was in his car heading back to Aosta did he finally turn his cell phone back on. A burst of sounds announced the presence of dozens of messages. He didn't waste time checking to see who they were from. He knew. His office, the prosecutor's office, and Anna. He called Officer De Silvestri.

"De Silvestri, I need you again."

"Tell me what you need, Dottore . . ." the old Roman officer replied.

"The guy I'm looking for is someone who couldn't put his nose out on the street."

"You're thinking about someone who was behind bars?"

"Or maybe who was just afraid to show his face. Which means there's something I need you to do . . ."

"A serious search. Find out who's just been released, who's escaped . . ."

"Have you ever seen a case where you cross-reference the information and you come up with something?"

"I sure hope so, Dottore. Just don't make the same mistake you just made."

"Which would be?"

"You came to Rome and you didn't even swing by to say hello."

"You're right, Alfrè, you're absolutely right."

CATERINA WAS WAITING FOR HIM ON PIAZZA CHANOUX, IN front of the bar. As soon as Lupa saw him emerge from Via di Porta Pretoria, she came galloping to meet him and leapt at him as if she hadn't seen him in a lifetime. Dogs have no sense of time. Whether their owner is away for five minutes or twenty years, like Ulysses in the *Odyssey*, it's the same to them. Especially for dogs like Lupa, who no longer really trust people.

"Thanks, Caterina. Was she a good girl?"

"She was a very good girl. We've become best friends. Isn't that right, puppy?" She smiled at the little dog as she wagged her tail and scampered around Rocco, whining and yipping. "Listen, Dottore—"

"Here we go again! We're on a first-name basis, not 'Dottore,' not 'sir'!"

"I'll try to do better . . . Listen, Rocco, Baldi is looking for you. A murder at the prison."

"A murder?"

"That's right. I don't know anything more than that. I didn't quite understand the message. Yesterday Italo had to run up there, along with the judge."

"And what does Italo have to say?"

"I don't have the slightest idea. I haven't seen him since yesterday, in fact."

Rocco nodded. "Wait, so, you weren't together yesterday evening?"

"He got his feelings hurt. He's all bent out of shape because he found out I told him a lie."

"You told him a lie?"

"Oh, yeah, technically. He wanted us to go to dinner at his aunt's house, and she's not feeling well, but I really didn't feel like it. I can't stand family dinners. Let's just say that I have my problems with the family as an institution. And he took offense."

"For a trifle like that?"

"Sometimes for much less!"

A crack in the wall, then. That relationship that looked so solid, diamond-hard—had it already started to creak and sway under the weight of time and routine? He felt ashamed to think it, but he couldn't lie to himself: if that couple was having problems, he could take advantage of the fact. "Did you have a fight?"

"Let's just say that . . . Dottore, maybe that's none of your business." And the deputy inspector started petting Lupa.

"You're right, Caterina. Excuse me. That's none of my business. Thanks for taking care of Lupa. I'll take her back to my room at the residence."

"When will you be coming into the office, sir?"

Rocco rolled his eyes. "Okay, Caterina, I give up. One of these days you'll get used to the idea of calling me by my name."

"That sounds like a threat!" said the woman with a smile.

"That's exactly what it is!" He whistled to Lupa and headed back to the residential hotel. Caterina stood there watching him go; then she turned and headed back to the cathedral, where she'd left her car.

HE'D JUST TAKEN A SHOWER AND PUT ON SOME CLEAN CLOTHES when someone knocked at the door.

"Who is it?" Rocco shouted.

No answer. The siege was under way again. It must be the guy from the reception desk. "Who is it?" Silence. Huffing with annoyance, he got up off the bed and went over to the door. "Who is it?" he shouted again, scant inches from the wood.

Silence.

He pulled the door open.

Standing before him was Officer D'Intino, looking at him out of empty eyes, holding his uniform cap in one hand. D'Intino, a native of the far-flung lands of Abruzzo, was the worst punishment that Aosta had held in store for him since his arrival at police headquarters. Worse than the snow, worse than the cold.

"Why are you here? What do you want? Didn't you hear me shouting?"

"But I used the secret knock." And he smiled.

"The secret knock?"

The officer raised his fist and gave three sharp raps on the wood, all the while smiling at the deputy chief.

"What are you talking about?"

"*Our* secret knock, no?"

"No. You and I don't have any secret knock. Plus, three knocks on the door, what kind of damned secret knock is that? D'Intino, for fuck's sake, you have to learn that when you knock on a door and someone yells out 'Who is it?' you're supposed to answer them!"

Lupa barked as if to emphasize the absolutely linear logic of the point.

"What a handsome boy," said D'Intino.

"What a pretty girl," Rocco corrected him. "She's a she!"

"Oh. What breed is she?"

"She's a Saint-Rhémy-en-Ardennes."

"A . . . ?"

"Saint-Rhémy-en-Ardennes. An extremely rare breed created by Baron Gaston de Veilleuse in the eighteenth century. Originally from the city of Sedan, it's not very well-known because it's a breed full of contradictions, but it's also excellent company. It alternates moments of enormous affection with outbursts of ferocity and an estrangement from the well-known instincts for fraternity and friendship normally found in the canine species. Therefore, I'd advise you not to venture too close, she might lick you or she might take your hand off at the wrist . . . Don't tell me you've never heard of a Saint-Rhémy-en-Ardennes, D'Intino!"

"No, no, now that I think about it, yes . . . Saint-Rhémy . . ."

". . . en-Ardennes. Now, would you care to tell me what you're doing here?"

"There's a thing . . . a bad thing . . . that happened at the prison in Varallo."

"All right. And now do you want to tell me what happened at the prison in Varallo?"

"A dead man!"

Rocco nodded. "You know something, D'Intino? At police headquarters, if you search carefully, there's a man. Easy to find, because he must weigh about 265 pounds. He has an agreeable face, cheerful, and very, very intelligent . . ."

"Deruta?"

"Didn't I say very intelligent? Do you think I just described Deruta?"

D'Intino said nothing.

"Fine. This man answers to the name of Carlo Pietra. He is the deputy chief of the Turin mobile squad. For the time being, you're going to have to speak to him because yours truly is on obligatory leave until he feels like coming back. Have I made myself clear?"

D'Intino stood in the doorway, mouth gaping open. "My good man D'Intino, which part of what I said isn't clear to you?"

"Dotto'. What isn't clear to me is what I'm supposed to do now."

"All right then, write it down. First! Go back to police headquarters."

Under his breath, D'Intino repeated: "Go back to police headquarters . . ."

"Second, speak to Carlo Pietra."

"Speak to Carlo Pietra . . ."

"Third, stop busting the balls of Deputy Captain Schiavone."

"Third, stop busting the balls of Deputy Captain Schiavone."

"All clear?"

D'Intino smiled. "I have to go to police headquarters, find Pietra, and tell him not to bust the balls of Deputy Captain Schiavone."

"More or less."

"So you're not coming?"

"Coming where, D'Intì?"

"To the prison?"

"Get out!" And he slammed the door in D'Intino's face.

End of his secret retreat. Life had come back, and it was demanding him in a stentorian voice. The following morning he'd have to go back to police headquarters.

"You're done goofing off, Rocco!" he said loudly.

ALESSANDRO MARTINELLI HAD GENEROUSLY PUT HIS OFFICE at the disposal of both Baldi and Pietra. The penitentiary guards, Mauro Marini and Daniele Abela, sitting in two wooden chairs, were gazing up at the gigantic chief of the Turin mobile squad as he stood by the window. Baldi, on the other hand, was toying with a Bic ballpoint pen, sprawled out in the warden's leather office chair, while the warden himself remained standing in the doorway, as if he were a guest. Italo Pierron stood behind him. He clasped his hands behind his back and observed the two penitentiary guards.

Marini was over fifty; the other man was under thirty. Both of them had sullen expressions on their faces.

"Would you explain to me, very clearly, exactly what happened?" Baldi began without looking either man in the face.

"Abela and I were summoned to put down a brawl that had broken out in the courtyard next to the door to Wing 2. Four or five convicts were fighting, so Daniele and I and other officers stopped them."

"Four Tunisians were sent to the infirmary," Abela went on. "The others were sent to solitary confinement. When the brawl was over, we noticed Cuntrera's body on the ground and we realized that he was dead."

"This Cuntrera . . ." asked Pietra as he looked out over the roofs of the prison from the office window, "did he take part in the brawl?"

"That we don't know. A few people said that he was minding his own business, smoking a cigarette."

Baldi shot a glance at Pietra, who continued to look out the window. "Who did you put in solitary confinement?"

"The ringleaders. One is Enrico Carini, a.k.a. Erik the Red. The second is Oluwafeme Chiama, a Nigerian former amateur boxer, and the third is Agostino Lumi, a.k.a. the Professor. They started the brawl. The real victims were Omar Ben Taleb and his cousin Aziz. Tarek Essebsy and Karim Lakal got off easy."

"Motive?"

"There's not much to it . . ." Marini started out. "I've been working in the prison system for twenty-five years now, Dottore, and riots and brawls are always about the same things. Money, narcotics, cigarettes, or when someone fails to show proper respect for their betters. Inside here, there's a whole other world, you know? And people will kill to make sure they're respected. There's a hierarchy of power, and the Professor with his two underlings are very high in the pecking order. Obviously, Omar failed to live up to some understanding. Or else, just as likely, he owed them money."

Baldi ended the conversation. "For now, you're free to go. Thanks." The two guards stood up and left the warden's office.

"Can I talk to the guy in solitary confinement?" the judge asked, looking at Martinelli.

"With all three of them?" Martinelli asked.

"Only with the boss. This Agostino Lumi."

"I suggest you take a look at my files. That might give you a sense of just what sort of person we're talking about." And he pointed to an old metal filing cabinet that had a letter of the alphabet for every drawer. Baldi gestured to Pietra, who immediately riffled through the folders for the letter *L*. The judge stood pensively gazing at the usual photo of the president of the Italian republic, the crucifix, the flag, and the small Ikea bookshelf with dozens of books packed together in no particular order. "Here you are. Agostino Lumi." The chief of the Turin mobile squad handed the binder to Baldi, who proceeded to open it.

"All right, let's have a look."

Agostino Lumi was a criminal who could fairly claim title to the term. Born in Varese in 1968, he had committed a dozen or so armed robberies, been involved in three shoot-outs with the Carabinieri, been charged with a double homicide for rubbing out a couple of the men in his gang, as well as an attempted murder, and then, along with those, assorted crimes such as theft and fraud, which netted him various sentences in his thirty-eight years of criminal endeavors and now added up to two separate life sentences without possibility of parole. The second of the two life sentences had been handed down while he was an inmate of the Viterbo house of detention. Later transferred to Varallo for disciplinary reasons, he had clearly reformed his little retinue of enforcers, a gang that would allow him to rule the roost within the walls of that prison, too. "Quite an estimable individual, in other words."

"Unless experience misleads me, Dottore, you're not going to get much out of a guy like that . . . and in any case I've already requested and obtained a transfer order for him," Martinelli said.

"Fine." Baldi sighed. "One last thing. Do you have the video footage from the security cameras?"

"Certainly. Do you want it?"

Baldi said nothing. He just nodded. Then he looked at Italo Pierron, who had remained silent throughout the questioning. "Pierron, arrange to take delivery of the material from Dottor Martinelli."

"Ah, Dottore," Pietra said. "Tomorrow I'm going to have to head back to Turin."

Baldi nodded. "Pierron, any news concerning the mental defective?"

Italo threw both arms wide, disconsolate.

"Officer, just remember that you promised to deliver him to me."

"Of course, Dottor Baldi! Don't worry!"

"Are you looking for someone who was behind bars?" Seated at her little writing desk in front of the window, Marina is doodling on a sheet of paper, random meaningless patterns. She doesn't like it here at the residence. Not much room—she feels confined. She'd like to go back to a normal living situation, I know that.

"Maybe . . ." I answer her. "Otherwise, why would they have waited so long to lash out at me?"

"Maybe they were just out of the country."

"Good point. That's another suggestion I'll have to give to De Silvestri."

"You never talk to me about your work."

"Because that's not my work. I'm talking about a son of a bitch who shot Adele to death when he was actually trying to kill me. It's called survival."

"Obfuscate," she says to me, pulling out her usual notepad. "Isn't that a lovely word? 'Obfuscate.' It gives the idea of someone scowling like a guard dog."

"But what does it mean?"

"You don't know? It's important, Rocco. Very important."

Sergio Mozzicarelli was looking at the sagging metal mesh of the bunk bed above him, bulging under the weight of Aldo, one of his cell mates. He lay there with both hands crossed on his chest. It looked as if he were praying. Instead, he was thinking. The night was silent. People were snoring. People were coughing. A mass of men, alone and forgotten, were trying to get to sleep, just as he was. Sergio rolled over, facing the empty bed, the bed that for a few days had belonged to Mimmo Cuntrera. They had taken away his sheets, and the thin mattress was folded over on itself, baring the metal mesh beneath. The two other men in the cell seemed to be deep in sleep. The moonlight bathed the walls and reflected off the green-painted window grates. The water in the drain of the little squat toilet was gurgling. He drew a deep breath. He tried to shut his eyes, to abandon his thoughts and pretend that the sound of the drain in the squat toilet was actually a high mountain stream, full of fresh flowing water, good to drink. But he couldn't do it: that sound remained a plumbing problem and he was still in a prison cell, not out in the meadows of some alpine valley. His eyes slid open as if there were a well-oiled spring behind them. He glanced at the bunk bed next to his. Karim seemed to be sleeping. Then he rolled over in his direction. Sergio saw the young man's eyes glittering in the dark. The Tunisian was awake. Their eyes met.

"You're not asleep?" Sergio whispered to keep from waking up Aldo, who was right above him, snoring and weighing down the springs with his two hundred pounds of flesh.

"No . . ." Karim replied, "and neither are you . . ."

Sergio turned over on his side. "How do you feel?"

"My mouth hurts a little . . . but that will pass." And the young man brushed his fingers over his jaw where he'd taken the hardest hit. "Those assholes. I'll make them pay for it."

"Never mind. If there's one reason I've lived to be sixty-eight, it's because I've often let things slide."

The North African nodded. Then he rolled over, turning the back of his head to his cell mate. A sign that he had no desire to speak. Sergio, on the other hand, would gladly have continued. He couldn't bring himself to be alone with his thoughts. And these weren't thoughts of yearning or dismay. There was no one outside of that prison waiting for him. His wife had remarried; his two children had jobs in other countries. His brother was serving a life sentence in Lecce prison, and the only way he was getting out was feetfirst. Sergio was alone in the world, and the burden of his solitude had never weighed on him the way it did that night.

Who can I trust? he'd been wondering obsessively for hours now. He needed to talk to someone, spit out the thing that had been killing him minute after minute. Because Sergio Mozzicarelli had seen.

He'd seen it all.

STRETCHED OUT ON THE EXTREMELY HARD MATTRESS OF HIS residential hotel, Rocco was staring, eyes wide-open, at the ceiling, illuminated by the neon light of a sign outside a pub down in the street below. It blinked at regular intervals, like a metronome, changing color as it blinked. Light pink, dark pink, purple. One two three, one two three. A waltz. Still midnight. How could it be? How could the nights in that residential hotel be so everlasting? One two three. One two three! He got up from the bed. Lupa looked at him, baffled. "I'm going out, Lupa. What about you, want to come?"

He put on his trousers. The dog was already standing next to the door.

It was a May evening, the stars were bright in the sky, and only the occasional straggler was still out wandering the streets of the city. He walked down Rue Piave, where he had lived for nine months. He looked up at the building. He looked at the downspout that the nameless murderer had used just a few days earlier to scale the wall and enter his apartment. There it was. Shutters fastened tight. Eyes closed. Dead and blind. Like Adele. Who was now sleeping forever in the cemetery of Montecompatri, near Rome.

"What's the name of the street where the police chief found me an apartment?" he asked Lupa, who was sniffing at a manhole cover. "Via Laurent Cerise . . ."

Lupa trotted along next to him. "Let's go over to Ettore's bar right now and ask him where it is . . ." And he headed off toward Piazza Chanoux.

VIA CERISE WAS A NONDESCRIPT STREET. ONLY A FEW HOUSES, none of them tall. He liked it. Above all, he liked the arch under the building where Via Archet ran through. He hoped that the street number with the apartment that the police chief had found him was right in that building. He walked up to the front entrance. On the large wooden door there was a "For Rent" sign, prominently displayed. Rocco Schiavone smiled. "So it seems this may be the exact building. We'll come take a look tomorrow, eh? Do you like it? It's nice. Look, there are mountains over there, and there are mountains over there, too. Not bad, not bad at all!" And he made a smart about-face and headed back to the residential hotel. But then he noticed that the street was directly behind the courts building. "What? Come live right next to the prosecutor's office?" he mused into the night. "Entirely out of the question!" He would be subject to every whim of Baldi and the rest of them, every minute of his life. "They're not getting me on this street, not if I was a cold, dead corpse!" Lupa barked in agreement.

Someone was waiting for him in front of the wrought-iron and glass door of the residential hotel. The shadow was that of a man. And he was smoking a cigarette. He would have expected Anna. And deep down, he was glad that it wasn't her; at that hour of the night he couldn't have withstood a heated argument about the future of monogamous relationships and couples in the society of the twenty-first century. In an automatic, instinctive reaction, Rocco put his hand underneath his loden overcoat. But he hadn't carried a pistol for years now. The shadow stepped forward, and under the glare of the pub sign it took on the semblance of Italo Pierron.

"Ciao, Rocco."

"Ciao, Italo. What are you doing here at this hour of the night?"

"When are you coming back to the office?"

"I don't know."

Lupa went over to sniff at the trouser legs of the officer in civilian clothing, who shooed her away with a faint lurch of annoyance. Italo didn't like dogs. "That business at the prison. It's serious."

"How serious?"

"Plenty serious."

"Give me a cigarette."

Italo pulled out his pack and Rocco's eyes lit up. "Camels? You bought Camels?"

"I was out of my usual smokes."

While he was lighting one, the deputy chief looked Italo in the eyes. "Are you trying to bribe me?"

"No, I'm not kidding around. I was at the cigarette machine, I was free to choose, and I said to myself, since I'm going to see Rocco anyway, why not just get the brand that he likes best?"

"Thanks. It's a very feminine thought."

"I'll take that as a compliment."

"How did you know that I would be awake?"

"Because since you've moved into the residential hotel, I've been calling the receptionist every day and by now I know your habits."

Rocco spat out the smoke, looking up at the sky that was spangled with stars. "In that case, let's come to the gravity of the matter."

"The dead man in prison. It's Mimmo Cuntrera."

At that name, Rocco shut his eyes. "Goddamn it to hell . . ." he murmured. "How can that be? Did someone murder him?"

"It looks like a heart attack, but the judge seems to be convinced that it's something else."

"Right. Mimmo Cuntrera isn't going to die like that. It would be too nice if pieces of shit like him were taken down by heart attacks. No, he's a weed, it's a lot harder to kill his kind."

"Rocco, maybe you'd better come back into the office."

Italo was right, and the deputy chief knew it. Mimmo Cuntrera was the irritating aftermath of the Berguet case. And of the investigations that Rocco had carried out in order to save the hide of the Berguets' daughter, Chiara. He couldn't just remain shut up in the Vieux Aosta. Adele was dead. And he felt personally responsible, even though his old friend Seba didn't see it that way. Those 6.35 mm bullets had been meant for him, for Rocco Schiavone.

"Put this in the log, Italo. On a May night, at . . . ten minutes past one, Deputy Chief Rocco Schiavone came face-to-face with a pain in the ass of the tenth degree!"

Italo smiled as he thought back to the chart that he'd hung up outside the deputy chief's office. "All right, I'll log it in tomorrow."

The deputy chief looked at him blankly, uncomprehending.

"So, Rocco, what are you going to do?"

"I'll sleep on it."

"Are you feeling sleepy?"

"No. Lupa's feeling sleepy."

It was true. The puppy had fallen asleep on his Clarks desert boots.

HIS THOUGHTS TURNED BACK TO MIMMO CUNTRERA. AND the story of the Berguet family. Something didn't add up in that coil of connections. There was one note that was out of tune in the musical score. Cuntrera had been discovered, Rocco and his officers had freed Chiara Berguet, the attempt of the Mafia conspiracy to take over Edil.ber had failed utterly, so why rub Cuntrera out? What had he known? Who wanted him dead? Drowning in his thoughts, he climbed the stairs and found himself once again lying on the hard-as-hell mattress of the Vieux Aosta. On the ceiling, the same old waltz of the three colors of the pub sign in the street below. "One two three, one two three . . ." And suddenly he was fast asleep.

FRIDAY

"Do you really think it's right that if I want to talk to you I have to get out the phone book and find the number of your residential hotel, and since it's an old phone book, it doesn't have the number, after which I have to go on the Internet and only after six different sites that no one's bothered to update, I finally get to hear your jerky voice in my earpiece?"

"What time is it?" asked Rocco.

"Seven thirty in the morning, may you die of cancer!" shouted Alberto Fumagalli. "Come to the hospital. I'm here working. And I've just witnessed something that, believe me, not even in a film by Spielberg . . . Hurry!"

"What do films by Spielberg have to do with anything?"

"It's straight out of a horror flick!"

"Spielberg doesn't make horror flicks, you ignorant lunkhead."

"Whatever, just get your ass in gear!"

"But wasn't Pietra on the case?"

"Pietra has gone back to Turin, he has a murder in Parella. I called the police chief, I called the judge. And they made an executive decision that your fucking vacation is over. Get moving!" And with that the pathologist ended the call.

Rocco rubbed his eyes. But he had no intention of hurrying over, the way Fumagalli had suggested. If life was sucking him back into the stream, he'd made up his mind he wasn't going down without a fight. Did they want to stick him with a royal pain in the ass of the tenth degree? Then he would go back to his longtime rhythms of existence: shower, breakfast at Ettore's café on Piazza Chanoux, police headquarters, morning joint. After that, and only after that, a visit to the morgue.

AND SURE ENOUGH, THAT'S WHAT HE DID. GOING BACK TO the office was like finding yourself face-to-face with someone who had been insisting for years that he was your friend, but who had never been your friend in the first place. The people from the cleaning crew had avoided dusting his furniture. He shut the door, flung open the window to the sweet smells of May that were being wafted into the room by a light breeze, sat down, opened the desk drawer, and lit the first joint after four days of abstinence. He leaned out the windowsill. The cars were going by on the street below; the peaks, still covered with snow, were gleaming in the timid springtime sunlight, while the shoulders of the mountains had turned emerald green. New grass, excellent fodder for the cows.

"You want to know something, Lupa? I could jump out my window. But I'd just land on the roof of the canopy over the entrance to police headquarters. It's not even a one-yard drop. At the very worst, I'd sprain my ankle. Just look . . ." The sky had opened up. The clouds were fluffy and white. He could see flowers on the meadows.

He inhaled another mouthful of smoke. Nice. Sweet and aromatic. The little electric trains started chugging again in his veins. His brain began spinning at a higher RPM; the pistons were puffing the dust away, the oil lubricated all the ganglions of his nervous system, and at long last Deputy Chief Rocco Schiavone felt that all was right with the world. Now, yes, now indeed he could go out and hear whatever news Fumagalli had, and all about his alleged horror films. He tossed the spent roach out the window, put on his loden overcoat, and opened his office door.

"It's a pleasure to see you again, Dottore!" said Casella. There they were, all lined up outside his door. Casella, D'Intino, Deruta, Italo, Caterina, and Antonio Scipioni.

"What is this?" asked Rocco. "Are you about to execute me by firing squad?"

"It's nice to see you again, Dottore! We missed you, you know that?" said Deruta. All their faces were beaming; they looked like a classroom of students who had just smeared glue on the teacher's chair and were eagerly waiting for him to sit down.

"Do you mind telling me what's gotten into you all?"

Italo winked and glanced archly at the wall to the deputy chief's right.

"What is it, Italo?"

"Just take a look . . ."

Rocco turned around. He hadn't noticed it when he'd first come in fifteen minutes earlier. There was a sign tacked up on the wall, divided into numbered quadrants. Up high was the title: "Major Pains in the Ass." Rocco stepped closer. His officers were snickering.

"Who did this?" he asked.

Italo raised his hand.

"Major pains in the ass . . ." the deputy chief started reading. Every once in a while his shoulders would shake. He was laughing. "Cafés that don't stock Algida ice cream, true enough. That's a huge pain in the ass . . . Oh, and Radio Virgin Mary, those pain-in-the-ass priests. All the zeroes on IBAN routing numbers . . . Wait, Italo, did you collect all these?"

"In the past few months," Pierron replied. "Then, as time goes by and we come up with others, I'll add them."

"Then you can add these five: Sixth degree, losing your place in a book you're reading. Seventh degree, put down waiting for your luggage at the airport. Or else seeing it arrive, but with a broken handle or zipper. Or not seeing it arrive at all. Eighth degree, put people who text you without saying who they are. Ninth degree, attending a performance of folk dances. Tenth degree, obviously, an unsolved case of murder. Speaking of which, Pierron, get ready, because we have to go. Fumagalli has something for us."

"Do I have to come, too? I already saw the dead body yesterday, at the prison."

"Your presence is essential!"

Italo nodded. Caterina walked over to the chart with a pen in hand. "Well, I'll add the new pains in the ass, then." And she started writing.

"Caterì, when you've finished this thankless task, do you think you could bring Lupa some water? She's asleep on the armchair in my office."

"Certainly. And where should I put waiting for your luggage at the airport, again? What level?"

"Seventh. Put that at the seventh."

"So are we certain that I absolutely have to come?" Italo insisted, hoping he could avoid this visit to the morgue. "I just had breakfast."

"Don't worry. I'm told that it's not disgusting, just horrifying."

"So, it's not going to make me throw up?"

"Exactly."

FUMAGALLI WAS WAITING FOR THEM IN FRONT OF THE MORGUE. He was looking up at the sky full of clouds that sailed along serenely, like so many little cotton balls, gliding on the calm spring winds. The snow, the cold, the black winter sky were all things that seemed light-years away. "Strange, isn't it?" said the medical examiner as soon as Rocco and Italo came within earshot.

"What?" asked the deputy chief.

"When you're in the middle of the winter, the days drag out and you get the feeling they're never going to end. And it seems as if the cold will never end, either. But then, look! Zap! You can't even remember when it was winter anymore."

"Speak for yourself. I can remember it perfectly. It was barely a week ago," Rocco replied. "Anyway, what about this horror flick?"

Alberto Fumagalli pressed his lips tight and gazed at the two cops with a serious expression. "Before you go in, Rocco, a word."

They stepped off to one side, leaving Italo standing alone in the middle of the plaza.

"Listen. It really is a rather distressing sight. I can just picture him"—and here he pointed at the Valdostan officer—"already stretched out on the floor. In other words, maybe we should leave him outside. Unless . . ."

"Unless what?"

"Unless you and me care to make a little bet."

Rocco looked the doctor in the eye. "I like it . . ."

"Let's say I give your officer six seconds."

"The odds are in your favor, Alberto. You already know what we'll be looking at, and I don't. That means that if you say six seconds, you have much better odds than I do. Which means I need you to give me a handicap."

"Like for instance?"

"I say it's going to be seven seconds. If Italo can hold out for only six seconds or less, then you win. From six and one hundredth of a second to when he finally does faint, which might not happen until ten seconds out, I win."

Alberto thought it over. "So I win if he passes out at the sixth second?"

"Or before."

"You've got a bet!"

"Okay, but what are the stakes?" asked Rocco.

"Dinner. At the Enoteca Croix de Ville."

"Appetizer, pasta, entrée, and dessert?"

"And an after-dinner amaro!"

Rocco shook the doctor's hand. They walked over to Italo while the medical examiner pulled his cell phone out of his pocket. He had no intention of calling anyone. He was looking for the stopwatch function, which he was going to start the instant that Pierron laid his eyes on what the doctor had described as something straight out of a splatter film.

"Let's go!" said the deputy chief, and the three of them trooped into the room.

ITALO LOOKED DOWN AT THE LINOLEUM FLOOR. ATTENTIVELY, Rocco studied the officer's face, which had already turned pale. In fact, as soon as he had entered the hallway infested by the metallic stench of disinfectant, he'd immediately started showing worrisome signs of heart palpitations. The deputy chief decided he'd been reckless in his betting tactics. Fumagalli opened the door to the morgue and, with a sadistic smile, said: "Be my guests . . ."

"Rocco, I . . ." Italo said under his breath.

"What is it?"

"I'd prefer not to."

"My ass, you'd prefer not to, Italo. You're a cop, learn how to do your job!"

They went in. Like a hovering, apprehensive mother, Rocco kept his eyes fixed on his favorite officer. He paid no attention to Alberto, who had in the meantime gone over to pull the plastic sheet off the corpse. The usual stench of rot mixed with alcohol that felt as if it would stick to their clothing forever. They went over to the autopsy gurney. Italo's eyes widened. The deputy chief attentively observed his partner, while the alert doctor had already started the stopwatch.

One second: Italo Pierron's pupils enlarged like oil spreading across water. Two seconds: his lips parted ever so slightly. Three seconds: his eyelids started to flutter hysterically. Four seconds: his forehead pearled over with drops of sweat. Five seconds: his eyelids started to lower. Six seconds: his eyeballs rolled upward. Almost seven seconds: Italo dropped to the floor.

"Fuck!" said Alberto as he hit the stopwatch. "Six seconds and fifty-five hundredths, goddamn it to hell!"

Rocco smiled and bent over to help his partner back up. "Good job, Italo! I knew you wouldn't fail me! Albè, you owe me dinner! Give me a hand here!"

"*Promissio boni viri est obligatio*," said Albert, quoting an old Latin saw about honoring your obligations. "And to think I lost by just fifty-five hundredths of a second, damn it all!"

Together they picked up the policeman and hauled him out of the morgue. They laid him down on a bench in the hallway.

"Now what are we going to do? Wait for him to wake up?"

"Don't be ridiculous. He'll be up and on his feet in two minutes," said Rocco. They left him stretched out on the bench with his feet elevated, and turned around and went back into the autopsy room.

This time, Rocco focused on the body.

Mimmo Cuntrera's corpse was a perfectly normal corpse, something that, sad to say, Rocco had already seen dozens of times before. The off note was that the body was already in a pretty advanced state of decomposition.

"I don't see anything out of the ordinary," said the deputy chief. "Well, I mean, he's a little bit rotten. Where is this horror flick?"

Alberto Fumagalli smiled. He went over to the table beside the gurney and picked up a white T-shirt. He picked it up, as if to show off how perfectly white it had come out in the wash. "Well?" he asked.

"Well, what?" He was starting to get on Rocco's nerves.

"They brought him to me from the prison with this T-shirt on him. A white T-shirt, made in China, if you ask me. Cotton. And it was still on him when I laid him on the gurney."

"I continue to fail to see what's so odd about it."

"Look here."

The stitches around the sleeves had been torn open at several points.

"So it's ripped. So what?"

"It's torn."

"In Rome, we'd say it was ripped."

"Well, you're in Aosta, so you can say that it's torn."

"Okay, all right, Alberto, it's torn. What about it?"

"Before I put him in the refrigerated drawer last night, it wasn't torn. So what happened?" The medical examiner's question hung suspended in the silence of the morgue.

"I don't know. Was he not dead?"

"Domenico Cuntrera was deader than Julius Caesar."

"Did someone sneak in here last night in a state of delirium and tear up his T-shirt?"

"No. There's only one answer."

"He's a zombie?"

"Oh, go fuck yourself, Rocco. He's not a zombie. This body swelled up on me."

"Isn't that what all corpses do?"

"Let me try to make myself clear. This corpse blew up on me to a ridiculous extent and then, in just a few more hours, it deflated."

"And what does that make you think?"

"I've never had anything of the sort happen to me before. I've been banging my head against it since this morning. Corpses just don't behave like this . . . and most of all, do you want to see the anus?"

"Can I skip that part?"

"As you like. It was just a matter of scientific precision. You see that he's already started to decompose? After just twenty-four hours?"

"That's the strange thing. And can you figure out why?"

"It's no easy matter. Not easy at all . . . I smell poison, though. I'm not sure exactly which, but if you ask me, it's poison!"

"Do you have a magnifying glass?"

"What do you want to look at?"

"The skin."

"Rocco, my friend, that's my profession. And anyway, I don't use a magnifying glass to look at skin." The medical examiner went over to a tripod. "Solenord fluorescent magnifying light."

He dragged it over to the corpse and switched it on. "Biconvex lens with a light intensity at fifty centimeters of 550 lux."

"Albè, it's not like I'm thinking of buying it." Rocco grabbed the swing arm and started examining the neck of the late Cuntrera.

"What are you looking for?"

But Rocco didn't reply. In silence he observed the pigments of the flesh, the moles. Then all of a sudden, he froze. "I need an expert opinion." And he handed the lens off to Alberto.

"Fucking . . ." said the medical examiner. "Fucking hell . . . it's tiny, it's really tiny, but I'll bet my retirement that this is an injection, or a bee sting."

"Do they have bees in prison?" asked the deputy chief with a smile.

"Okay, that changes everything. Injection mark on the jugular. Bingo!"

"So now what are you telling me?"

Alberto jerked upright. "That things are starting to become clear. Now I need to get busy, and fast. If you want to stay, be my guest. But I need to cut my patient open and, believe me, for someone like you, that's not an entertaining spectacle."

"I'll get going." Rocco headed for the door while Alberto reached across the table to gather the tools of his trade. "So what's the plan?" asked the deputy chief, turning around once he'd reached the doorway.

"I need to take a few bits of good old Mimmo here as samples and send them out to be tested. I need a first-class toxicologist, someone skilled. This is something that I personally have never seen before. And I'll tell you the truth, I find it extremely exciting!"

"Exciting?"

"That's what I said."

Rocco nodded. "Exciting. All right, well, you owe me a dinner." He opened the door.

"Oh, Rocco?"

The deputy chief stopped and turned back. "Yes?"

"Any news about the son of a bitch who broke into your apartment?"

Rocco limited himself to shaking his head.

"When you catch him, give me a shout. Because, and let's keep this between us, I'd love to have him as a patient for a couple of hours."

When Rocco got out into the hallway, he went over to Italo, who was starting to regain his senses. "Come on, Italo, let's get back to the office. I'll drive."

Italo nodded and handed the keys to the deputy chief. "I'm sorry, it's just that I really—"

"Don't sweat it, you earned me a dinner!"

THE SEA WAS CALM. A VAST SILVERY GRAY EXPANSE THAT, toward the horizon, almost verged on purple. The constant low waves broke gently against the rocks. The occasional seagull glided solitary through the air. In the distance a ship had turned athwart the horizon line. Corrado Pizzuti was standing outside his café, arms crossed on his chest, his gaze lost in the panorama before him. He'd considered reporting Enzo Baiocchi to the police. All things considered, Corrado was an innocent man. All he'd done was drive Enzo to Aosta, so was that a crime? He'd had no advance knowledge of the reason for that drive—that's what he'd tell the police. Which, after all, was the truth. If he'd understood that bandit's intentions along the way, he would have torn out of there, leaving Enzo in some service area along the highway. The real problem was: Would they believe him? Corrado had spent time in prison on two separate occasions, once for defrauding an insurance company and once for peddling narcotics. What would his word be worth to a policeman? Less than zero. Especially given the evidence of that damned receipt he'd had them issue at the hotel. How could he have made such a stupid mistake? The umpteenth mistake of his life.

He had to get rid of Enzo.

It's him or me, he decided.

"Here's your espresso . . . ristretto, the way you like it."

Tatiana had joined him outside, with two demitasse cups of espresso.

"Thanks . . ."

The woman placed her lips against the rim of her demitasse. "The sea is beautiful today, isn't it? The winter is over. Soon it will be warm and the season will begin."

Corrado smiled as a motor scooter shot noisily past along the waterfront. "It's true. And then the noise will start up again and I won't be able to get to sleep before three in the morning."

"Hey, what's got into you?"

At last, he turned to look at her. "Oh, just foolish thoughts in my head."

"You want to tell me about them?"

"It's nothing much, don't worry about it."

"No, I *will* worry about it. Since that trip you took last week, you've been odd. What happened to you?"

"Oh, nothing, like I told you. Every so often I think about Rome. And I get a little homesick, that's all. Then I get over it."

"Tonight, I'll take you out to dinner."

Corrado smiled. "What about the CPA De Lullo? Are you going to leave him all alone at home?"

"What if I do? One evening alone won't kill him."

"What's the name of the city you come from? I always forget it."

"There's no way you could remember it. Vsevolozhsk . . . near St. Petersburg."

"What if we went and opened a café back there?"

Tatiana burst out laughing. "You wouldn't last three months. It's too cold for you there. But why? Don't you like it here?"

"Not anymore . . ." And he stepped around the woman and went back into the bar.

Tatiana heaved a sigh just as Barbara the bookseller stepped out of her store. "Buongiorno, Tatiana . . ."

"Buongiorno."

Barbara looked around. She seemed to have something urgent to say to the Russian woman. She shot a glance around the inside of the café. "I need to talk to you," she told her in a whisper, without stepping any closer.

"So talk to me."

"Not here. Later. I have to run now." And she hurried away.

Everyone's getting strange, Tatiana thought to herself.

Corrado had started making panini. Slowly, methodically. A slice of bread, a dollop of mayonnaise, a leaf of lettuce, the tuna, another leaf of lettuce, another dollop of mayonnaise. While he was working on his third prosciutto panino, he suddenly froze. He looked down at the yellow-handled knife that he held in his hand and resumed the train of thought that his business partner had interrupted. He didn't have any other solutions. He couldn't go on living in that nightmare, blackmailed by that piece of shit. He had to do it. He had to prepare everything with calm and care and then strike unexpectedly. When Enzo least expected it, when Enzo was defenseless. Otherwise he'd never be able to beat him. A quick, accurate, lethal blow and all his problems would be over. He just needed to find the courage. Maybe help himself out by snorting a line or two before going to bed so that he'd remain wide-awake and clearheaded once the time came to drive the point of the yellow-handled knife into the monster's body.

BEFORE ENTERING HIS OFFICE, ROCCO NOTICED THAT CATERINA had updated the chart of pains in the ass. He smiled at the painstaking work his deputy inspector had done.

"Dottor Schiavone!"

Officer D'Intino's high-pitched unpleasant voice echoed down the hallway. Rocco turned around.

"What do you want, D'Intì?"

"The dog."

"What about her?"

"It's inside. It's still sleeping. It's not feeling sick, by any chance?"

"She's just a puppy. Sleeping is one of her favorite activities."

"Listen, there are at least six phone calls from Judge Baldi. He's been looking for you like a crazy person."

"What time is it now?"

"Five o'clock."

Rocco rolled his eyes. "I need to go to the prosecutor's office."

"Do you want me to go with you?"

"God, no."

"Do you want me to look after the dog?"

"No, absolutely not."

"Do you want me to do anything else?"

He was about to retort: "Yes, get the fuck out from underfoot." Instead, an idea came to him, unlooked for, but it lit up his brain as only genuine strokes of genius are capable of doing. "D'Intino! I have something important for you and Deruta to do. It's a fundamental mission!"

The officer snapped to attention. "You do? You do! I'll call Deruta?"

"Here he is now!" said Rocco. And in fact, Deruta had just emerged from a side door. "Deruta! Come here, please."

"Right away, Dottore." And wobbling on his undersized feet, he walked toward them.

"All right, then, Deruta and D'Intino, there's something very important and delicate that I need you both to do for me."

"At your service, like always," Deruta blurted.

"Now, first of all, and this is a very important point: you must always report directly and exclusively to me. No one else at police headquarters. Is that clear?"

Both heads bobbed affirmatively in unison.

"It's a tough, challenging, difficult task, but I know that you can pull it off. You always have in the past, as far as that goes."

A small grimace of skepticism twisted Deruta's mouth.

"What's wrong?"

"Well, actually, Dotto' . . . one time you sent us out in search of a lock that you gave us the key to and they practically beat us both to death."

"That's true," added D'Intino, "and another time you sent us to spy on some narcotics dealers and I broke two ribs . . ."

"Plus, also just last week up in the mountains in the middle of all that snow so that they almost had to cut off D'Intino's frostbitten big toe."

"I'm still limping a little from that!"

Rocco listened and then replied: "But this time it's much harder than that. Still, if you don't feel up to it, that's okay. I'll just ask Scipioni, this kind of thing doesn't scare him!"

"Don't say that even in jest!" Deruta's pride rebelled at the thought. "Give us our orders!"

"Wednesday, May 9, and Thursday, May 10 . . ."

"Last week . . ."

"Very good, Deruta. I need you to make the rounds of all—and, I repeat, all—the hotels and bed-and-breakfasts in Aosta and surrounding provinces and get a list of all the guests who stayed there. Avoid luxury accommodations and three-star hotels. Search two-star hotels and down. In other words, cheap and cheerful."

D'Intino lowered his voice. "Who are we looking for?"

"You go search. Most of all, keep your ears open for any mention of someone who comes from Rome. This is important, get the lists and bring them to me. To me and me alone. Have I made myself clear?"

They both nodded again. "When do we start?"

"Right away, Deruta. This minute!" And he pulled open his office door to go through it. He turned again to look at the two officers, who still stood, anchored to the spot, in the middle of the hallway. "Well? What are you waiting for? Get going!"

"But if we're going to do this job, though . . . then there's something we need!" And Deruta looked at D'Intino in search of some sign of assent.

"What do you need?"

Deruta held up his right hand with four fingers in plain view. "Four highlighters!"

"One pink, one yellow, one green, and one blue!" D'Intino summed up.

Rocco furrowed his brow slightly. "Why, though, don't you have any in the office?"

"No," Deruta replied tragically. "They never approved them for us."

Rocco threw both arms wide. "Will ten euros be enough?"

"Certainly."

The deputy chief put his hand on his wallet. He didn't have a ten-euro bill. So he gave them a twenty-euro banknote. "Buy yourselves four highlighters apiece!"

D'Intino and Deruta emanated joy from their eyes, from their skin, and from their hands as they hastily grabbed at the twenty euros. Effusively thanking him and already deep in conference, they hurried out of the office.

"Huh . . ." Rocco murmured and went into his office.

LUPA WAS STANDING BY THE DOOR. SHE WAS WAGGING HER tail, and it smacked rhythmically against the back of the couch she'd fallen asleep on. She'd heard the deputy chief's voice. "Ciao, Lupacchiotta, how are you?" Rocco picked the puppy up and hoisted her in midair, gazing into her eyes. "Now you and I are going to have to have a serious conversation. Papà might have to go away for a few days. Are you going to be a good girl?"

Lupa licked his nose.

"I'll take that for a yes. Now will you come with me to see the judge?"

Lupa licked his nose again.

"But you have to behave yourself, understood? Let's go, forward march!" And he set her down on the floor, whereupon Lupa ran straight out of the office and disappeared down the hallway.

LUPA WAS PARTICULARLY INTERESTED IN THE FRINGE OF THE faux-Bukhara carpet in Baldi's office. She was ripping the tassels of fringe one by one.

"Dogs aren't allowed in the prosecutor's office building," Baldi told him.

"I know that. But downstairs they made an exception."

"She's stinking up my office."

"Lupa doesn't stink. If anything, she smells of popcorn. Especially when she's asleep."

Baldi shook his head. "Just tell me if you've come up with an idea, Schiavone."

"First of all, let me extend my compliments."

The judge listened attentively.

"If you hadn't insisted on bringing the victim's body immediately to the morgue where Fumagalli could take a look at him, we would never have noticed."

"Noticed what, Schiavone?"

"You were right. This was no heart attack. Cuntrera was murdered."

"I knew it, I knew it!"

Rocco shot a quick glance at Lupa, who continued to chew on the carpet.

"Only I wish you'd explain better."

"Fumagalli discovered a strange reaction taking place with the corpse during the night. And as a result of that, he's now examining exactly how that corpse, in fact, became a corpse."

"Excellent!" And Baldi slammed his fist into the desk, making the photograph of his wife jump, along with all the pens and an old brass calendar that was still set to June 2005. Lupa, however, did not allow herself to be distracted. She went on munching on the Bukhara rug. Baldi suddenly leapt to his feet. He strode around the desk. "That carpet is state property, and if your dog won't stop, I'll make you pay for it."

"Lupa!" And the dog shifted her attention to Rocco's Clarks desert boots, methodically ripping the laces to shreds.

"So that means we're looking at a murder. And whoever did the killing might be our mysterious puppet master, right?"

"That's right. The self-proclaimed Carlo Cutrì."

"Self-proclaimed, you got that right. Now listen carefully . . . Let me bring you quickly up to speed. Domenico Cuntrera belonged to the gang that was extorting the Berguet family. But we need to assemble the puzzle pieces. Important puzzle pieces. The first piece: Cuntrera's papers, the ones we arrested him with at the border. Well, I'm working on it . . . and there are plenty of things that don't add up. But those are complications with the banking system that are of little interest to you . . ."

"If you say so . . ."

"The reason they don't add up is, if you chase after various numbers and numbered accounts, you get very high up the totem pole, Dottor Schiavone."

"You don't strike me as someone who has a fear of heights."

Baldi burst out laughing. "I love it, I'm going to steal that line. But now let's move on to the second puzzle piece: the Vallée Savings Bank. Do you remember them? They were lending money to Pietro Berguet's company, Edil.ber. The bank had shut off the spigots of funding to the building company. And so Pietro Berguet started borrowing money from Cuntrera, which means 'Ndrangheta, and once Cuntrera got his nose under the tent flap, he was trying to take over the whole company."

"I remember perfectly, Dottore. It's only been a couple of days."

Baldi paid him no mind. "Then you discovered that no fewer than seven of this Cuntrera's victims, all of them small businessmen who owed him money, had one thing in common: namely, a bank account with the Vallée Savings Bank. Are we on the same page so far?"

The deputy chief did no more than nod.

"And so I started digging into the papers of this bank, whose director, Laura Turrini, you've already met. And here's the second puzzle piece: Dottoressa Turrini . . . Well, she's no longer employed by the bank. Fired, given her pink slip in the course of a single afternoon."

"That sounds odd."

"And now let's move on to the third detail, which is the most concerning one. Specifically, Carlo Cutrì. Who is supposed to have been the accomplice of the late Cuntrera."

"Right. A resident of Lugano, no?"

"Carlo Cutrì doesn't exist."

Rocco's eyes opened wide.

"No," Baldi specified. "No such person. At his address, there is a French family, and there isn't the faintest shade of any Carlo Cutrì in the lists of Lugano residents."

"What does that mean?"

"I don't know. It means that Carlo Cutrì is a fake name for someone else who controlled Mimmo Cuntrera and who organized the kidnapping of poor Chiara Berguet."

Rocco lit a cigarette. "Or else it's a real name, but now he's hiding behind a fake one."

"Right."

"A fine mess, Dottore."

"I have the distinct sensation that we're always several steps behind."

"Behind who?"

"That's what I don't know, Schiavone! If I did know, I would have solved the case by now, don't you think? The sensation I have is that we're closing the stable door—"

"—after the horse has bolted. Yes, and it's a nasty sensation."

"And put out that cigarette. Who told you that you could smoke in here?" Rocco obeyed with a grimace as the judge went back to his desk. He noticed that the photo of the judge's wife had fallen facedown. The judge picked it up, and for the first time since Schiavone had set foot in that office, he turned it to face his interlocutor. He made the introductions: "My wife . . ." Rocco smiled. Maybe the judge's marriage was intact after all. After all the back-and-forth since September with the photograph traveling from drawer to trash can and then back onto the desktop, but only facedown, after months and months, peace and serenity seemed to have returned to the judge's little family. Baldi leaned over to make sure the dog wasn't doing any damage to the furnishings of his office.

"What breed is it?"

"She's a Saint-Rhémy-en-Ardennes."

"A what?"

"A very rare breed. And bipolar, into the mix. They can be extremely accommodating or else terribly aggressive. It all depends on the owner's personality."

"In that case, remind me never to pet her. Saint-Rhémy-en-Ardennes . . . that strikes me as complete bullshit. In any case, if we find out who killed Cuntrera . . ."

"Then we can track back to the mastermind. Cuntrera had just been transferred to the prison, so it seems a little early for him to have made any mortal enemies, at least to this degree."

"I couldn't agree more. And then, as I said, the papers that Cuntrera had with him were pure dynamite! Tremendously explosive. I think the brains behind this murder can be found somewhere in those documents. I'm sure of it. How do you intend to proceed?"

"Investigating inside a prison is a very challenging thing to do. The rule of silence is more powerful than the prison walls themselves. No one would breathe a word to me, no one would make any false moves in my presence. I'd have to undertake the investigation from outside. But if there's one thing I've learned in life, it's that if you're going to dig into filth and shit, then you're going to have to climb down into the sewers yourself, roll in the stuff, until you start to reek of it."

"How about a disguise?"

"It would be pointless, Dottor Baldi. The convicts would figure out immediately that I'm not one of them. And anyway, I'd need time. No, what I'm going to have to do is go in and pretend that I'm there on some routine assignment. That's the only way I can hope to win some friends, get someone in there to like me. If you can help me with the warden, persuade him to give me all the help possible."

"Consider it done."

ALL HE WANTED WAS TO RETRIEVE A COUPLE OF LINEN SHIRTS and his disposable razors. He stealthily entered the old apartment on Rue Piave like a thief in the night. First he went into the bathroom, and then, after counting to three, he went into the bedroom. He was afraid. Afraid that the mattress might still be there, with the patches of rust on it, rust that wasn't really rust at all. Afraid of envisioning Adele's body again, riddled with the bullets that someone had fired into the poor woman that Thursday night. He opened the door and lunged at the clothes closet without turning around, without thinking, rapidly, holding his breath, as if the air itself were still befouled with that murder. The shirts were there, on the second shelf. He took them and quickly exited the room. He shut the front door behind him without even stopping to double-lock it. He went down the steps again without breathing and found himself back in the street. At last, he breathed in, his mouth wide-open, and started toward his car. Sitting on the still-warm hood of his Volvo was Anna, arms crossed.

"How are you?" she asked him.

"Been better. You?"

"Been better."

There was a strange light in her eyes, and Rocco couldn't tell whether it was a gleam of anger or profound sadness. She was dressed in black. The sweater over which a handsome silver pendant hung was black. The knee-length skirt was black. The ankle-high shoes were black. She wore no socks. She reached up and brushed her hair back. "I've been waiting for you for days."

"I know. I only went back to the office today."

"Are you free this evening?"

"I'm always free."

"We're having a party. Will you come?"

"I'm not in the right mood for a party."

"You'll like this one. The crème de la crème of Aosta's high society will be there."

"Will your lover be there, too?"

"*You're* my lover."

"No, I mean your official lover. That architect Bucci Something-or-Other."

Anna smiled. "Bucci Rivolta, is it really possible that you can't get that name into your head? I don't know if he'll be there. But you need to relax. He's not my lover anymore."

"You know what? I'm starting to get a little tired of people who want to shoot me!"

"Don't worry, he doesn't even have a permit to carry a gun. Eight o'clock at my place?"

Rocco nodded.

"Do you have a black suit?"

"What, are we going to a memorial service?"

"No, it's just that it's formal, and black is elegant."

"Black isn't elegant. Black is funereal. I'll come dressed as nicely as I know how." Then he pushed the button on the remote and the running lights on the Volvo blinked on and off.

"And with that the conversation is officially over," Anna said to herself. "One thing, please, if you're going to run late or not come at all, will you call me?"

"Of course, of course." Rocco climbed into the car. Anna knocked on the window. Rocco opened it. "Yes . . . ?"

"Would it be out of line to ask you for a kiss?"

Rocco leaned out, barely brushed his lips over hers, and put the car into reverse.

"I've kissed warmer gravestones," Anna murmured.

"Excuse me?"

"Nothing," the woman said as she turned on her heel and headed for home.

"But why? Why!" shouted the deputy chief as he slammed his hand down hard onto the steering wheel.

THE ONLY TELEVISION SET WORKING AT POLICE HEADQUARTERS was the one in the waiting room. Rocco chased out two officers who were resting up after a twenty-four-hour shift. While Italo was working with the cables around the video equipment, Antonio Scipioni walked in with a packet of DVDs in one hand.

"All right." Rocco walked to meet him. "Are these all of them?"

"These are the recordings made by security cameras numbers four, five, and six out in the courtyard."

"Excellent. Are you done, Italo?"

Pierron turned to look at the deputy chief. "All done."

"These are hours of video!" Antonio exclaimed. "They start twenty minutes before the discovery of the corpse and they end an hour later."

"What happened afterward is of no interest to us." And Rocco cracked open the first DVD case. "What we're interested in is before."

"Are we going to watch them all in order?"

"You're going to watch them all in order," Rocco mocked him in a singsong. "Minute by minute. And mark down anything interesting that you notice."

The grimmest dismay was stamped on Italo's and Antonio's faces. "What's wrong?" the deputy chief continued. "Did you have other plans for today?"

"But . . . I'd say . . ."

"Antonio, a nice long day at the movies with a friend, what more could you ask for?" And with a smile he left the two officers to that thankless task.

AS THE DEPUTY CHIEF STRODE DOWN THE HALLWAY, HE SAW Casella emerge from an office. "Casella!"

The officer came running. "Yes, sir, Dottore!"

Rocco pulled out his wallet and extracted a twenty-euro banknote. "Go to the pastry shop. Get a nice big tray of finger pastries and take them up to Antonio and Italo, in the waiting room."

"Why?"

"Has it really come to this? Are you seriously asking for an explanation of a direct order from your superior officer?"

"No, it's just that, seeing that I've got a stack of important documents here, I thought that . . ."

"Well, you thought wrong. Go on, get going. Ten minutes tops and I expect to see you back here. I might have other things for you to do!"

"I'm on my way!"

Casella grabbed the twenty-euro bill and headed for the exit.

Before going into his office, Rocco stopped and shot a glance at the chart of pains in the ass. He pulled a pen out of his jacket pocket. He had one in the ranking of sixth degree: buying pastries for Sunday lunch. Then he went in, followed by Lupa.

He shut the door, and the noise of the panel slamming against the door jamb coincided with the ringing of the telephone on his desk. He grabbed the receiver. "Who's busting my balls now?" he shouted.

"Schiavone? It's Farinelli . . ."

It was the chief detective of the forensic squad in Turin. "Ciao."

"How are you?"

"Better than yesterday . . ."

"I'm always waiting for the day when you answer 'Doing fine!' That'll be the day that I bet all my savings on the Powerball."

Rocco sat down in his leather desk chair. Lupa leapt up onto the sofa. "That day will come only once the primordial waters have taken back dominion over dry land, and the planet is finally safe from humankind!"

"Excellent. You seem to be in fine fettle. So listen: something's stirring."

"I'm all ears."

"We're talking about the pistol that was fired in your apartment. The 6.35 mm. I've done some cross-referencing and you know what? That pistol was used three years ago, in an armed robbery in a bank in Cinecittà, and someone was shot to death. The victim was called Ugo Ferri, a retiree. He just happened to be in the wrong place at the wrong time, his bad luck. Caught in the crossfire."

"Go on."

"Two bank robbers. One was arrested, the other one got away, and that pistol was never recovered. And now here it is again, in the hands of the mysterious murderer of your poor late friend Adele."

"Do you know the name of the bank robber who was arrested?"

"Hold on, I've got it right here . . ." Rocco heard the sound of shuffling sheets of paper. "Now, where the fuck . . . Ah, here it is! Now then . . . Pasquale Scifù . . . he died in prison a few years later."

"And the other one . . ."

"Nothing. Scifù never talked."

"Were there any witnesses, anything that might help me?"

"Not much to speak of. The only thing is that while Scifù was of relatively normal stature, we hear that the other guy was a giant. He's the one who fired."

"Thanks. You've been invaluable."

"Useful?"

"I certainly hope so."

"At last! He's finally starting to see the glass half full!"

"What glass?"

ANTONIO SCIPIONI AND ITALO PIERRON WERE GAZING AT THE television set, and had been for three hours now. Their eyes were starting to blur, as lines and colors merged together.

Rocco Schiavone strode into the room like a gust of wind.

"How are we doing?"

"Ah, thanks for the pastries . . . they were excellent," said Antonio.

"Rocco, we can't take it much longer. We've been looking at the same things for hours . . ." Italo replied, rubbing his face.

"And do you mind telling me what you've seen?"

"Let's do this, sir. We'll show you the images on fast-forward, and while we watch we can give you a running commentary."

"Antonio, but weren't you on a first-name basis with me, just like Italo?"

"Ah . . . yes . . . it's just that in the office . . ."

"If there's no one else, then what do you care?"

"You're right, Dottore. So, shall I go ahead, sir?"

"Go on."

Antonio pushed a button on the remote control, and the black-and-white images started up.

"This is video camera one."

Sped up like this, it was like watching a Soviet formalist film.

"All right. So here's the brawl. You can see the three convicts here at the left of the screen attacking the Moroccan."

"Tunisian," Italo corrected him.

"Right. Then these two other North Africans come running to help the Tunisian, you see? One of them jumps onto the back of the scarface . . ."

"Erik," Italo specified.

"And then the other assumes karate stances as he tries to hit the negro."

"The black man, Antonio, 'negro' is offensive," Rocco corrected him.

"Right you are. The black man. Anyway, he swells up his face like a rubber dinghy."

"Wow, that's a right hook. The African can throw a punch, eh?"

"Right. Then . . ."

"And then," said Italo, taking over, "we have another North African coming to the rescue, this guy here, you see? I think his name is Aziz, and he takes quite a beating from Erik."

"Erik delivers quite a punch, too, eh?"

"And now here are the convicts hurrying to put down the brawl. And then the guards come in and settle things quickly."

They went on watching the footage.

"Who's this third guy attacking the Tunisian?"

"That's a guy they call the Professor. He's the mastermind behind the group," Italo replied.

"There, now we're on it!" Antonio pointed to the right-hand side of the television set. "You see the people starting to assemble? Back here is the body of Mimmo Cuntrera."

"And why can't we see him?"

"Because that's a blind area."

Rocco touched his chin. His two days' growth of beard sizzled at the contact like hot oil in a frying pan. "What about the other video cameras?"

"None of the six video cameras was taping this corner of the courtyard."

"So, wait: You're telling me we don't have any footage of the man falling to the ground?" Rocco asked.

"No."

The deputy chief stood up.

"It would have been too easy, right?"

The two officers exchanged a glance as if it was somehow their fault.

"So we already know one thing. Whoever killed the guy knows the prison like the back of their hand, as well as the video camera surveillance system. Which means it's someone who's been in there for a good long time already."

SERGIO MOZZICARELLI RETURNED TO HIS WING. HE WAVED hello to the sentinel standing guard. He didn't feel like staying out in the courtyard. Not after what had happened. Not after what he had seen. He leaned his back against the hallway wall and started considering his fellow prisoners in that wing.

Who could he tell about this?

He immediately ruled out the foreigners. He never spent time with them—he didn't know them at all. Romanians and Albanians spoke only rudimentary Italian. Africans couldn't speak it at all. All that remained, then, were the Italians, a tiny portion of the prison population. He could have talked to Cavabucion, the former bartender from Padua—whose moniker meant "corkscrew"—but he didn't even know his real first name . . . That was out of the question. How about Federico? He would certainly have misinterpreted Sergio's approach, assuming that it was nothing more than a sexual advance. And then Federico would start coming up with a series of heavy-handed double entendres about the possibility of having sex in the showers or else in his cell during the "socializing" hours. Or else Mariano? The truck driver who had murdered his wife and her lover in a single night of violence? No, not him, either. That left Marco. Too young. All he ever thought about was the children he'd left behind and the days he counted down until he could return home. All he was good for was making leather bracelets with his astrological sign engraved in a black stone. After that, he had run out of fellow Italians. Few in number and none of them reliable or willing to share his secret and keep it jealously to themselves. Worst of all, none of them capable of offering him any advice.

Just don't give a damn about it! his head told him. Just don't give a damn about it, Sergio, you saw it, so what? Mind your own fucking business. In a year you'll be out and you can try to enjoy the last scraps of this shitty life you've made for yourself.

"I'm just going to get myself into a world of trouble . . ." he said in a low voice as he looked down at the floor. And for what?

Domenico Cuntrera hadn't even been a friend of his. In those few days they'd exchanged, at most, three words. All he knew was that Cuntrera was Calabrian, that every night he prayed to the Madonna, and that they were planning to transfer him in the next few days. But they hadn't been quick enough about it.

Just don't give a damn about it.

But he couldn't get that face out of his mind, that poor wretch as his features turned deathly blue, his staring eyes seeming to beg for help as his life fled his body, hasty and cowardly as all lives end. The foam on his lips, his death rattle. And what had Sergio been able to do? How had he responded to that desperate plea? He'd hidden behind the reinforced concrete column to make sure he wasn't seen while a gang of assholes were beating each other bloody at the far end of the courtyard.

Just remember not to give a damn about it.

"Inside! Gates are closing!" shouted a guard. Sergio slowly returned to his cell, along with Aldo and Karim. With the noise of clanking, clattering metal, the gates slammed shut. Soon they'd bring their dinners.

Just don't give a damn about it.

IT WAS 8:30. ROCCO WAS RUNNING LATE. HE'D WASTED TIME calling Brizio and telling him the details of the pistol and the armed robbery and associated murder in Cinecittà. His friend had assured him that he would get busy and let him know. Though Brizio had to say, he'd never heard of this Neapolitan Scifù. Rocco was galloping toward his residential hotel, with Lupa trotting after him, tail wagging happily. He had to take a quick shower and get dressed. But the idea was already starting to surface in his head of calling Anna and standing her up at the last minute—a move of colossal oafishness. He entered the residential hotel and went to the desk to ask for his key.

"You're unbelievably late!"

He turned around. Behind him, sitting on one of the sofas in the lobby, was Anna. Lupa ran straight toward her, barking. Anna greeted the puppy with open arms—"Lupa! Are you happy to see me?"—and she bent down to pet her, then looked up at Rocco. "She's happy to see me. Take a lesson from Lupa."

"It'll take me three minutes, I'll get changed and be right downstairs. Do you think the dog can come?"

"I don't think so."

"I can't even bring the dog . . . Well, okay." Rocco whistled, and Lupa followed him up the stairs.

HE OPTED FOR THE USUAL DARK-BROWN CORDUROY SUIT WITH a light-blue shirt and no tie and, of course, his Clarks desert boots. "Now you go nighty-night," Rocco said, pouring the doggie kibble into the pink plastic dog bowl. "All right? I'll be home soon." Lupa lunged at the food. Rocco put on his loden overcoat, left the table lamp on for the puppy, and shut the door softly behind him.

"THANKS FOR COMING TO PICK ME UP HERE AT THE RESIDENTIAL hotel. I was running late."

Anna looked Rocco up and down. "So you think that's elegant evening attire?"

He made a poor showing compared with the woman's getup: she wore a simple black tube dress, adorned with a necklace shaped like a grape vine with red stones peeping out among small gold grape leaves, a cyclamen jacket tapered at the waist by bone buttons, and a pair of black python ankle boots. "You're dressed for the office."

Rocco looked at himself in the reception desk mirror. He hadn't even brushed his hair. "You think?"

"You didn't even shave! Let's go, or we'll be late. Shall we take your car, or are you going to make me drive all the way there?"

"All the way where?"

"Outside of Aosta. Toward Rumiod."

"Do you know the way?"

"Sure. We're going to the house of Berardo Turrini."

"That surname isn't new to me. Any relation to Laura Turrini, director of the Vallée Savings Bank?"

"He's her husband. The head physician."

To call the residence of Berardo Turrini a house was certainly reductive and clearly inadequate. You entered the property through a double gate surmounted by six antique wrought-iron lamps. Rocco and Anna drove along a narrow lane lined by a double row of poplar trees, their white trunks standing out like skeletons in the dark of night. The villa was gigantic, illuminated brightly for the party. Rocco stopped to observe it after parking the car on the lawn amidst other vehicles, each of which was worth more than the GDP of an African nation. Three stories of modern architecture, a spectacular triumph of glass, wood, and stone. "Not bad, eh?" said Anna, taking care where she stepped, lest she sprain an ankle in her high heels. But the lawn was solid, an expanse of green velvet.

They walked along a gravel driveway and finally arrived at the front door of the home, which was an enormous glass arch leading into the rooms on the ground floor. A lively crowd of people were milling around with glasses in their hands; uniformed waiters fluttered here and there carrying precariously balanced trays. As soon as the couple entered, an elderly, completely bald waiter extended his arms to take their overcoats and then turned to go. "Are we going to see them again, those overcoats? I left my wallet in mine," Rocco said. Anna didn't even dignify it with a response.

Soft diffuse lights gently illuminated the artworks hanging on the walls. Rocco jerked in surprise as he approached a canvas with a slash at the center. The rest of the paintings were every bit up to the same level. A Burri, a Boetti tapestry, a considerable number of pencil drawings by artists ranging from Miró to Léger.

"Does a head physician really make this much money?"

"It's family money, Rocco. Now stop drooling over these things and let's go introduce ourselves."

"Anna!" A man in his late fifties approached with both arms thrown wide-open. He was bronzed, with gleaming white hair and a black suit worn casually over a simple T-shirt the same color. "At last!"

"Berardo!" They embraced. The usual double kiss, one on each cheek. "May I introduce Dottor Schiavone?"

"I know him by reputation," the man said, with a faint smile. They shook hands. Rocco took in the house at a glance. "So does a person have to buy a ticket to come see you?"

Berardo broke into a deafening laugh. "I see that you appreciate contemporary art. Come along, let me introduce you to my wife."

They walked through a living room the size of an apartment and approached the wine table, where Laura Turrini was chatting with a woman well into her seventies. A spiderweb of wrinkles on the face clashed with the lips newly redone by a cosmetic surgeon. "Laura, guess who's here?"

"Anna!" Laura broke away from the table with a glance of apology to the older woman. "Anna, how nice to see you." They embraced. Then Laura's gaze turned sad when she saw Rocco. "Dottor Schiavone . . ."

"So you've already met?" Berardo asked.

"Yes," Rocco replied. "How are you, Dottoressa Turrini?"

"Tonight we can be on a first-name basis."

"How's it going, Laura?"

"Fine. I see you're in fine form!"

"Don't lie," Anna broke in. "He looks as if he's just gotten off a forty-eight-hour stakeout!"

"Have you seen the Berguets lately?"

Laura turned pale. Her husband took it upon himself to intervene. "Don't even talk about it . . . What happened to them . . . was . . . unpleasant?"

"Just 'unpleasant'?"

"Well, of course. Is 'terrible' more like it?" asked Berardo.

Laura regained her normal coloring. "What do you think? I'm so sorry for what happened to the Berguets! I've been friends with Giuliana and Pietro for years now. The bank that I represent has always been close to the Berguets."

"Except for the last little while."

Anna rolled her eyes. "Excuse me. Rocco, do you really think this is the time and place to talk about this sort of thing? We're at a party!"

"Anna's right!" Turrini added. "I have other guests, please excuse me . . ." And displaying a mouthful of teeth that gleamed like ivory, he abandoned the trio.

"May I offer you some wine?"

"Gladly," said Anna, and chatting in a low voice with Laura, she walked away from Rocco. The deputy chief didn't follow the two women. He stood there watching them as they approached the buffet table.

What the hell am I doing here? he asked himself.

SOMEWHERE THERE HAD TO BE SPEAKERS PLAYING MUSIC. IF the master of the house showed a certain eye for the visual arts, the same could not be said of his ears. Rocco thought he could recognize the saccharine notes of "Strangers in the Night" as mangled by the Italian saxophonist Fausto Papetti. He scrutinized the faces of the guests. The men were atomizing sheer arrogance from the pores of their skin. The women, in contrast, were exuding botulinum toxin. All the women seemed to have the same face. A face that had been re-created in an operating room. A democratic standardization of facial features, eliminating any diversity of race or physiognomy, making those faces smooth, glistening, and expressionless. A house full of reptiles.

"Well, are you going to take the apartment?"

The friendly voice of Police Chief Costa made him turn around to look at one of the three big windows that dominated the room. "Dottore, buonasera."

"I heard that you're back in the office. That makes me happy. But at the same time, I'm saddened by the knowledge that you didn't come upstairs to see me. And yet you know that I was trying to get in touch with you. Have you seen the newspapers?"

"I'd say so."

Costa straightened the glasses on the bridge of his nose. "Don't be offended by the things they say about you."

"Are you referring to Buccellato? She's going a little heavy-handed, don't you think!"

Costa grunted. His hatred for those *news vendors*, as he called them, showed no sign of abating, still as strong as when he originally conceived it, after his wife left him for a reporter in Turin. Then Costa shook his head to clear it of the columns, the fonts, the articles above and below the fold, the jump lines, the editorials, and the bylines that danced before his eyes, mocking not only him but also his office and his efforts. He gave Rocco a level look. "How are you, Schiavone? Do you feel like you're up to coming back to work?"

"No, Dottor Costa. I'd say that I'm not."

"I understand. Are you going to bring me the son of a bitch who broke into your apartment?"

"I certainly hope so," Rocco said, thinking back to the muttered promise he'd made to his friend Sebastiano that if he ever found Adele's murderer, he'd turn him over to his friend so that Sebastiano could put an end to that matter with his own bare hands. So Sebastiano could avenge his girlfriend's death in cold blood.

"I'm relying on you." Costa recovered his smile. "Well then, are you going to take the apartment on Via Laurent Cerise?" the police chief asked. "It's eight hundred fifty square feet, the rent is eminently affordable. If you like, it's already furnished. It's on the fourth floor, and it has a burglar alarm and grates on the windows."

"It only has one shortcoming, but it's as big as the Matterhorn."

"And what's that?"

"It's right around the corner from the prosecutor's office."

Costa looked at Schiavone. "If anything, that strikes me as a feature."

"I know. That's why we'll stay friends. We have two very different views of life."

Costa nodded. "You can bet on that. Speaking of views and visions, what do you have to say about what happened in prison?"

"I don't know yet. In any case, it was certainly a murder; Cuntrera, the Mafioso who was blackmailing the Berguet family, was murdered."

"An ugly story, in that case. Oh, and speaking of the Berguets, look over there . . ."

The police chief jutted his chin toward a specific point in the living room. Standing next to a tapestry was a man. Small in stature, fair-haired, light-colored eyes. A charcoal gray suit draped over his frame without a crease or wrinkle.

"Who's he?"

"Luca Grange."

"The one who was awarded the construction contract by the regional government instead of Edil.ber?"

"Right. The party is partly for him."

"Ah. How nice to know that Signora Turrini is *such* a close friend with the Berguets."

"Yes, *such* a close friend," Costa commented sadly. "But life goes on, doesn't it?"

"I see it differently. It's more a case of the victor's carriage being the most comfortable one."

"That's always the case, except for in one field: soccer. I will always remain a Genoa fan, in victory and in defeat."

"And since when has victory ever favored your team?"

"Let's forget about it, Schiavone, and just focus on your own team."

"Right you are. Tell me a little something more about this Luca Grange."

"He's a young businessman. His father had contracts with the township of Aosta to clean the public transit vehicles. But Luca is an architect, he founded the company, and apparently not even two years later, he's ready to make the great leap."

Rocco Schiavone had no trouble whatsoever classifying Luca

Grange in his mental bestiary. His ice-blue eyes, focused and still, perfectly suited to the snows of the endless tundra, and his white teeth and small, sharp nose made Luca a Siberian husky, the dog originally from Siberia trained to pull sleds, the protagonist of the greatest novels of the northern frontier.

"So it certainly seems that Luca Grange is a young man who'll go far . . ." Schiavone muttered.

"So it would seem."

Now Fausto Papetti was squeezing out a version of "Killing Me Softly." Costa smiled at Rocco. "I need to go find this stereo and put on some different music."

"That's something I'd appreciate deeply, Dottore."

With a smile, the police chief walked away.

"HEAVENS! OF COURSE, I'LL TAKE YOU TO SEE HIM!" BERARDO Turrini was shouting in the center of the living room with a wineglass in his hand. "Everybody, come with me!" And he headed for the door. A group of six people followed him. Rocco looked over at Anna, who shrugged and tailed after the group. Rocco did the same.

"Where are we going?" he asked her.

"I don't know. To see something very important, I think."

The group, which now numbered fifteen people, went out the back door of the house, and like the rats following the Pied Piper of Hamelin town, they followed the master of the house in single file. They turned down a little lane, and only the sound of gravel crunching underfoot broke the nocturnal silence. A narrow road illuminated by beautiful lampposts led to a cluster of reddish buildings.

"The stars are out," said Anna.

"Don't look up," Rocco warned her. "On those heels, you'd wind up in the trauma ward."

"I think that there are at least three orthopedic surgeons at this party! In fact, why don't you have them take a look at your back?"

The odor of horses, mixed with leather and fodder, became increasingly strong as the group approached the stables. In the distance, on the left, the light-blue color of a brightly lit swimming pool promised the arrival of summer.

A short, powerfully built man came forward to greet the group. "Here's Dodò . . . the best groom in the whole valley. Dodò, these are my friends."

"Buonasera . . ." said the little man. From his wrinkles, it looked as if his face had been folded and refolded countless times, like an old road map.

"They want to see Winning Mood."

Dodò smiled and raised his right arm, pointing the way. "Over here . . ."

The heels of the guests echoed on the cobblestones. From inside a stall a horse was delivering powerful kicks against the structure. Another horse, farther away, was neighing, perhaps because he'd been bothered by that noise in the night.

Followed by the guests, the groom threw open a double sliding door, and they were all immediately enveloped by the dampness and stench of equine urine. Then the groom turned on the lights, illuminating a long hallway. Every thirty feet or so there was a door with bars. It looked like a wing in a penitentiary. "Winning Mood is in the last stall," said Berardo Turrini, by this point incapable of further restraining his excitement. "Come on, come on!"

To the right and left, there were sleeping horses, and here and there horses with their heads bowed, munching on the fodder scattered over the floor. A gray stallion pushed his muzzle out through the hatch in the door. He kept his ears back and gazed out at the group of rubbernecking intruders with a blank gaze. At last, Berardo came to a stop.

"Dodò!"

The groom, who had seized a rope, opened the door and walked into the stall.

"Ladies and gentlemen, allow me to present Winning Mood!"

At Berardo's gesture, the little man emerged, leading a bay stallion on a halter.

"Here he is, ladies and gentlemen!"

He was an enormous animal. Gleaming, powerful, with a long mane and strong, muscular legs. His hooves seemed to set the stone floor aflame.

There was a chorus of appreciative "Ohs!" from all the onlookers. Except for Rocco, who knew less about horses than he did about women.

"He's marvelous!" cooed a blonde matron at the head of the group.

A bespectacled fellow walked up to the horse and started stroking him. "With a horse like this, what's to stop you?"

"Right," said Berardo, and he smiled complacently. "We're going to run him for the first time at Cattolica, at the end of the month."

"Who are you going to have ride him?"

"I still don't know . . . Maybe Rodrigo . . ."

"Nice, isn't he?" a woman said to Rocco, trying to engage him.

"Fantastic," replied the deputy chief.

"He's the grandson of Chandelier!" said the woman.

"Fantastic," said Rocco again.

"He'll win plenty of national races, even if he's only three years old!"

"Fantastic!"

Anna leaned over and whispered into Rocco's ear: "Don't you know how to say anything else?"

"It's like the old joke . . ." Rocco whispered back. "'Fantastic' is just a nice way of saying 'Who gives a flying fuck!'" The deputy chief turned around and realized that they weren't in the very last row. Behind them was Luca Grange, glass in hand, laughing softly.

"I couldn't help but overhear," he said.

From up close he looked even more like a sled dog.

"I didn't mean to be offensive."

"Don't give it a second thought. I don't know anything about horses, either. They're like a fever: you either have it or you don't." He extended his hand. "Luca Grange."

"Rocco Schiavone. This is Anna . . ."

"Cherubini!" She filled in the name that he had clearly forgotten as she shook Luca's hand. Rocco was ashamed of himself. Forgetting a woman's last name was an unforgivable slight. And Anna made that clear to him, glaring fire at him. "Shall we go in?" Rocco suggested to Anna.

"You go ahead. I want to stay here to look at Chandelier's grandson."

"Fantastic!" said Rocco, but Anna didn't laugh.

THERE WAS NOTHING LEFT FOR HIM TO DO BUT TO WANDER through the house all on his lonesome. He was suddenly reminded of the film where Peter Sellers, mistakenly admitted to the party of a wealthy movie producer, bumbles into an endless succession of embarrassing gaffes. Rocco had one of the servers pour him a glass of red wine, and then he grabbed an hors d'oeuvre off a tray, a small tart of a vague color, hard to pin down exactly. "What is this?" he asked the server.

"Salt-cod paste with a corn polenta purée and . . ."

He gulped it down in a single mouthful. It was exquisite. He had just managed to swallow the food when his throat locked tight. At the far end of the room, standing and talking with two smiling ladies, was Walter Cremonesi, an old acquaintance of his. The right-wing terrorist, an extremist who'd been in Italian prisons since 1976, had a criminal record as long as his arm, featuring burglaries, armed robberies, and a couple of murders. The deputy chief hadn't seen him in years. He was pushing sixty, but he looked hale and healthy.

What's he doing in Aosta? Rocco wondered. And his mind flew straight to the thought of Adele murdered in his bed.

Drawn closer like a moth to a flame, he didn't even realize that he'd come within a few yards of the man, who stood almost six feet tall, skinny and lithe. All that remained of his dangerous years was a small scar under his square jaw. There was no need to expend any effort to give him the appearance of a specific animal. He'd always known it: Walter Cremonesi was a *Dendroaspis polylepis*, better known as a black mamba. His eyes were lively and wide-set, his mouth was lipless, and his lean body seemed ready to dart forward from one moment to the next. But the thing that he most had in common with the reptile was the shape of his head. Like a coffin. Walter swiveled his small dark eyes toward Rocco, and a barely perceptible light seemed to flash in his irises. The close-shaven top of his head reflected the halogen spotlights illuminating the little corner bar. Rocco furrowed his brow.

"Rocco Schiavone! I'm delighted to see you again."

Rocco drew even closer. The two women who were chatting with Cremonesi had lost their smiles. They seemed embarrassed. They ventured only the slightest nods of the head to greet the new arrival.

"I'm much less delighted than you are, Walter Cremonesi. Much less delighted. And I don't remember that we were ever on a first-name basis."

Walter nodded, maintaining a half-hearted smile. His upper lip pulled back, briefly displaying a mouthful of teeth as small and sharp and straight as knife blades.

"May I introduce my friends?"

"If they're friends of yours, I'll have to decline the honor."

"Oaf!" said the taller of the two women, who then left the little group. The shorter one, a few years younger, seemed amused.

"That's just the way our friend the policeman is. A little brusque, but he's always been tons of fun, you know that, Amelia?"

"Ah, so you're a policeman?" asked the young woman. "Pleasure to know you, my name is Amelia." And she extended a handful of inch-long Ferrari-red fingernails. She'd had some work done on her mouth by a plastic surgeon, while a tattoo artist had put a small bee on her neck. But Rocco didn't shake hands; he just threw back the glassful of wine.

"Do you like my tattoo?" the young woman asked.

"No. I like bees, though."

"So do I. And do you know why? Because they flit from flower to flower." And with a faint smile she took her leave of that individual with a two-day growth of whiskers and a corduroy suit, so completely out of place at such a chic gathering. "See you around, Dottor Schiavone . . ." said the young woman as she brushed by, just inches from Rocco's nose.

The scent of tuberose flowers. Too much of it, thought the deputy chief.

"Pretty, isn't she? Do you want to take her out for a spin, Schiavò? A girl like Amelia, though, might be a little much for a deputy chief. Or maybe not. Are you still rounding out your salary these days?"

"You know something? Seeing you a free man out on the street is worse than a curse word in church."

Walter turned serious. "I've paid my debt to society."

"I doubt that very much. I think you had a couple of centuries to serve, if my memory doesn't deceive me."

"What about good conduct? I served ten years. Doesn't that seem long enough?"

"Go tell that to the bank teller you murdered on Via Nomentana."

"That wasn't me."

"And I'm just waiting for my invitation to play tournament tennis at Wimbledon."

"Anyway, I'm a free man now, no different from you."

"You may well be a free man, but you're not even fucking remotely like me. What are you doing in Aosta?"

"I live in Val d'Aosta, Deputy Chief. I make wine. In fact, what do you think of it?" And he pointed to the glass that Rocco was still holding in one hand. "I make it. I have a vineyard. What you just tasted is my Primot red. A wine that's holding up its end of the bargain. Do you have any other questions for me? Because my concept of an enjoyable evening isn't being subjected to the third degree."

"I'd very much like to know where you were on the evening of Thursday, May 10."

This time Walter burst out laughing. "I can't believe it. Is this seriously an interrogation? Here? Now? At a party?"

"Do you remember, yes or no?"

Walter rolled his beady eyes, merrily and mockingly. "May 10, May 10 . . . No, I don't remember. I might have been at home. I might have been at the club, or I might have been overseas, I'm just not sure. I might have been fucking your wife."

Rocco stared him in the eyes. Then with a quick swipe of his tongue, he cleaned the wine off his lips. "This is good wine. All things considered, I'm happy they let you back out on the street again, Cremonesi. Fucking you over another time will be a real pleasure."

"If you want, you can talk to my lawyer. In fact, just look!" And he pointed to a sofa in the living room. "He's that guy, the little short one with the mustache, talking to Judge Messina. His name is Ferretti. Counselor Stefano Ferretti. Maybe you even know the judge, he works at the Aosta courthouse. You could ask him!" And he walked off, shaking his head.

Rocco stood there. He exchanged one last glance with Amelia, who smiled at him, narrowing her eyes a little. He could have gone over to her, struck up a little conversation, spent an enjoyable evening. Instead, he preferred to wait for Counselor Ferretti to leave the sofa and then go over to talk to Baldi's colleague. "Everyone's here this evening. Even you . . ."

The judge waved for him to sit down beside him, patting the cushion with his hand. "Do you remember me, Schiavone?"

"And why shouldn't I, Dottor Messina?"

"I see that you know Cremonesi."

"Yes. I threw him behind bars once. And believe me, seeing him back out on the street isn't my idea of a good thing."

Messina stroked his thick black beard. "There's no prison sentence that can hold up if you can afford a good lawyer and you're dealing with the Italian system of justice."

"Coming from you, that's cold comfort."

"Right. Do you want to know why Walter Cremonesi isn't behind bars anymore?"

"That would be nice, for starters."

"He makes wine. He owns a vineyard and a winery. Primot is the varietal. And you know what? He runs the place with a group of convicts that are working to rehabilitate themselves. A nice little cooperative. What's more, you're probably familiar with the Gozzini law?"

"Refresh my memory."

"For us citizens who are free to roam the streets, a year is made up of twelve months. But for those who are behind bars, serving out their sentence, a year is made up of just nine. If the convict is cooperating with the process of reeducation and rehabilitation, his sentence is reduced by a month and a half every semester. And that's how we get to nine months. Participating with the process of reeducation, however, hardly demands who knows what efforts. It's enough that you refrain from murdering or raping anyone, and that's the bar you have to meet. In other words, cause no overt trouble, and you've done your part. When you're serving out your last four years, lo and behold, a correctional order is served and off you go home, to serve out the rest of your sentence, there or performing some public service. Simple, no? And let's not forget the amnesties!"

"The guy was a terrorist . . . He's killed people, committed armed robberies . . ."

"One of these days come down to the courthouse with me. I'll show you how it works. The only ones who go to prison are the losers. Four trials, judicial review court, statute of limitations. This is a government that hands out absolutions and immunity, Dottor Schiavone."

"And you continue to work as a judge?"

"What alternatives do I have?"

Rocco sprawled out on the backrest of the three-seat sofa. "He might have been the one who snuck into my apartment . . ."

"I doubt it. Cremonesi has become a businessman. He's a member of high society here. If you ask me, those are the kind of things he's left behind him."

"No. He's a weed, a bad seed. And a bad seed is what he stays until the end of his days."

Judge Messina smiled. He stroked his beard again and said nothing.

THE NIGHTS IN PRISON WERE LONG. ALWAYS HAD BEEN. BUT for Sergio Mozzicarelli the nights he was living through now were interminable. He tossed and turned in his bed without being able to get a wink of sleep. How the hell was Aldo able to sleep on like that? But then, Aldo hadn't seen what *he* had. And Karim? He, too, seemed wide-awake. He narrowed his eyes, squinting to see through the dark. Karim was writing something on the wall.

"What are you doing?" asked Sergio in a low voice.

"I'm writing my name."

"Why?"

"Because if I stare hard at it, I might start to feel like sleeping."

Sergio sat up in bed.

"Why can't you sleep, Sergio?"

"Because . . . Karim, I saw something."

The Tunisian turned over. His eyes were glistening. He was crying. "What did you see?"

"The other day, down in the courtyard." He lowered his voice and whispered: "I saw who killed Cuntrera."

The young man heaved a deep sigh. He ran his hand over his face. "Where I come from, we say that the fruit of peace hangs from the branches of the tree of silence."

"Still, I can't help but think about it."

"Think about it, but don't tell me. I don't want to know about it. I don't want to know about anything. I count the days, Sergio, and I can't wait to get out of here. And when I'm out of all this," he said, taking in the little cell with a glance, "it isn't going to be anything more than a bad memory."

Sergio nodded. "What would you do in my situation?"

"I'd get some sleep."

"DON'T YOU WANT ANYTHING, ROCCO?" ANNA ASKED HIM AS she munched on a small plateful of grape leaves stuffed with black rice, apparently now having forgiven him for his gaffe in the stables.

"How do you know these people?"

"My ex-husband. He used to socialize with them before moving to Geneva. High finance. The Turrinis are a very wealthy family from Milan. They own shops, apartment buildings. Berardo's grandfather owned steel mills."

"Yes, but why do you keep frequenting them?"

"I don't know. Could it be because I'm bored? You want the truth? You see that guy who looks sort of like Giuseppe Verdi?" She turned her eyes to a little short man dressed in a charcoal-gray three-piece suit, with an overripe yellow flower in his buttonhole. He was talking animatedly to a woman as skinny and dry as an olive branch.

"Well?"

"He's a gallery owner. I want to go talk with him, maybe he'll hold a show for me. He has a gallery in Turin and another in Milan. And he's a partner with one of the biggest art salons in Berlin."

"Fine, you go get busy with Giuseppe Verdi. I'm going home."

Anna looked at him askance. "Why?"

"Because I'm starting to feel like throwing up. Because this place disgusts me and shit is oozing out of the walls, because I don't want to have anything to do with these people, and because I consider that the fact you brought me here amounts to a grave insult. See you later!"

He turned on his heel and left Anna standing there with the plate of stuffed grape leaves in her hand.

"PLEASE GIVE ME MY COAT, IT'S A LODEN."

"Right away," replied the attendant, ducking behind a brocaded curtain.

He could feel the floor burning under his feet. The music of Fausto Papetti was echoing in his head. The lights and the smells of food were suffocating him.

"Is this it, Signore?"

Rocco grabbed it. He checked to make sure his wallet was still in the pocket. The attendant smiled. "Don't you trust us?"

"No! I don't, and if you want some free advice, go get a job somewhere else."

"I have three children."

"Then just keep your dick in your pants!"

AS HE WENT BACK OUT ACROSS THE GARDEN, HE PERCEIVED a presence, someone observing him. The deputy chief turned to look back at the villa. At a second-floor window a blond head was looking out. Smoking a cigarette. The face was in shadow, but then the figure leaned out and caught the light. It was Max. Rocco raised a hand to wave. Max waved back lazily.

"Well? Aren't you going downstairs to the party?"

Max shook his head no.

"Why not? There's lots of lovely people!"

Max shrugged his shoulders and withdrew to his room, shutting the window behind him.

THE NIGHT WAS CHILLY, AND THERE WAS NO ONE OUT AND about. Rocco was angrily chewing on a dry and flavorless sandwich he'd bought at the train station café. He thought back to the evening he'd just spent. He thought about Anna, who regularly forced him into situations that had nothing to do with him. And especially he thought about the fact that right then he was alone, late at night, without a single car at the nearby intersection, not a single light in the windows above. An easy target, a fish in a barrel. He looked around. His would-be killer could be hiding right around the corner of the yellow building. Or hunkered down between the car and the now-closed pharmacy. Or else he could be standing right behind him, merging into the shadows of the fir trees. Maybe he'd never even left Aosta, the man who'd crept into his apartment. He'd just hidden out in some out-of-the-way little hotel, waiting for an opportunity like this. Waiting until Rocco Schiavone was alone, without a witness, unarmed and distracted, when he'd finally be able to complete the work he'd undertaken. The deputy chief threw both arms wide. He turned, slowly. Aside from the occasional branch tossing in the wind and a light that came on in a fourth-floor window, nothing happened.

And so he shouted: "Here I am! I'm right here!"

"And who gives a flying fuck!" replied a distant voice.

A familiar voice.

Rocco burst out laughing. From the street in front of his residential hotel a man emerged. He was smoking. He had a quick, on-edge stride and not a hair on his head.

Furio!

"What are you doing there?"

"Being an excellent target!"

They hugged. His friend dropped his cigarette to the ground. "Your cell phone? Don't you turn it on anymore?"

"Why are you in town?"

"Passing through. On my way to France."

"To do what?"

"The less you know, the better. Listen, do you know a quieter place?"

"Quieter than this? Not possible!"

"In the middle of the street?"

"So what?"

Furio looked around. He nodded. Then he grabbed Rocco by the arm. "Come on!"

He led him to a dark corner under a portico. "Do you mind telling me what's going on?" Rocco asked. "What is it you want to tell me?"

Furio slid a hand into his jacket pocket. "I don't want to tell you anything. But if you stay here, out in the open, that guy might come back. And I can't stand to think of you in the middle of the street acting like a fool. So I'm not letting you expose yourself like this." And he handed him a 9 mm pistol, placing it in Rocco's hands. The deputy chief looked down at it.

"I don't carry a handgun anymore."

"I know, but if you have this, I'm going to feel a little less worried. I haven't been sleeping well for days on your account. It's a Ruger semiautomatic. Seven shots, 9 mm, it's small and it weighs less than a pound."

Rocco took it.

"The release is on the left side, the magazine has an angled heel on the grip."

"You sound like a salesman," said the deputy chief.

"Most important of all, this little girl is a virgin."

"Listen, Furio, even if you leave it with me, I'm still not going to use it."

Furio grabbed him by the lapels. "Listen up and listen good, you dickhead. This isn't playtime. Somebody's out to kill you, and you'd better get that through your thick skull. Keep a weapon within reach, always. I'm sick and fucking tired of going to funerals!"

Rocco looked his friend in the eyes. Then he nodded. "All right, Furio. All right."

Furio straightened the lapel of Rocco's loden overcoat. "Excuse me."

"Speaking of pistols. Have you heard from Brizio?"

"Yes, he told me everything. That the gun used to shoot Adele was previously used in an armed robbery in Cinecittà."

"Which means that the bastard comes from Rome. At least that's a lead."

"You'll see, we'll track down the guy that used this gun, Rocco."

"Right. So, you want to get a drink? Ettore is still open."

"Sure, but just one, I still have to drive . . ."

They emerged from the portico and headed toward Piazza Chanoux. "You know who I ran into this evening?"

"No."

"Walter Cremonesi."

Furio froze in the middle of the street. "I don't believe it."

"I swear."

"And what is he doing here?"

"Making wine."

"Do you believe it?"

"The way I believe that Catanzaro can win the Scudetto."

"So was it him who shot Adele?"

"I don't know. But I have to assume so."

"Keep an eye out for him. That guy is a cobra."

"No, he's a black mamba, it's obvious that you don't know a fucking thing about animals!"

THE SNORING FROM THE OTHER ROOM WAS FOLLOWING THE rhythm of the waves on the beach. A slow, elderly pace. The light from the streetlamps filtered faintly through the venetian blinds, transforming the white bedcover into a zebra skin. Corrado lifted the sheets. Lowered his feet to the floor, which was ice cold. He stood up. The bed barely creaked. He remained motionless, listening. From the other room, Enzo Baiocchi's deep breathing went on, slow and regular. He crept forward through the shadows. Since midnight, he'd kept his eyes open to accustom them to the darkness, and now he could see like a cat. The glare from the streetlamp outside made everything so much simpler. He put his hand on the doorknob. He'd left the door ajar to avoid making noise. He opened it slowly, and the hinges that he'd oiled while the other man was taking a shower obeyed silently. He was in the hallway now. He knew that hallway by heart, and he knew that it was only seven short footsteps to the living room. One foot in front of the other, careful and precise, he reached the door that gave onto the little parlor where Enzo was fast asleep on the sofa bed. He touched the door handle. He gripped it and slowly lowered it. He'd oiled that door thoroughly as well, and he managed to open it wide without so much as a squeak. The sea kept lashing the beach with its waves, at the same rate as Baiocchi's breathing. An odor of armpits and cigarettes penetrated his nostrils. It hovered in the room as if it were a thick and greasy fog. There the monster lay, blanket over his chest, in a tank top T-shirt. His arms were thrown wide like some savage Christ. His mouth hung open and his breathing was lifting and lowering his hairy chest. It was all a matter of a minute, no more. A single minute, a leap in the dark, and then it would all go back to how it had been before, before Enzo Baiocchi had invaded his life. He reached back and put his hand on his buttocks. He felt the handle of the knife, held snugly by the elastic band of his underwear. It was cold, colder than the blade. Or maybe it was his blood that no longer pumped through his veins. One foot in front of the other, precisely, never once taking his eyes off the man on the sofa bed. He'd done this once before, in the country, with a hog. It had been easy. He'd pushed his blade against the hog's throat and had driven it in, with a sharp, accurate movement. The hog had squealed and stretched its legs four or five times; then it had lain there, dangling and spraying blood out of the cut like an open faucet. Enzo wouldn't even scream. He wouldn't have time. Corrado would sink the knife right into his heart, with both hands, with all his weight and all his rage. These are the last breaths you're ever going to take, you piece of shit, he thought to himself.

The shutters in the living room were half open. A cold blade of light illuminated a quarter of a face. Enzo Baiocchi was sleeping. Corrado laid the knife against the man's neck.

All it takes now is some pressure. A simple thrust, sharp and decisive. Now!

A sudden stab of pain burst out next to his belly button. Corrado's eyes bugged out. He stared at Enzo. He, too, had both eyes wide-open now, his mouth twisted in a silvery leer. His face had filled with wrinkles. Corrado dropped the knife and staggered backward. Baiocchi's hand, dripping with blood, held the switchblade tight, and the blade was sunk deep inside him. Corrado could no longer breathe, much less talk. A scalding column of vomit was rising up his esophagus. With both hands, he tried to grab Enzo's hands, to tear that fire out of his stomach. That was when the killer got to his feet and stood facing Corrado. He caught a whiff of the stench of Enzo's armpits and the gust of onion on his breath. With a single yank, Enzo hauled the knife up toward Corrado's sternum, while he covered his mouth with the other hand. Corrado was filled with an immense pool of pain as he felt the hot, sticky blood gush out, running down his hips and legs.

Then his vision blurred until it all disappeared, the moon outside, the room inside, the fading smell of armpits and cigarettes. He flopped to the floor like a discarded apple peel.

Enzo wiped his blade on Corrado's T-shirt. Now he needed to get busy. He couldn't leave the place like this. The first thing he did was to wrap the body in the sheets from the sofa bed. He'd lost a lot of blood, the bastard—he'd have to clean up afterward. He needed to take advantage of the darkness. Like a spider in its lair, Enzo turned the bloodstained bedclothes into a white cocoon. Hastily, he got dressed. He found the keys to Corrado's car, which was parked right outside the living room window. He'd have to move quickly and silently and hope that the sleepless eyes of some retiree or some youngster coming home from a late-night drinking spree didn't catch sight of him.

"Fucking dickhead . . ." he murmured as he looked down at that cocooned body sprawled out at his feet. Then he picked it up. Luckily, Corrado Pizzuti didn't weigh much. At least he wouldn't sweat. With his burden of horror he went over to the window. He opened it and peered out into the street. Empty. No cars in sight. Only the sound of the waves behind the changing booths along the beach, now locked up for winter. He tumbled the dead body out the window. It dropped with a dull thump onto the dark sidewalk next to Corrado's car, a green Fiat Multipla. All he needed to do now was take him far away from there. He took the house keys and went out. He'd dump the corpse somewhere in the countryside, on the gravel riverbanks, deep in the canes and mud where no one would ever think to go looking for it.

SATURDAY

The first rush of breakfast customers had come and gone, leaving the counter strewn with crumbs and stacked espresso and cappuccino cups and saucers in the sink. Decaf espressos, caffè macchiatos, cappuccinos, pastries without custard filling or filled with marmalade, elephant ears, strudels, a surging river of requests that Tatiana had managed to satisfy by leaping madly back and forth from the Faema espresso machine to the cash register to take payment and give change. By nine in the morning Corrado still hadn't shown up. His cell phone was turned off. Such a thing had never happened in all the time they'd run the bar together. If he was going to be late, he'd always let her know, if only with a text message. He only lived a ten-minute walk away from the café.

What's happened to him? Tatiana kept wondering as she leaned against the sink, sipping her third espresso and staring at a random point on the floor, next to the ice cream freezer.

She didn't notice that Barbara had come in. "Buongiorno, Tatiana!"

The Russian returned to earth and smiled. "Ciao, Barbara. Buongiorno."

The bookseller walked up to the counter. "Where's Corrado?"

"Exactly. Where is he? Espresso?" The customer nodded, and Tatiana swiveled around to make an espresso for her friend. "Nobody's seen him."

"What do you mean, nobody's seen him? Did you call his cell phone?"

"He's turned it off." She emptied the portafilter and then filled it again. "Not a text, nothing at all."

"He must have been out late last night and he's probably just still sleeping."

"Sure." A rivulet of frothy hot espresso started dripping into the demitasse. "It's like you say." She picked up the demitasse and turned toward Barbara. "Do you want a pastry? A lemon braid?"

Barbara didn't answer. She poured half a packet of cane sugar into her espresso and started stirring it. "Listen . . . I need to talk to you."

"Go on."

She took a first sip, set down the cup, and looked the Russian woman in the eye. "I have a suspicion."

Tatiana's stomach hollowed out. She knew that Barbara liked intrigues and mysteries and that she frequently amused herself by glimpsing plots everywhere, but still, in that morning charged with tension and anxiety, the bookseller's words had the effect of a warning siren. "What suspicion?"

"I don't think Corrado's alone at home."

"What do you mean?"

"I'll explain. Yesterday evening I could see light filtering out through the shutters. But Corrado was still here at the bar with you."

Tatiana shrugged. "So what? Maybe he just forgot and left the light on."

"No. Because I saw it as I was driving by in my car, taking Diego to soccer practice. Then when I went back by ten minutes later, the light had been switched off. I went back to the bookstore, and only then did I see Corrado leave the bar. I tell you, there's someone in there." And she finished the espresso with the eyes of someone who's discovered buried treasure and can't wait to get her hands on it.

Tatiana pushed back the lock of hair that had fallen in front of her eyes. "Maybe . . . someone could be in there, but a she, not a he." And she realized with what a heavy heart she had uttered that unremarkable statement. A woman. It had never occurred to her that Corrado might have a girlfriend, a sweetheart, or even just a young woman to spend a few hours between the sheets with. It was an image she didn't like. Not one bit. A subtle, electric shudder ran down her throat and burst in her heart.

"Do you think that he has a girlfriend?" the bookseller asked skeptically.

"No!" She was tempted to add: "I hope not." But she didn't.

"Listen, when he shows up, why don't you ask him some questions?"

"What questions?"

"Like: 'So, Corrado, has your mother come to stay with you?'"

Tatiana grimaced. "I don't think that he has a mother, and if he does, he's never mentioned her to me."

Barbara nodded. She could do better. "Try this one: 'Corrado, why don't you rent out a room to make a little more money? Don't you find it lonely, living alone?'"

"There's only one bedroom in Corrado's apartment!"

"Then tell him that your sister is coming to stay for a few days and ask if he can let her sleep at his place."

"I don't have a sister!"

"What a pain in the ass!" The bookseller huffed in annoyance. Where were all the detectives and inspectors that she had devoured in years of bookish cannibalism now that she needed them and their insights? "Here, I have it! Tell him this: 'My husband and I are celebrating our second anniversary. You and your girlfriend are officially invited over to dinner tonight!'"

Tatiana thought it over. "Then what if he asks me, 'What girlfriend?'"

"Then you look him in the eye and you say: 'The one you've had staying in your apartment since you got back from your mysterious trip! I want to meet her!' And this is important, watch his reaction carefully. If he touches his nose, if he looks away, if he drops his eyes or avoids the subject, then you can be sure he's lying!"

It seemed like a good tactic. Clear, direct, unequivocal. "You think?"

"I saw it on a television series, a guy who could uncover lies just by observing people's facial expressions! You'll see, he'll smile and thank you and he'll say: 'Of course, what's-her-name and I would be delighted to come!' And you will have discovered the truth!"

"Then that's what it is."

"What is?" asked the bookseller, placing a euro on the counter.

"That's why he's so pensive and always seems to have his head in the clouds. That's what he's hiding. A woman!"

"You see?" And with a smile, Barbara went back to her bookshop.

A woman. Corrado had a woman. Tatiana clenched her teeth, but she couldn't keep a solitary tear from sliding down her cheek.

Rocco Schiavone was sitting at the usual café table on Piazza Chanoux, before the delicious breakfast that Ettore had just brought him. The air was sparkling, the meadows were emerald green, and the snow that just a few days earlier had fallen in the city had now fled the valley, taking refuge high on the peaks. The sun was shining high above in the sky. Its rays caressed the building and the mountains that wedged Aosta in like a picture frame. A May morning, the weather so lovely that all the tables were crowded. The customers were all beaming happily, some of them luxuriating in the luminous slaps of sunlight, sprawled back in their chairs with their eyes closed. It looked like a lazy Sunday morning. The time had not yet come to doff their winter jackets, but their bones were starting to suck in the warmth. Rocco looked down at his feet. He smiled down at this most recent pair of Clarks desert boots, which might now have a reasonable hope of surviving much longer than the other twelve pairs that had been destroyed in little more than eight months.

He saw her go by about thirty feet from his table. Even wearing jeans and a jacket pulled tight at the waist, she made quite an impression. The woman recognized him and smiled, reversed direction, and approached him. "So, are we enjoying the sunshine this morning?"

"Before going into the office . . ."

"You weren't in the right mood last night, Deputy Chief Schiavone."

"No, Amelia. I certainly wasn't. Let's just say that the people you were with aren't exactly my type."

Amelia pulled out a chair and sat down at the table.

"Shall I have Ettore bring you something?" Rocco suggested.

"No, I've already had breakfast. And this lovely dog?"

Lupa, sprawled out on the sidewalk, limited herself to rolling her eyes at the new arrival.

"What's its name?"

"Lupa!"

"Oooh . . . how sweet. What breed is she?"

"A Saint-Rhémy-en-Ardennes."

Amelia looked at him before bursting out laughing. "Never heard of that breed!"

"I may not be much of a clotheshorse, but when it comes to dogs I think I hold my own."

"A Saint-Rhémy . . ." Amelia shook her head.

The woman's tuberose-scented perfume reached Rocco's nostrils. It was a little too redolent for his tastes. "Have you known Walter Cremonesi long?"

"No. I've only met him a time or two. I'm a friend of Dr. Turrini's. And Signora Turrini, too, to be perfectly clear."

"Are you from Aosta?"

"You remain a policeman even when you relax!"

"Occupational hazard of the profession. By the way, what do you do for a living?"

"I'm in charge of PR for Luca Grange. You met him, right? Last night . . ."

"Ah, yes, the rising star of the local business community."

The woman smiled. "I'm thirty-four and I'm from Gruskavà."

"You're not Italian?"

Amelia smiled. "In Italian, it's Groscavallo; in Provençal, it's Gruskavà . . . In Turin province. I'm completely Italian." With a quick swipe of the hand, she brushed back a lock of hair. "I lost my folks years ago and I moved to Aosta. Anything else you want to know?" And she looked at him with her big brown eyes.

"No. That should do it, thanks."

"There are men who might have taken advantage of the situation to ask me for my cell phone number."

"I'm not one of them."

Amelia laughed as she touched her neck. "I assure you, you're actually all the same. Maybe you're just a little more skillful than all the others, but you want my cell phone number, and how!"

Rocco smiled, narrowing his eyes as he did so. "Instead of your cell phone number, why don't you tell me whether that bee on your neck is the only tattoo that you have."

Amelia leaned closer to Rocco and whispered: "There's only one way to find out . . ." She got up. "I wish you a very nice day, Dottor Schiavone."

"Same to you, Amelia . . . Amelia what, by the way?"

"Amelia is enough." She shot him a wink and walked away. Rocco forced himself not to turn to watch her ass as she walked off. He gave in after just three seconds.

She had two exquisitely perfect hemispheres.

LUCKILY, THE THIRD LIGHTER WORKED. HE'D GIVEN THE first two to Lupa, who liked to disassemble them, grasping them between her paws as she chewed on them. With his first long drag, he realized that the case he had before him was a tough one, and that it wasn't going to be easy to crack it. Only a few cars were going by on Corso Battaglione Aosta. He opened his office window and tossed the roach out onto the canopy roof. His curiosity piqued, he looked out. Right there, outside the window and on top of the canopy over the front entrance to police headquarters, he noticed an indecent quantity of roaches from previous joints. All tossed out there by him, day after day, since September of the year before. They formed a pile that might attract attention. If the police chief happened to lean out his office window on the third floor, he would certainly ask just what those little dots of paper piled up down there might be. Rocco needed to tidy up after himself. He swung his leg over the windowsill and looked down. Less than a yard below him was the roof of the canopy that covered the entrance to police headquarters, protecting it from the unending rains of Val d'Aosta.

Deputy Inspector Caterina Rispoli had chosen to walk to the office that day. She was eating a diet bar as she crossed the street. Police headquarters was right there, in front of her. She was in a foul mood. The night before she had quarreled with Italo. The usual issues. The usual problems that plague young couples everywhere. Italo wanted them to move in together. To Caterina, that sounded worse than a threat. It wasn't that she was afraid. Rather, quite simply, she preferred to leave things the way they were now. She liked living in her little apartment, with her own spaces and her own books. The mere idea of having Italo in her home—with his messiness, his underwear, his pee stains all over the toilet rim, his PlayStation constantly on—horrified her. Like having to live with a teenager.

"You're afraid to take a perfectly simple and natural step that any two people who are in love ought to be willing to take without even having to talk about it," Italo had shouted at her.

"The idea of living together makes me anxious," she'd told him. "Then we'd start neglecting each other, taking each other for granted, and the next thing you know you're going to bed in droopy pajamas and woolen slippers, bundled up like so many Santa Clauses. After which, it's good-bye, sex."

Italo had done his best, unsuccessfully, to point out to her that when you love someone, all these things are a normal part of life, living together, doing things together, and maybe even paying just a single rent.

"Then that's really the heart of the problem!" she'd started shouting back at him. "The rent! I can't believe it."

"Wait, don't you like being with me?"

"What does that have to do with anything? Sure, I like being with you, but I want to live alone. I need that."

"Are you seeing someone else?"

"Have you lost your mind?"

"Do you or don't you have another boyfriend?"

"What other boyfriend could you be thinking about, Italo? You're more than enough!"

Maybe it would have been better if she'd told him that she'd never had a real family of her own, that the only reason her parents lived together was to maul each other mercilessly, that her father had been a brute, and that if she shut her eyes and thought back to that man she'd stopped calling Papà at the age of six, she felt like vomiting.

"Caterina, I'm sick of this kind of relationship. I don't like it, it feels distant and cold."

"What are you trying to tell me?"

"What kind of future do we have?" Italo had asked her, staring her firmly in the eyes.

"I don't know, it's not something I worry about. I'm fine for now, just the way things are. Why do you want to get in a rush and ruin everything?"

"Because you need to live your life with an eye to the future! Look at our deputy chief."

"What does he have to do with any of this?"

"He has a plan for the future. He wants to go and live in Provence, he's doing everything he can think of to change his life. He's working for an idea!"

"What the fuck are you talking about?" Caterina never used curse words, but this time Italo had dragged it out of her. "The deputy chief is mentally ill. He's a miserable wretch who lives all alone, in a city where he's a stranger, pursued by people who want to rub him out, and he has a gang of friends who I wouldn't trust as far as I could throw them."

"I like Rocco!"

"Then go ahead and move in with *him*!"

With the echo of that screaming fight still echoing in her head, Caterina looked up. On the roof of the canopy over the front entrance to police headquarters was none other than the deputy chief himself.

"Dottore? What are you doing up there?"

Rocco looked over the edge. "Ah, Caterina, ciao."

"What are you doing up there on the canopy?"

"Nothing in particular. I don't have a balcony. I wanted to get some fresh air."

This guy really is out of his skull, Caterina decided. "Are you crazy? You could fall over the side!"

The deputy chief looked around. "No. This canopy is just three feet below my window."

"Sure, but then if you fall off the canopy, it's at least ten feet."

"But I'm not going to fall."

"What are you putting in your pocket?"

"I just dropped some spare change."

Caterina shook her head.

"Oh, and, Caterina? Could you add one more pain in the ass to the chart?"

"Certainly. Name it."

"People who don't mind their own fucking business. And put it at the eighth degree."

"Got you loud and clear . . ." And the deputy inspector walked into police headquarters.

Schiavone got both hands on the windowsill and pulled himself up. He was struggling to clamber through the window to get back into his office when Italo threw open the door. "What on earth are you doing, Rocco?"

"Oh, so it's a family defect, then . . ."

"What are you talking about?"

"Your wife asked me the same thing just a minute ago."

"She's not my wife. And anyway, since when is it a defect to ask questions?"

"No, Italo, it's a defect not to mind your own fucking business. What's up?"

"Apparently there have been dozens of phone calls for you. But why don't you turn on your cell phone?"

"To avoid receiving dozens of phone calls. And I can see that you persist in the error of your ways, failing to do what I just instructed you to do."

"Namely, to mind my own fucking business?"

"Exactly!"

"Okay, but still, call the judge back. Otherwise, he's going to ruin my life."

Rocco let himself drop into his chair. "Are you afraid of being transferred? It's not so bad. After all, take a look at me: a new police headquarters with lots of interesting people to spend your days with, cheerful folk, likable, extremely stimulating. I'd never have met a D'Intino or, say, Deruta, to say nothing of Casella. Who wouldn't want to work with people like that? And then there's this city! Warm, welcoming, lively, full of vim and vigor and sunshine! Let me say it to you with my hand on my heart: I wouldn't trade it for any other city on earth!"

Italo looked at him for a couple of seconds in silence. "Are you making fun of me?"

The deputy chief didn't answer.

"You're wrong, Rocco. Just think how much worse it could have gone."

"Oh, really?"

"You could have wound up in Sacile del Friuli!"

"Which is where I could suggest Baldi send you! Okay, I'll call him later, and that's a promise."

Italo leaned on the desk. "But aren't you afraid, Rocco?"

"Of what?"

"The way that guy tried once, he could try again."

Rocco pulled out a cigarette. He lit it. "No, Italo. Not right away. It's too hot right now. Later, maybe, when the waters have subsided, he'll give it another try. But I'm going to catch him before he gets a second chance." He took a puff and exhaled the smoke in a plume toward the ceiling. "Instead, why don't you tell me something. How are we going to catalogue this new case in Varallo? This is a tenth degree, because it means I still have to investigate the Mimmo Cuntrera murder, but it's something more. Because it's inside a prison."

"A ten, summa cum laude?"

"We've used that before. Let's try a ten, ne plus ultra, this time. Add it to the chart."

"I'll make sure I do. By the way . . . there's a person waiting for you, out in the hall."

Rocco rolled his eyes. "Who is it?"

"Giuliana Berguet, remember her?"

"Of course I remember her. What does she want now? Her daughter's back home, isn't she? Please, I just don't have the strength. Tell her I'm not here. Tell her I imploded, that I tumbled into a space-time wormhole, that—"

"Rocco, do you want some advice? Talk to her for a few minutes. It's worth it."

"Why?"

Italo smiled slyly. "Judge Baldi really wants you to." And he left the room without closing the door behind him. Sure enough, just a few seconds later, Giuliana Berguet came through it. Rocco stood up and walked toward her to shake hands with her. "Signora Berguet, I'm delighted to see you!"

The woman's face was more relaxed than the last time he had seen her; the bags under her eyes were gone now, but a dark light poured from her veiled eyes. She smiled only with her mouth, and she blinked slowly as she did. "Dottor Schiavone, please forgive me . . . I hope you'll forgive me for intruding upon you in your office."

"What can I do for you, Signora?"

"You've already done so much." Giuliana Berguet sat down across the desk from him. Rocco sniffed the air quickly. The cigarette had covered the penetrating odor of grass that so often wafted through the air between those walls. "I just came to thank you. You've given me back my daughter."

"How is Francesca?" Rocco asked, taking a seat.

"Chiara," the woman corrected him.

"Excuse me, of course, Chiara. How is she?"

"I don't really know . . ." she said, drawing a deep sorrowful breath and emitting a groan, the kind that only a mother thinking of her children's fate can expel. "She won't go back to school, she hardly speaks, she eats even less. She doesn't want any psychological counseling. My husband claims that time is the best medicine."

"Don't believe him," retorted the deputy chief. "All time will do for you is make you get older."

"There's a real desire to meet you and thank you in person. But there's not the level of strength required to leave the house."

"Excuse me, but are you talking about Chiara or your husband?"

"Chiara. My husband . . ." And here she emitted a second groan.

Different, sharper. This one was a wifely groan. "My husband, I'm not sure about. He isn't the same person anymore, hasn't been for a few days now. They expelled him from the competition for the bid, and now he spends most of his time out and about, who knows where. He doesn't go to the office, he seems to have lost all interest in the company's future."

Rocco wasn't much when it came to marriage counseling. He limited himself to nodding, with the expression of someone who understands and empathizes.

"He snaps at the slightest thing," Giuliana continued. "He seems to have lost his mind. I even tried talking to his brother Marcello about it . . ."

"How is Marcello?"

"He seems to have reacted better. But Pietro . . . I'm really very worried. In any case, I won't take any more of your time. I just wanted to say hello. By the way, that horrible thing I read about in the newspaper, the murder in your home. How terrible!"

"Right. I'm working on it."

"Are you thinking this might be part of a vendetta?"

"It most assuredly is, Signora. But not on the part of the people who were trying to extort your husband. It's something else, and eventually I'll figure out what."

Giuliana nodded. The deputy chief assumed that the two of them had nothing else to say to each other, and so he extended his hand to the woman. "Let me thank you again, then, and please give my best regards to your husband and your daughter." But Giuliana didn't stand up. She looked at him, her eyes puffy with tears. She barely opened her mouth and in a faint voice said: "Help me."

Rocco furrowed his brow. He didn't understand. "How can I help you, Signora Berguet?"

"I'm losing everything. My daughter, the company, my husband.

Please. I know that Pietro is seeing another woman. He's chilly and distant. He's no longer himself. I'm begging you."

"Signora, that's the kind of work that private detectives do, not the state police."

"Can I hire you?"

"No. I'd say that you can't."

Giuliana looked at the floor. "Chiara, her at least. She won't talk to me anymore. She only told me that she really wished she could thank you, but she doesn't have the courage to come in to police headquarters. I'm begging you, go see her. Just once."

"I'll try . . ."

"No. Trying's not enough. You need to promise me!"

IT HAD BEEN SERGIO MOZZICARELLI'S SHIFT IN THE INFIRMARY. He'd been sent out to bring a meal to Omar Ben Taleb, the Tunisian who'd been beaten badly a few days earlier by the Professor and his friends. He made his way through the armored doors that the guards opened for him, one by one, without a word of greeting. It wasn't that they had any bad feelings about him, either way; it was just that they couldn't remember his name, in spite of the fact that Mozzicarelli had been an inmate of that house of detention for seven long years. Sergio was an invisible man. A face in the crowd, of ordinary height and stature, an undistinguished gaze. He was a fleeting shadow, a breath of wind. In the past, this quality had come in handy when he wanted to hide or avoid arousing suspicion. And even in prison, never being at the center of attention was, all things considered, a distinct advantage. Being an anonymous character, a mere cameo in the lives of others, had come naturally to him. He was at his ease in that transparent body that no one ever took aim at, of which no one ever asked a favor. But now, he thought, that very same transparency was dragging him into real trouble because it had allowed him to see everything, to know everything. Shadows don't have consciences, he kept telling himself, but somehow he couldn't master that anxiety; he couldn't manage to keep to himself the nugget of information that could pin down a killer, bring him to justice. He got to the last barred gate, the one that gave onto the infirmary ward. Officer Tolotta, tall and imposing, smiled as he opened the door for him. This guard, like all the others, couldn't remember his name. "Is this for Omar? Let me take a look." He studied the tray. Next to the bowl of minestrone was a slice of light-colored meat. "What is it?"

"I don't know . . . beef . . . pork."

"Pork? Have they lost their minds in the kitchen? He can't eat pork. Well, anyway . . . you tell him that it's beef . . ."

Sergio smiled as Federico Tolotta snapped the lock open.

The only patient in the six-bed ward of the infirmary was Omar. Mozzicarelli walked over to him. The young man lay there with his eyes shut. His face was swollen. His lips were split, his nose was bandaged, and he had two black eyes. One hand was wrapped in gauze dressings. In the other arm was a needle and an IV tube.

"Time to eat!" said Sergio. He set the tray down on the nightstand. "Are you strong enough, or do you need me to call a nurse for you?"

Omar barely opened an eye. He looked at the other inmate. "Sergio . . . you're Sergio, right?" he said.

Sergio was astonished. "Yes, that's me. Why?"

"Mind your own business, Sergio. Don't talk to anyone. Keep to yourself the things that you've seen . . . and . . ." But he didn't finish the sentence. He shut his eyes again. Sergio stood, frozen to the spot. How could Omar know? How had he heard about it? he wondered. Then, suddenly, he knew. Sergio had mentioned it to his cell mate Karim, and sure enough Karim had then informed Omar. Everyone knows that prison radio, as they called it, could be as slow as a sloth or as fast as a cheetah. But the idea that two people knew now left a bad taste in his mouth. He went back to the door. Federico was waiting for him to come out so he could relock the door. "Sergio! That's your name!"

"We've known each other for years and you only just now remembered my name? Ah, so you were eavesdropping, weren't you?"

Tolotta smiled at him. "Did you tell him it's beef?"

"Federico, that guy can barely even drink water. Send him a nurse to feed him, take it from me."

Instead, Tolotta slammed the barred door shut with determination. "Have you lost your mind? Do you want to talk to the unions? Go on, Sergio, go on back to your wing. And take care of yourself."

Sergio stuck a cigarette in his mouth and walked away from the ward.

"And don't you dare light that thing until you're outside!" the guard shouted after him.

The inmate lifted a thumb and replied: "Got it. My last name's Mozzicarelli, by the way."

"DON'T EVER TELL ME FRIENDS AREN'T ANY USE TO YOU," said Officer Italo Pierron, tossing a small-format newspaper filled with photographs onto Rocco's desk.

"What's all this?"

"Take a look on page twelve."

Rocco leafed through the newspaper. It was a publication of an Aosta real estate agency. "Page twelve. So?"

"Look right here." Italo stepped close. "Bedroom, living room, bathroom, kitchen, and office. Top floor in the city center for just six hundred fifty euros a month. Via Croix de Ville! It's yours!"

The deputy chief lowered the newspaper. "Do you get a kickback?"

Italo turned pale. "Have you lost your mind?"

"So what you're telling me is that you decided to find me an apartment?"

"Exactly."

Rocco looked at the newspaper again. "All right. Do me a favor. Hold on . . ." And he pulled out his wallet. He extracted his checkbook from the wallet and signed one check. He detached it and handed it to Italo. "Here. It's for the rent, the security deposit, or whatever else you need. Oh, Italo, that's a blank check, do your best not to lose it."

Italo nodded. "What if you don't like the place, though?"

"Take Lupa. If she barks, the place is fine. If she won't go in, forget about it."

"I don't really get along with Lupa."

"Then let Caterina handle it."

Italo made a face. "Caterina, actually . . ."

"What?"

"We have some problems. In fact, I don't know if you can give me some advice . . ."

"Oh my God, what a pain in the ass! What is this? Have you all taken me for a marriage counselor?"

"Why?"

"Signora Berguet tells me that her husband is seeing other women, that he has various lovers."

"Well, is it true?"

"How would I know?"

"Before I forget . . . Judge Baldi wants to know if—"

"Yeah, yeah, I know. I know. I have to go to Varallo. Call Antonio and Caterina. We need to have a chat."

Italo snapped to attention and started to leave the office. But the instant he opened the door he froze to the spot. "Rocco . . ."

"What's wrong?"

"Don't you think it might be dangerous?"

"What? Going into the prison?"

"Right . . . What if the guy who broke into your apartment knows someone who's in prison?"

"That's just a risk I'm going to have to take. By the way, have there been any calls from Rome for me?"

"No, nothing."

"Then I'm going to give you an important assignment. I want you to answer all phone calls that might come in to me from Rome. Specifically, from the Cristoforo Colombo police station, in EUR, from Officer Alfredo De Silvestri."

"Got it." And Italo finally left the office.

The deputy chief opened the drawer. He saw the Ruger pistol that Furio had given him the night before. He didn't even touch it. Instead, he picked up an already rolled joint and put it in his pocket. Then he locked the drawer back up.

Antonio Scipioni, Caterina Rispoli, and Italo entered the room. Lupa barked and ran straight toward the deputy inspector. She seemed to remember that this was the woman who had saved her from the snow. Lupa licked Rispoli's hands while the policewoman took the puppy in her arms.

"Now listen carefully. Italo has already told you that I'm going to have to be away for a while . . ."

The blank looks on Caterina's and Antonio's faces clearly said that Italo hadn't. "Again?"

"Yeah, it's just that I have to go to the prison to get things straight concerning Cuntrera's death. What I want you to do while I'm gone is this: stay in touch with Baldi. He's taking a look at the papers of some guy called Luca Grange, the one who landed the public works contract that the Berguets thought they were going to get. The thing smells, and nobody thinks it adds up. Italo and Caterina, you need to do whatever Baldi tells you."

"All right . . ." said Rispoli, with her wrist clamped between Lupa's jaws. "Do you want me to look after your dog?"

"That would be great. I don't think I can take her with me."

Italo made a face. Which escaped the notice of neither Rocco nor Italo's girlfriend.

"Any particular problem, Italo?"

"I don't like dogs!"

"What do you care? After all, she's sleeping at my place, not at your place."

"With a dog but not with me?"

"Oh, God, you're relentless!"

"That's enough!" the deputy chief interrupted them, clapping his hands. "That's enough, listen to me carefully. Now we're moving on to the hard part. There's a man, Walter Cremonesi . . . he's a former terrorist whom our nation's correctional system seems unwilling to keep safely separate from the rest of society. Now he owns a vineyard just outside of Aosta, called Vini Primot."

"Do I need to keep an eye on him?" asked Antonio.

Rocco nodded. "But be careful. He's a vicious beast. Before tailing him, read up on his record. I'll just say this: when you were still sucking on your mother's tit, Cremonesi was already shooting people." Rocco stood up. "One last thing. Give me the DVDs from the closed-circuit surveillance cameras. I'll take them with me."

"I'll make sure you have them," said Antonio. "How long are you going to be away?"

"I hope not long. It's not as if they list Varallo prison as a Club Med vacation spot."

TATIANA RANG THE BUZZER BY THE FRONT GATE FOR THE third time. She waited for ten seconds or so.

Nothing. Corrado wasn't answering. Sitting behind the windowpane was the second-story neighbor, a little old lady with an enormous pair of eyeglasses whom Tatiana had never seen out on the streets of Francavilla al Mare. She waved to her to open her window. The woman seemed not to understand.

"Open the window!" she shouted. The woman got up out of her chair, slowly turned the handle, and pulled the window open.

"What is it?"

"Do you know Corrado Pizzuti? The guy who lives on the mezzanine floor?" And she pointed up at the closed windows.

The woman barely smiled. "Yes."

"Do you know where he is? Have you seen him?"

"No."

"Could you open the gate for me, please? That way I can cross the courtyard and go over to his staircase and call some other neighbor?"

"No."

"There she is, the slut!" A high-pitched voice echoed across the courtyard behind Tatiana. She turned around. Another old woman had appeared in the second-story window of the apartment building facing the first, Staircase B. This woman's hair color verged unexpectedly on pale green. "What are you doing sticking your face out the window, you slut!"

She had it in for the woman on the second floor of Staircase A. "Go back inside, you disgusting slut, you and your cats!"

The two women glared daggers at each other. Tatiana looked back and forth, first at one and then at the other, baffled.

"You just need to shut your trap!" shot back the little old lady on the second floor of Staircase A, plucking at her cardigan sweater. "And worry about your husband!"

"I guess you'd like to worry about him for me, wouldn't you?"

"Fuck yourself!" shouted the woman with the oversized eyeglasses and shut the window. She vanished, swallowed up by the dark room behind her. Tatiana looked up at the neighbor woman on Staircase B. "Buongiorno, Signora."

"Why were you talking to that slut?"

"I wanted to know if you'd seen Corrado. Corrado Pizzuti, the guy in the mezzanine apartment on Staircase A."

"What, are you his girlfriend?"

"No. His business partner, we run the Bar Derby on Piazza della Sirena."

"Slut. You're a slut, no better than my sister!" And with these words, she, too, slammed her casement window shut and withdrew into her apartment. Tatiana threw both arms wide in helpless frustration. Then she turned her eyes up to scan the other windows in the apartment building. Except for the ones on the second floor, they all seemed abandoned. She rang the buzzers of all the other apartments, but no one answered. Except for the little old lady on the second floor, who reappeared in her window. Tatiana gestured to her in an appeal to buzz her in, but the woman did nothing other than to vanish again.

"Where could you be?" she said in a low voice. It occurred to her to search the area around the apartment buildings for Corrado's green Fiat Multipla. The surf was rough. During the night a north wind had sprung up that was now shaking the palm trees and pushing the waves into roaring breakers. Tatiana put on her baseball cap. She walked around the block three times, but there was no trace of Corrado's car. Anxiety was by now a constant knot at the center of her chest, blocking her windpipe. She leaned against a wall, trying to get a breath of air. She could feel it. Something had happened.

"*Chto mnye delat'?*" she said to herself in a faint voice, speaking her native Russian. "What am I going to do?" There was nothing left but to go to the Bar Derby. Open the place up for business. Then wait till nightfall. And if Corrado hadn't given any signs of life by then, she'd go to the police.

DEPUTY CHIEF ROCCO SCHIAVONE HAD BEEN SITTING ON THE little yellow settee outside Judge Baldi's door for the past ten minutes. Lupa had dropped off to sleep, and he had already read everything there was to read. A copy of *La Stampa* that was three days old; two magazines published by the Guardia di Finanza, Italy's financial police; a pamphlet for a hotel in the ski resort of Courmayeur that somebody had forgotten there; all of the notices posted on the walls and even the label on the fire extinguisher. The door was still closed. There was nothing left for him to do but kill time by studying the swirls and whorls of the knots in the wood, hoping to discover some mysterious hidden figure in them. He was still focusing on this task to pass the time when the door finally swung open. Judge Baldi appeared in a herringbone jacket from the eighties and the gray skin tone of someone who hasn't had a breath of fresh air in hours. Behind Baldi, Rocco was able to glimpse the bearded Judge Messina sitting in the office and a black uniform bedecked with glittering silver insignia.

"Schiavone! I'm going to be busy with this for quite some time. Can we postpone till later?"

Rocco got to his feet. "I just wanted to make sure everything was taken care of. I'll go to Varallo tomorrow. Did you talk to the warden?"

"Certainly . . ." He turned around and looked at the room behind him, then slowly shut the door. "This meeting is never going to end. But we're doing great things, you know that?"

"I don't doubt it."

"Cuntrera's papers . . . the documents we found on his person at the border . . . are looking like they're going to be decisive!"

"Am I wrong, or is there a carabiniere in there?"

"That's right, a colonel." And he looked at the deputy chief. "I can't say much. But this time, thanks to you and that mental defective Cuntrera, we're going to be able to nab a fair number of people. And as we were saying the other day, very highly placed people, too! So now I'd like you to solve the problem at the prison."

"ROS?" asked Schiavone.

"Excuse me?"

"That colonel . . . is he ROS? Special Operations Group?"

Baldi nodded. "They're giving us a hand now."

"If you need me, you know where I am." Rocco shook his hand, and then, with a soft whistle, he summoned Lupa. "Shall we go, pup?"

"Schiavone?"

He turned around after walking halfway down the hall.

"Keep your cell phone switched on."

"You can count on it."

EVENING HAD FALLEN AND WITH IT THE TEMPERATURE. During the day, the sun provided warmth, but the minute it ducked behind the line of the mountains, the chill that had dogged Schiavone's footsteps for months now spread back out into the streets and piazzas of Aosta. The icy embrace of an unwelcome, intrusive old friend. He was planning to eat dinner in a trattoria, but first he'd make sure to feed Lupa. He walked into the brightly lit residential hotel and stepped up to the reception desk for his key. The receptionist greeted him with a smile, then jutted his chin to direct his attention to the sofa behind him. Rocco turned around. Sitting in front of the now-cold fireplace was Anna. He went over to her.

"What am I supposed to think?" she asked him without standing up.

"That's a little generic. Give me the topic."

"You and me, Rocco. What am I supposed to think?"

Lupa was trying to get Anna to pet her, but there was an electric charge running under the woman's skin powerful enough to light up a desk lamp. The dog wandered away and curled up at her master's feet.

"Last night at the Turrinis' house, you left without even saying a proper good-bye. I'm not talking about love or us being a couple, I'm just talking about basic good manners!"

"I'm not a guy with manners of any kind, you ought to know that by now."

"Right, you just do whatever you feel like, without a thought for the consequences."

"That's a problem I have."

But Anna still wasn't done. "Do you know how I got home? Or is that a problem you haven't even considered?"

"Someone must have given you a ride?"

"Asshole!" Anna dropped her gaze.

Here we go, thought Rocco. Tears were rolling down her cheeks, even as Anna struggled against it. "What did I ever do to you, Rocco?"

Rocco sat down beside her. "Nothing. You didn't do anything to me. Unfortunately."

"Then would it have cost you that much to make a phone call? Or even just drop by to make sure I made it home safe and sound?"

"You have a point about that. That was a shitty group of people. I shouldn't have dumped you there. Even though you did seem completely at your ease."

"All the same, that shitty group of people was talking about you. The Turrinis, for instance, even though you made damned sure not to even say good-bye to them."

"Don't worry, I'll find a way of making it up to them," Rocco replied without bothering to conceal the irony in his voice.

"Or else that friend of mine, the gallery owner, who really wanted to meet you."

"But I didn't want to meet him. Doesn't that count for anything?"

Anna opened her handbag. She pulled out a handkerchief. She rose quickly to her feet and walked away, turning her back on him. She was drying her eyes. The receptionist at the desk looked down in embarrassment. Then Anna turned back around. "When Nora told me what an asshole you were, she wasn't telling me half of it!"

The deputy chief heaved a sigh.

"Now I need you to tell me: What was I for you? Just a quick fuck?"

"Two, actually."

"Right. Two." Anna laughed, with a note of hysteria in her voice. "And not even especially memorable ones, trust me."

"Never claimed any different. Listen to me, Anna, sit down for a second."

"No!"

"Please."

The woman shut her eyes, took a deep breath, and went back to sit down next to Rocco. "Listen, let's just think of it as a scale, with two pans. On the one side is you, and you've loaded up the pan, while on the other side is me, and I've put in practically nothing. So this is what happens." He fluttered both hands. "You see? There's no balance. If we want to get some balance, there's only one of two ways. Either you remove some weight from the scale, or else I add some . . ."

Anna looked him in the eyes. "So you can't do it?"

"I can try. But you need to give me some time."

Anna nodded. "Why did I ever fall in love with you?"

"You can't ask the innkeeper if the wine he serves is good!"

The woman finally smiled, and her eyes became enormous. "My mother always told me: 'Anna, stay away from the men who make you cry and only chase after the ones who make you laugh.'"

"Your mother was a wise woman."

"You're sort of a mix of both kinds, the crying and the laughing. Shall I sleep at your place?"

"And then what? We'll just be back where we are tonight, and instead of two quick fucks we'll be up to three. But nothing will have changed."

"Have we come to this? Are you actually giving me the 'I don't deserve you' line?"

"No, I'm just trying to explain the way I see things between us without hurting your feelings."

"So basically, you don't love me. Say those words, and we can call it quits."

Rocco took a deep breath. He took both of Anna's hands in his. "I don't love you."

Anna reeled from the blow. She shut her eyes, and two tears leaked out from under her large eyelids. "It hurts a little to hear you say it, but at least you said it." She opened her eyes again. "Thanks."

"For what?"

"For the honesty." She picked up her purse and got to her feet. "I hope you have a good night, and a very nice day tomorrow."

"Like fun. I'm going to prison tomorrow."

Anna looked at him for a couple of seconds. A half smile flickered across her face. "The idea of you going to prison isn't all that ridiculous after all."

"You've got a pretty good sense of humor yourself, you know."

"Take care of yourself, Rocco." She turned on her heels and strode to the residential hotel's glass front door. Her eyesight must have been blurred by streaming tears because she came dangerously close to smashing into the glass doors, which had opened automatically but not quickly enough for her. She could have marked her exit with a cathartic burst of laughter, but instead, she just kept walking and vanished into the street. The deputy chief looked at Lupa. "Hey, you! Let's go get some sleep. What do you think? Did I just fuck up?"

Lupa stood up and put her head up near Rocco's lap, and he immediately scratched her head. "I guess I did, right? I fucked up. Just look at what's become of me, having to ask a dog for advice." Going out for dinner was out of the question now.

"Come on, let's go to bed!"

WHEN HE SAW TATIANA AND BARBARA COME INTO THE OFFICE of the town constables, Ciro got to his feet and flashed his brightest smile. "Tatiana! Dang, if Luca finds out that you came in on the day he went home early, he'll tie a rock to his ankles and jump into the river, no doubt."

The Russian woman didn't smile. Her eyes were gloomy and haggard, and her face was pale. Barbara was there to offer her moral support and was walking just a few inches away from her friend, convinced she might collapse at any instant. "What's happened?" asked the constable. "Why are you here? Do I need to be worried?"

"I need to file a criminal complaint, Ciro!"

Ciro's eyes bugged out. "A criminal complaint? Why?"

"It's about Corrado," Barbara broke in.

"What's he done?"

"He's vanished." And Tatiana finally broke into tears.

"Oh, Jesus . . . Sit down! Sit down!" And the constable went to fetch a chair. "Let me go get you a glass of water . . . Wait, wait right here . . . And you, Barbara, stay close to her, okay? Hold on while I go call Lisa, too . . ." Then he turned toward a door and yelled, "Lisa!" He quickly shoved his hands in his pockets, pulled out a plastic key, and headed for the vending machine. "Lisa!" he called again. "Could you come out here please!"

The door swung open and Lisa emerged with a sleepy face. "What's happening?"

"Tatiana's here . . . and she says that Corrado has disappeared!" he shouted over his shoulder while jabbing at the buttons on the vending machine. "Damn it to hell! . . . I jabbed the wrong button. Is a Coca-Cola all right?"

"Don't bother, Ciro!" said Tatiana. But the constable had already shoved his hand inside the flap.

"Anyway, Coca-Cola has plenty of caffeine and it'll pep you up!" He yanked the pull tab, took a glass from the desk, and emptied the can into it.

"Disappeared? Are you sure?" asked Lisa, adjusting her hairdo, freshly tinted with reddish highlights. You'd almost expect the dye to come off on her hands, it was such a radical shade of Titian red.

"I haven't talked to him since yesterday. I've been calling him continuously, but his cell phone is always switched off."

"Maybe he had to leave town!" said the constable as he handed the glass of Coca-Cola to the Russian woman.

"He'd have told me. He's never gone away without telling me. Last week he was out of town for two days and he called me without fail to make sure everything was okay. Corrado is . . . apprehensive, that's the word."

"All right, then, let's proceed methodically." Lisa went over to sit behind the desk. "When is the last time you saw him?"

"Yesterday evening, right before closing time."

"That's not very long. I mean, are you ready to declare him a missing person? Maybe he's at home even as we speak!"

"Listen!" Barbara broke in. "Last week, Corrado was gone for two days, but since he got back he's been very strange, and when I say strange, I mean *strange*." Barbara seemed to have been possessed by the spirit of Inspector Maigret. "And he wouldn't talk. He was on edge, and he'd snap at the drop of a hat."

"So he was dropping his hat? Maybe he's losing his hair!" Ciro replied.

"You idiot," his partner upbraided him.

"I was just trying to lighten the—"

"Just keep your trap shut. Go on, Barbara."

"Now, as long as I've known him, Corrado has always lived alone. But just the other day I discovered"—and here she lowered her voice to just above a whisper—"that there was someone else in his apartment. And Tatiana and I are certain of that."

"A lady?" And Ciro winked at Barbara.

"Then why would he be keeping his shutters closed?" the bookseller continued. "Let's say it was a lady. Did she live in the dark? Why? What was he ashamed of?"

"Maybe the lady is married, and she didn't want to be seen in that apartment." Ciro was still clinging to that hypothesis.

"Or else something else."

"You know that Corrado had a criminal record, right? And who knows . . ." While Tatiana said these words, she trembled. ". . . who can say . . . maybe a fugitive from justice!"

There was a dense, compact silence.

"A fugitive from justice?" Lisa echoed her.

"Why not?"

"Then that would explain everything!" the lady constable realized. "If he's a fugitive from justice, then he could hardly say: 'I'm going to be out of town, so you need to help me hide this man' . . . It's clear, isn't it? These are things that people do in secret!"

"Not so!" Barbara objected. She had taken the reins of this investigation well in hand, and a quick glance at her spirited eyes showed that she was thoroughly enjoying herself. "Who says? If you're going to do something secret, then it's best to do it in the light of day, you just call over to the bar, you say that a commitment of some kind—anything will do, you make something up—requires you to go to . . . oh, I don't know, to Ancona, and you go. Otherwise you're just going to kindle suspicions!"

"No, that's right. Barbara has a point," said Tatiana, who hadn't touched a drop of her Coca-Cola. "Just disappearing like that, without warning: it doesn't look good!"

"Did anyone else have the keys to his place?" Ciro broke in.

The Russian woman gestured disconsolately. "Please . . . I can tell. Something's happened to him!"

Lisa took the situation in hand. "All right. Let's go in the back office and take down the details of this criminal complaint."

"Then what happens?" asked Tatiana as she got to her feet.

"We'll inform the various police headquarters, then the prefect will contact the special commissioner for missing people and the investigation gets under way."

"Let's just hope it's nothing, eh?" said Ciro, opening the door to the office. Barbara and Tatiana went in. The constable looked at his colleague. "You know something? Tatiana is in love with Corrado."

"Jesus! Luca's going to kill himself!"

SUNDAY

Alessandro Martinelli ushered him promptly into his office.

He had spoken with Baldi and he'd been more than willing to help.

"Where do I sleep?" the deputy chief had asked.

"Three rooms right next to the office. It sort of resembles a cell, but all things considered, that's just part of the package, right?"

"I'd agree. Just one more favor."

"If I can."

"I'm going to need a television set in my room, if it's an old one that doesn't matter, and a DVD player."

"I'll have them bring in the TV set from the rec room on the ground floor. Anything else? I don't know, a wake-up call at a certain hour? Breakfast in bed?"

Rocco took a deep breath. He looked down at his feet, then looked back up at the warden. "I'm not asking you any special favors to make my stay in this shithole more agreeable. I'm doing it so I can do my job. That being said, if you'd be so kind as to take your sarcasm and stuff it up your ass, we'll get through the coming hours in a relatively rapid and painless fashion."

The warden cleared his throat. "They'd told me that you were a guy who didn't mince words."

"I'm happy to mince words all afternoon if you feel like it. But what I don't like is when people like you think that they're dealing with some poor fool they can dangle on a string. Now, if it's not too much trouble, I'd like to speak with Agostino Lumi before he's transferred. Do you think that might be possible?"

Martinelli smiled. "Certainly. And it won't be necessary to fill out forms in triplicate, either."

"That's good to hear."

"I've put him in solitary confinement. He's in the wing for sex offenders. While I make the necessary arrangements, why don't you read up on his criminal record." And the warden gave Rocco the binder, slamming it down on the desk. The room wasn't brightly lit, so the deputy chief stepped over to the window. From there he enjoyed a panoramic view of the house of detention.

"All right then, I'll get going . . ."

"One last thing. I'll also need to be able to move around the prison."

"Sure, I'd thought of that, what do you think? You'll have one of my men at your disposal at all times to escort you wherever you need to go. He's right outside, whenever you need him." Then he pulled open the door to leave. "See you soon. Make yourself right at home." Rocco rolled his eyes and decided to ignore that last gratuitous bit of sarcasm from the warden.

This was the time of day when all the inmates were free to roam around their respective wings. They were socializing, as he had been informed. Rocco took one last look at those gray buildings, which reminded him of a working-class quarter on the outskirts of Rome; then he started leafing through Agostino Lumi's binder. He wasn't interested in the bastard's criminal record. He wanted to find his weak point.

"Well, lookie lookie . . ." he said to himself with a smile as he went on reading.

He set the binder down on the desk. He opened the door. Waiting for him was a prison guard reading the newspaper. It only took a quick glance for Rocco to classify him in his own personal bestiary. That guard was a *Myocastor coypus*, also known as a nutria. The big nose and handlebar mustache gave him the smiling, cunning air of a retired Prussian colonel.

"What's your name?" Rocco asked.

The guard leapt to his feet. "Mauro Marini . . ."

"You're the one who found Cuntrera's body, if I'm not mistaken?"

"You're not mistaken, Dottore. I was with my colleague Daniele Abela . . ."

"Would you take me out to the courtyard?"

"Come right this way . . ."

And the two men started walking down the long hallways as the metal doors opened and closed as they went past. "This way, follow me . . ."

"Listen, Marini, what do you think?"

"About Cuntrera's death?"

"No, about the going-out-of-business sales in January."

Marini looked the deputy chief in the eyes. A smile played under his luxuriant mustache. "What do I think? Like I told the judge, I've been working in correctional institutions for many years now. Sometimes, all it takes is a glance, a word out of place, or an insult, and . . . bam! The feuds begin."

The air was redolent of soup and disinfectant. The smell came off the floors, the walls, the guards' uniforms, and even from his own jacket. The two men finally emerged into the open air.

"Here we are, this is the courtyard. Down there is a soccer field, do you see?"

"And that building on the right?"

"It's a workshop. That's where we found Cuntrera, near Wing 3." And the guard pointed to a perpetually shadowy corner. Rocco walked over beside him. He looked around. Hurricane fencing and enclosure walls. The guard towers.

"And the guys who started the brawl, where were they?"

"Down there, by Wing 2." And Marini pointed to a wall on the far side of the courtyard. More than three hundred feet away. Rocco paced out the distance. Then he stood on the ground where the brawl had broken out. He looked around again. Still the same hurricane fencing, the same enclosure walls, the same guard towers looking down. From here he couldn't see the corner where Cuntrera had been killed. "Who was on duty in the guard towers?"

"I don't know. But I'll find out."

"Thanks. And I want to talk with whoever was on those two guard towers down there. I don't need anyone else. Tell me about the schedules . . ."

"Certainly. All right, then, from nine until eleven and then in the afternoon from one until three, the inmates can come down here for some fresh air."

"And what do they do?"

"People do different things, they chat, they play soccer, they go over there, you see? To the workshops. We have two computer workshops and one for woodworking. From five in the evening until nine they can stay in their sections and socialize. But they can't leave the section. At ten o'clock we shut the armored cell gates and then it's lights out."

"What about meals?"

"We serve lunch from eleven o'clock to twelve noon, and dinner's at six thirty. We have a library and a gym and those are the two most heavily used spaces."

"What time was it when Cuntrera died?"

"Two thirty?"

"Are you asking me?"

"No, no. Two thirty," the guard hastened to state.

"Let's go back upstairs . . . This courtyard is disgusting."

"I know. But you ought to see the cells. They're even worse. The real problem here is health. We've had cases of tuberculosis, and even inmates with full-blown cases of AIDS. But with all the cuts in funding . . ."

"Listen up, are the four North Africans still in the infirmary, or have they returned to their cells?"

"Only Omar's still in the infirmary. Two of them have gone back to their section, whereas the one who got the worst beating, Aziz, is in the hospital."

"There's something I need to understand. How do you get into this? What are the points of access?"

Marini nodded. "Every section has its own entrance. See? There are three. But the inmates restricted to solitary confinement have a section all their own, and they don't come into this courtyard; they go to the covered yard, over there."

Rocco went back to the corner where Cuntrera had given up the ghost. A recess, just yards from Wing 3. "What about this entrance? Where does it lead?"

"It's the third wing."

"And was that where Cuntrera had his cell?"

"Yes, he was in that section."

"So when he was killed, he was very close to the entrance to his detention wing. Fine. Who was at that door on the day of the brawl?"

"I don't remember. But I think Tolotta. Federico Tolotta."

Rocco stepped closer to the gate. "Why don't you have them open up, please."

Marini picked up his radio. A moment later, the gate leading into the section opened. A short, balding guard with a sad face appeared. "I'm Deputy Chief Schiavone. Are you Tolotta?"

"No. I'm Biranson. Tolotta is my colleague, he comes on duty tomorrow."

Rocco, followed by Marini like his shadow, stepped into the hallway. Straight ahead were the stairs. On the right a metal door. "What's this?"

"That door leads to an internal corridor," replied the diminutive Biranson.

"And where does this corridor lead to?"

"To the other side," Marini replied. "Open up, Bruno, let's show the commissario just where this corridor leads."

"Let's show the deputy chief," Rocco corrected him.

"Ah, of course, excuse me."

Bruno slid the key into the lock, turned it three times, and pulled open the metal door. "If you please, through here."

It was a long, curving, narrow passageway, barely more than a yard wide, and on either side extremely high blank walls that were topped by a metal mesh that served as a roof. "There, you see? It's a passageway that we never use, it's just for us guards, only in case of accidents or emergencies. A single man can just fit through." Biranson, followed in single file by Rocco and Marini, was walking along, stepping on the weeds that had sprung up in the cracks in the cement. "But we never use it."

They came to another door. This one, too, all in metal. "Here we are. The corridor ends here." Biranson pulled out his keys and opened that second rusted entrance. "After you . . ."

They found themselves just outside of the recreation courtyard, near the location of the brawl, facing Wing 2. "So, if I understand completely, this corridor links Wing 3 with the outside of the courtyard."

"That's correct, right next to Wing 2," said Marini. "And there, you see? It's right where Omar was attacked. In other words, it's helpful for going around to the other side without having to go across the open plaza."

"But we practically never use it!" Biranson said again.

"Biranson, the concept is clear to me," Rocco said. "Now tell me, who has the keys to these doors and to the doors to the wings?"

"Saint Peter himself!" Biranson replied, hoisting two bunches with a dozen or so keys in all. "Anyone who's at the courtyard gate is assigned to have the keys to the armored gates"—and here he raised the first metal ring—"and to these two metal gates"—and then he displayed the two remaining keys. "Dotto', the same is true for the other gates—the ones leading to the other sections, I mean to say. There, too, they have an internal passageway, just like this one." And he knocked his knuckles against the metal door. Rocco nodded.

"Do you want to go see this section?" Marini asked.

"No. I want to go talk to Agostino . . ."

"IT'S AN HONOR TO MAKE YOUR ACQUAINTANCE, DOTTOR Schiavone. I've read a great many things about you."

Agostino Lumi, a.k.a. the Professor, had the kind of eyes that Rocco had seen on the faces of the worst bandits and armed robbers. Still, dead eyes, without a glimmer of expression, dry black river rocks. "You're a talented policeman. Somebody just killed a friend of yours, a woman, right in your home, isn't that right?"

"Nice to see you keep up with the news."

"I read the newspaper every day. A German philosopher used to say that reading the newspaper—"

"—is the realist's morning prayer," Rocco finished his sentence for him.

"I see that we both studied the humanities."

"Absolutely. Which is the best kind of studies. Is that why they call you 'the Professor'?"

Agostino Lumi started rolling himself a cigarette. "Do you mind if I smoke? You know, talking to a person like you in here isn't the sort of thing that happens every day. Mostly, I deal with rough, ignorant people, illiterates. Foreigners, for the most part. And donkeys. Donkeys that amble and graze the soil in the courtyard. Instead, I sense that you and I can have a lovely chat. So this woman they murdered in your home, was she your girlfriend?"

"No."

"Ah, of course, after your wife's death, you devoted yourself to a chaste, uncommitted life, didn't you?"

"Why, you certainly do read a lot of newspapers!"

"I read and I conjecture. When you have lots of time on your hands, you know how it can be. And yet you're still a young man, women must happen along. What do you do? Don't you even fuck anymore?"

"Are you gathering notes for your regular evening masturbation?"

Agostino smiled, but only with his lips. "And have you come up with some ideas about who might have killed your friend?"

"Yes," Rocco lied.

Agostino Lumi clapped his hands like a little boy watching a puppet show. "And when do you expect to arrest him?"

"I'm not planning to arrest him." Rocco leaned in close to Agostino's face, close enough to perceive the stench of garlic and tobacco smoke on his breath. "Arresting someone like that is just doing them a favor. I don't do favors. For anyone." Then he leaned back out to a safe distance.

Agostino Lumi furrowed his brow. "That's not the sort of thing a conscientious policeman would do."

"The idea that I'm a conscientious policeman is something you've come up with on your own."

"Tell the truth. The real target wasn't your girlfriend, was it? It was you, right?"

"Do you know anything about it?"

"I can guess . . ."

"How did that brawl go the other day?" Rocco inquired brusquely.

Agostino licked his cigarette. "Ah, you're referring to that little dustup in the courtyard. I wouldn't go so far as to call it a brawl. It was nothing special, just the usual roosters skirmishing in the courtyard."

"There were three of you trying to massacre a young man . . ."

"A narcotics dealer, actually, deputy chief." Agostino lit his cigarette. "A dealer who's bringing narcotics into this prison."

Rocco nodded. With a quick glance he took in the cell that housed Agostino. A bed, a small window, a private bathroom. The walls weren't flaking; they'd just been repainted with the usual bureaucratic pale green. There was a shelf full of books with tattered spines. "So what exactly are you? Some kind of internal prison policeman?"

"I'd really rather be thought of as someone who cares about law and order. I'm just trying to keep this place clean."

"An honorable ambition." Agostino smiled and took a drag on his cigarette.

"How does this Omar manage to get the narcotics inside?"

"With his little third-world boyfriends on the outside. They smuggle them in through the visiting room. Evidently there are guards willing to turn a blind eye in exchange for gifts. And then Omar, Tarek, and Karim deal the shit. There are two hundred prisoners in here, all of them bored and depressed. An excellent client base, don't you think?"

"I don't know. I've never done time behind bars," Rocco replied.

"I think that every policeman ought to spend some time behind bars, actually, maybe in disguise. You can figure out a lot of things by just spending a month or so in prison, and it might come in handy for the work you do."

"For example?"

"You'd get a much better understanding of the psychology of criminals."

"I really don't give a flying fuck about the psychology of criminals."

"You aren't following me. I'm just saying that if policemen did a little bit of prison time, they'd work more effectively and they'd be quicker to understand the moves and the intentions of guys like me. But I'm speaking against my own self-interest!"

"There's no need to serve time in prison to understand you. You all have pretty basic psychological makeups, believe me."

Agostino put out the cigarette. He smiled. But, again, only with his lips. His eyes remained dark and motionless, like two glass marbles. "But from the way you're doing your job as a policeman, if you ask me, sooner or later, a little time in here is something you're going to be looking at."

"Right? That way, maybe you and I will have lots of time to chat. But now, let me tell you a story. I was born in Trastevere, and you may or may not know that Regina Coeli prison is right there, at the foot of the Janiculum Hill, the Gianicolo. Let's just say that I had lots of bad influences, questionable acquaintances, and so one time my father took me up on top of the hill, looking down on the prison. Regina Coeli stands just two hundred yards under the terrace with the panoramic view. You know what was going on up there? The prisoners' wives, often clutching the railing of the parapet that stood above the sheer drop down to the prison, were talking with their husbands, shouting down to the barred windows. That way they could converse, exchange information, say that they loved each other, or maybe even talk about minor domestic issues. That day a woman was there, in her early thirties, and she had a little boy by the hand, maybe eight years old, at a guess. The woman was talking with her husband. 'Aldo!' she yells. 'Listen, your son got straight Ds on his report card!' After a couple of seconds Aldo's voice comes up from the outermost wing of Regina Coeli: 'Goddamn it to hell . . . where is he?' and his wife replies: 'Right here with me! He can hear you!' And the husband replies: 'Tell him that the minute I get home, I'll take my belt to him, and that'll make him feel like studying!' And the wife: 'Before you get home, your son will be out of college!' My father looked at me and took me back home. There, you see? I didn't need anything more than that. Of course, I always gave my father some trouble, some concerns, but he knew that that day I had understood." Rocco looked at him, a long, intense look. He got out a cigarette and lit it. Nice and slow, prolonging that silence as much as possible.

"So?" asked Agostino.

"So our little conversation is all done now, and you and I are sitting in a cell, in the solitary confinement wing, talking like two men who delve into the filthiest shit every day of our lives. All right, then, can I speak, or do you still want to persist with these personal questions to see if you can piss me off? No? Shall I go on? Fine. Will you tell me who the fuck told you to unleash that mess in the courtyard, then?"

"So we're on an informal basis now?"

"We're on an informal basis now."

"Are you still talking about that little dustup, Rocco?"

"That's right. But listen, strictly speaking, even though you don't have to call me 'sir,' it still doesn't authorize you to actually call me by my first name. To you, I'm just Schiavone."

"What the fuck do you want from me, Schiavone? Do you want me to tell you things that I don't know, and that you're going to need to find out for yourself? It makes me laugh to watch you spinning the treadmill, uselessly, just like a hamster, you son of a bitch, fucking whoremonger."

"Speaking of which, how's your sister?"

For the first time, there was a darting sign of life in Agostino's eyes, rapid and almost invisible. "Why do you want to know?"

"What do they call her? 'Cri-Cri'? Why? Isn't 'Carmela' chic? Doesn't it sound sexy? Or is she ashamed because it was her mother's name?"

"Actually, policeman, my sister isn't a very interesting topic."

"I disagree. I mean, word is that Cri-Cri is quite the little cocksucker."

Agostino smiled. He rocked his head to the right and the left, making the bones in his neck crackle and snap. "My sister lives in Varese and she's a schoolteacher. You'd better double-check your information, Schiavone."

"Your sister was a working whore in Milan, at Corso Como 12, in the basement apartment where you hid out a couple of times to avoid arrest. Now I hear that she still sucks cocks, but only in the very best hotels."

The Professor was starting to look like a pressure cooker.

"Cri-Cri has climbed the ladder, no doubt of it. Where did she learn her skills? From her sainted mother?"

Agostino lunged, but Rocco was ready for him. He slammed the palm of his hand into Agostino's face, right under his nose. The inmate dropped to the floor. Rocco got up and delivered a sharp kick to his ribs. "Where are your friends when you need them, eh, Agostino?" He let fly with a second kick. "Where are they?" Then he sat down again. Marini appeared in the grate. He saw the inmate on the floor. He was turning to get his keys, but Rocco halted him with a gesture. "Everything's fine. Don't worry."

The worried guard vanished back out into the hallway. The deputy chief lit a second cigarette. Slowly, Agostino moved. He held his hand over his bloodied nose. He raised his head; then on all fours he made his way to his cot, where he grabbed a washcloth to stem the nosebleed. "Piece of shit . . ." he snarled, looking at the deputy chief, who sat smoking, unconcerned. He picked up his eyeglasses and put them back on.

"Professor, now let me tell the way I see things."

Agostino said nothing. He looked at a fixed point on the floor. He hoisted himself up and sat down on the cot.

"Someone told you to unleash all that hubbub. Someone suggested it. You did it, and maybe you didn't even know why. But the guy they killed in the cell was a made man in the 'Ndrangheta. People like that eat people like you for breakfast. So if you think back on it, and if something occurs to you that you might want to tell me, go ahead. It just might save your ass." Rocco stood up and walked over to the barred door.

"If you so much as lay a hand on my sister, I'll—"

"I wouldn't touch her even if I was triple-wrapped in condoms. But there are other people, guys who do this stuff for a living, who might make sure she's found spread open like a sofa bed, fileted like a fish. Think it over, carefully. Everybody knows where to find a whore." He dropped the half-full pack of cigarettes on the floor.

"Here, smoke something decent for a change, not that shit that you roll, ineptly, if I might add." Then he shouted: "Marini, open this door!"

THE PRISON INFIRMARY WAS DOWNSTAIRS FROM THE ADMINISTRATIVE offices. It must have been recently repainted because there was still a distinct odor of paint. Green walls and fluorescent lights tinged the skin with an unhealthy grayish hue and left circles under the eyes like out of some film by Murnau. There were three wardrooms, each with six beds. In the first wardroom, Rocco glimpsed a skinny young man who was staring at the ceiling and barely breathing. Dr. Crocitti and Marini both greeted the inmate, but he didn't reply.

"What's wrong with him?" Rocco asked.

"Acquired immunodeficiency syndrome. We're going to take him down to Turin, to the infectious-diseases ward. He needs to be in isolation, we're not equipped for it here. Do you know how many prisoners with AIDS we have in this prison?"

"No . . ."

"Seven. And sometimes we don't even have an aspirin to give them if they catch a cold . . . Oh, well, forget about it. You know something, Dottor Schiavone? I'm waiting for my pension. Then none of this is my business. Only I'll take all of this"—and he looked up and out, his gaze taking in the whole hallway—"with me, for the rest of my life. Until the day I die."

Crocitti was frighteningly skinny, with a haggard face and lemur eyes bugging out of their sockets. His gut spoke eloquently of an absolute lack of physical activity. His thick curly hair, sprinkled with gray, looked like a camouflage helmet.

Marini was toying with his keys. He had an array of bunches of keys. They crossed paths with a male nurse. He was carrying a vial. "Doctor, I just changed Omar's IV . . ."

The doctor nodded and kept on walking alongside Rocco and the guard. In the second room as well there was only one patient.

"Here we are. Omar Ben Taleb. Three guys beat him up. But he's recovering. A few fractures, but nothing serious, I'm glad to say."

Marini pulled out a key. He opened the barred door. "Do you want to be left alone with the kid?" he asked him. Rocco nodded his head and walked into the room. Marini shut the barred door behind him.

Omar was wide-awake. On his nightstand he had a bottle of water and an old Roy Rogers comic book. His face, his lips, and his eyes were blackened and swollen.

"Can you talk?" he asked him.

Omar nodded.

"Will you tell me what happened?"

Omar raised his bandaged hand and touched his lip to stop the throbbing that was bothering him. "I don't know. They just started threatening me . . ."

"Why?"

"They said I was smuggling hashish into the prison . . . and they wanted it . . ."

"And do you bring hash in?"

Omar shook his head.

"Omar, you're behind bars for dealing controlled substances, so don't try to feed me any bullshit . . . Just tell me the truth. We're talking about a dead man."

Omar took a deep breath. "Now and then. Because I don't have any family here. And without money, life is terrible in here. Eating nothing but the garbage they make in the kitchen isn't something I'm interested in. So I have to buy food . . ."

"You ever get any weed?"

Omar looked at the deputy chief uncomprehending. "Weed—marijuana, you mean?"

"Exactly."

The young man shook his head.

"Too bad. So tell me, were you expecting any that day?"

"No. Nothing. I swear to you, Commissario—"

"Deputy Chief."

"What?"

"I'm a deputy chief, not a commissario. What is it that you think happened?"

"No idea. All I know is that I was unlucky, Dottore. I used to be a mechanic. But then the garage went out of business. What was I supposed to do? Go back to Tunisia and starve to death?"

"Did you know Mimmo Cuntrera?"

"Who's that, the guy who died?"

"That's right."

"No. I don't know anything about him. I've never even heard his name before."

"Had you ever had any trouble with those guys before?"

"What, are you crazy? I've never even talked to them. Erik, the black guy, and the Professor are people you steer clear of if you happen to cross paths with them. I don't know why they attacked me that day. I really don't know . . ."

"How long do you have on your sentence?"

"Two years. And you know what? I'm going back home. I don't want to stay here anymore. Better to starve, you know? Where I come from, you can already go swimming in May. It's starting to get hot and the melons are ripe."

"I understand, Omar. But you're not hiding anything from me, are you?"

"What would I want to hide from you?"

A tear rolled out of the young man's blackened eye. Rocco got up, put the chair back where it belonged, and left Omar to his memories.

Rocco, Mauro Marini, and Dr. Crocitti were standing on a catwalk each smoking a cigarette.

"How do you see it? Difficult?" asked the prison doctor.

"Are you married?"

"More or less," the health services director replied.

"That's how I see this situation. More or less difficult. Are you the only doctor here?"

"Well, besides me, there's the doctor from IMAS."

"IMAS? What's that?"

"The Integrative Medical Assistance Service. He came the day after the brawl in the courtyard . . . Then there's a psychiatrist, a dentist, an immunologist, and four male nurses who work alternating shifts."

Rocco flicked the cigarette to the floor. "Would you show me where you keep the medicines?"

"Sure. Come with me . . ." And Marini flicked his cigarette to the floor, too. Then he and Crocitti led Rocco away.

To get to the pharmacy in the house of detention, the doctor opened an armored door, turning the key three times. Rocco took a close look at the lock. It hadn't been tampered with.

"Please, go ahead in . . ."

It was a room with an examination bed, a table with an EKG device, a large glass-front cabinet with boxes and bottle of medicines inside.

"But as I was telling you earlier, we only have emergency and first aid pharmaceuticals. Are you looking for anything in particular?"

"No. Unfortunately I really have no idea. Syringes?"

"They're here . . ." And he pulled out a key and opened a drawer. That lock, too, seemed untouched. "They're all sterile, single-use syringes . . . I also see a few cannula needles, for IVs . . . In other words, it's all here."

Rocco nodded. "How many people have access to this room, to these pharmaceuticals?"

"Only the doctors. The nurses have to speak to us for anything they might need."

Rocco ran his hand over his unshaven whiskers. "Listen, Dr. Crocitti, can I have a list of everyone admitted to the infirmary in, say . . . the two weeks prior to the day of the brawl?"

Crocitti looked up. "There's no need, I know it by heart. Aside from the poor kid you saw in the other room, we've had Ilie Blaga in here, a Romanian, for a case of dysentery. We sent him to the hospital, too, and he should be back in the next few days. There was Aziz Ben Taleb for an abscess and, last of all, Sergio Mozzicarelli, an old inmate being checked out for kidney stones."

Rocco took a deep breath. "Thanks. You've been very helpful. Shall we go, Marini?"

"At your orders!"

ON A WOBBLY PLASTIC CHAIR, THE WARDEN HAD HAD AN OLD television set with a cathode tube set up, along with a DVD player that had been repaired with duct tape. Perfectly in keeping with the room around it. A bed, little more than a cot with a small, flat pillow, and a nightstand made out of an old filing cabinet, were the only furnishings in the room. On one wall hung a Carabinieri calendar and a terrifying painting that depicted a smiling clown with a handful of juggler's balls. The deputy chief had put the DVD with footage of the brawl in the player. He hit PLAY.

Here was Omar being beaten by the murderous trio to the left of the screen; here were Tarek and Karim running to his rescue. Then Aziz's arrival. But there was no sign of Mimmo Cuntrera. And none of the inmates were going anywhere near that blind spot to the right of the TV screen where the Calabrian might have already been breathing his last. From that corner he saw an inmate emerge, hurrying to put down the brawl, followed by a guard and two other inmates. He froze the picture. He knew just how pointless it would be to ask around whether anyone had seen anything. Anyone who knew anything said nothing. Or else they'd present themselves of their own free will when the time came.

"Shall we go to dinner?" asked Marini, poking his head in the door. Rocco nodded.

"Marini, come here for just a second, please . . ."

The other man came over.

"Look carefully." And he pointed to the still on the TV screen. "Who is this?" And he pointed to the spot behind which Cuntrera must have been already lying on the ground. "Who's this inmate?"

Marini looked at the still picture. "That's Radeanu."

"What about this great big guy here, this guard running from the right of the screen, where I'd expect Cuntrera to be, who's that?"

"That's Federico Tolotta, a colleague. He was on duty in Wing 3 and in fact he's coming from the right of the TV screen."

"And instead, over here, on the left of the screen, this is you . . ."

"Right."

"Congratulations, you look good on TV. So who is this other guy?"

"My colleague Abela. We were both coming from outside the courtyard, near Wing 2."

Rocco let the video run. The figures resumed movement. While Abela and Marini put down the brawl with the help of other convicts, Tolotta picked up a bunch of keys from the ground and used it to hit the Nigerian in the back of the neck. Agostino Lumi and Erik the Red were immobilized by Abela, while three other guards came running to help their colleagues. The last punch was thrown by Marini, and it caught Erik square in the jaw and knocked him flat.

"Nice right hook, Marini!"

"Thanks!"

"Tomorrow morning, I want to talk to the Romanian Radeanu and to Abela. And also to Tolotta, if he deigns to make an appearance."

"He just had the day off today."

Rocco turned off the television set. "What's for dinner?"

"I'd recommend avoiding the pasta. And the entrées, too."

"What's left?"

"Side dishes and fruit. You can't go wrong."

"I'm laughing as hard as I can."

"You're in prison, Dottore, what did you expect? Rainbow trout?"

"CORRADO HAS VANISHED. I WENT TO HIS PLACE, BUT WHEN I rang he didn't answer. His car isn't there, either." Tatiana was serving her husband a plate of lightly scorched Hot Pockets. The CPA Arturo De Lullo had a woolen cap on his head in spite of the spring-like temperature. He coughed three times and then slowly lowered himself into the chair at the table. "They're burned, Tatiana . . ."

But the woman didn't even reply. "So I went to the police and I filed a missing-person report!"

De Lullo was suddenly overcome by yet another coughing fit. He turned red in the face, and seemed as if he was going to spit up his soul any second now. Once the convulsions had calmed down, he breathed in slowly and then said: "You went to the police? Aren't you overdoing it a little? Have you tried his cell phone?"

"It's switched off."

The CPA had never much liked that Corrado Pizzuti, from the day he'd arrived in town from Rome three years earlier. The man had never really appealed to him. De Lullo expected him to pull some unethical move at some point, sooner rather than later, probably. Tatiana had insisted on going into business with him on the Bar Derby, in spite of the fact that De Lullo was opposed. But he couldn't really tell her no. Tatiana was his last woman. The last woman he was ever going to make love with, the last woman he was going to kiss, the last woman who'd make him dinner, the last woman to smile at him. The woman who was going to close his eyes when he died, gently, without making a scene, as one more inevitable passage of life. If he thought about his two nephews, who hadn't called him in months and who were incapable of doing anything but defaming Tatiana and inquiring about the market value of the tiny 1,100 square feet of his apartment, he always sank into a fit of hoarse, rheumy coughing. Tatiana was going to be his last companion before chronic obstructive pulmonary disease finally shuffled him off this mortal coil. And he certainly owed something to this last angel who had willingly taken on the task of seeing him to the end of his road.

The burned Hot Pocket was as hard as a slab of wood. "Is there dessert afterward?" he asked her.

"If he'd left me his house keys, I could have just gone in. Maybe he's sick," the woman replied, going over to the pantry. She'd brought home two custard doughnuts from the bar. She set them down in front of Arturo. He immediately grabbed one.

"What if his neighbor has a set of keys?"

"That woman does nothing all day but quarrel with her sister who lives in the apartment facing her. You should hear the things they say to each other!"

Arturo wiped the custard filling off his chin. Still chewing, he said: "The Iezzi sisters have hated each other since they were small . . . Don't worry, my love. This evening we can watch that program on TV with all the dancing! You like that show so much . . ."

Tatiana sat down. She poured herself a glass of water.

"Aren't you going to eat?"

"I'm not hungry, Arturo . . ."

THE DINING HALL WAS A BIG ROOM WITH A DOZEN OR SO TABLES. On the right side were the counters where the food was dished out. In the middle were two cement columns that held up the ceiling, a good thirty feet high. Rocco hadn't followed Mauro Marini's advice and had decided instead to risk the chicken breast. At the other end of the table, two guards in their late twenties sat down. "Ciao, Mauro . . ."

"Ah, it's you two. Dottore! This is Mattia and this is Ugo. They were on the guard towers the day of the brawl." Then he spoke to his colleagues: "Why don't you move a little closer . . ."

The two men picked up their trays and slid along the bench until they were next to Rocco and Mauro. "Allow me to introduce Deputy Chief Rocco Schiavone . . . from Aosta police headquarters."

They shook hands. Rocco noticed that the two new arrivals had opted for the chicken breast, too. "How is it?" asked Rocco, pointing to their plates.

"Well . . . at least it's grilled, with a little lemon . . ."

Rocco took a bite. It tasted of hospital. "It's stringy," he said.

"I told you to stick to the side dishes!" said Mauro Marini, and shrugged his shoulders. At the far end of the room, an old man in a shiny tracksuit and a white T-shirt stood looking at the deputy chief. Rocco look up and met the man's glance. The man smiled at him, then darted into the kitchen like a mouse.

"What can we do for you?" asked Ugo, fair-haired and freckle-faced.

"When that brawl broke out, you had a good vantage point up there to see the whole courtyard."

"Certainly," the other guard replied: Mattia, dark-haired and with an enormous nose. He, too, started chewing on the meat.

"Didn't you notice anything? Cuntrera collapsing to the ground? Maybe someone who had approached him?"

They both shook their heads in unison, like a couple of plush dogs on a car's rear dashboard. "No. Nothing. To tell the truth, I was keeping an eye on the outside of the prison. There was a car that was having mechanical problems," said Ugo.

"I had my eye on the courtyard. But to tell the truth, I saw those inmates brawling, I sounded the alarm, and I didn't look in the other direction where the dead man was lying. It was only Mauro, who went over with a young colleague . . ." And he looked at Marini. "Who was it? Abela?"

"Exactly," he replied.

"All right, Dottore, it wasn't till then that I looked over there, when Marini and Abela went over to figure out what had happened and why that guy was lying on the ground."

"At first I thought it had something to do with the brawl," Marini went on, biting into an apple and getting bits all over his mustache, "even if that struck me as odd. In other words, Cuntrera was just a hundred yards away from the fighting, right?"

"That's right," said Schiavone. "Near Wing 3. The brawl was on the other side, in front of the door to Wing 2. In any case, one thing is clear. When you went in, Cuntrera was already dead. Which means the murderer did his work earlier."

"That's right, earlier . . ."

They went on chewing in silence. "I need to talk to Tolotta . . ."

"Tolotta comes on duty at six . . ." said Marini. "I know that because he relieves me."

He expected to hear snoring, the heavy breathing of more than two hundred men in confinement, packed together like sardines. Compressed, ready to explode. But instead, there was nothing. From the hallway only the distant tapping of some electronic device or other. Not the sound of a car, not the noise of footsteps. And in spite of that surreal silence, he couldn't seem to shut his eyes. He'd been tossing and turning on his cot for hours. The cot was uncomfortable, too short, with just a single blanket and a flat pillow that might as well not have been there. He got up and went over to the window. The sections were shrouded in darkness. The stars were watching from over the mountains, outdazzled by the enclosure lights that drooled their yellow glare over the fields around the prison. A car accelerated toward the city. A delivery van came puttering toward the house of detention. Who could say how many others, like him, were lying awake. The guards, certainly, weren't sleeping. And in the sections, the inmates lying on their cots, eyes open, as they remembered well-known faces, distant and unattainable.

He switched on his cell phone. A crazed carousel of beeps announced the presence of dozens of messages. Nearly all of them missed calls. A message from Deputy Inspector Rispoli: "Lupa is fine. She's eating and sleeping!" One from Italo: "How's it going?"

And, finally, a text from Alberto Fumagalli: "Damn you! Call me the minute you read this message!" Then, just half an hour ago, a phone call. Anna.

He looked out the window again. It was almost midnight. He saw his face reflected in the glass of the windowpane. He switched his cell phone back off and went back to bed.

He finally fell asleep around three.

A SHIVER RAN DOWN OFFICER ANTONIO SCIPIONI'S SPINE. The clock on the car's dashboard said it was twenty-two minutes past midnight. He'd already been staked out in front of the Ristorante Santalmasso, a short distance outside Aosta on the road to La Salle, for three long hours. Walter Cremonesi had gone in at ten o'clock and still hadn't come back out. The mountain hut that housed the restaurant had all its lights brightly burning, and the luminous sign was reflecting off the bodywork of the four luxury automobiles parked outside. He was starting to feel the tingling of pins and needles all down his left leg. His foot had gone to sleep entirely. He decided to get out and take a peek at the dining room from the side window. He grabbed his compact camera and opened the car door. He stamped his foot on the ground three times, and a stab of sensation lanced upward into his brain. Then he twisted his aching neck, put both hands on his hips, and arched his spine backward. He heard a vertebra crack, then another. He took a nice deep silent breath and approached the restaurant. He cautiously peeked inside. Walter Cremonesi was sitting at a table, along with two other men and a woman who immediately attracted his attention. Silky black hair, red lips, a small fine nose, a red dress that put a substantial pair of breasts on display with a plunging neckline. As she sipped her wine, she left the stamp of her lipstick on the rim. Otherwise, the dining room was empty. A waiter with a flower-print vest approached the table bearing three saucers with dessert. Officer Scipioni heaved a sigh, because that endless dinner seemed to be drawing to its conclusion and soon he would finally be able to go home and get some sleep. He took pictures of the foursome, though only after making sure that the flash was turned off. He put the little Nikon back in his pocket, stepped away from the glass pane, and retraced his steps. Outside the entrance was a lit-up wooden vitrine, and in it, on display, was the restaurant's menu. Antonio leaned forward curiously. He grimaced when he read the prices of the appetizers. Entrées came in at more than twenty euros. Not the kind of restaurant he could afford. He went back to the car and lit a cigarette. The night was clear, but a light chilly wind found its way down the collar of his leather jacket, raising goosebumps on his flesh. The cold glittering stars dotted the dark vault of the sky. He got back into the car and cracked the driver's side window open just wide enough to let the smoke stream out.

"Put both hands on the steering wheel," said the voice behind him, making the hair stand up at the nape of his neck. "Guaglio', did you hear what I said? Get rid of your cigarette and put both hands on the wheel!" He tried to glance up at the rearview mirror, but the man was hidden behind his headrest.

"What the fuck . . . ?"

"Do it now!"

Slowly, Antonio tossed the cigarette butt out the window; then he grabbed the steering wheel. The man emanated a smell of cheap cologne.

"Who the fuck are you?" Antonio asked.

"Who the fuck are *you*?" the other man asked. Antonio started to turn around, but the cold metal pressed against his cheek persuaded him to desist. Out of the corner of his eye, Antonio glimpsed the barrel of a handgun.

"I'm going to ask you just one more time. Who the fuck are you?"

Antonio swallowed. "Officer Antonio Scipioni, from Aosta police headquarters . . ."

"And what are you doing here at this time of night?"

"I'm working."

"Oh, for fuck's sake . . ." And the man opened his door and got out of the car. Antonio saw half the man's body reflected in the side-view mirror. The man walked forward. Tapped on his window. At last, Antonio rolled down the glass. And finally he could see him. In his early fifties, hair neatly combed, a mustache and a goatee. He smiled in at the officer. "Captain Pietro Andreotti . . ." And he extended his hand.

Still baffled, Antonio shook it. "Captain?"

"Carabinieri, guaglio' . . . All right, so why are you staking out this restaurant?"

"Orders from my deputy chief. That is, though, I'm not actually staking out the restaurant. I'm tailing Walter Cremonesi."

The officer nodded. "Why don't you do this. Go on home. And forget about Cremonesi." The carabiniere gave him a wink and vanished into the dense stand of hedges that surrounded the parking lot. Scipioni heaved a sigh and touched the pocket of his heavy jacket where he had his camera. It didn't strike him as a particularly good idea to tell the carabiniere about the pictures he'd just taken. He started the car and left the Ristorante Santalmasso with his head full of unanswered questions, worse than the stack of bureaucratic files awaiting him on his desk.

MONDAY

When Rocco finally got to sleep, it proved to be short-lived. At five o'clock he leapt to his feet as if the fire alarm had just gone off. Instead, there was complete silence, except for someone going by in the hallway. He dressed hastily, grabbed a towel, and left the room. The hallway was illuminated by fluorescent lamps. He decided to head down to the dining hall. Maybe they made their coffee better than they did their chicken breasts.

In the kitchen they were already at work on breakfast. There were two men cooking; a third was loading trolleys.

Schiavone picked up a metal pitcher, poured a black liquid into a plastic cup, and the aroma of coffee wafted into his nostrils. It was black, piping hot, and, not least, excellent. He left the kitchen and followed the signs to the showers.

"Excuse me . . . the locker room?" he asked a guard.

"Ah, certainly . . . that way."

He went down the stairs and opened a double door that led into an enormous room lined with dozens of metal lockers. Two guards were undressing; another one was already in the shower murdering a song by Lucio Dalla. Rocco thought he recognized Mauro Marini's voice. He looked at two other guards who were stripping off their uniforms. "No, let's face it, the Sanremo Music Festival isn't in his future," said the younger guard.

"Wait, is that Marini?" Rocco asked.

"Yup," commented the other man, disconsolately.

"Marini, you sound like a walrus in heat!"

The other man stuck his head out of the shower. "Ah, Dottore, it's you! My shift is over, I'm going home."

"That doesn't authorize you to massacre our eardrums!" shouted one of the younger guards.

"Can I take a shower, too?" asked Rocco.

"Be my guest. If you like, there's shower foam and deodorant in my locker. It's the first on your left."

"Thanks!"

Marini's locker had the usual deplorable calendar featuring a girl with big tits sitting on a motorcycle, but these days those photos were there more out of a sense of duty than any real desire. Change of clothes hanging up, a pair of clogs, talc shower foam.

Rocco pulled it out and started getting undressed. By this point, Marini had moved on to covers of Queen.

"After Queen, the next item in the repertory is *Rigoletto*."

"We're climbing the ladder, aren't we?"

"No matter how high you go, you'll still be able to hear Verdi turning over in his grave!"

As if he'd taken the suggestion, Marini went on to the work of the Swan of Busseto, specifically *Rigoletto*. "*Cortigiani vil razza dannata, per qual prezzo vendeste il mio beneeee . . .*"

The two young guards closed their lockers and left the locker room, hands over their ears. Rocco stepped into the shower.

After a hellish night, the shower felt like a pleasant massage. He ran the water over his hair, shoulders, face, and ears.

Marini shouted a series of guttural sounds.

"I don't understand!" responded Rocco, doing his best to overcome the auditory blur of the rushing water.

"Toltt!"

Rocco turned off the faucet and stuck his face through the shower curtain. "Marini, I don't understand!"

The man was drying his intimate parts with a rough violence that only made Rocco fear the worst. "Soon Tolotta will be here. He's the one I wanted you to meet . . . my colleague from Wing 3 where we first found the corpse. I'll turn you over to him."

"Ah . . . right . . . that way I can talk to him."

"Yes, in fact, here he is!" the mustachioed guard announced. "Ciao, Federì!"

Federico Tolotta was enormous. Six foot four, not a hair on his head, a pair of Dumbo ears. A large nose but, all things considered, in keeping with his face, which was pink and round. Definitely tipping the scales at over 225 pounds. His eyes, rimmed by dark circles, unquestionably placed him in the family of the *Ailuropoda melanoleuca*, the giant pandas of Sichuan. He had two lockers. His jacket alone was enough to fill one of them.

"Hey, Federì, Dottor Schiavone needs to talk to you."

Tolotta smiled. "Sure. Anything I can do to help . . ."

"So, this is Deputy Chief Schiavone. He's here from Aosta police headquarters."

"I imagine for that nasty business with Cuntrera."

"And you imagine correctly!" Rocco stepped back under the rushing jet of water.

"I'VE BEEN ASSIGNED TO ACCOMPANY YOU ANYWHERE YOU need to go . . ." said Tolotta, opening the armored gate.

"Right," Rocco replied. Another hallway. He was starting to get his orientation in that labyrinth of doors and rooms separated by heavy metal gates. "Will you tell me about the day of the brawl?"

"Sure. I was on duty in Wing 3. The one that's closest to where they found the corpse . . ."

"I saw it in the video. Go on."

"I heard shouts, then a colleague behind me shouted that they were killing each other. So I unlocked the armored gate and went running out into the courtyard. I rushed toward—"

"Hold on," the deputy chief interrupted him. "Did you close the gate?"

"Of course. Behind me. Then I ran straight toward the brawl."

"And you didn't notice Cuntrera on the ground?"

"No. I didn't notice him."

"Were there other people running toward the brawl with you?"

"Naturally, a bunch of inmates and colleagues. When we got there, we pulled them apart and—"

"Yes, I saw the rest in the footage from the closed-circuit security cameras. But tell me, nothing strange happened?"

Tolotta stopped in the middle of the hallway. He thought it over. "No. Nothing strange. Then in the end Abela and Marini started shouting and we found Cuntrera's corpse. In the corner. About thirty feet from the gate I was guarding."

"Do you mind coming with me to my guest quarters? I want to show you something . . ."

ROCCO TURNED ON THE TELEVISION SET. HE RAN THE RECORDING from one of the closed-circuit security cameras. "This is during the heat of the brawl, you see?"

Agostino Lumi, Erik, and the Nigerian were beating the Tunisians bloody. Other convicts were hurrying over. Then the guards arrived.

"There, that's you!" And he pointed to Tolotta as he ran toward the brawl. He froze the picture. "Right back here, on the right of the screen, from where you appeared, in this area, Cuntrera is dying."

Tolotta nodded.

"And you didn't notice him when you passed by?"

"No, I told you. I didn't notice him. You see, along with me there are two other inmates hurrying along, and this other guard here—he's named Guidi, I think. They ran right in front of me and maybe that kept me from seeing that there was a man on the ground."

"Can you tell me why this corner isn't covered by security cameras?"

Tolotta smiled. "That's not right, actually. There is a security video camera, right here, you see it?" And he placed his finger on the screen, right on top of a huge lamppost. "Right on this lamppost . . . it covers that corner and the gate to Wing 3. The door I just ran out of."

"Then why don't I have the recording?"

"Because that security camera has been broken for the past week and we're still waiting for them to come fix it, that's why."

Rocco nodded. "And the same way you know that fact . . ."

". . . everyone else knows it, too, Dottor Schiavone. That corner hasn't been covered by the video cameras for the past week. If you only knew the things the inmates have been writing on the walls there!"

Rocco ran back the video. "You approach the brawl . . . Here you pick up the keys . . . You grab them and you hit Oluwafeme in the back of the head."

"That's right. I figured that with the keys in my hand, the punch would be more effective. I mean, that guy is *big*."

"And in fact you can see the Nigerian is staggering after you hit him. A little unfair, to hit him like that, don't you think?"

"Desperate times, desperate measures, right?"

The video continued. "There, now you've subdued them, you take Erik into custody . . ."

"That's right . . . we were just taking him away when—"

"When Marini and Abela start shouting, attracting your attention because they've just found Cuntrera dead. You can only see the back of one of them, and you head straight over in that direction. Here, on the right of the screen."

"But how did Cuntrera die, anyway?"

"Of homesickness."

The giant panda didn't get the joke.

"I was just kidding. Someone gave him an injection of some kind . . ."

"And no one else saw?"

"Strike you as strange, too, Tolò?"

HE'D TYPED INTO THE SEARCH ENGINE: "ESCORT AOSTA." A website had come up with lots of photographs and cell phone numbers of beautiful women. All with their faces blocked out. But their breasts, their legs, and their lingerie could have aroused a corpse.

But are these photographs real? Alessandro Martinelli, warden of the house of detention of Varallo, was wondering. Maybe they'd just copied them out of fashion magazines, and then you went to the appointment and found yourself face-to-face with a skeletal junkie or, even worse, a transsexual. He lingered over one girl who seemed really promising. It listed her cell phone and three other photos of the woman, still with her face blocked out, in various poses. But she was never naked. Always fully dressed, maybe just a glimpse of breast, a bit of thigh. She was in the Top Escort category.

Expensive stuff. Hundreds and hundreds of euros. And maybe she was worth every cent. He read her profile.

Ciao, I'm not for just anyone, only for a discerning, refined customer. Time to spend and generous gifts should be among your virtues. I don't reply to anonymous messages. At my place or in third-party offices. Seriously, though, only write me if you're interested. My time is precious to me. But wait and see, you won't be sorry that you called. The only risk is that you might fall in love with me, with my lips, with my breasts, with my theighs.

Martinelli was a stickler for good spelling, and that last error shattered his excitement. Someone knocked at the door.

"Come in!" shouted the warden, and with a click of his mouse he closed the escort website, replacing it with a drab and bureaucratic email from the Ministry of the Interior.

The office door swung open and the bearded face of a guard appeared. "Dottore! Mozzicarelli, the inmate who asked to see you, is here."

"Send him in."

The guard gestured and Sergio came in, his shoulders bowed, his hands in front of him, and his head hanging low.

"Well, what is it?" snapped the warden, out of sorts, without inviting him to sit down. "You've been asking for this meeting since yesterday. I hope it's something important."

"Dottore, I . . . I have to see someone."

"Mozzicarelli, this is a prison, not a hotel. Who do you need to see so urgently?"

"The deputy chief."

Martinelli narrowed his eyes. "Do you mind telling me why?"

"No, Dottore, I mean yes, I do mind. It's something that . . . in other words, I can only tell him."

The warden nodded seriously and seemed offended. "All right. We'll take care of it later. Now go back to your cell and don't worry about it."

"Actually, today I'm on cafeteria duty."

"Even better, so go to the cafeteria, and if Dottor Schiavone has time to see you, I'll let you know."

"Make sure you tell him that this is something he'll be very interested in."

"Mozzicarelli, if this is to waste the deputy chief's time and mine with some delirium of yours, say so immediately and we don't have to discuss it ever again."

"Dottore, you and I have known each other for many years. And I've never asked you for a thing. If I tell you that it's urgent, trust me. It's urgent and it's very, very important."

"Sollima!" shouted the warden. The door swung open again and the guard's bearded face reappeared. "Take the inmate back to his cell."

"To the dining hall, actually," Sergio corrected him.

"Wherever it is!"

The two men left the room. Martinelli went back online to get the photo of that Amelia. In any case, he wanted to make a note of the girl's cell phone number.

Deputy Inspector Caterina Rispoli entered the conference room in police headquarters where Antonio and Italo were waiting for her. She carried two small plastic cups.

"What am I going to tell Schiavone?" she asked as she set the espressos down for her colleagues.

Antonio grabbed his espresso. "What do I know? Just tell him what happened to me. Anyway, the Carabinieri were there and they're following Cremonesi. Then Schiavone can figure what it all adds up to."

"It's a strange thing," said Italo after sampling the cup of bilge from the vending machine. "It seems to me that there are maneuvers going on here that we don't understand. What should I do? Report it to the judge?"

Caterina thought it over. "No. For now, let's just tell Schiavone about it. But he insists on keeping his cell phone switched off."

"Okay, but what am I supposed to do?" asked Antonio. "Do I go on following Cremonesi?"

"Forget about it. Let's wait for Rocco," said Italo, tossing the little plastic cup into the trash can.

"Anyway, I printed the photos I took of those four people."

"Put them in the deputy chief's drawer. We'll show them to him as soon as he gets back," Caterina ordered. Antonio nodded.

"I have something to say . . . but, actually, it's a little embarrassing, you know?"

"Go ahead, Italo," Antonio urged him.

"Yesterday I had to take some medicine to my aunt up in Nus. I was on my way back when I saw Pietro Berguet, Chiara's father."

"What's so strange about that?" asked Caterina.

"The strange part is that he was coming out of the Hotel Pavone . . ." And he shot a little smile at Antonio.

"Why are you laughing like a fool?" Caterina upbraided him. "Well?"

"Oh, come on, Caterina, don't you know? The Hotel Pavone is famous, or at least notorious."

Caterina shook her head. "Famous for what?"

Antonio came to his colleague's rescue. "It's a love hotel. Guys take their lovers there."

Caterina incinerated Italo with a glare. "And how would you know about this?"

"Everyone knows."

"Everyone who engages in this filth!"

"Well then, you can get mad at Antonio, too. He knows about it."

"What did I do wrong?" Scipioni asked defensively.

"Yeah, how come you know about it?" And now the poison darts that seemed to be pouring out of Caterina's eyes were targeting the Sicilian-Marchesan officer.

"Caterì, everyone knows."

The deputy inspector made a face. "Because you're animals!"

"Listen, the guys that go there go with women. Whether they're their lovers or something else."

"Their lovers are just pathetic fools, tricked by guys who squire them around promising them the moon and the stars. And in any case, you're all still animals!"

"If only I were an animal," said Italo calmly, "then by now maybe I'd be sleeping under the same roof as you!"

Caterina said nothing in response. She just swept out of the room, slamming the door behind her.

HE'D TALKED TO THE ROMANIAN INMATE WHO HAD WALKED by Cuntrera's corpse during the brawl, but he hadn't managed to get any interesting information out of him. Mimmo Cuntrera seemed to have died in some parallel dimension that made him invisible to the others. Standing in front of a vending machine that had just dispensed an espresso, on the second floor of the office wing, the deputy chief was stirring his plastic cup with a plastic stirrer stick and looking young Abela right in the eyes.

"That's how it was, Dottore. I was in the courtyard, next to Wing 2, when I heard the shouting and I saw the brawl. So, along with Marini, I ran over to help. I took Agostino Lumi into custody and handed him over to my colleagues."

"Yes. I saw that in the footage from the security camera."

"Then Marini called me, because he'd seen that man on the ground . . . that Cuntrera."

Rocco took a sip of espresso. It tasted like a chicory broth. "What the fuck . . ." And he flung the still half-full plastic cup into the trash can. "So it won't do any good to ask you questions. You were on the far side, opposite from where Cuntrera was killed."

"Yes."

"So you didn't see anyone approach him and talk to him . . ."

"No, Dottore. Truth be told, I was just getting a breath of fresh air outside of the office and thinking about my summer vacation. I'm taking it in June!" he said with a hint of pride.

"Dottor Schiavone!" From the end of the hallway, Tolotta, the giant panda, was calling for the deputy chief's attention. "There's a phone call for you. From Aosta."

Rocco rolled his eyes. "Where should I take it?"

"I'll put it through to you in the warden's office. He's out doing his rounds and the room is empty."

Rocco nodded. He slapped Abela on the back and took the stairs to Martinelli's office.

"Dottore, do you mind? I'm going on my lunch break. You can find me down in the dining hall."

"All right, Tolò . . . see you later."

"LISTEN, TELL ME SOMETHING, DO YOU HAVE A PROBLEM WITH your thumb that keeps you from turning on your cell phone? I've been trying to reach you for hours! I called police headquarters and I spoke to one of your officers, and it took an hour before he'd agree to give me the phone number of this fucking prison!" Fumagalli was shouting into the receiver that Rocco was holding a good five inches from his ear as he sat in the warden's office. He was looking at a framed photograph. Three little kids. All three were blond and all three wore red-and-white-striped overalls. "Didn't you see the texts I sent you?"

"Yes, I saw them."

"Then why didn't you call me?"

"Because I didn't feel like it."

"What are you doing in prison?"

"Are you done asking questions, or do you plan to go ahead for half the day?"

"I have something extremely important to tell you, you asshole. Do you want to know it or not?"

"So go ahead and tell me!"

"Open your ears good and wide . . ."

"Okay, but you stop yelling at me, Albè."

"This is about Cuntrera . . . All right, so you remember? The corpse swelled up, then it shrank back down to normal, and so on and so forth?"

"Yes, I remember all of that. God willing, I haven't come down with Alzheimer's yet."

"I sent the glands to two of my colleagues in Brescia. Two luminaries. They're the only ones capable of it."

"Capable of what?"

"Capable of identifying the substance that killed Cuntrera. You probably ought to be sitting down for this: ethyl carbamate!"

Rocco furrowed his brow but said nothing.

"Oh, did you hear me or not?"

"What the fuck is ethyl carbamate?"

"May God incinerate the ignorant!"

"I have a computer in front of me. Do you want me to go on the Internet, or are you going to tell me yourself?" And he touched the mouse with one hand. The screen lit up.

"Structurally speaking, it's an ester of carbamic acid . . . You can even find it in wine, it develops independently . . . It's also known as urethane. You ought to know that certain carbamates like neostigmine were also utilized in pharmacology."

Rocco smiled. On the monitor of the warden's computer he saw the last search the functionary had done: "Escort Aosta."

What a sterling husband and head of household, Rocco thought.

"Oh! Are you listening to me?"

"Yes, sorry . . ."

"You know what it does, Rocco, if it's injected in massive doses?"

"You tell me."

"It kills you on the spot! But it's just that it has another characteristic: it's volatile. And if we hadn't performed that autopsy, we'd never have known."

Rocco was distracted by the escort's web page. He was about to read the welcome message, but it struck him as more important to focus back on what Fumagalli was saying. "Let me get this straight . . . They injected him with this urethane, the guy died, and the killer was expecting a distracted, half-assed autopsy, in other words, hoping they'd give it a glance and move on, hopefully two days after his death . . ."

"Exactly, and in that case it would have appeared that Cuntrera had died of natural causes. A nice fat heart attack, just to make it perfectly clear . . ."

"The volatile chemical substance would have vanished . . ."

"And we would have just held a funeral and buried him. Most importantly, we'd never have noticed that sudden crazy swelling of the corpse, which was a result of the garbage they injected him with."

"Where can a person get their hands on this urethane?"

"It's not easy. No one uses it anymore. There was a time when it was prescribed for multiple myeloma, but nowadays we know that it's highly toxic."

"In other words, laying your hands on it is no simple matter . . ."

"No, not at all. Listen, maybe you can still find it in circulation for veterinary applications . . . but like I said, it's hard to obtain. Meaning, it's not as if you can go to the pharmacy and go up to the prescription counter and—"

"Albè, I get it!"

"It was useful, right?"

"You bet it was useful. It means that whoever killed Cuntrera had an accomplice outside of these walls. Thanks."

"When are you coming back to Aosta?"

"Why?"

"Because I owe you dinner. I pay my debts and I pay my bets!"

"As soon as I get back I'll call you."

He hung up the phone. A detail of the photograph in which the escort in a garter belt with her face blanked out was giving it her all made the deputy chief smile. A little bee tattooed on her neck. Rocco recognized that tattoo. "Nice work, Amelia," he said, under his breath. "'I'm in charge of PR for Luca Grange' . . ." Then it occurred to him that, in a sense, that was a form of PR, wasn't it? Just a question of nuance.

He turned off the computer. He got up from the leather office chair and headed for the door. He pulled it open. He came perilously close to a head-on collision with Alessandro Martinelli, who was returning to his office.

"Ah, Martinelli. They put a phone call for me through to your office."

"Yes, in fact, they told me about it. Listen, Dottor Schiavone, earlier an inmate came to see me. Sergio Mizzica . . . Mozzica—I can't remember his exact name right now. He wanted to talk to you."

"To me?"

"That's right, he wouldn't tell me what it was about. But trust me, as often as not this stuff is nonsense, the inmates have to find a way to pass the time, they make up stories as long as it gives them some margin of prestige inside the prison."

"This Mozzica, Mizzica, or whatever his name is, who is he?"

"He's an old inmate. Doesn't have any family, I believe. He's been here for many years. Do you really want to talk to him?"

"Well, you know what they say, right? Wardens come and go, but the inmates stay on!"

"You can say that again."

"Where would I find him?"

"Downstairs, I think, in the cafeteria. He was on duty."

AS SOON AS HE ENTERED THE STAFF DINING HALL, THE MIXED odors of minestrone and fried onion filled his nostrils. Of the ten tables, only three were occupied. Tolotta had his mouth full, and he waved hello to him from the far end of the room. He recognized Biranson, the little guy from Wing 3, and young Abela. Rocco went over to his personal sherpa. "Tolò, I'm looking for an inmate. Mizzica . . . Mozzica . . ."

Federico swallowed his mouthful. "Sergio Mozzicarelli, a little old guy. He's over there, in the kitchen." He jutted his chin toward the double doors behind the food counter. "Why?"

"None of your fucking business."

A FAT AND SWEATY COOK WAS STIRRING AN ENORMOUS CAULDRON with a scorched bottom. He had a cigarette in his mouth, and his bovine eyes were gazing into the horrendous concoction. "Who are you?" asked a faint voice from somewhere behind Rocco. It was a small, dirty man who was drying his hands on a tattered, mended rag.

"Deputy Chief Schiavone, state police. I want to talk to Sergio Mozzicarelli."

"Are you from Rome, too?" the little man asked.

"Yes."

"I'm from Frascati!" he said with a hint of pride.

"Frascati isn't Rome. It's Frascati. So where's Mozzicarelli?"

The kitchen attendant was clearly offended. He retreated to a hurt silence and jutted his chin toward a cluster of stainless steel prep tables against the far wall. A man with his back to them, dressed in an old shiny tracksuit, was cleaning the tabletops. Rocco went over to him.

"Mozzicarelli?"

Sergio jerked, startled, and emerged from his reverie. "Yes . . . ?"

Rocco had already seen him, his first day in the cafeteria. That man had smiled at him, and had then retreated to the kitchen. "I'm Deputy Chief Schiavone. You wanted to talk to me?"

"Me?"

"Yes, you. You went to the warden's office because you wanted to see me . . ."

Sergio glanced around—"No, it was nothing, I must have been confused"—and went back to wiping the stainless steel work surface with his wet rag. Rocco grabbed him by the arm.

"Mozzicarelli . . . what was it you wanted to say?"

"Why, no, it was nothing. Nothing important. I mean it was trivial."

The deputy chief dropped the inmate's arm. "Let's hear it."

Sergio drew a deep breath. "If you can help me with the warden, I could be very useful to your investigation."

"What could you tell me?"

"Cuntrera was my cell mate . . . He never uttered a single word in those three days. He didn't get any packages . . ."

"Mozzicarelli, cut the bullshit."

"Can't you help me? It's tough in here. If I could just get some furloughs, some time on the outside . . . I'm an old man and I really need to get out of my cell."

Rocco turned around. The cook went on stirring. The little man from Frascati was peeling potatoes. Nobody seemed to be paying any attention to their conversation. "Tell me the truth, what do you want from me?"

"I told you! Nothing. Just a little help. Give me some help."

Rocco heaved a sigh. "Who's threatening you?"

"Threatening me? Why would anyone want to threaten me?"

"Because all you're telling me about is nonsense and you won't tell me the serious things."

"There's nothing!" Sergio raised his voice. His chin was trembling, and his eyes had hardened. "If you don't want to help me, don't. Now let me get my work done, or else I'll lose my kitchen-work rights and I'll have to go back to my cell."

Schiavone stepped closer to the old convict. "Do you want to talk to me somewhere other than the kitchen, or else in private? I can make sure that no one touches you. I guarantee it."

Sergio stepped around him and strode, his mind made up, toward the double doors. "Leave me alone!" And he went through into the dining hall. But Rocco hurried after him. He grabbed him by his arm. In a low voice he whispered again: "I could have you transferred to solitary confinement, you'd be safe there."

Sergio looked at him for an instant, eyes filled with desperation and fear. "Leave me be!" he shouted, but nothing in his face indicated an actual, sudden, internal rebellion. "I haven't done anything wrong and I don't know anything!" Mozzicarelli's piercing voice echoed through the dining hall. The old man shook loose of Rocco's grip and walked quickly away toward the food counter. The guards sitting at their table observed the scene curiously. Abela was smiling; Biranson quickly dropped his eyes when he saw the deputy chief looking at him. Tolotta, in contrast, was fooling around with his smartphone.

"Come on, Tolò . . . we need to get back to the courtyard."

AT THAT TIME OF DAY, THE PRISON COURTYARD WAS DESERTED. The inmates were all in their cells, waiting for their scheduled time to be outside getting fresh air. The day was sunny, not even a cloud in the sky, and the wind was wafting in the scent of fields and flowers.

"Spring is here," said Tolotta as he followed Rocco over to the spot where Cuntrera had been found dead. He looked over toward Wing 2, on the far side of the courtyard, where the brawl had broken out, then toward the door to Wing 3, right behind him. He looked up at the sky. He shot a glance over to the guard towers.

"How far would you say it is from here to the guard towers?"

"At least five hundred feet . . ."

Then Rocco looked down at his shadow on the ground. He checked the time.

"Take me to the entrance and give my regards to the warden. He's been very kind."

"What . . . are you leaving?"

"Yes. This place is too damned depressing . . . I'll swing by my room, just the time to check one thing, and then I'll see you at the front gate in fifteen minutes."

Tolotta raised his right hand to the visor of his cap, in an imitation military salute.

"At ease, Tolotta, at ease . . ."

"So let me get this straight, Mao Tse-tung . . . and try to stick to Italian, or else I'll have to give you a smack so hard that I'll shut those squinty eyes of yours once and for all." Sebastiano was leaning over Guan Zhen as he sat behind the cash register of his little shop on Via Conte Verde.

"I already told you, Sebastiano . . . all I knew, I already told police. Three years ago, maybe more."

Seba balled his hands into fists. Brizio intervened before the angry bear had a chance to wreak havoc on little Guan and the second-rate merchandise on display in his shop. "So would you mind telling us the same thing? Nice and slow."

Guan looked up. Seba laid a hand on the counter. His hand was much bigger than the Chinese shopkeeper's face. "All right then . . . three years ago, the armed robbery in Cinecittà, right? Two men. A Neapolitan who was called . . . Just a minute."

"Don't pretend you can't remember, Mao Tse-tung!" And Seba's fist slammed down on the glass next to the cash register.

"Yes, yes, now I remember. Pasquale Scifù . . ."

"That guy's in the boneyard now. There was another guy. A big guy. The one who shot and killed the retiree. Who was that?"

Guan Zhen thought it over. "I don't know exactly. People say . . ."

"Then you just tell me what people say," said Brizio, keeping his cool.

"First people were saying this one. Then that one. Who can say which is the truth?"

For half an hour now they'd been asking that man the same question, and all he would do is smile back with his rotten buckteeth. And for the past half hour he'd always said the same things. Seba had already lost his patience just a minute in, while Brizio was starting to feel that by now he, too, was nearing his limit. But if he lost control, then he could kiss good-bye whatever information they might hope to obtain. His bearlike friend would reduce Guan to a bleeding heap of flesh and buckteeth. "Then you just tell me both names, Mao Tse-tung."

"Anyway, my name is Guan. Guan Zhen."

"Who the fuck cares what your name is," said Brizio. "Tell us who you think did the shooting!"

The Chinese shopkeeper thought it over. "And in exchange?"

"You get to live," Seba grunted.

"All right then, Guan, or whatever the hell your name is. You see my friend here? Someone killed his wife. And if you give us a hand, you can keep your little shop open and no one will come around bothering you. But if my friend doesn't find out who it was, you and your little shop are going to disappear once and for all."

"You Brizio threatening me?"

"Yes. I'd definitely say so."

The Chinese shopkeeper smiled, shaking his head. "You know who is my friend?"

"I know. And I don't give a fuck. Because, you understand,

Sebastiano here doesn't have a thing to lose. You do, though. You have the shop, a wife, and two kids. That's a lot to lose, isn't it?"

Guan seemed to be convinced. "All right then, the two names. First people were saying it was . . . him . . ." And he pointed his finger with the black-and-yellow one-inch nail at Sebastiano.

"Me?" asked Seba. "They say I pulled the robbery in Cinecittà? What the fuck are you talking about, Mao Tse-tung?"

"In fact, that's what people were saying. And if they were saying your name, then the other name is fake, too, if you ask me."

"You tell us that name, and we're a step ahead."

"If you don't believe in one, then why believe in the other?"

Seba looked at Brizio. "I'm going to slaughter this guy!"

Brizio blocked his friend's arm. "In fact, we don't believe it. But just tell us the name."

The Chinese shopkeeper shot a glance at the door. Then he lowered his head. He unfurled a sarcastic smile stocked with cavity-filled teeth. "Go fuck yourself!"

Brizio went to the front of the store and pulled down the metal roller blind. Meanwhile, Sebastiano grabbed Guan by the lapels of his jacket and hauled him up off his chair. He hit him hard with a head butt, and the nose of the Chinese shopkeeper made an ugly sound. A gush of blood immediately poured out of his nostrils. Not satisfied, Sebastiano hit him again. This time, Guan passed out. They left him lying on the floor. Then Sebastiano and Brizio readied the chair and the duct tape.

ROCCO THREW OPEN THE DOOR TO HIS LITTLE ROOM IN THE prison. He immediately turned on the television set, slipping the DVD into the slot in the player. All he needed now was a confirmation. There had to be a detail that he'd overlooked, simply because he hadn't grasped what was happening. Now that things were finally clear, he'd watch with a different pair of eyes. Because now he knew: the killer was on that video. He pushed the PLAY button. Right at the beginning, when the brawl had first broken out and the first two guards, Marini and Abela, came bursting onto the scene from the left of the screen, directly out of Wing 2. He froze the frame. He stepped closer to the TV set. He narrowed his eyes. He extended his forefinger, as if to touch the object that had attracted his attention. "There it is!" he said. On the ground, at Abela's and Marini's feet, was a bunch of keys.

WHEN THE TRAFFIC LIGHT TURNED GREEN, ITALO SHIFTED into first gear and pulled out. "Let me see if I have this straight," he said to the deputy chief. "You know who it was, but we aren't going to arrest him?"

"That's right . . ." Rocco pulled a pack of cigarettes off the dashboard of the police department vehicle. "Have you started up with these pathetic excuses for cigarettes again? Hadn't you switched over to Camels?"

Italo said nothing. "So how are we going to proceed?"

"Before we proceed, we need to figure out who wanted this murder to happen. We're talking about the mastermind, Italo. I still don't know who that was. Even if I do have my suspicions."

The people on the street were wearing lighter clothing now. Jackets and calf-length overcoats had given way to short windbreakers and green, red, yellow, and blue pants. Everyone had begun to bloom into colors like a meadow full of wildflowers. And though no one ever realized it, even sidewalks and meadows resembled each other closely.

Rocco was pleased. Because any time human beings rediscovered the fact that they were part of nature, he knew that there was still a glimmer of hope.

"You're smiling," Italo told him. "Usually when you solve a case, you're sad and pissed off."

"That's true. But we're still only halfway there."

"Whoever it is, I would arrest them immediately and not waste any time!"

"I never would have thought it could turn so beautiful around here. Aside from the mountains, which still turn my stomach, the meadows . . . the meadows are a shade of green that no one's ever seen in Rome."

Rocco had mentioned Rome. Flashing red light! Alarm bells! Italo felt a hollow in the pit of his stomach. From one moment to the next he could expect to hear Schiavone's nostalgic litany begin to unfold, and he wasn't sure he'd be able to take it. Since September he'd been sitting through one or even two a day. First the sky of Rome, then the buildings of Rome, and the colors of Rome, and the women of Rome. An infinite list of wonders that the nation's capital, according to the deputy chief, revealed only to those capable of glimpsing them.

"Have you ever eaten filetti di baccalà?" Rocco asked him without warning.

"No. What's that?"

"You know what baccalà is, don't you? Dry salted cod? In the old days, we only used to eat it in Rome at Christmas. My grandmother, for example, used to make it with fried artichokes. Which, as you ought to know, are Article 4 of the Roman constitution."

Italo could already recite the first three articles by heart, as instructed by Rocco. Now he mentally added the fourth to the list. "We're talking about the one written by you, right, Rocco?"

"Exactly. Article 5 reads as follows, in fact: 'Never shake the breadcrumbs off your tablecloth onto the balcony, unless you're hoping to breed pigeons as livestock.' And Article 6? 'Never go to the sushi place near Piazza Vittorio, because they're Chinese and they have no idea how to make real sushi.' To come back to the filetti di baccalà, now you can find them year-round, not just at Christmas. And you know the trick for making them the way God commands? It all depends on how you remove the salt from the salt cod. Nonna used milk to desalt her cod, not water. She'd soak it for almost three days!"

"Sure, but what do dry salt cod filets have to do with anything?"

"If you leave the fish soaking in the water for less than forty-eight hours, then the cod will be too salty and you can't even eat it. You have to leave it soaking and be patient, until it's nice and tender. Then you fry it. Understood, Italo?"

No. Italo didn't understand at all. "Since when are you a cook?"

"Since never. In fact, cooking is another thing I consider a tremendous pain in the ass. And if you stop to think about it, in the ranking of pains in the ass, the chart you hung up outside my office door, you need to add recipes and chefs." And he lit one of Italo's Chesterfields.

"All right. At what level?"

"Eighth degree, solid. Chefs . . . in the old days, we just called them cooks. Only, if they let us call them cooks, they won't be able to charge us two hundred euros for dinner anymore."

"Speaking of restaurants," said Italo, honking at a car that seemed to have fallen asleep in the middle of the road, "what do you think about what happened to Antonio?"

"His little encounter with the Carabinieri corps? I was fully expecting it. Didn't he get a chance to take any photos?"

"Yep. He printed them out and left them in your desk drawer."

"Not the one that's locked!" Rocco exclaimed, nervous at the thought of his weed.

"No, because that drawer, in fact, is locked, Rocco. How do you think Antonio could have gotten into it?"

"How do I know? Are you aware of just how many policemen behave like thieves, some even better than thieves?"

Italo looked at him. "I know one very well."

Rocco tapped the ash off his cigarette without a word.

"In any case, all that Scipioni said was that, Cremonesi aside, there were two men and a woman, apparently very beautiful. But from the way she was dressed and made up, Antonio says that she was more of an escort than anything else."

Rocco cracked his window slightly to let the smoke out.

"Speaking of escorts, you want to know something? In Nus I spotted Pietro Berguet leaving the Hotel Pavone," said Italo.

"What's that?"

"Oh, well, you're Roman, you can't be expected to know. It's a hotel, or really it's just a love nest. He had a girl with him . . . He went all the way to Nus to avoid being noticed. But if you ask me, everybody in town already knows."

"So what's become of the proverbial Aostan discretion?"

"There never was such a thing. You're convinced that around here everyone's silent, discreet, and peace-abiding. You couldn't be any more mistaken, Rocco. In Aosta, like everywhere else, people don't generally mind their own business. Do I really need to remind you how Nora found out that you were cheating on her with Anna? Wasn't it the baker?"

"True . . . and as far as that goes, I can tell you something, too. When Pietro Berguet's wife came to police headquarters the other day, if you ask me, she already knew. And now I'm even going to have to go talk to the daughter . . . Why did she have to ask for me?"

"Because you saved her life, Rocco."

"Maybe so . . . whatever happened with the apartment on Via Croix de Ville?"

"I went to see it. With Lupa, just as you told me. Well. I went in. Lupa barked."

"But did Lupa go into the apartment?"

"Certainly. She went in, she sniffed around, and then, all of a sudden . . . plop! She took a shit right in the middle of the living room!"

"No!"

"I swear it!"

"Well, I hope you took the apartment."

"Of course, I did. Shouldn't I have?"

Rocco smiled. He slapped the officer on the knee. "That's great news! She took a shit in the living room! An auspicious beginning!"

Italo went around the traffic circle, and finally the police headquarters building appeared in all its dreariness. A concrete box, square and graceless, enough to wipe the smile off your face even on a lovely spring day like that.

"Ah! I get it!" Pierron suddenly shouted, so loud that Rocco dropped his cigarette.

"What the fuck are you shouting about, you moron?"

"That thing about the dry salted cod! You've caught the killer, and now you're going to let him soak until he's just right . . . is that it?"

"Well, you get there late, but eventually, you get there."

"Now then, Dottor Schiavone." Costa took off his titanium-frame eyeglasses and set them down on his desk. "I'm not going to conceal the fact that this silence of yours has been keeping me on pins and needles. I'm not going to bore you with the story of how hard I've been working to avoid the news vendors in this city, or go on at length about the gold-medal-worthy slaloms that I have to undertake on a daily basis, now that you've stopped bringing me reports and results. But for now, I'm successfully holding them at bay. I hope that you have something for me."

"Certainly, Dottore. The only thing is that I have to ask you to wait before calling a press conference. For now, we're going to keep an eye on the man who committed the murder in prison, keep him warm. Until I finally identify the mastermind."

Costa smiled. "All right. I'm listening!" he said, in excitement, as he rubbed his hands.

"You don't need to listen to me. You need to watch this video." Rocco got up from his chair and slid the DVD into the slot on the police chief's computer. A few taps of the mouse and the DVD was ready for viewing. "What I'm showing you, Dottore, is footage from the closed-circuit security camera of the prison courtyard. Watch carefully."

To the left of the computer screen, the brawl broke out, with Oluwafeme, Agostino, and Erik against Omar. Here were Tarek and Aziz, who came running. The penitentiary guards Abela and Marini trying to put down the brawl. The bunch of keys on the ground. More prisoners; then Tolotta, the enormous guard, plunged into the out-of-control fray, grabbed the keys, got a good grip on them, and hit the Nigerian in the nape of the neck.

Rocco halted the video. "Did you notice anything?"

"No," said Costa. "What should I have seen? There's a fight, people hitting each other, guards separating them, and other guards taking them into custody."

"In fact, I had to watch and rewatch the video multiple times. But I finally understood. Do you see, Tolotta, this guy, the size of a bear, as he comes running in?"

"Yes . . ."

"Good. He's the guard from Wing 3. So you see—he shows up, he takes a few punches, then he bends over and picks up the bunch of keys."

"He must have dropped it!"

"In fact, that's what he told me. You see? He uses the keys to hit the Nigerian, then he pockets them. That's his bunch of keys! Why is it lying on the ground before he gets there?"

With interest in his eyes, Costa looked up at Schiavone as he sat back down at the desk. "You need to know that those keys open the doors in Wing 3. And especially one particular door, a small metal door that is almost never used. It leads to a corridor, a passageway not even a yard wide that takes you from Wing 3 over to the door to Wing 2. It's a passageway for the guards to go from one side of the courtyard to the other, without having to go through it."

"Let me go back to the earlier question: Why were Tolotta's keys there on the ground before he arrived?"

"Because he didn't have them, someone else did. Someone who kills Cuntrera outside the gate to Wing 3, hurries down the passageway that runs around the courtyard, and then emerges outside Wing 2, right next to the brawl."

"Christ . . ." said Costa, starting at the screen. "So the brawl was nothing but a diversion . . ."

"That's right. Organized by the very same guard. As soon as Agostino Lumi, Oluwafeme, and Erik get busy, he acts right in time with the brawl. He kills Cuntrera and emerges on the other side, without anyone noticing."

"Which guard is it? The old one? The young one?"

"At first, I thought it might be the old guard, Marini. Because whoever killed Cuntrera knew that that point wasn't being covered by the security cameras, and Marini knows this prison like the back of his hand. Then I stopped and thought it over. You see? A longtime inmate, Mozzicarelli, knows something. He wanted to talk to me, and I went and had a conversation with him in the cafeteria. And as soon as he saw me, he changed his mind. He was terrified, he was wetting his pants. He did everything he could to shout right in my face that he knew nothing about the case, and he did it in the dining hall. In front of everyone. To make sure he was heard. Right then, the guards in the dining hall were Biranson, Abela, and Tolotta . . . On the day of Cuntrera's murder Biranson wasn't on duty. So who's left? Those two guards killed Cuntrera. Abela committed the actual murder, Tolotta was his accomplice for the keys."

"And why do you think they did it?"

"There has to have been a mastermind, someone who ordered the murder. First, because Abela has only recently started working at the prison. Second, because Cuntrera didn't know anyone in the prison and had only even been there for three days. What I have to find out is who paid them, where they got the urethane, which certainly isn't the kind of thing that could have been found in a prison infirmary. Who benefits from this murder?"

Costa smiled. "My dear Schiavone, thank you. It's a pleasure to have you back in our midst."

"I never left. Now I'm just going to have to ask you to maintain the utmost confidence."

"What the fuck, Schiavone!" Costa shouted. "I'm a police chief, not a goddamned gossiping concierge!"

"Excuse me, sir, you're right."

As quickly as he'd flared up, the police chief calmed back down. "So do you have an idea?"

"A vague one, a very, very vague one. But most likely it has something to do with the public works contract and what happened with the Berguets. That's where we're going to have to do our digging."

Costa made a face. "Maybe you'd better drop that lead."

"Why, Dottore?"

"Well, while you were away, some things have happened that . . . Well, anyway, you'd better forget about it."

"Are you referring to the presence of the ROS in the prosecutor's office and the Carabinieri who are keeping Cremonesi and company under surveillance?"

Costa looked him in the eye. "How on earth do you know these things?"

"I keep my eyes open, I ask around, I observe, I catch whiffs, I look at details . . ."

". . . and you bust balls," added the police chief in a mocking singsong. "Just drop the case of the hospital-construction contract. We have people working on that, trust me."

"I'll try. But I have the feeling that I'm going to wind up wallowing in it up to my ears."

"No, just keep your ears clean, and you'll be happier, believe me. So you aren't taking the apartment on Via Cerise after all?"

"No, I found a fantastic place on Via Croix de Ville."

"Nice! In the middle of town!"

"And far from the courts building."

IT HADN'T REQUIRED A VERY LONG TREATMENT. GUAN HAD folded the minute he set eyes on the scissors that Brizio had pointed right under his left eye. The name of the second armed robber in Cinecittà had popped right out of his mouth. "Paoletto Buglioni," he'd said. They'd released him from the chair and then they'd stepped out onto the street.

"What do we do now?" asked Brizio as he looked out at the city under a sudden driving downpour. Sebastiano said nothing. The only sound was the scraping of the windshield wipers and an odor of stale smoke in the car.

"Shall we go see him tonight?"

"What time does he get off work at the discotheque?"

"Five in the morning."

"Let's go get something to eat."

"I'm going to text Rocco." And Brizio reached for his cell phone.

"No!" shouted Sebastiano. "This is my job. Not Rocco's. Leave him out of it."

"But Seba . . . he said . . ."

"This is the way it's going," the big man shouted. "I have to find whoever shot Adele. We only need to tell Rocco about it when it's all said and done. You feel like a bowl of pasta cacio e pepe?"

"Sure, I guess. Where? Roma Sparita?"

"Why, is there anyplace else knows how to make it?"

"WHAT ARE ALL THESE PAPERS ON MY DESK?" SCHIAVONE shouted as soon as he stepped into the office. Deputy Inspector Caterina Rispoli hurried in from the hallway. "Welcome back . . ."

"What a mess . . . And where's Lupa?"

"Lupa is at my cousin's house. She has a garden, so Lupa's happy there. These papers are from Deruta and D'Intino. They wouldn't tell me what they're about, apparently they're only allowed to report to you."

"Of course not, the last thing they would do is tell you about it . . . but what is it?" He took the first sheet of paper off the top of the pile. It was a list of the guests in the city's hotels for the ninth and tenth of May. A lightbulb lit up in the folds of his memory. The two policemen, loyal and conscientious, were tracking down all the hotel guests in Aosta and surrounding areas during the two nights of the murder in the apartment on Rue Piave, the killing of Adele.

"But that's a huge job!" Caterina said.

"It certainly is. But just think how many days we've had them out from underfoot, right?"

Caterina smiled. "Is this work good for anything, though?"

"Absolutely not," said Rocco, tossing the sheets of paper back on his desktop. "All right, now. Why don't you update me on the latest developments while we go over to the Berguets'."

"To the Berguets'? To do what?"

"I have to keep a promise. And if she sees a woman there, too, Chiara might just relax and put her trust in us. Come on! The quicker we get there the sooner we can leave."

IT HAD BEEN TWO DAYS NOW. SPENDING HER TIME BEHIND THE counter serving coffee and pastries just made her feel as if she were wasting her time. She hadn't given up, though, and since Sunday she hadn't stopped calling Corrado's cell phone. But the answer never varied: "The customer you're trying to reach isn't accepting calls at this time." That morning, Tatiana had also gone back to Via Treviso, in hopes that she could speak to another neighbor, but aside from the two Iezzi sisters, who just kept bickering and trading insults, she hadn't found anyone else. Corrado's shutters were still shut tight. Then she'd taken the CPA De Lullo's old bicycle and she'd ridden up and down every street in Francavilla in search of Corrado's Fiat Multipla.

Nothing.

"But do you at least remember the license plate number?" Barbara the bookseller asked her as she sipped the last tea of the day. Since the day Pizzuti had disappeared, there had been a new light in Barbara's eyes. She seemed almost happy to be able to plunge into that mystery worthy of her favorite novels.

"No . . . Wait!" And she ran over to the cash register and flipped through a notebook tucked away underneath it. She found an auto insurance bill and two receipts for premiums paid. "Here we go!" the Russian cried, beaming with satisfaction. She read them.

"Let's take this to the constables. To Ciro and Luca. If the car has been abandoned somewhere, then they'd have a record of it, right?" said Barbara.

"Good idea!" said Tatiana. Then, like a short sharp punch to the solar plexus, she was struck by a sudden gust of fear. What if they had found the car? Abandoned who knows where? What would that have meant? That Corrado . . . She shook her head to drive away those horrible thoughts. She rushed to the telephone to call the office of the municipal constables. But even before she could dial the number, the constables' Fiat Punto pulled up in front of the café and parked. Ciro and Luca got out, beaming. They walked in and said hello to Tatiana. "Buonasera, lovely ladies!"

"Buonasera!" the two women replied.

"So, what's new?" Ciro asked. "Any news about Corrado?"

Tatiana shook her head.

"Could you make us two nice shots of Sambuca?"

Tatiana went behind the counter. "I was just about to call you . . ."

"Why, did you change your mind? Have you decided to go out to dinner with me?" Luca unfurled the most dazzling smile in his repertory.

"We thought it might be best," Barbara now weighed in authoritatively, well aware that she enjoyed the two officers' full and unalloyed respect, "if we gave you his license plate number, seeing that the car has vanished, too."

"Excellent idea, right, Ciro?"

"Excellent idea." And the two constables stepped close to the bar to take their glasses of Sambuca. Ciro drained his in a single gulp. Luca nursed his, taking tiny sips. "Let's issue this criminal complaint, then. Tatiana, will you come into the office to fill out the forms?"

"I'll come!" said Barbara, who was starting to be fed up with the constable's insolence. But he just smiled and took another small sip of the liqueur.

"Worst case, you could go on that missing-persons program on TV, right? What's it called again . . ."

"So you think this is something to crack a joke about?" Tatiana snapped. "Huh? This is serious business!" And the town constable blushed. "Corrado is missing! And so is his car. And he's not answering his cell phone. And he wasn't alone at home. Corrado has been in trouble in the past, serious trouble, and he's even been in prison. That's why you shouldn't be laughing, you should be taking this seriously, seeing that you're wearing a uniform!"

"Calm down, Tatiana," the bookseller broke in. "Luca was just kidding around. Right, Luca?"

"That's right . . ."

"Do us this favor, go to the office, and issue this report."

"Happy to do it!" Ciro reiterated. "We love you, Tatià, and we feel the same about that loser Corrado. Now, let Luca finish his Sambuca, then we'll head over to the office and take care of everything . . ."

Luca drained off his glass and then reached for his wallet to settle up.

"No, Luca, it's on the house," Tatiana said, calmer now and sorry for the outburst she'd just unleashed. "And excuse me. I'm just a little bit on edge."

Luca took the insurance receipt and with his partner walked out of the bar.

Tatiana crossed her arms and leaned against the espresso machine. In silence, Barbara finished her tea. Only then did she realize that the Russian woman was weeping. "Tatiana!" And she ran around behind the counter. "No, Tatiana, no."

Instead of calming her down, the bookseller's embrace had the opposite effect. Tatiana released the brakes and subsided into a river of tears. Her knees gave way beneath her and she fell to the floor. She hung there, supported by her friend's arms, like a rag tossed by the wind.

"My friend . . . you'll see, we'll find him. You'll see."

"No, Barbara, no," she replied through her sobs. "I know it. I can feel it. Corrado is dead. He's dead!"

CHIARA AND ROCCO WERE SITTING ON THE BED. CATERINA was sitting in a swivel chair at the girl's desk, which was covered with photographs and CDs. At the door, Giuliana was looking at her daughter with such intensity that seemed to be trying to transmit nothing but positive thoughts and a lust for life to her. But Chiara instead was distracted by the landscape outside the window. Pale and serious, she had her knees pulled up to her chest, her chin resting atop them. Night had fallen, and the only light illuminating the bedroom was the lamp on the nightstand, shaped like a hot-air balloon.

"Can I get you anything?"

Chiara started clutching at her knees with an obsessive rhythm.

"No, Signora, grazie," Rocco replied. But Giuliana wouldn't leave.

"A cup of tea?" the woman asked the deputy inspector.

"Grazie, Signora, nothing, really."

"Mamma, they don't want anything, please!" Chiara said in a faint voice. Giuliana lowered her head and left the room, closing the door behind her.

"Jesus, what a pain in the ass!" Chiara blurted.

Rocco looked at Caterina. Then at the girl again. "You're a bit of a wreck . . ."

Chiara didn't answer. She kept looking out the window.

"It's normal for your mother to worry, you know that, right?"

"She just keeps hassling me! It's all she knows how to do."

"That's her job," said Rocco.

Chiara smiled. "Right."

There was a book in French on the bed. A book of fairy tales. Rocco picked it up. "Are you reading this?"

"French homework. It's a fairy tale by Anatole France . . ."

Rocco picked it up. "*Abeille* . . . what does that mean?"

"'Bee' . . . 'little bee' . . . It's a fairy tale, like I told you. But I don't know why, I can't seem to concentrate. I read a line and then . . ."

"And then?"

"And then my mind starts to wander. I'm back in that garage in the midst of all that snow."

Rocco set the book down. "A girl all alone in the woods, a captive of the evil ogre, and then Prince Charming comes along and saves her."

Finally Chiara looked at the deputy chief. "And are you supposed to be Prince Charming?"

"In the fairy tale, sure. In reality, not so much. I'm just a policeman."

"Right, and in fact, I imagine Prince Charming a little different from you."

"I know. He looks a little more like Max Turrini, right?"

Chiara bit her lip. "Right. Max keeps coming over. But I don't know. Tell me the truth, Dottor Schiavone. They raped me, didn't they?"

Caterina tried to catch her boss's eye, but instead, he just answered without paying the slightest attention to her. "Yes, Chiara. They did."

Chiara sniffed loudly, then wiped away a tear. "Thanks. You're the only person who tells me the truth."

"In many cases, that's a benefit. Other times, it's best to say nothing. But I think it's best if you know what really happened. Anyway, the two sons of bitches are dead."

"They are. But what about the person who sent them?"

"So is he. Murdered in prison."

"Good, I'm not ashamed to say that I'm happy to hear it."

"Do you know what I'd do if I were you?"

"No."

"I wouldn't go back to school this year. I'd take a sabbatical. And I'd travel. I'd go out and see the world. London, Paris, Amsterdam . . . just between you and me, they have marijuana in Amsterdam that's unbelievable. Have you ever tried the Grand Mix?"

Chiara smiled. "To hear this from a policeman . . ."

"Look." Rocco stuck his hand in his pocket. He pulled out a big joint, ready rolled. Caterina's eyes bugged out. So did Chiara's. Rocco lit it. He took a long drag.

"Ahhh . . . I feel better already." And he handed the joint to Chiara, who sat there, on her bed, both arms wrapped around her knees. The girl looked over at the deputy inspector as if asking permission. Caterina, frozen in place on the leather swivel chair, didn't move a muscle. Slowly, the girl reached out her hand, took the joint, lifted it to her mouth, and inhaled. She shut her eyes. Then she slowly exhaled. "Nice," she said.

"It is, isn't it? This comes from Amsterdam, just to give you an idea."

Chiara finally burst out laughing. "I can't believe it. A deputy chief of police handing me a joint."

"Right? This is reality, too. That is, a Prince Charming who does drugs really doesn't strike me as believable."

Chiara took another drag and shyly passed it to Caterina, who shook her head.

"Caterì, just a drag never killed anyone."

"But I don't . . . I haven't since I was in high school . . ."

"Exactly."

Caterina took the joint. She eyed it. "It certainly smells good," she said. Rocco gave her a wink. The deputy inspector raised the joint to her mouth, holding it between thumb and forefinger, as if she were afraid of getting her fingers dirty. She rounded her lips into an O, and then took a long drag. She swallowed the smoke. She didn't cough. "Thanks," she said, turning red. Then she handed it back to Rocco.

"So a sabbatical year, is that what you're suggesting?" Chiara asked.

"Why not? You're doing fine at school, I know that you have excellent grades. You can afford it. Put off university for a year. What's so bad about that? Think about Max, he's twenty-one years old, and even this year he's not going to be graduating."

"Yeah, if his parents don't grease his teachers adequately, he'll be graduating from high school with his children."

All three of them laughed. Rocco passed the joint back around to Chiara, and this time she took a drag without much hesitation. "I realize that this is something I can tell you." She stood up. She grabbed the crutch that leaned against the nightstand, hobbled over to the armoire, and opened it.

When she got back to the bed, she was carrying a ream of paper.

"Have you written a book?" Rocco asked her, frightened now.

"No, don't worry. These are photocopies that Max made." She sat down with her legs crossed, the paper in her lap. "These are things he found in his father's office. Because for some time now, he's thought things aren't really adding up."

"I'm not following you."

"His parents . . . he hates them. He hates that bitch of a mother and that whoremonger of a father. The Turrinis are nasty people. And they hang out with nasty people."

"I know that from personal experience," Rocco said.

"They have some strange frequentations. Max xeroxed the documents that his father had in his safe, and he brought them to me because he doesn't understand a word of it."

"And what did you understand?"

"Not much. But . . ." And she started leafing through. "There's one thing that's pretty clear. His father owns a dozen or so companies, half of them in Switzerland. And it's not clear what they're for. Moreover"—and she handed a sheet of paper to Rocco—"you see this document? It's a contract with a building company . . . the one that screwed Papà out of the project."

"Chiara, these are extremely sensitive matters."

"Take these documents to Judge Baldi. He'll listen to you."

"And how are we going to explain to the judge that we came into possession of these documents?" Caterina asked.

"Caterì, that's the least of our concerns. Baldi is used to this sort of thing, at least he's gotten used to it since we started working together." He handed the sheet of paper back to the young woman. "Let's do this, Chiara. I'll take this stuff to the court building. I'll leave out your name and Max's. And in exchange I want you to do something for me."

"What's that?"

"Dress up nice, go back to being as attractive as you are, get out of this room and away from the fairy tales of Anatole France, go back to school, say so long to your classmates, and leave, or else sit down and go back to doing what at your age you do best."

"Which would be what?"

"Living your life."

Caterina looked over at Deputy Chief Schiavone, who was stroking the girl's hair. She couldn't say why, maybe it was that gesture, the words that she'd heard, the joint that she'd smoked, but something happened in the center of her chest. She didn't know if the lurch she felt was the result of some emotion or a simple heart flutter. She smiled and discovered that a tear was welling up in her right eye. She quickly wiped it away. It might have been due to a surge of emotion, or it might have been some component in the marijuana that she was allergic to.

"WHERE ARE YOU GOING, SIR?" CATERINA ASKED THE INSTANT Rocco stopped the car outside the deputy inspector's apartment building.

"I still have a visit to pay. You should get home, the working day's over."

Caterina looked at the apartment building's front door. "How do you know that this is where I live?"

"I've been following you for months," Rocco replied seriously.

At first, Caterina turned pale; then she got the joke and smiled. "Then you no doubt know that I go to bed late . . ."

Why did you say that? Caterina asked herself. What got into your head? Have you lost your mind? Are you flirting with him?

A series of thoughts that followed one after the other at the speed of light, but the inappropriate phrase had already left her lips.

"I didn't know that you had a hard time getting to sleep. You need to find someone to keep you company."

Caterina looked Rocco in the eyes.

Oh my God, is he about to try something? she thought in horror.

"Go on, Caterì . . . Otherwise we'll wind up falling asleep right here in the car."

The young woman nodded. Smiled. Opened the car door and got out. Rocco accelerated and tore out of there, tires screeching. He didn't even stop to check whether or not she had her house keys.

And that lack of gentlemanly attention bothered her. But then, as she inserted her key in the lock, she felt a swirl of confusion.

I'm a cop, I'm his professional partner, I'm not a woman that he's just taken home after going out to dinner together, she said to herself.

But you're still a woman, aren't you?

You can't just decide you're a cop or woman according to which comes in handy.

The thing is, you're both.

All right, then, let's get one thing clear: with him I'm a cop.

Wrong!

Finding herself torn between such opposing thoughts, slapped from one side to another by her own considerations, was proving to be more tiring than the workday itself.

"Oh, for God's sake," she said as she unlocked the front door on the street and climbed the stairs, "get a hold of yourself! First you're dying of embarrassment, then before you know it you're complaining that he didn't even tell you good night . . . This is the first and the last time that I smoke a joint. No matter what happens!"

"And right you are, Caterina!" Signora Cormet said to her, on her way downstairs to take out the trash. Caterina clapped both hands over her mouth. She'd said it loud and clear.

According to Giuliana Berguet, even though she couldn't be sure, Pietro still ought to be in the offices of Edil.ber, the construction company. When Rocco pulled up, the light was on on the second floor. Rocco got out of the car and walked toward the front entrance. He went in. There wasn't a soul around. Not even a night watchman, nothing. Everything was turned off, lights, office machinery. He stepped into the elevator and rode upstairs.

In the circular landing, only a single light filtered from Pietro's office. Muffled music was coming from inside. Rocco knocked at the door. No answer. He knocked harder. Someone turned off the stereo, interrupting a song by Grover Washington Jr. "Who is it?"

"Schiavone, state police . . ." And he opened the door.

Pietro Berguet was sitting behind his desk. In shirtsleeves, his collar unbuttoned. His tie was draped over the back of a chair. His jacket lay on the floor. He was alone and was smoking a cigar that had befouled the air. Outside, far away, set like gems in the mountainside, a manger scene of twinkling house lights. Pietro narrowed his eyes. "Ah, it's you. I thought it might have been the night watchman."

"No. And now that you mention him, I didn't see him anywhere."

"He must be making his rounds," Pietro replied.

"But just the same as I was able to enter, anybody else could get in, couldn't they?"

"And do what? What do I have left to lose?" And he gestured to Rocco to take a seat. Rocco sat down on the sofa where, just a few days earlier, Cristiano Cerruti had been sitting. Cerruti, Berguet's right-hand man. Cerruti, who had sold Pietro out to the highest bidder.

"Say, by the way . . . nasty thing that happened at your house," Pietro commented.

"Yes. Nasty thing." Rocco paused, then observed, "But then it's not as if anybody's laughing themselves to death around here, either!"

Pietro lifted the stubby cigar into the air. He observed it. He turned it in his fingers. "No. I guess not." Then he crushed it out on the glass desktop. "They've crushed my spirit, that's for sure."

"And what are you doing about it?"

"I'm smoking a cigar."

"You could do something else."

"Like what, for instance."

"Like for instance you could go check up on your daughter."

"Sure." Pietro stood up. He went over to the window. His rumpled shirt, untucked, hung low over his trousers. "Chiara . . . she's probably the one who's paid the highest price. Quite a failure, don't you think?"

"What are you referring to?"

"Myself. As a father, businessman, husband . . ."

Sitting on the desk was a box, and next to it was the wrapping paper, ready to be snugged around it.

"Do you ever feel sorry for yourself, Dottor Schiavone?"

"Like everybody. But then something clicks inside me and I decide that I've had enough." He stood up. Went over to the window. "Do you want to know what's happening while you're sitting in here being depressed?"

Pietro looked him in the eyes. His eyes were dry. But the skin under the eyelids was twitching.

"You're wrapping presents for who knows who . . . What is it, a bottle of perfume, there on your desk?"

The CEO of Edil.ber swiveled around and looked at the box. "Yes, it's a bottle of perfume," he admitted.

"Carnal Flower . . . and if you ask me, it's not for your wife."

"I think you ought to mind your own fucking business."

"I really can't do that, seeing that the women in your household have dragged me into this matter yet again. Giuliana is at her wits' end, and you know that. Your daughter, on the other hand, who is an amazingly strong individual, gave me something, something that I'm going to take to the judge tomorrow."

"And just what would that be?"

"A lead. Maybe a faint one, just a hint of a lead, but it might be something that could help you. Something that might finally discredit Luca Grange and his little team of assholes."

A dim light flickered on deep in the man's eyes. "What did my daughter give you?"

"Some documents, very interesting ones."

"Why didn't she give them to *me*?" Berguet whined.

"To you? To a father who doesn't know which way to turn, and who spends his time with whores when he's not at work?"

Pietro took a breath and said nothing.

"What would you have done with them? You would have just screwed things up, I'm here to tell you. Instead, the girl, who is smart, very smart, believe me, gave the papers to *me*. And thanks to her, there may still be hope for you, for your family, and for this construction company."

Pietro recovered his smile. "And you can't tell me what—"

"No," the deputy chief interrupted him. "I'm afraid not. The less you know about it, the better. Just one piece of advice, and this is as a friend, not as a policeman. Go home, be with your family. You can't even begin to imagine how lucky you are. And keep an eye on Chiara. Take care of her. Not like a drunk, not like an angry nut. Like a man." Rocco headed for the door. When he got to the middle of the room, he turned and pointed to the box and the wrapping paper. "This perfume . . . throw it away, or give it to your wife. Even if you didn't buy it for her, she still might like it. Obviously, by the way, I was never here."

"Obviously," Pietro agreed. "But what am I supposed to do, Dottor Schiavone? Should I call my lawyers?"

"Clearly you haven't understood a single thing I said. Don't do anything. You trusted me once, right? Do it again."

He left the office. He got back in the elevator. On the ground floor, the lights suddenly turned on. A man in the uniform of a security guard with a flashlight in his hand stood looking at him. "Who are you? What are you doing here?"

Schiavone didn't even dignify him with a glance. "Sure, don't worry about it . . . good night!" And he left Edil.ber.

He had just disgusted himself. All that false optimism, where had it come from? That surge of love toward the Berguet family? What were they to him? Little more than a case solved. People he never wanted to see again as long as he lived. And so? He'd felt like an idiot, after speaking words of wisdom to that desperate fool, who was half in the bag. What was becoming of Rocco Schiavone?

"Are you turning into a sentimentalist, Schiavò?" he asked, glancing into his rearview mirror as he started the car. "Damned springtime . . ." he muttered, as he put it into reverse.

LUPA WAS SLEEPING AT THE FOOT OF THE BED. NOT ROCCO. He had decided it was time to get back to reading some healthy books. He held the book upright on his stomach and smiled at every page.

"WHAT ARE YOU READING?"

"Carl Hiaasen. Ever hear of him?"

"Tourist Season . . . *No, I've never read it. How is it?"*

"Not bad . . . what about you?"

Marina is lying next to me. She has her cheek braced on the palm of her hand. "I'm looking at you."

"See anything interesting?"

"Especially these wrinkles you're getting around your eyes." She extends a finger. It seems as if she's about to touch the wrinkles. Instead, she retracts it, the way snails retract their eyes. "Are you moving to that apartment where Lupa marked her territory?"

"Of course I'm moving there. I'll take care of a couple of things, get rid of a few items, and I'll move. I've already put down the deposit."

"Six hundred and fifty euros a month! Right in the center of town. In Rome you couldn't rent a garage for that money. Not bad, is it?"

"We're in Aosta, which isn't exactly Rome."

She heaves a sigh of annoyance. "When are you going to learn to live where you live?"

"Why, what am I doing wrong?"

"You're pretending. You have to decide whether to jump into the fray or stay out of it. You can't always play it both ways."

What a pain in the ass.

"And don't say, 'What a pain in the ass!'"

"I didn't say it, Marì . . ."

"True, but you thought it. You know I can read your mind."

I look at her. I think I'm going to have to start wearing glasses for my farsightedness, because Marina's features, just like the pages of the book, are getting blurry. And I'm not crying.

"It's just because your eyesight is getting worse . . . a perfectly normal thing as you get older . . ."

"But you've always worn eyeglasses."

"Stop right there! I'm nearsighted. Plus, I had contact lenses. With glasses on I look like a toad."

"I like the way you look with glasses."

"You used to. Italian has some rules, at least try to respect the tenses."

"I like the way you look with glasses," I insist. "Don't you wear them anymore?"

Marina falls back on her pillow and looks up at the ceiling. "I don't need them. They can't do me any good. Rocco . . ." When she calls me by my name and uses that exact tone of voice, that note, that hue, I always get a hollow in the pit of my stomach.

"What?"

"I'm not coming to the new place."

There's something stuck in my throat, something I can't swallow. And yet I haven't eaten dinner. "What do you mean, you're not coming?"

"I'm not coming. I'm not coming anymore. Maybe when you come back to Rome, if you ever do, I'll see you there. But there's nothing left for me to do here."

"Nothing left for you to do here? You need to stay with me."

She runs a hand over her forehead. She's white as the snow, and light as the pollen. "I'm tired, Rocco. Do you believe me when I say that I just can't keep it up anymore?" She turns her head. The muscles strain in her neck. She narrows her eyes. "And you can't keep it up anymore, either, my love."

I clench my jaw. Twice, three times. "What do you mean, I can't take it anymore? I can take it easily . . . I can."

"No. You can't keep it up anymore, either." And she extends a hand. She wants to caress me. I shut my eyes. This time I feel her! I feel her hand on my cheek. I feel her skin, her warmth, her veins, and her blood, flowing fast. She's here. She's here again, with me. Forever.

"Ciao, Rocco . . . buonanotte."

I squint my eyes. I don't want her to see me cry. Not now. She doesn't deserve that. I want to take her hand. But I just touch my cheek. I can feel my whiskers. I open my eyes. She's gone. She's not there anymore.

Marina? Talk to me again, my darling angel . . .

TUESDAY

Paoletto Buglioni got off work at 4:30 in the morning. He'd climbed into his Smart car, and at the sight of him getting in, any ordinary observer might well have bet good money that that huge creature stuffed into that little vehicle wouldn't be able to get the door shut. From the Lungotevere he headed for Testaccio, and then he turned onto the Via Ostiense. At Ponte Marconi he made a left onto Via Cristoforo Colombo. At that time of the day, those unlucky souls who had to go to work were still finishing their breakfast, while a very few were coming home after a night out painting the town red. Paoletto yawned and tried turning the volume of the radio up high. That helped to keep him from flopping over fast asleep. He drove past the Rome beltway and came to the turnoff for Tre Pini. There he veered to the right, continued along a road that just fifteen years earlier had been little more than a country mule track, and after that turned left up a stunningly steep road that led directly to his quarter, Vitinia. A cluster of houses, more than half of them villas and apartment buildings dating back to the seventies, built in violation of the city code and crisscrossed by a network of one-way streets. He parked his Smart car. It was a parking spot reserved for handicapped drivers, but no one in the quarter, not even a constable, would have dared to say a word to him about it, much less write him a ticket. He got out of the car and pulled out his house keys. He walked through the front door. He climbed a flight of stairs and finally stood in front of Apartment 3, where he lived. He opened the door and switched on the light. He hung up his heavy jacket on the coatrack and entered the living room. Sitting comfortably on the sofa were two men.

"What the fuck . . . ?"

"Ciao, Paolè," said Brizio. "Do you remember? This is Sebastiano."

Paoletto recovered his cool. "Certainly I remember. But what are you two doing in my home?"

"Well, you have a piece-of-shit burglar alarm," Sebastiano replied seriously.

"I'm tired, I want to get some sleep, so tell me what you want right away and then get the hell out from underfoot."

"Sure, we'll tell you right away, won't we, Seba?"

Sebastiano got to his feet. Same height as Paoletto. He looked him calmly in the eye. "At that bank robbery in Cinecittà three years ago, with Pasquale . . . you were the other guy."

"Me? What the hell have you got into your head?"

"Listen, that wasn't a question, understood?" Sebastiano went on. "That's a statement. Mao Tse-tung told us so."

"Guan Zhen," Brizio corrected him from the sofa. "He has a little shop on Via Conte Verde, property of the family of the late and lamented Pasquale, one of his longtime friends."

"Guan? Never heard of him."

"But he knows that it was you. You fired that gun and you killed that poor retiree."

Paoletto touched his nose. "Brizio, let me tell you something. I don't know what the fuck you're talking about, it's past five in the morning, I've been working all day, and now I'm going to get some sleep. There are beers and even milk in the fridge, so take your choice: breakfast or a nightcap. When you leave, close the door behind you. I may have a shitty alarm, like Seba says, but I'd feel just a little bit safer if you shut the door when you leave." And in order to give some credibility to his stated intentions, he took off his jacket and stood there in a white shirt. Under the cotton, the enormous muscles of the bouncer from Hysteria pulsed and twitched.

"We don't give a fuck whether or not you killed someone. All we want to know about is the pistol that you used . . ."

"Here we go again!" said Paoletto, rolling his eyes. "I didn't have anything to do with it!"

"Who'd you give the gun to?" Sebastiano insisted. "Your brother?"

"My brother?"

"That asshole Flavio? Did you give it to him?"

Paoletto leaned in, just inches from Sebastiano's face. He wasn't afraid of him. "What the fuck does my brother have to do with any of this? Flavio lives with Mamma, and she's eighty-five years old."

They looked like a couple of mountain goats about to lock horns. On the one side there were muscles and long hours in the gym, on the other stifled rage. Brizio did his best to keep them from reaching the point of no return. "Paolè, I told you, we don't want you, we don't want your brother, all we want is the gun that you used."

The bouncer continued looking Sebastiano in the eyes. He

ground his teeth. "If I told you I don't know a fucking thing about it, it's because I don't know a fucking thing!"

"You know what your problem is?" Seba asked him calmly.

"No, what is it?"

"When you stand up to someone face-to-face, there are two things you need to remember. The first one is to brush your teeth. The other is never to turn your front toward them. Never ever. Always at an angle, turned to one side. Always . . ." And with an extremely rapid move, he grabbed Paoletto's testicles until the other man shouted in pain. Seba was clenching them so tight that the enormous bouncer slowly sank to his knees. Seba's gigantic hand was a hydraulic press, the veins swollen with blood and the skin red with effort. Brizio didn't stir from the sofa. He limited himself to observing the scene. Paoletto continued shouting, "Let go of me! Let goooo!" but Seba wasn't listening. It wasn't until the complexion of Paoletto's face veered toward a purple hue that the Marsican brown bear released his grip. Buglioni remained on the floor, curled up, his hands on his testicles and a mask of gasping pain on his face. He rolled back and forth on the living room carpet, cursing the Holy Trinity. Slowly Seba climbed up on top of him, immobilizing both Buglioni's hands with his knees. Towering over him, he spoke in a calm voice: "The pistol. Who did you give it to?" And he accompanied the question by pulling back his fist, a brutal iron mace, ready to smash down into Paoletto's face.

"I gave it back to my . . . my brother . . . Flavio. He'd given it to me in the first place."

Seba nodded. He stood up. He brushed his trousers off at the knees. "If I find out that you called him, we'll be back. And we won't be waiting for you sitting on your sofa."

"What he's saying," said Brizio as he stood up, "is that if you see us again, you're about to die. Ciao, Paoletto." And he stepped over him and went out the door. Sebastiano shot one last glance at the bouncer still sprawled on the floor, then followed his friend.

"If your dog wants that carpet, I'll give it to him as a gift." Judge Baldi had leaned over the edge of his desk to observe the painstaking work Lupa was doing to unweave the imitation Bukhara.

"Lupa!"

The dog stopped chewing and laid her muzzle on the floor, gazing up guiltily.

"Please excuse her."

"So, what about these papers?"

Rocco extended the sheaf of paper that Chiara Berguet had handed over to him. "Here. There's lots of interesting stuff."

"How did you happen to lay your hands on them?" Baldi grabbed the documents and started reading through them.

"Max, the Turrinis' son. He photocopied them and gave the copies to Chiara. Because he may not be a rocket scientist, but he did understand that there's something rotten going on in that house, and clearly he was disgusted by it."

A blazing, radiant smile lit up Baldi's face. "There's lots of lovely stuff in here . . ." And then, "Ah!" he shouted suddenly, jabbing his finger down onto a slightly rumpled sheet of paper.

"What is it?" asked Rocco, almost frightened. Lupa, too, had pricked up both ears.

"It's nothing. I knew it. I knew it!" And he stood up suddenly from his chair. Then he sat right back down. His excitement was unmistakable in every fiber of his body. "This is useful, this is exactly what we needed!" And he looked at Rocco. "That the Turrinis were in cahoots with Luca Grange was something we'd known for a while. Who besides Chiara and you and me has seen these papers?"

"Just Chiara and you and me. And Max, but that's like saying that a blind man has seen them."

Baldi went on reading the document. "Six companies in Switzerland . . . I know this one, and I know this one, too . . ." It was like watching a little kid eagerly trading baseball cards. "I already have this one . . . and this one . . . Ah! This one I'm missing! The Viber company! Fantastic! Fantastic! Fantastic! Schiavone, this is manna from heaven. Blessed, and welcome, and very, very important." He laid down the documents. "What can I say? Thanks!"

"You're quite welcome. Now, I have a question to ask you . . . An officer of mine happened to make the acquaintance of a carabiniere while he was tailing Cremonesi."

"I know. We all know. We're working that side of the street."

"We who?"

"You know perfectly well. You saw them the other day here in my office. Don't ask questions, and instead, tell me . . . the problem at the prison?"

"Solved."

Baldi clapped his hands and then rubbed them together. "What is it today? Christmas morning? You actually know who murdered Cuntrera?"

"Yes. But what I haven't identified yet is the mastermind. Or rather, I should say, I do have my suspicions . . . There are only two pieces of the puzzle I still have to find."

"With your work today, you've redeemed yourself for months of irritability and judicial blasphemy! What else can I do to help you?"

"Nothing. Now it's my problem to solve. There's a detail I'm still missing." Rocco raised a finger in front of his face and twirled it as if trying to kick up a whirlwind. "I can sense that this detail is spinning round and round and round in my brain, but it's going so fast I can't quite grab it!"

D'INTINO AND DERUTA HAD PILED UP DOZENS MORE PAGES with lists of the guests at local hotels and motels on the nights of the ninth and tenth of May, as ordered by Rocco. The commitment they were devoting to the task was deeply moving. They'd even come up with a variant that, in their fervid imaginations, was meant to simplify the deputy chief's work, by highlighting the women in pink and the men in blue. It wasn't clear to him yet what they were trying to communicate with the green and yellow highlighters. Rocco made a mental note to ask the next time he saw them. Antonio Scipioni and Italo were in his office. Rocco opened the drawer that was normally locked. Inside he found the Ruger, still there, along with the four prerolled joints. But this wasn't the time for that. He was looking for Scipioni's photos from the restaurant. "Where are they?"

"I put them in the middle drawer. I never touch the locked drawer, you know that!" Scipioni replied.

"Right you are!"

He reached in and picked them up. Four people sitting around a table. Very first thing, he recognized Walter Cremonesi and Amelia. The others, with their backs to the camera, were unrecognizable. "Who are these two?" And he flipped the photo over to Antonio.

"I don't know. I never saw them before. One of them has blue eyes . . ."

"Does he look like an Alaskan husky?"

Antonio thought it over. "One of those sled dogs? Yes, I'd say so."

"Then he's Luca Grange. What about the other guy?"

"He's a little short man, kind of rough-looking."

"Wrinkled as hell?"

"Yes . . . wrinkled as hell, and he walks with his legs all bent, like this." Antonio tried to bend out his thighs so that they looked like twin parentheses. "Oh, heck, it's not quite right, but you sort of see what I mean . . ."

"Like a soccer player?" asked Italo.

"Yeah, like a guy who used to play soccer . . . but with Sandro Mazzola, because he's at least seventy years old."

Rocco gazed at Scipioni with a serious expression. "Are you mocking Sandro Mazzola?"

"Me, never, I wouldn't dream of it. Why?"

"Because Sandro Mazzola is as close as you can get to the pure essence of soccer as anything this country has ever had. Mark these words clearly in your brain, scratch them into the walls of your bedroom, buy a poster of the champion and venerate it every blessed day of your life."

"He played for Inter, though," Italo objected, "not for Roma!"

"Imbecile! When you're talking about a champion of this level, the color of the jersey is an insignificant detail. He's a part of the heritage of all humanity, understand?" He went back to look at the photo. "But in your opinion, why would someone take a groom to dinner?"

"What's a groom? Some kind of Val d'Aosta specialty?" Scipioni asked in perfect earnest.

"No. Italo, you tell him."

"A groom? It's one of those things, a whatchamacallit . . . the thing that has those something-or-others . . . no?" And he raised his hands into the air, describing a sort of circular shape.

Rocco rolled his eyes. "Disgusting ignoramuses. Groom, ostler, hired hand, or in our case . . . stable boy. So, let me ask again: Why should two businessmen and a courtesan take a stable boy to dinner?"

"A courtesan?"

"That's right, Italo. Because that's what Amelia is. So?"

"I don't know. Maybe they want to talk about horses?"

"Or else because this little fellow right here is something more than a groom, no?"

If it had been in decent shape, recently washed and maybe given a solid, polished coat of wax, if the side-view mirror had been intact, if the windshield hadn't had a crack running from one corner to the other, if the wheels hadn't been naked, unprotected by hubcaps, if the lightbulbs of the back-up lights and running lights hadn't been stripped of their plastic covers, if the tires themselves hadn't been underinflated, the rubber cracked and scuffed, no officer of the highway police in Pescara would have ever given a second glance to the green Fiat Multipla parked for the past two days over by the bus station. Instead, that ramshackle jalopy had attracted the attention of law enforcement. And soon a report that Corrado Pizzuti's car had been found reached the barracks of the municipal police of Francavilla al Mare, in the province of Chieti. Things had thereupon immediately gone terribly downhill. All the comforting words that Ciro and Luca had lavished on Tatiana had done absolutely no good, and neither had the hugs and smiles of the bookseller. It was clear to everyone that this abandoned vehicle marked the beginning of something tragic, dark, and frightful.

"Why would he have left it there?" the Russian woman kept asking as she leaned against the railing of the pier overlooking the sea. The wind was tossing her hair and drying her tears. She'd locked up the bar and was standing there with Barbara, trying to figure out what she thought now.

"At the bus station. Does that mean he took a bus? Or what?"

"It just might be . . ." Barbara guessed, but more in an attempt to comfort her than out of any real conviction, ". . . that someone stole the car and then dumped it there so they could get back home."

"Then why would they have stolen the car in the first place?" Tatiana asked with a glimmer of hope.

"Maybe it was just some drug addict who wanted to get to Pescara, saw that piece of junk, and stole it. Corrado was the kind of guy who left . . . I mean, who leaves his keys in his car."

"And someone would risk going to prison just to avoid taking a bus where no one ever checks your tickets and that takes you to Pescara in less than half an hour?"

"What if he drove around first? What if he used it to commit an armed robbery?"

"A Fiat Multipla that's barely even running?"

Barbara knew that there had to be another explanation. She didn't know which one, as long as it was anything but the one that she and Tatiana had already understood for some time. She tried playing one last card. "Listen. What if he just wanted to disappear? What if he did something in Rome that he just couldn't tell anyone else? Do you remember, in the last few days, he was frightened, lost in thought . . ."

Tatiana looked her in the eye. "Meaning that the reason he didn't take the car was to make sure . . ."

"To make sure no one ever found him. And he dumped his cell phone somewhere, too. Exactly for that reason: to make sure nobody could track him down. So you know what we can do? We can go to the bank and ask whether by any chance he made a sizable withdrawal in the last few days. My friend, if he did, we've found the lead to the solution! Corrado has a big problem on his hands, but he's still around, still hiding out somewhere trying to come to terms with it. If you ask me, pretty soon we'll hear from him!"

She couldn't even say how she'd been able to bolster her friend's spirits, but a faint smile appeared on Tatiana's face. The glimmer of hope sparkled even brighter. Barbara silently thanked Simenon, le Carré, and P. D. James, and she accompanied Tatiana to the local savings bank to delve into this hunch. If the bank teller confirmed her intuition, then that would deal them a whole new hand, and it would restore Corrado Pizzuti to the ranks of the living.

THROUGH THE OPEN WINDOW CAME THE PERFUME OF MEADOW flowers. It managed to overpower the stench of exhaust fumes from the passing cars. All winter long he'd smelled nothing but the odor of burning firewood. And the resin of the pine woods. Snow, too, ought to have had a smell. But Rocco had never managed to catalogue it, occupied as he was with cursing that crisp white blanket as it devoured one pair of desert boots after another. Only now that the threat had receded did he try to give it a name. But he couldn't come up with one. He decided that, just as the Newton disc sums up all colors and transforms them into white, so it was with the scent of the snow that summed them all up, only to zero them out in its blinding whiteness. Even though someone had once managed to explain that smell to him. A carpenter, in a town in Valtournenche. Who knows why he gave him that example. Perhaps moved to pity by Rocco's light loden overcoat, his shoes drenched by snow, he'd taken a clump of snow in one hand; then he'd crushed it and held it up to his nose. "There are people who can smell the forest in snow," he'd told him. "Others smell a rose. To me, the snow smells of cream." And he'd extended the palm of his hand so Rocco could smell it. But all that Rocco could smell was the scent of wood that issued powerfully from the man's hands, mixed with glue and wet sawdust. Still, the old man seemed perfectly sincere. He could smell cream in the snow. He smiled at the thought that he, too, could smell Marina's distinctive scent every time she came to see him. Cream, pine needles, Marina. When all is said and done, everyone smells the odors and scents they like best.

He went back to his desk. He picked up his cell phone. He dialed Amelia's number, which he had obtained from the website. The phone rang twice; then a woman's voice replied, as warm as an embrace. "Ciao . . ." she said. "Who's this?"

He hadn't thought of a name to use. "A friend."

"And just what does this friend want with me?"

"He wants to drop by and get to know you."

"When, my love?"

"Right away would be good by me."

"Oh, oh," the woman laughed. "We're in a hurry, are we?"

"Yes."

"And do you want to get to know me at my place or yours?"

"At your place. I don't have a home here."

"Then you're not from here."

"Otherwise, I'd have to be a homeless person, right? And a homeless person isn't likely to be able to afford someone like you . . . Amelia . . ."

"You're sweet."

"Listen. The pictures on the website . . ."

"Yes?"

"Is that really you? It's not like I'd show up there and then find a surprise?"

"Sweetheart. You're talking to a professional!" She playfully acted stern. "It's me, a hundred percent. The only thing you can't see is the face. But that's reserved strictly for someone who . . . I think you know what I mean, right?"

"Of course, I know what you mean. So can I have the address?"

"Do you have a pen?"

"Right in my hot little hand . . ."

"All right then, come on up to Arpuilles . . . on the regional road . . . As soon as you're in the village, third house on the left. It's a red house. But you have to tell me when you're coming. Are you in town?"

"Yes. As long as it takes me to get in the car . . . shall we say in fifteen minutes?"

"All right, then, I'll be expecting you . . ." Then the voice turned cold and professional, like an announcer at the end of an advertisement for a pharmaceutical product. Speaking rapidly, she said: "I accept only cash, no credit cards, no debit cards, no checks, payment must be complete before services will be provided."

"Do you offer student discounts?"

Click. Call ended.

SEBASTIANO AND BRIZIO HAD GONE LOOKING FOR FLAVIO Buglioni, who lived in the Ostiense quarter, but they'd only found his mother. A woman eighty-five years old who couldn't even hear the cars honking downstairs at the traffic light.

"Signo'!" Brizio shouted as the woman listened to him with a foolish smile on her face. "We're here to see Flavio! Flavio, understood?"

"Flavio is my son!" the mother proudly announced. "Do you want an espresso?"

"No, we don't want an espresso. We want Flavio!"

"Flavio is my son!"

"Christ on a crutch!" Sebastiano broke in. "We get it, we know that Flavio is your son, but where is he?"

The woman signaled in dumb show that she hadn't understood. Sebastiano repeated the words, using his right hand to accompany every word with an act of mimicry. "Flavio"—and here he pointed to the photo on the marble-topped side table by the front door—"your son"—and he pointed his index finger at the little old woman—"now"—and he indicated his watch—"where is he?" he asked, bunching all the fingertips of his hand together and shaking his hand up and down.

"I don't know what time it is. You have a watch on your wrist, young man." Sebastiano shut his eyes.

Brizio weighed in again: "Signora, do you know how to read?" And he pointed to her eyes. "I mean, can you see okay?"

Flavio's mother shrugged her shoulders. Brizio put his hand in his pocket. He pulled out an old receipt, took the pen from the side table, and wrote: "Where is Flavio?" Then he handed the little sheet of paper to the woman, who held it at arm's length from her face to read it.

"Ah!" And she smiled. "So you want to know where Flavio is?"

Seba practically hugged her.

"No idea. He left three days ago!"

That exchange, carried out at the top of their lungs, had tested the vocal cords of the two friends. Brizio decided not to abandon the new communications strategy he'd just discovered, because at least it seemed to work. He found another scrap of paper and wrote: "Where did he go?"

The woman read that note, too. "No, young man. I don't know," she shouted. "Maybe to go see his brother. Or maybe to stay with some friend."

Brizio wrote: "Did he pack a suitcase?"

"You've got me! I didn't see. He left while I was out shopping for groceries. Do you want an espresso?"

"No, thanks," Sebastiano shouted.

By now, Brizio had run out of receipts from his wallet. "Seba, give me something to write on."

His friend pulled a receipt from a mechanic out of his jacket pocket. Brizio wrote, again in front of the old lady's attentive eyes: "Do you have your son's cell phone number?"

The woman took a while to read it. "Don't be silly! I don't even have a phone in the house! No, no, I don't talk with those gadgets. Flavio has one, but I wouldn't even know where to look for the number!"

Exhausted, they gave up the chase. The last message that Brizio wrote was: "Arrivederci, Signora!"

"And if he comes back, who should I say came to see him?"

It was Sebastiano who answered: "Jerry Lewis and Dean Martin."

The woman smiled, nodded in gratitude, and accompanied the two men out to the landing.

"Fuck you very much!" Sebastiano shouted with a smile.

"Thanks. Same to you, and to your family." And Flavio's mamma gently shut the door.

"After all, she's deaf as a doorpost," the bear muttered. They started down the ramshackle stairs, stained with humidity and mold. "Paoletto didn't warn him. If he's been gone three days, then it wasn't Paoletto who warned him . . ."

"Maybe," said Brizio. "Or maybe not. What counts is the fact that Rocco and I talked to Paoletto about the pistol last Wednesday. And who knows whether he sounded the alarm and Flavio, to avoid trouble, didn't just decide to disappear for a while."

They walked out into the street, greeted by the stench of auto exhaust and the noise of traffic. "Do you want to go pay another call on Paoletto?" Sebastiano shouted, to make himself heard above the roar of the intersection.

"No. Let's wait. Maybe we really ought to talk to Rocco. Then if we don't find out anything more, in a day or two we can go back and see Paoletto and leave him lying on the floor."

Seba nodded. They went back to the car in silence, their cheeks burning red.

THIRD HOUSE ON THE LEFT ALONG THE REGIONAL ROAD. It was a red, single-story house. Rocco parked. He turned around. On the back seat, Lupa was curled up with a rubber bone between her paws. "Chew on that, not on the steering wheel or the gearshift, because this is a Volvo and spare parts are very pricey. Be a good puppy, understood?" And he cracked the windows just enough to let in some fresh air and got out of the car. The house had a small front yard with a well-tended garden, surrounded by a white picket fence. A lovely place, sunny, surrounded by fields, quiet. The roses were just starting to bud, along with other yellow flowers dotting the metal arch over the front gate. The bell had no name next to it. Just two initials: "A.A." Rocco smiled. That's how they started classified ads, to make sure they're first, listed alphabetically. He pushed the buzzer. The electric lock buzzed loudly and the gate swung open. He walked up a short gravel path and arrived at the front door. He rang the doorbell there again. A few seconds passed, and then the woman opened the door. When she saw Rocco, she betrayed no reaction. She just smiled. "Come in," she said to him. "You see that I was right? That you wanted my cell phone number?"

Rocco went in.

A modern house, with a central fireplace, a chesterfield sofa, and paintings hanging everywhere. A quick glance was sufficient to catalogue them: uninteresting mountain landscapes, a dime a dozen. Amelia was wearing a very serious knee-length gray skirt suit. "I'd recognized your voice on the telephone," she told him and kissed him on the cheek.

The scent of tuberose flowers, by the ton.

"Yes?"

"That's right . . . so do you want something to drink?" And she gestured for him to have a seat on the sofa.

"No, thanks."

"Is this your first time?" she asked him.

"First time what?"

"First time you've made an appointment like this?"

"No."

"How did you manage to find me?"

"Like the bees, you buzz from flower to flower. But you leave your traces," he said to her.

Amelia smiled. She sat down. "Do you have any preferences?"

"Are you referring to your services?"

"Exactly."

"So what are the specials of the house?" Rocco asked.

"Double penetration? Are you into bondage? Are you a masochist? A sadist? Do you love a golden shower? Do you like things *en travesti*?"

Rocco stretched his neck to one side. "Would fucking be too simplistic?"

"No. I'd say that's an option. Do you have any preferences as to attire?"

"Usually I'm not wearing any. Neither is my sex partner."

Amelia smiled. "Sure, okay, but do you have any fetishistic fixations? Fishnet stockings, garter belts, waist cinchers, stiletto heels, balconette bras?"

"No. The way your mother made you . . . does that constitute a perversion?"

"I don't really know . . . but I wouldn't think so." And she stood up. "Because usually they have a regular laundry list. Last night a client asked me to dress up as a policeman. I had to handcuff him."

"Nothing special about that. I do it all the time." He said it with a vague hint of menace, but Amelia seemed to miss that overtone entirely.

"All right, listen, I'm going in the other room. Could you . . . ?" And she extended her hand. Rocco understood immediately. He pulled out his wallet and counted out four hundred-euro bills. He gave the woman the cash. "Can I get a receipt?" Rocco asked.

Amelia smiled and left the living room, disappearing behind a door. "I'll be back as soon as I'm ready."

He'd only have a few seconds.

He stood and hurried over to the purse he'd noticed on his way in. Inside, nothing but makeup and a comb. No wallet. He opened the drawer of the cabinet. Two sets of keys and a thin silver ribbon for gift wrapping. He left the front hall and went to the galley kitchen. He searched all the drawers there: they were empty. Likewise empty were the cabinets. He looked around. There were two other pieces of furniture with drawers. One by the sofa, the other next to the fireplace. But there, too, all he found were little dust balls and a metal paper clip.

It wasn't a lived-in apartment. There was still the mailbox, outside in the front yard, but he didn't have time for that. The woman, dressed in a filmy negligee, called to him. "I'm ready."

I'm not, thought Rocco.

"Do you want to take a shower first?"

"Do I stink?" he asked her.

"No. Maybe we can start with a nice hot bath and then . . . we'll see how it goes."

"That strikes me as an excellent idea," he lied. But at least that would give him a little more time.

"I'll go draw a bath," she said and vanished behind the door again. Rocco moved quickly. He silently opened the front door. He left it just slightly ajar. He went to the mailbox, which fortunately wasn't locked. Catalogues, flyers, mailers. Nothing, not a bill or a certified letter. He went back into the house. He softly shut the door and decided to take a look at the rest of the place.

He could hear the water splashing in the bathroom. He opened the first door and found a pink bedroom. There were just two side tables, no armoire, no dresser. The side tables were empty, too. The second room was a sort of office, the walls lined with photos of a trip to India. The desk drawers were empty, too. The third door was the bathroom. Sitting on the edge of the tub, Amelia was dipping her hand in the water, lost in thought.

"*De qué hes? Apéra'm s'as besonh d'ajuda.*"

"I don't understand . . . what did you just say?"

"Did you find what you were looking for?" she asked.

"No."

"Do you need help?"

"Why would you frequent people like Cremonesi?"

Amelia didn't take her eyes off the water in the tub. "Because they're so generous."

"They're not nice people."

"Do you know any nice people?"

"What are Cremonesi, Grange, and Dr. Turrini doing together?"

"Business."

"What kind of business?"

"I couldn't say. I'm not on such intimate terms with them."

"But you go to dinner with them."

At last Amelia looked up. "Did you have me followed?"

"Let's just say it was a coincidence . . ."

"Dottor Schiavone, are we going to fuck today, or would you rather summon me to police headquarters, accompanied by my lawyer?"

"I imagine I wouldn't get my four hundred euros back."

"You imagine accurately."

"Then let's forget about the poetry and just fuck."

"Let me warn you, I don't kiss."

"Neither do I."

HE WAS GIVING IT HIS ALL. AMELIA WAS SWEET, GENTLE, sensitive, and clearly at least somewhat experienced. She touched where touching was appropriate; it was delightfully easy to penetrate her. And while he was possessing her, he looked her in the face. She kept her eyes shut. Her generous bosom seemed even more attractive now that it didn't have to battle the law of gravity. Her skin was well cared for, without stretch marks, and her legs were muscular. The tattooed bee on her neck was pulsating over her veins, and a light patina of sweat had appeared on her forehead. Her black hair spread out on the pillow seemed to be moving with the wind. He didn't need to think. Just feel her body. He caressed her arms, grabbed her breasts, massaged her thighs. His penis was burning in spite of the condom, but it was a faint, almost tender burning sensation.

He shut his eyes. The images came pouring in like an avalanche. Caterina's face, Lupa's tail, Marina's hair and her pale diaphanous hand, Giuliana Berguet adjusting her necklace, Adele laughing, Lupa's tail again, Cuntrera's corpse, the perfume of the tuberose flowers, the scent of the meadows, the book by Anatole France, the Turrinis' Fontana paintings, the police chief's eyeglasses. He opened his eyes again. Now Amelia was looking at him. She seemed impatient. He decided it was time to be done with it, and he came.

AS HE GOT DRESSED AGAIN, HE DIDN'T SAY A WORD. THE woman lay on the bed, illuminated by the light from the window with the pleated pink curtains. He laced his Clarks desert boots, stood up, and put his hand on the door handle. "I think we'll be seeing more of each other," he told her.

"Why? Were you satisfied?"

"No. If you ask me, at four hundred euros you're overpriced. I'm thinking more about down at police headquarters. Ciao, Amelia." Before leaving, he offered her a tip, free of charge: "By the way, there's no *e* in 'thighs.'"

"Well, Italian isn't my native language. I grew up speaking Provençal . . . *Dab plasèr* . . . it's been a pleasure!"

WHAT REASON THERE COULD HAVE BEEN FOR ALL THOSE IMAGES to flood through his mind he just couldn't say. Were they mental notes, so many Post-its stuck to his brain? The police chief and his eyeglasses were certainly a reminder of some kind—he was almost certainly trying to find Rocco. Marina and Caterina, too easy to find an answer to that one. Lupa's tail? Why Lupa's tail? Giuliana Berguet and her necklace . . . Why had Chiara's book of fairy tales surfaced in his mind? They're just images, he thought to himself, like frames of an old movie. A friend of his who'd been a psychiatrist, now dead, but with whom he'd spent many wonderful evenings, had explained to him that thoughts and dreams are very rarely random products of chance. Often images and concepts remain buried under the ashes, but all it takes is a breath of wind to bring them back to life. He got back into his car. Lupa had licked the side window extensively. Delighted to see her master returning to the car, she leapt into the front seat and greeted him, sniffing vigorously at his neck and face. "What is it, do you smell a strange scent?" he asked with a laugh. Lupa barked. "Are you jealous? But you know the way things work, don't you? That's just the way males are . . ."

The rapidly growing puppy continued licking him.

"Males have two brains. One up top, the other down below! And more often than not, the second one has more control than the first." He inserted the electronic key into its slot next to the steering wheel. The minute that the various lights and gauges lit up on the control panel, he had the distinct sensation that dozens of little lights had flicked on in his brain as well. He'd realized: The book by Anatole

France on Chiara's bed! The fairy tale. *Abeille*, which means "bee." A doubt surfaced. He grabbed his cell phone and called Italo. "Do you speak Provençal?"

"No. I speak patois. It's a little different, but still, more or less, yes . . . why?"

"You need to tell me how to say 'bee' in Provençal."

Italo said nothing. Then: "I'll ask my aunt. She's from Castagnole Piemonte, you know?"

"Who the hell cares where she's from. Just get busy!"

He ended the call. He didn't have to wait a full minute. A chime announced the arrival of a text message. It was from Italo. "Bee is abelha. That's what my aunt remembers."

Bee. Abela. The surname of the young guard at Varallo prison. "A.A." written on the young woman's doorbell. "Amelia Abela?" Maybe the picture finally had a frame.

"OUT!" SHOUTED THE CHAIR UMPIRE. HUNDREDS OF MOTHS were fluttering around the halogen spotlights illuminating the tennis court.

"What do you mean, out!" protested Vittorio Abrugiati, who had clearly seen that the volley was inside the line.

"Papà, if it's out, it's out," his son replied from his perch on the chair.

"Vittò, don't even try. It was out," said Dario Cantalini, who'd outpaced Vittorio in the first set with a clear lead of 6 to 1 and was leading in the second set 2 to 0, his serve. Vittorio delivered a kick to his bag, which flew through the air, spitting out three yellow tennis balls and a towel. "Fuck, though, it was in by a yard!"

His son, who was refereeing the game with the help of two friends, and who understood tennis better than his father, since he was currently leading the Abruzzo regional series, rolled his eyes. "Come on, Papà, it was out!"

Dario Cantalini rubbed his hands. "Forty–love, and I have three balls for the third game, my friend! And don't forget, you're going to have to wash my car inside and out, eh?"

"Not necessarily!" Vittorio protested. "Though if I even have the chair umpire against me, maybe so!"

"Papà, cut it out, or I'll give you a warning!" shouted his son Carlo.

Vittorio got ready to receive the serve. Dario blasted a ball that skidded on the line, and Vittorio didn't even try to hit.

"Ace! Dario's game, three to zero, changeover!" called Carlo.

"Oh, go fuck yourself!" Vittorio hissed through his teeth. "But I can't see a thing with these electric lights!" he protested, heading over to the chair to dry off the sweat.

"So now it's the electric lights, and then the balls are deflated, and the racket needs tightening! You want the truth, Vittò? You don't have a chance against me! . . . Your father has a lot to learn!" Dario and Carlo laughed loudly, in unison.

"Buonasera!" Vittorio looked up. Behind the fence around the court were two women. Barbara and Tatiana.

"Ciao, Barbara . . . buonasera . . ." Vittorio replied.

"Afterward, do you have two minutes for me?" asked the bookseller.

"If you wait five minutes, I'll finish him off and you can have him for the rest of the evening!" Dario shouted to her as he opened a bottle of mineral water.

"Umpire, time!" Vittorio called, and then went over to the two ladies.

"What's going on?"

"Sorry, we went to the bank, but it was already closed. So

Federica told us that we could find you here . . . and actually . . ." Here she cupped her hand in front of her mouth and shouted to Carlo: "Your mother said that she needs the car tonight and can't let you borrow it!"

From high atop his chair, Carlo grimaced in annoyance. "Then how am I supposed to go to Pescara? Papà, will you lend me yours?"

"The volley was out, right? You've just answered your own question!" The teller from the savings bank turned back to Barbara and Tatiana.

"Listen, there's a problem. Corrado has been missing for two days now . . ."

"What do you mean, missing?"

"Nobody knows what's become of him," said Tatiana. "He's not home, his cell phone is switched off, and they found his car near the bus parking area, in Pescara."

"Oh, fuck . . ."

"Listen, Vittorio, by any chance, did Corrado come to the bank recently? Did he make any large withdrawals . . ."

The teller looked at Barbara. Then Tatiana. She had dark circles under her eyes. "Yes, he came in . . ." he replied. "Four days ago." An electric shock writhed under the Russian woman's skin. "But he made a deposit. Two checks." He thought he could see the young woman deflate a little.

"No withdrawals?"

"No. Why?"

"Because if he had withdrawn cash, it might have meant that he'd gone on the run to hide out, who knows where . . ."

"On the run? To hide out? What on earth are you talking about?"

"It was just a supposition," Barbara replied.

"No. I'm sorry. Tomorrow morning I can check and see whether he used an ATM anywhere."

"Would you do me that favor?"

"Certainly, glad to. Of course, I never said a thing to you."

"Absolutely not."

"But has something happened?"

"We don't know, Vittorio. He's been strange for days, now. And he just left, dropping everything, without so much as a word."

"Well?" Dario shouted from the court. He'd already taken his position. "Are you going to let me win by default?"

"Go play your tennis match, Vittò . . . and thanks," the bookseller said, giving him a kiss on each cheek. Tatiana limited herself to a handshake. "I'll keep you posted . . ." And with a series of darting leaps, Abrugiati went back to his game, gathering tennis balls as he went. It was his serve.

Barbara and Tatiana left the blazing glow of the spotlights illuminating the tennis court and plunged back into the darkness of the tennis club, following the little lane that led back to their car. "I'm sorry," said the bookseller. "I'm so sorry."

"We did our best." Tatiana tugged at her jacket as if she'd just been run through by a shiver of unexpected cold. But the air was warm, springlike, and a light breeze brought the scent of the sea and the coming summer. "I hope they find the body, at least."

This time Barbara lacked the strength to contradict her. She had no arguments left to make. Only fleeting hopes. And she knew that hope, when pitted against logic, usually loses.

"I WASN'T EXPECTING YOU AT THIS HOUR OF THE DAY," SAID Alberto Fumagalli, shutting the door to the morgue behind him. "But tonight I can't take you out to dinner. I have other plans." And he shot him a wink.

"You have a woman?" Rocco asked.

"What woman! Poker, four of us, to the death. It's me, the head physician in traumatology, an anesthesiologist, and a damned male nurse who skins us alive every time."

"What are the stakes?"

"A thousand euros!"

"Really?"

"At ten percent," the medical examiner modified the statement.

"Wait, a hundred euros? All this ruckus over a hundred euros? When you decide to raise the stakes, give me a call."

Alberto put his hands on his hips. "So let me get this straight . . . are you saying that at a thousand euros you'd join the game?"

"I'd join the game and clean you out."

"Don't worry. I'll organize it!" And he raised his hand in a feigned karate chop to threaten the deputy chief. "Look out!"

"Listen, Alberto, I have an important question. That pharmaceutical, the medicine you found in Cuntrera's body."

"Hold on! Let's be specific. We established that it was urethane from an examination of the glands. But the substance is extremely volatile. We're still waiting to get a trace of the actual poison."

"Well, so what are you saying, was it or wasn't it?"

"It was!"

"My God, it's hard work talking to you."

"Don't I know it. Well, what do you want to know about it?"

"Where did you say you could find it?"

"It's rare . . . Nobody uses it anymore. There are people who might still use it for veterinary applications, but like I said, it isn't easy to find it. It's very complicated. That is, if you think there might be a pack of it in Varallo prison, you'd be wrong. Or in the hospital. Or in this morgue."

"Understood. Veterinary applications, you said?"

"Yes. But why?"

"Because little by little, your favorite deputy chief is putting together all the pieces of the puzzle. Good luck on poker night."

Alberto scratched his nether regions.

THE STACK OF PAPER ON HIS DESK HAD GROWN EVEN TALLER. D'Intino and Deruta were carrying out their assignment with Germanic precision. He poured a handful of dog kibble that he kept in the office into Lupa's bowl, and then glanced over at those endless lists. Hostellerie du Cheval Blanc, HB, Le Pageot, Milleluci. They'd even gone to the Vieux Aosta, his residential hotel. The cretins had underlined his name three times and added an exclamation mark. Who knows what that was supposed to mean. Italo walked in without knocking. "Hey, can I bother you?"

"Come on in." And he set down the sheets of paper. His favorite officer was gray in the face and had circles under his eyes.

"May I?" Italo asked, pointing to the sofa.

"I have to warn you that that's Lupa's sofa. If she jumps on you, don't blame me."

The officer sat down, and not three seconds later, the puppy had jumped up next to him, asking to be petted. Italo refused. "Don't worry, I have much more serious problems."

"Like what?"

"Caterina . . ." Italo said.

Rocco threw both arms wide. "What's the matter with you people? Are you taking me for a marriage counselor, too? All right, let's hear it, what's the problem?"

Italo sniffed loudly. "The problems, Rocco. Plural. First of all, she doesn't seem to me to be particularly interested in starting a family. And she doesn't want me to move in with her."

"Eminently understandable. Have you taken a look at yourself?"

"Why don't you take this seriously for once? She says that she needs some space. She doesn't want me around the house, she likes being on her own. I say she has another man!"

"You don't understand a thing. You've only just begun, you have to give a relationship time to grow, don't you know that? The two of you are like onionskin paper, you set something down on it that's a little too heavy and CRACK! The whole thing rips in half."

"How long?"

"How am I supposed to know, Italo? Wait and see, she'll ask you when she feels ready."

"But then what if I'm not ready anymore?"

Rocco burst out laughing. "Italo, you're never going to find another girl like Caterina. Calm down and get a hold of yourself!"

"You know what I say? I say that I'm not sure if I want to go on like this."

Rocco interrupted him brusquely. "If you take a look at the chart that you yourself hung up outside my door, you'll notice that advice to the lovelorn, if I'm not mistaken, ranks up there at the ninth level of pains in the ass. So do your best to appreciate just how hard I'm trying here. Now I'm going to ask the question that ought to constitute the acid test so that you can resolve this matter once and for all: Can you imagine a life without her?"

Italo thought it over. He looked at his hands. "A life without her?"

"Exactly!"

"I don't know."

"Well, when you have the answer, come on back and we'll finish the conversation. But it has to be an honest answer. Considered and reconsidered. Is that clear?"

"That's clear . . ."

He knew that it created a certain awkwardness just to ask the question. Few males would know how to answer that question with any certainty. And he could see that Italo Pierron's uncertainty was, for him, tantamount to opening a big clear highway straight to Deputy Inspector Caterina Rispoli.

"Now listen. Do you have anything to do tonight?"

Italo threw his arms wide.

"Fine. Then you and I have a date. Make sure you're wearing plainclothes. Black, if you can manage it."

A gleam of excitement appeared in Italo's eyes. "Are we going to make some money?"

"No. We're going to find something out. This is work, my friend."

"Too bad. There's not going to be a shot at any more money, is there?"

"You picked up several thousand euros not even a week ago! Or have you already forgotten that bucket full of cash that we found behind Mimmo Cuntrera's restaurant? Try to be patient. And remember not to be too greedy."

Beethoven's "Ode to Joy" suddenly rang out, making Rocco's cell phone vibrate on his desktop. "Where the hell is it?" as he searched under the sheets of paper Deruta and D'Intino had brought him. "Where the fucking hell is it?" And at last he extracted it from the tangled mess of paper. "Schiavone here . . ."

"Ciao, Rocco, it's me, Furio!"

"Hey, my friend . . ." And the deputy chief waved Italo out of the office. He waited until the officer had shut the door behind him. "What's happening?"

"Listen up. Seba and Brizio have managed to track down the pistol that shot Adele."

"That's good news. So . . . ?"

"Paoletto Buglioni had used it. Then apparently he gave it to his brother."

"Flavio?"

"Exactly. There's just one thing. Flavio seems to have disappeared. It's clear that he gave it to Adele's killer. But now he's holed up somewhere. And if you ask me, we're not going to be able to find him."

"Still, that's a big step forward. A very big step forward. Are you in Rome?"

"I have been for a few hours now. Seba and Brizio didn't want to drag you into it, but I figure these are things you need to know."

"Why would they have kept me out of it?" Rocco asked, his voice growing louder.

"Seba . . . is convinced that if you find the killer, you'll send him up in front of the judge. But he wants to have a little talk with him first . . ."

"Understood. I don't know myself what to hope for."

"That he gets there first, Rocco. He's the one who has paid, in person, and more than anyone else."

"Actually, that would be Adele," the deputy chief corrected him.

"After Adele, of course."

WEDNESDAY

Cigarette smoke had filled the car. The night was passing quietly, and it seemed as if all they did at the Turrini residence was throw parties. The lights were still on, and there were a dozen or so expensive cars parked on the gravel driveway. A Labrador retriever was curled up under an outdoor light and was chewing on something red. A rubber ball, maybe.

"How much longer are we going to have to wait?" asked Italo.

Rocco stretched his legs. "Until the guests go away."

The clock on the car's dashboard read three in the morning.

"Why did you ask me that thing about the bee?"

"I needed to know . . ."

"Can I at least turn on the radio, Rocco?"

"No!"

Italo heaved a tired sigh. "My balls are aching," he complained. "Sometimes they tingle. Does that ever happen to you?"

"No. It happens to my ass cheeks."

"Can I get out and stretch my legs?"

"Stay inside!" the deputy chief snapped seriously. Then he pointed his finger at a spot at the foot of the hill where they had parked. About thirty feet from the low wall around the Turrini villa, there was a dark-blue car with its lights out.

"You see them?"

"Who is that? Bodyguards?"

"No. It's the cousins."

Italo looked at him blankly.

"The Carabinieri."

"Ah! Still? Are they keeping an eye on the villa?"

"If you ask me, it's the same people who stopped Antonio."

A silvery laugh, sudden and distant, caught their attention. A number of people had stepped out of the front door to the villa. "Luca Grange, and maybe his wife . . ." Rocco began.

"Cremonesi and two women . . ."

"I know the one on the right," said Rocco. "Her name is Amelia."

"Not bad."

"She turns tricks for four hundred euros!"

"And how do you know that?"

"I just do . . . Who are those others?" asked the deputy chief.

"All right, so the guy in the gray jacket . . . Fuck! He's one of the commissioners for public works."

"With his wife, I'd say . . . and the two at the door are Signore and Signora Turrini . . ."

"Look!" said Italo and pointed again at the Carabinieri's car. Even if it was a good fifty yards away, it was clear to see that the man in the passenger seat had rolled down his window and was taking pictures. "They're definitely spying on them . . ."

"Sure enough . . ."

"But are we here for the same reason?"

"No. We have to do something much cooler than that. Trust me!"

The guests climbed into their cars and one after the other left the Turrini villa. They drove out the main gate and turned onto the road to Aosta. The owners of the house, on the other hand, had gone inside and had already turned off the ground-floor lights. Now only the lights on the second floor and the little tower were illuminating the darkness.

"Have they gone beddy-bye?" asked Italo, lighting his umpteenth cigarette.

"Yes, but let's wait just a little longer . . ."

THE CRY OF A NIGHT BIRD ECHOED IN THE DISTANCE. THE tree branches minced up the light of the almost-full moon. The two policemen's breath was a dense mist. At night, the temperature dropped almost to the level of the winter that had just ended. They moved forward silently, and only a branch snapping underfoot now and again gave away their presence. They reached the villa's outer perimeter wall, directly behind the main entrance. Rocco looked up at the stone wall. It wasn't much higher than a couple of yards, but lining the top of it were shards of glass from broken bottles. He spotted a gap between the stones, wedged the toe of his shoe into it, and hauled himself up by the strength of his arms. He gazed down carefully at the sharp blades of glass. "Pistol," he whispered down to Italo. Italo handed him his gun. The deputy chief slid back the barrel to make sure there wasn't a bullet in the chamber, pulled out the magazine, extracted a handkerchief from the pocket of his jacket, which he had chosen to wear on that expedition in place of his faithful loden overcoat, and wrapped the handkerchief around the first shard of glass. With four blows from the butt of the pistol and very little noise indeed, he succeeded in shattering the cemented base of the bottle. He moved on to the second broken bottle.

"How long is that going to take?"

"As long as it takes, you ballbuster!"

Six minutes to clear a decent open space so there was no danger of ripping open one's flesh when scrambling over the top. Rocco handed the pistol back to Italo, who put the magazine back into the grip while the deputy chief leapt over and found himself on the far side of the wall. Shortly thereafter, he was joined by his partner. They were then on the grounds of the Turrini property. "Are there dogs?" asked Italo, clearly frightened.

"Certainly. He has a Labrador retriever and a German shepherd. So try to keep quiet."

They crept through a grove of fir trees. A couple of linden trees stood at the edge of the grove. The villa, beyond the trees, stood dark. Aside from a solitary light in the turret, there was no sign of life. "All right, move fast!" And the deputy chief and his junior officer, bent over, moved rapidly across the meadow, which glittered with the reflected light of a spotlight glaring from atop the wall about sixty feet away. They reached a stone building. "All right . . . let me see if I can remember . . ." Rocco looked around. Then he made up his mind. "That way . . ." And he moved off toward the right. Italo, who still didn't understand what they were doing there, followed him faithfully. The stench of horse urine and feces, mixed with straw, was increasingly overpowering. "All right . . . now through here!" Rocco hissed. At last they reached the stables. Somewhere a horse was rhythmically stamping a hoof on the pavement. The deputy chief leaned against the wooden gate. He turned the handle and slowly opened it inward. It was creaking. The operation demanded more time than expected. Schiavone pushed slowly until he had wedged open sufficient space to make his way into the stables. Then, like two nocturnal fish, rapid and silent, the two policemen slid inside. The deputy chief pushed both sides of the heavy wooden gate behind him. In front of them was a long corridor with the stalls of the individual horses on the left and right. A black horse with a long mane had appeared, checking out the new arrivals. As the deputy chief went by, he stroked the horse's muzzle. "If they pull their ears back, never pet them!"

"I wouldn't dream of it!" said the officer. "You want to tell me what we're looking for?"

Schiavone said nothing. They went past all the stalls. At the far end of the structure there were two doors. He tried to open the first one. No luck. He pulled out his Swiss Army knife while Italo continued looking nervously behind him. "If they catch us, we're in serious trouble, Rocco!"

"*If*, in fact, they catch us."

A horse whinnied. Italo started and practically lurched into his superior officer's arms. "Unless you tell me what we're doing here, I'm leaving!"

"Go ahead, be my guest."

Rocco inserted the blade into the keyhole. He forced it two or three times. It snapped open. He opened the door and went in, followed closely by Italo. The room had no windows. Confidently, Rocco switched on the light.

Saddles. Hanging off hooks screwed into the wall, made variously of black and brown leather; the odor of greased leather predominated. On a table sat horse girths, sheepskin saddle pads, gel saddle pads, saddlecloths. On either side were two large trunks. They bore labels with the names of the owners: Max and Laura Turrini. Rocco opened them. Jars, brushes, and grease for the horses' hooves, a riding helmet, a couple of riding crops, gym shoes, riding boots, an empty document case, a dark-blue jacket with a coat of arms stitched onto the chest. "Nothing!" They switched off the light and left the room. They were back in the dark corridor, which took its illumination from the outdoor lighting and from the moonlight coming in through the higher windows. A little bird flew from one rafter to another. Once again, Pierron started in fright. "What the fuck, Italo, you're just a jittery cream puff! Man up!" Rocco went over to the second door. This one wasn't locked. That room, too, had no windows, and once again, they turned on the light. Harnesses, reins, manila ropes, carabiners, and riding crops. On another wall, there were martingales, headpieces, fetlock boots, and bell boots. A set of shelves packed with jars of hoof grease. Horseshoes piled up in a corner. Two folding lounge chairs and three rakes with stalks of hay caught in the tines. "Not a fucking thing in here, either."

"That depends how you look at it," said Italo. "I see lots of things." Rocco's only response was to turn out the light.

They were back out in the long corridor lined with stalls. There was also a third room without a door, but it was merely a place to park two wheelbarrows and a lawn mower. They headed back. Another horse poked his head out. This one was gray with black spots. As if he had caught his fellow horses' attention, three other horses followed suit. "We've woken them up . . . now they think it's time to eat. Hush, be good boys and go back to sleep," Rocco said, tapping them lightly on the nose. At the center of the corridor was a larger stall than all of the others. Outside was a nameplate that read "Winning Mood."

"This one seems to be a champion. A horse worth many hundreds of thousands of euros." And Rocco glanced inside to get a look at the horse.

"Would stealing him be out of the question?" asked Italo.

The horse was on its side. It had been sleeping. Eyes wide-open, it was looking at the face of that intruder, come to disturb its nightly sleep.

Rocco noticed that the next stall was empty. After the sliding gate, they had built a wall complete with an armor-plated door.

"And what about this?" The deputy chief pulled open the sliding gate and went in. He touched the wall. He looked at the door a little closer. "Take a look at this lock!"

"Do you know how to pick it?"

"It's not going to be easy. It's a Mottura." The two wooden walls that supported the jambs showed cement underneath the boards. "No, I thought I could remove the wooden facing of the wall, but there's cement underneath. It's an armor-plated room, in any case . . ."

"So what are we going to do?"

"That I don't know," Rocco replied. Then he glared at that obstacle made of metal and wood with hatred. He kicked at it. "This makes everything much more complicated . . ."

"So now what?"

"So now we go and look for the keys." And he said it with simplicity, as if someone had just suggested they go to the bar for a drink.

BESIDE THE VILLA, ABOUT A HUNDRED YARDS AWAY, A SMALL structure served as a garage for the cars. The garage doors were open. Inside were a Jaguar, an SUV, and a small four-wheel drive vehicle. Above the garage, three windows with lots of curtains. Rocco and Italo, hidden in a thorny dog rose bush that was just putting out its first blooms, eyed the building. "We have to hope that he lives there," said the deputy chief.

"Who?"

"Dodò."

"Who's Dodò?"

"The groom."

"Ah!" said Italo, who still remembered what he'd been told at police headquarters. "The one who was at dinner with them?"

"Exactly, Italo. Are you starting to understand?"

"Absolutely not."

They slipped outside.

THE DOOR TO THE LITTLE APARTMENT WAS LOCKED TIGHT. The deputy chief tried to turn the handle a couple of times, but there was nothing doing. "We're going to need to get up on the roof."

"On the roof?"

"That's right . . . Haven't you noticed something?" And without bothering to wait for an answer, he darted around the corner of the little stone house. Italo had no option but to follow him.

Rocco picked up a small metal outdoor table and carefully positioned it next to the wall. He climbed on top of it. He reached up with both hands and got a grip on the rain gutter. "Let's hope this holds," he whispered to Italo. "If not it's going to make a tremendous ruckus!" He pulled himself up. The gutter creaked, but it supported his weight. The deputy chief was on the roof. "Come on, don't sweat it, you weigh less than me."

Italo heaved a sigh of annoyance and imitated his boss. With some difficulty he pulled himself up, and then they were standing on the terra-cotta roof tiles of the little outbuilding. "Walk gently now. One foot after the other, and test the tile to make sure it's solid, otherwise don't rest your weight on it."

The two shadowy shapes slowly began making their way across the roof. One step after the other, balancing carefully, gingerly trying not to slip or knock anything off, for fear of waking up everyone in the house. After a few minutes they came to a halt. "There you go, right here," said Rocco, bending over a skylight. "You see? It's open!"

Inside, the outbuilding was dark. Italo turned to look at the villa. Even the light in the little tower was switched off by then. A dog barked in the distance. Schiavone already had his Swiss Army knife out and was undoing the screws that fastened the plastic skylight to its fixtures. "Done!" he said, and pulled off the plexiglass cover. Now they could get into the house. Rocco was the first to lower himself inside.

He found himself in a small room with a washing machine, a sink, and a set of shelves packed with detergents and dirty clothing. He gestured for Italo to lower himself after him. His partner obeyed. Slowly he helped him to set his police boot on the lid of the washing machine, holding him by the waist until the officer set foot on the floor. The deputy chief opened the door to the little room. They entered a small living room with a fireplace; there were embers still glowing.

"What are we looking for?" asked Italo in a low voice.

"Keys . . ."

From the adjoining bedroom came a slow and regular snoring. Dodò was sleeping. Luckily, the task proved very simple. Next to the front door, on a wooden panel covered with hooks, there were six bunches of keys. Three sets of car keys, the others unidentified. Rocco immediately recognized the key to the armored door in the stables. Gently, he slid it off the hook. He showed it to his partner, who gave him a wink. One object struck Italo's attention. On the table by the front door, lying in plain view, there was a wallet. Italo grabbed it. Rocco noticed and tore it from his hands. "I wasn't going to steal it," said the officer.

"I know. But I wasn't trying to keep you from doing it. There's just something I need to see." He opened the wallet. Only a little cash but, more importantly, the thing that Rocco was looking for. The Swiss driver's license belonging to the groom, who continued to snore in the adjoining room. He read the name. "Dodò, my ass!" he said. "You want to see what our little friend is named?"

Italo squinted and managed to read in the dim light from the fireplace: "Carlo . . ."

"Cutrì!" And the deputy chief looked the officer in the eyes. "Do you get it now?"

Italo nodded. "Fucking . . ."

"Right." And Rocco put the wallet back where it had been. He opened the front door of the little house and left.

"Come on, let's get moving."

"Are we going to leave everything like this?"

"I'll finish up later. Now get going!"

THEY WENT BACK TO THE STABLES. THE HORSES WERE STARTING to wake up. Many of them had put their muzzles outside the half doors and were stamping their hooves. Rocco and Italo reached the stall next to Winning Mood's stall and went into it. The deputy chief inserted the key in the lock and pulled open the door to the little secret room.

Ten feet by seven, a refrigerator, English prints of horses hanging on the walls. Rocco opened the refrigerator. The dim bluish light illuminated his face. The fridge was full of pharmaceuticals. Phenylbutazone, Zylkene, Equanimity, Calmitan, Equiworm . . . Rocco examined them box by box. He would read the label and then put the package back. Stanozolol, Tefamin. Bronchodilators, corticosteroids, anti-inflammatory drugs, and hormones. Rocco was no expert in sports medicine, but he'd dealt with a few cases. Half the pharmaceuticals in that refrigerator were banned substances, products used for doping, things you'd definitely keep under lock and key. Then one box in particular caught his eye. Drontal Plus, a dog dewormer. He knew about it—he'd given the same stuff to Lupa. He picked up the package. It seemed odd to find that pharmaceutical in the midst of all those horse medicines. Under lock and key, and in a refrigerator.

He opened the box. Inside were three glass vials. And they were labeled: "Ethyl carbamate." Urethane.

"Bingo!" said Rocco. He put the medicines back into the refrigerator. "Now we've got to get moving, Italo. I have to put everything back where it was, and soon it'll be daylight. Let's lock up here, and then we can meet at the enclosure wall."

"Where are you going?"

"To put the keys back and screw down the skylight."

BACK ONTO THE ROOF. THE SKY WAS BEGINNING TO LIGHTEN. On the one hand, that was a good thing, because it helped him to carry out the challenging task of screwing back together the opening mechanism of the skylight. On the other hand, however, if someone woke up and looked out the window, they'd spot him immediately. He was as unmistakable as a drop of blood on fresh snow. He took a deep breath and tried to stay calm. He had put the keys back and had shut the door to the outbuilding behind him. Up on the roof, with all the chill and the damp that had seeped into his bones during that long night, his hands seemed to be tied in knots. It was hard to get his fingers to move, and the screws were only about an inch long. He'd already driven home the first two. He moved on to the third screw. He silently hoped that Italo had made it back to the place where they'd crossed the wall and climbed over to the other side by now. At least that way, if he was captured, he'd be able to take full responsibility, without having to put poor Pierron in harm's way. The third screw slipped into place as well. He pulled out the fourth. But the forefinger and thumb of his right hand refused to obey his mental commands. The screw slipped out of his grasp and bounced across the terra-cotta tiles. It continued its progress toward the rain gutter, landing with a metallic clang.

"Fucking hell!"

He couldn't afford to waste time looking for it now. He'd necessarily have to abandon the task when it was only three-quarters finished. He stood up. Step by step, he crossed back over the roof, taking care not to slip. The smooth soles of his Clarks desert boots weren't especially well suited to the purpose, but fortunately he managed to make it intact through the ordeal. He lowered himself from the rain gutter to the metal table, and then put the table back where it belonged. He was done! He was moving away from the outbuilding when something caught his eye. Looking out the window on the second floor of the villa, Max was watching him. Rocco stopped in the middle of the lawn. He looked up at the boy. Max slowly lifted his hand and waved to him. Rocco waved back. Then Max opened the window and gestured for him to come over. The deputy chief looked around. There was no one else on the lawn or in the house. He moved quickly over to the foot of the building. The young man had the appearance of someone still wandering in the world of dreams.

"Hi."

"Ciao, Max."

"Did Chiara give you the documents?"

The deputy chief nodded his head.

"And were you able to find anything?"

He nodded his head again.

"Make them pay, Dottore!"

"You understand that your father and mother are part of the group."

"I know. But I didn't give a damn. They can do what they want, but not with my life."

"Are you sure? If they get tangled up in all this, what are you going to do?"

The boy shrugged his shoulders. "I don't know. I'm legally an adult. I could go to America and stay with my uncle. Or maybe I'll finally graduate from high school. If there's anything you need, you know where to find me. And don't worry, I never saw you here!" With that he shut the window. Rocco smiled and quickly darted behind the bushes. As he was running toward the enclosure wall, he marveled at that young man in whom he hadn't at first detected any noteworthy qualities. He regretted his hasty and superficial judgment of the young man. It's typical of the old to dismiss and condemn the young. But it's only jealousy of the things the old have lost forever.

How much had that decision cost Max? How many nights had he lain awake eavesdropping on his parents, their friends, and that whole clan of wrongdoers that were milling around in his home? They had forced him to mingle with people like Walter Cremonesi, Carlo Cutrì, and that asshole Luca Grange. Other young men would have looked the other way, interested only in getting a new car and a couple of credit cards in their wallet. But not Max. He'd made the decision to uproot his life, a change that he knew would soon turn into sheer hell. But at least he'd be able to sleep at night, in his own bed, and not sit up restlessly smoking at the window, eating his heart out.

"It's six thirty in the morning, Schiavone!"

"Did I wake you up, Dottor Baldi? I'm already in the office . . ."

"You're not a normal person. You either disappear for days on end or else you're in the office at ridiculous times of the morning. I hope you have something really important to tell me."

Rocco propped his soaking-wet Clarks desert boots up on the windowsill. "Well, let's just say that I've found Carlo Cutrì. Is that sufficient?"

From the other end of the line came a moment of silence. "Where?"

"He works as the stable boy at the Turrini estate. He goes by the name of Dodò."

"Are . . . are you certain?"

"I swear it, by all that's holy. I need two warrants. Daniele Ábela and Federico Tolotta. For the murder of Domenico Cuntrera."

"Hold on, hold on, hold on, what are you talking about?"

"The mastermind, and this is the most interesting thing, is none other than Carlo Cutrì. Through the agency of Amelia Abela, the prison guard's sister, an escort by profession."

"You're vomiting a series of details that I—"

"That I'll explain clearly to you at the courthouse. But I need the warrant right away."

"And this isn't a dead end?"

"No, Dottore." Over the phone, Rocco heard a distant car horn. "Wait, Dottore, you aren't at home?"

A moment of awkward silence. Then: "No . . . listen, Schiavone. We can't meet at the prosecutor's office right now. This isn't the right time."

"This isn't the right time?"

"No. Now just do me a favor, wait until after lunch. Then you'll see that I'll explain everything clearly to you as well."

"You're starting to worry me, Dottor Baldi."

"I'm not the one who needs to worry, and neither are you. It's someone else. We'll talk later." And he ended the call.

Rocco stood there with the cell phone in his hand, not sure what to think now. Lupa looked at him, her muzzle wedged between her two front paws. "Oh, well . . ." he said to her. "Maybe he was just over at his girlfriend's house and wanted to cut the conversation short." Someone knocked at the door. Lupa barked.

"Come in!"

Deruta and D'Intino made their entrance. They were gray, wrecked, and carrying a notepad. "Dottore! Here we are! Ciao, Lupa!"

"What's up?"

"We're done. We only have Val d'Ayas and Cogne left." And they laid down a sheaf of twenty pages or so on the deputy chief's desk. "We're dead tired, but we've done a good job, haven't we?"

"Sure," said Rocco, looking at the stack of lists they'd just set down. Including the lists dotted with colorful highlighter stripes. "Can you tell me why you highlighted all the names?"

"Certainly," said D'Intino. "So, pink is the females, blue is the males, green is the families, and yellow is the foreigners. Sharp, right?"

"Male foreigners or female foreigners?" asked Rocco.

D'Intino turned and looked at his colleague with a glance of despair. "All the foreigners."

"And if I were looking for a male foreigner, or a foreign family, or a foreign woman, what am I supposed to do?"

He had posed them quite a problem. "What are you supposed to do?" D'Intino asked rhetorically, stalling for time.

"You can't," Deruta admitted in defeat. "You'd have to read them one by one."

"No, no, that just won't do," said Rocco. "No, no, you have to come up with a method."

"I've got it!" Deruta burst out. "Now we'll list all the foreigners on another sheet of paper, with hotels and times, and then we'll make the males blue, the females pink, and the families green."

"Then that means you wouldn't use yellow at all anymore?"

"I'm afraid not, Dottore."

"Fine. It strikes me as a good idea!" Rocco scooped up the

sheets of paper and handed them back to the two policemen. "All right then, get to sorting."

"Grazie!" the two officers replied happily.

"But first, give me back the yellow highlighters!" and the deputy chief held out his hand.

With a grimace of annoyance, D'Intino pulled them out of his jacket pocket and handed them over to Schiavone. "Here you are, Dotto' . . ." he said, gazing down at the two highlighters like a mother watching her son leave forever.

"Then we're all good. Get to work, now!"

"Ciao, Lupa!" D'Intino sadly bade the dog farewell, and together the two men left the office.

That was a nice little assignment that would keep them occupied for at least another couple of days.

Now the desk was free of the papers of the De Rege brothers, the official nickname of the D'Intino–Deruta duo. Rocco saw a note from Caterina: "De Silvestri from Rome. It's important!"

Rocco looked at the clock. It was too early to call the Cristoforo Colombo police station in the EUR district. And Rocco didn't have the Roman officer's home number. The fax was blinking: he only noticed it at that instant. Rocco got up. He went over to the machine and tore loose the sheet of paper.

Dear Dottor Schiavone,

This may not amount to anything, or perhaps it actually may prove useful. A report came in about a missing person. The name made me sit up in my chair. I hope it can be of some use to you. Corrado Pizzuti. He seems to have disappeared last Saturday from his home in Francavilla al Mare, in the province of Chieti. I remember this man very clearly, as I feel sure you do. In the meantime, I'm continuing my search for people who may have escaped or been recently released from prison and who might have anything to do with you. I'll get back in touch as soon as I have news.

Yours, Alfredo De Silvestri.

Rocco crumpled up the sheet of paper. Corrado Pizzuti! Of course that name meant something to him. It was the seventh of July 2007. And he'd been driving the car.

It would take him almost eight hours to get to Francavilla al Mare. There was no time to waste.

FLAVIO BUGLIONI HAD BEEN RINGING THE BELL FOR HALF AN hour. Luckily a woman walked out the front door and warned him: "Listen, that intercom doesn't work."

"I have to go to Roberta Morini's place . . . Is she in?"

"How would I know?" she replied. "I'm not her damned mother!" But then, with unexpected courtesy, she left the front door open. "She's on the third floor!"

"Grazie."

The apartment building was an unsightly structure dating from the seventies, and the staircase hadn't seen a paint job in all the years since. An abhorrent array of cracks, stains, and chunks of plaster that had simply fallen off was covered with a map of giant graffiti informing the residents "Bebbo and Marta, together since 11/27/2010" and "I cant stand being without you," without an apostrophe. He decided that taking the elevator would be too risky and instead climbed the two flights of stairs. The tenants had decided to take their own individual and idiosyncratic approaches to nameplates. Some had made them out of paper, others in metal, and a few had simply written their names directly on the door itself. Apartment 7 on the third floor had two different surnames: Morini and Baiocchi. Flavio leaned his ear against the door and pushed the doorbell. He heard it ring inside the apartment. At least this one worked. Rapid footsteps. Then a woman who looked to be forty-five or so opened the door. Half her hair was black from the roots up; the rest was a stringy blonde. Her face looked tense, her eyes were reddish, and she wore a pair of jeans and a green sweatshirt with "University of Ohio" written on it.

"What is it?"

"I'm Flavio Buglioni. I was looking for Enzo . . . Enzo Baiocchi."

"My father isn't here."

"Listen, I'm sorry to bother you, but it's something pretty serious."

"Well, I can tell you that I don't give a flying fuck about my father. Or about anything he might have done. For all I care, he can drop dead in the middle of the street!" And she tried to shut the door. Flavio leaned in on it. "No, hold on, hold on. Please, let me come in!"

She looked out at him: the man was polite, and he had a look of despair on his face. She couldn't even say why, but she let herself be talked into opening the door and standing aside. "Okay, but let's make this quick, eh? I'm cleaning house."

The stench of spinach and onions was infesting the air. A little kid, maybe nine years old, was sitting at the kitchen table—or in a room that served indifferently as kitchen and living room—with several pens in his hand. A notebook lay on the table in front of him. The boy looked up at him without a smile.

"You, Tommà, do your homework! The boy wouldn't go to school today. He says he has a fever . . ."

At last the child smiled. He was missing an incisor from the front of his mouth. He started writing again. "All right, go ahead."

"In front of the boy?" asked Flavio.

"In front of the boy," replied Roberta.

"You don't know where I can find your father, do you?"

"No. Who are you?"

"I'm a friend. He came to see me ten days ago. Since then, I haven't seen him."

"Does he owe you money?"

"That, too . . ."

"Yeah, well, you can go whistle for the money. Chalk that up as a lesson." Roberta looked at the man's hands. He had a tattoo on his thumb. Five dots. He wasn't from the police. "Anyway, he was here, just ten days ago. He slept here, too. Then, God willing, he left and he isn't coming back."

"And you haven't heard from him since then?"

"If he ever decided to call, I'd hang up in his face. Can I ask why you're looking for him? Aside from the money, I mean . . ."

"It's a nasty story. The less you know about it, the better. Do you have any idea where he might be?"

"No. I don't know. As far as I know, he was supposed to be behind bars. But instead, he's out on the loose. So he must be hiding out somewhere. If you happen to find out where he is, let me know. That way I can tell the police and they can put that rat back in prison where he belongs!"

Flavio knew that Enzo Baiocchi tended to leave a bad taste wherever he'd been, but to hear what the guy's own daughter thought of him shook him up a little. "Aside from you, Signora, does he have any other family?"

Roberta thought it over. "No . . . I don't think so. Aside from an elderly cousin, a lady who lives in the country, and who knows if she's even still alive. When I was a little girl, I went to see her once. Half crazy, she was. Lived with twelve cats and a nanny goat. She was his aunt's youngest daughter. But she's gotta be dead by now."

"In the country, where?"

"Huh . . . hold on a second and let me think . . . see if I can remember." Then she turned to look at her son. "Tommà, what's the name of that town where your grandpa's cousin lives? The one I told you about, who lives with all the cats and the nanny goat?"

The little boy thought it over for a second. "Pitocco!" he said, in a low, rheumy voice, the last sound you'd have expected from him.

"There, that's right. Pitocco."

"Where's that?"

"Near Guarcino."

Flavio smiled faintly. "Do you remember the name of this aunt of his?"

"No. But you just ask where the house of the crazy woman is. They'll be able to point you in the right direction. Want some free advice? Just forget about my father. He's nothing but trouble."

"Yeah, I sort of noticed . . ."

IT WAS ALMOST FOUR IN THE AFTERNOON WHEN ROCCO FINALLY pulled up in front of the barracks of the constables of Francavilla al Mare, practically next door to Pescara but technically in the province of Chieti. He'd spent longer than he'd expected taking Lupa out for various walks and poops and pees. It seemed as if there were some kind of curfew in effect in the little town. Except for the fact that there were some stores still open, not a living soul could be seen out on the streets. Just a few sickly-looking trees, tested by the winter and not yet recovered, withered palm trees on a narrow waterfront embarcadero, as lifeless as the apartment houses, all of them clearly vacation homes locked up tight until the sun came out and the weather warmed up. Breakers were smashing down heavily against the rocks and the sand.

Ciro Iannuzzi, bored and tired, was leafing through a motorcycle magazine and not bothering to look up at the person in front of him. "Go ahead . . ."

"I need some information," said Rocco, leaning closer to the glass partition.

"There's a tourist office," Ciro replied, chewing his gum. The sound of someone talking while snapping a cud of chewing gum was one of the things that turned Rocco Schiavone's blood jet-black. He held his breath and then asked again. "This has nothing to do with tourism. It's a sensitive matter, so if you don't mind, I'd like—"

The constable looked up at Rocco. He smiled. "Is this about your wife?"

"What, do they make you learn stand-up comedy before you can work as a constable around here?"

"Listen here, my good man, unless you have something urgent, you can just hightail it out of here . . ." And he pointed him to the door.

"Shall we start over from scratch? All right, then, buonasera. Now, Mr. Constable, sir, it's your turn to say buonasera."

"So you've studied stand-up, too, haven't you?"

"That's right. At the police academy." Rocco looked at the constable, who narrowed his eyes, uncomprehending. "I'm a deputy chief of the state police, my name is Rocco Schiavone, and you can just thank the good Lord above that there's a pane of glass between us, otherwise by now you'd be picking your teeth up off the asphalt. Did you think that was funny?"

The constable turned serious. He stood up. "Couldn't you have said so right away?"

"Why, you fucking stupid dickhead? There isn't supposed to be any difference between me and someone who isn't a member of the police, as far as you're concerned, asshole! Do the job they pay you for. So do I have your full and undivided attention, now? Do you think you can answer my questions?"

"Go right ahead."

"Corrado Pizzuti."

"Certainly, Corrado! When was it, Saturday? Tatiana reported him as lost!"

"What is he, an umbrella?"

"I mean to say, no one can find him."

"Who's Tatiana?"

Just then, Lisa, the lady constable with dyed-red hair, came in with a smile on her face. "What's going on, Ciro?"

"The gentleman here is looking for Corrado." Then he lowered his voice "He's a deputy chief of police . . ."

"Ah!" said the lady constable. "Yes, Tatiana reported him as a missing person."

"Yes, we've established that. Where can I find this Tatiana?"

"Down at the Bar Derby, on Piazza della Sirena. It was Corrado's bar. But now she's running it."

"Grazie." Rocco turned to go.

"So, Dotto', is it something bad?" asked Ciro.

TATIANA AND BARBARA, THE FIRST WITH TEARS IN HER EYES, the other with a distinct quiver of excitement, had told the deputy chief everything they knew. Their suspicions, their suppositions, the days of anguish, and then the news of the discovery of the car at the long-distance bus station in Pescara. "Did you know Corrado?" Tatiana had asked him.

"Let's just say that my life and his intersected a few years ago . . ."

"He had some bad priors, didn't he?" asked Barbara as they

walked along the waterfront esplanade on their way to Pizzuti's apartment.

"Quite a few" was all Rocco had to say in reply. He certainly couldn't tell her about the seventh of July of six years ago. That was something personal, his own private matter, something that only De Silvestri at the Colombo police station and his friends Seba, Furio, and Brizio knew about. Lupa trotted along after the little trio, attracted by smells she'd never breathed in before. Behind the low wall of the promenade was the beach, and beyond the beach was the sea. Every so often the little puppy would climb curiously onto the parapet and observe that strange gray-blue liquid that made so much noise and sprayed white foam in all directions as if it were ravenous for a biscuit.

Via Treviso was deserted. "Here, this is the front gate of the apartment building. Corrado lives on Staircase A, on the mezzanine floor. Shall we ring the doorbell and get them to let us in?"

Rocco nodded. Lupa caught up with them.

"Signora, I'm Tatiana, Corrado's friend. Could you let me in?"

"No!" replied a bitter voice, curdled by the passing years. The woman hung up the intercom. Rocco sighed. "What a pain in the ass." He rang the buzzer again.

"I said I'm not opening up!"

"State police, Signora, open up this fucking gate!"

The woman on the other end of the intercom thought it over. "Police?"

"That's right. Do it now!"

The old woman on the second floor did as she was told. They went into the courtyard and headed for Building A, and the woman looked out the window to keep an eye on them. As soon as Barbara looked up, the old woman withdrew behind the curtain.

They buzzed up to the tenant again to ask her to open the

apartment house entrance, a glass-and-metal door. This time the old woman didn't even reply. She just buzzed the door open.

"Where are we going to go now, though?" asked Barbara. "We don't have the keys."

Rocco said nothing. Corrado's door was the first one on the right. "I'm going to wear this damned thing out," said Rocco as he pulled out his Swiss Army knife. For a while now it seemed as if he hadn't been doing anything but picking locks. The good thing was that he was getting his old skills back.

"What are you doing?" asked the bookseller with a smile.

"What do you think, Signora?" And twenty seconds later the mechanism clicked the door open. Barbara and Tatiana exchanged an uncertain glance. Finally Barbara worked up the nerve to ask the question. "Can we be certain you're actually from the police?"

Rocco, with the door half open, looked at her. "Yes, Signora, do you want to see my badge?"

The policeman's glare set her back on her heels. "Stay outside, the both of you, what's inside here may not be a pretty sight."

He turned on the light. The two women did as they were told, but they still peeked in the doorway to see what they could see. Rocco went into the kitchen. There were two plates in the sink and a dripping faucet. Outside the breakers roared. Lupa followed him with her nose to the floor. She had turned into a veritable vacuum cleaner. In the bedroom the bed was unmade. In the bathroom he found a toothbrush and various toiletries. An empty bottle of hydrogen peroxide lay on its side in the bidet. The bathrobe that hung on a hook on the back of the door was dry. As was the shower stall. He went into the living room. There was a sofa with pillows on it. An old television set. A cabinet with bric-a-brac of various sorts. Next to the sofa, on the light-colored tiles, there were some very distinct dark stains. They looked like rust. Rocco bent down. He imitated Lupa and put his nose to the floor. No doubt about it.

Blood.

He prevented Lupa from licking the blood, and together they all left the apartment. He locked the door behind him. The two women's eyes were four question marks. "You don't think he was alone, do you?"

"No. There was someone with Corrado. But what did you find?"

Rocco's only response was to reach for his cell phone. "I'm calling police headquarters in Chieti . . ." he said.

Tatiana and Barbara listened in silence. Barbara threw her arms around her friend.

"Deputy Chief Schiavone . . . put me through to the mobile squad . . . Francè? Rocco Schiavone here . . . Fine, thanks . . . We've got a problem here in Francavilla. Via Treviso, 15 . . . I'll wait for you here . . ."

"What sort of problem?" Tatiana asked in a quavering voice, even though she already knew the answer.

"Signora, we're not going to be seeing Corrado again."

Only then, once she finally had the answer to the nightmare that had been dogging her footsteps for days, did Tatiana roll her eyes upward to the heavens and drop to the ground like an old used tissue.

LUPA RAN FREE ON THE DESERTED BEACH, HAVING THE TIME of her young life. She darted toward the water, barked at the waves breaking nearby, and tried to bite them. She was flabbergasted when she realized that the waves had no bodies and simply dissolved the minute she tried to sink her teeth into them. Rocco was sitting on the low wall, having turned over responsibility for the investigation to his colleagues from Chieti. Corrado Pizzuti had been murdered. But by whom, and for what motive? Searching the apartment, rummaging through all the drawers, in the armoire, and even in the washing machine, he'd found nothing of any interest except for the two plates in the sink and the blood on the floor. He could feel the burden of exhaustion settling down on his shoulders. The wind was tousling his hair. Far off in the midst of the waves someone was having fun launching a sailboat at full speed.

Beethoven's "Ode to Joy" on his cell phone shattered his thoughts. It was the office.

"Rocco, where are you?"

"In Abruzzo, Italo."

"In Abruzzo? Doing what?"

"A hefty helping of my own fucking business. What do you want?"

"Utter mayhem has broken loose back here! The police chief is trying to find you, the judge is trying to find you. An enormous development. There's a press conference in half an hour! Haven't you been listening to the radio?"

"No. Why?"

"There's been a roundup. The ROS have arrested the Turrinis, husband and wife, Walter Cremonesi, Luca Grange, and a couple of city commissioners over the thing with the public works contracts. This is serious business! When will you be back?"

"Fuck!" said Rocco. And ended the call.

BARBARA HAD PUT TATIANA TO BED. THE CPA DE LULLO was watching a TV program on Canale 5.

"Let's let her rest," the bookseller had said, and De Lullo had picked up the remote control and turned off the television set.

"So he's dead?"

Barbara nodded.

"Tatiana sensed it."

"Right."

"Why was he killed?"

"I don't know, Signor De Lullo, I can't figure it out. There was someone in the apartment with him, and probably whoever that was murdered him. I think it has something to do with his past."

A convulsive cough shook the CPA. Barbara ran to the kitchen, but by the time she got back with a glass of water, the tempest had subsided. "I'm sorry, I'm so, so sorry," he said, wiping his lips with a handkerchief. "I never did like that Corrado. But Tatiana did."

The bookseller lowered her eyes.

"Can I tell you a secret?" he continued. "No, I didn't like him one bit, but he was important. Because I don't have long to live. And knowing that Tatiana wouldn't be left all alone was a source of happiness to me. In other words, when your times comes and you have the luxury to tidy things up, you want to leave things behind you in some sort of order, no?"

"Please, let's not talk about this sort of thing, if you don't mind."

De Lullo laughed quietly, keeping his mouth shut. "What else would you expect from an accountant? It's a depressing subject, but why not talk about it? That's life." He looked around the apartment. "I'm leaving her this apartment. Now that the papers are ready, she can receive a small pension. But the thing that keeps me awake at night is this. Can she find anyone to take my place?"

Barbara didn't know what to say. She didn't want to answer that question.

"I mean it. For me, Corrado was a sort of insurance policy on Tatiana's happiness. She deserves it, you know? She hasn't had an easy life. All she's done since she was a little girl is work. All she did was study and work. She brought home money and good grades."

De Lullo looked at his own face reflected in the empty cathode tube. "She deserved something more than an old, dried-out husk. You know something, Barbara? I'm so rotten that they don't even want my spare parts."

"Should I make something for you to eat?"

"No, I'll just heat up a 4 Salti in Padella dinner. I have a box of gnocchi alla sorrentina."

In the other room, Tatiana had heard every word. Along with the tears she was shedding for Corrado's death, more tears ran down her face for the CPA. Then the two streams of tears joined together until they dried each other up. She got to her feet. She adjusted her blouse, pulled up the waist of her jeans, put on her slippers, and went into the kitchen to make dinner. If there was one thing her husband hated, it was 4 Salti in Padella.

ANOTHER SEVEN HOURS ON THE ROAD, FROM ABRUZZO BACK to Aosta, chased the whole way by the night, a healthy carrier of blinding headlights, and sudden surges of sleepiness. Lupa, covered with sand, was sleeping in the back seat. Rocco received five long and intricate phone calls, and he blessed the memory of whatever mysterious engineer had invented Bluetooth, allowing him to speak directly to his car radio and hear the voice from the other end of the line right through his stereo speakers, instead of drilling through his ear out of the earbud. The first, extremely lengthy phone call with the chief of police lasted from the Teramo exit to the Ancona South exit. Costa was bitterly bemoaning the fact that Schiavone hadn't been able to attend the press conference for the arrests. "The result of the concerted efforts of law enforcement, working together, Schiavone, including you!" Then there were the three phone calls with Baldi. The first lasted from Senigallia to Rimini North, with the judge thanking him for those documents and for the stunning revelation concerning Carlo Cutrì. "Don't worry," he had told him. "I won't mention your name. You won't be in any news articles tomorrow morning!" The second call lasted from Imola to Modena, and during it Rocco had had to explain to him every detail of what had happened in the prison, in the exercise courtyard, and the matter of the keys to Wing 3, four separate times. The third phone call with Baldi lasted the whole distance from Reggio Emilia to Milan South. In that phone call, the judge made it clear that the problem of arresting Cuntrera's murderers needed to be solved, and quickly. Now that the masterminds had been put behind bars for other crimes, the operation had to be carried out before the subjects could take fright and flee. Finally, at Pont-Saint-Martin, ravaged by the many miles driven in a single day, at 1:30 in the morning, as his eyelids drooped and his eyes grew puffy with sleepiness, there was the fifth phone call, this time with Anna, a call made up of silences, sniffing and blowing of her nose, lines like "I don't even know why I called you." After an initial aggressive onslaught that verged on the hysterical, it had slowly morphed into a confession. Anna was unhappy, she felt a void, both physical and existential, she was afraid that she'd lived her whole life the wrong way around, she no longer felt so much as a crumb of self-esteem. Finally, once Rocco had managed to direct the conversation onto the dead track of the final good-bye, Anna had unleashed a new and ferociously aggressive diatribe that had ended with the words "Go fuck yourself, Rocco!" minced through clenched teeth, and then a sudden end to the call. By the time Rocco parked his Volvo outside the Vieux Aosta hotel at 2:15 a.m., he knew two things: he needed to go to sleep, and he was never going to look at another woman as long as he lived.

THURSDAY

HANDS OVER THE CITY

Yesterday the officers of the DIA, or Anti-Mafia Investigation Directorate, under the command of Colonel Gabriele Tosti and the forces of the ROS, or Special Operations Group, carried out a roundup, arresting the members of a Mafia-connected profiteering ring that had taken control of numerous local public works contracts and had operated in the shadows, using as fronts a series of Italian-Swiss shell companies. A startling number of prominent local names were involved: Luca Grange and his brother-in-law Daniele Barba, chairman and managing director of Architettura Futura respectively; Dr. Berardo Turrini, head physician at the Aosta hospital, and his wife, Laura, former director of the Vallée Savings Bank; Walter Cremonesi, now a vintner, but also a former terrorist with ties to the Milanese underworld; and last of all, Carlo Cutrì, ostensibly Dr. Turrini's stable boy but actually a member of the Calabrian 'ndrina of the Mileto clan, tied to the kidnapping of Chiara Berguet, daughter of the well-known local businessman and builder Pietro Berguet, a kidnapping that in not even two weeks was resolved successfully due to the efforts of the officers at Aosta police headquarters. At the center of the investigation is the assignment of public works contracts for construction on the hospital and the regional medical clinics. Architettura Futura had won those contracts, scooping them out from under the nose of Pietro Berguet's Edil.ber.

It's a fine, memorable day for our city, but this cancer that had metastasized in the good and honest part of our society and which has been extracted by the painstaking and heroic work of Judge Baldi of the Aosta prosecutor's office ought to be a warning to the . . .

Rocco turned the page. He ought to have gone to sleep, to catch up on the hours of backlog; instead, by six in the morning, he was already on his feet and sitting down at the bar. Ettore's espresso hadn't helped him to regain consciousness, and reading the newspaper was even more boring than a dance recital.

COULD THE CUNTRERA MURDER BE RELATED TO HIGH-LEVEL ARRESTS?

And while the prosecutor's office and the DIA carry out high-level arrests throughout our city, harvesting the results of months of investigation and hard work, one is tempted to wonder just what has become of the case of Rue Piave. The murder of Adele Talamonti in the home of Deputy Chief Rocco Schiavone remains shrouded in mystery. No news escapes the black box of police headquarters. That case is being handled by Carlo Pietra, adjunct deputy chief of the Turin mobile squad, who has, however, been absent from Aosta for days now. The only news to emerge is that Schiavone has been sent to Varallo prison to investigate the murder of Domenico Cuntrera, a man with ties to the organized crime 'ndrina of the Mileto clan, responsible for the kidnapping of Chiara Berguet. One cannot help but wonder whether this prison inmate was linked in some way to the Mafia-connected profiteering ring that for some time now had been calling the shots and ruling the roost here in Aosta. At the prosecutor's office, however, lips are still stitched tight concerning the Talamonti case. That murder, possibly being covered up by the police force itself, is something that we never tire of asking about in the pages of this newspaper, loudly demanding explanations and results. Once again, yesterday, Police Chief Costa made no mention of the case, and in response to our insistent questions he responded

> evasively or simply chose not to answer at all. What is hidden behind the Talamonti case? What plots are being hatched in the highest offices at police headquarters in order to avoid exposing one of their own men to objective responsibilities and criminal sanctions? What are they waiting for at police headquarters and in the courthouse of this city? Why don't they begin a serious investigation and try to put a name and surname to the killer of the unfortunate Adele Talamonti?
>
> ——SANDRA BUCCELLATO

Maybe the time had come to go pay a call on this journalist. The woman wouldn't stop attacking him. But there was one thing he'd learned in all these years: Never respond. Never dive into the fray. That was exactly what Buccellato wanted. She was seeking a reaction, and if he stumbled into the trap, the woman would dine out on it for another three months. Instead, Schiavone had chosen the silent approach. Remote and unapproachable. Ignore those articles, go high when she went low, and thereby reduce those journalistic cannonades to mere blanks, loud bangs with no projectiles. To an attentive reader who had never seen a response from the deputy chief in the pages of that newspaper, it would be clear that the policeman wasn't going to waste his time getting into snarling matches, but instead was at his desk, working hard, bringing in results and earning his salary. Still, his fingers were itching. He'd love to get his hands on her. If the journalist had been a man, he would have gone straight up to the newsroom, he'd have grabbed him by the lapels, and he would have given him a sharp, hard head butt right to his nasal septum. But that wasn't something he could do with Sandra Buccellato. He crumpled up the newspaper and stood up from the little café table. "Let's go, Lupa!" The dog followed him, her muzzle dirty with pastry crumbs from the sidewalk.

HE SMOKED THE JOINT ON THE WAY FROM PIAZZA CHANOUX to the courthouse. It wasn't as nice as sprawling listlessly in his leather office chair, but it was still better than nothing. When he entered the prosecutor's office, the jolt of adrenaline prompted in the staff by the arrests of the day before hadn't entirely subsided. Dozens of people were circulating from one office to another, voices chased after each other in the hallways, a couple of Carabinieri in uniform were transporting file folders along with a court clerk. The door to Baldi's office was wide-open. The judge stood, bent over his desk, checking documents. Lupa lunged at the carpet to continue her labors where she'd left off.

"Schiavone!" Baldi walked over to greet him with a broad smile on his face—"What a day!"—and shook his hand.

"Yes, a really beautiful day. The sun is shining and—"

Baldi burst out laughing. "Who gives a damn about the sunshine! I was talking about the arrests!"

"Right. But there is still one thing—"

"Don't ruin it for me, please. I have some wonderful news for you. The public works contract is back on the table and Pietro Berguet is in the running. Happy?"

"Delighted. But now listen—"

"What?"

"The Cuntrera case."

Baldi leafed through dozens of documents until he found the two sheets of paper he was looking for. "*Promissio boni viri est obligatio!*

My word is my bond. Here are the arrest warrants for Daniele Abela and Federico Tolotta."

"Fine. But it's late, considering that news of the link between our investigations in prison and the roundup that you've carried out was already in this morning's newspaper. So there's someone that's leaking to the press."

"No one in the prosecutor's office!" As usual Baldi defended himself against such charges with all his body and soul.

"And no one at police headquarters. I can say that because no one at police headquarters even knew about it. All right, Dottore, it's the same old story. But like I was telling you on the phone last night, I need to add a third arrest."

"A third arrest?"

"Right. Amelia Abela, an escort by profession. She was the connection between the masterminds and the murderers."

"But this Amelia . . . Abela. Any relation to Daniele?"

"His sister. I checked it out."

"And just who are the masterminds behind the murder?"

Rocco thought it over. "Cutrì, Cremonesi, Turrini . . . all of the people involved in the thing with the public works contracts?"

"Why are you asking me?"

"Because there's something that—"

Baldi interrupted him, throwing both arms wide: "No, Schiavone, do me a favor! Banish all doubts! Don't rethink it all. Have you come to a conclusion? Well then, let's close the book on this matter, I say!"

"Yes, Judge, maybe you're right. Even though there's one thing that still doesn't add up, as far as I'm concerned."

"Let's hear it," Baldi said patiently. Rocco noticed that the photo of his wife had once again disappeared from the judge's desk.

"If we arrested Cuntrera and he had some papers with him that allowed you to make all those arrests, then why go to the trouble of eliminating him?"

Baldi shrugged. "Vengeance? Fear? In any case, Cuntrera was someone who knew too much. Maybe he'd threatened them, maybe he was blackmailing or extorting them: 'Get me out of jail or I'll ruin you once and for all . . .' And who knows what secrets he took with him to the grave. Secrets that it's going to be our job to uncover, by putting that little gang of sons of bitches that we've thrown behind bars to the third degree! What do you think, that when you arrest four people the war has been won? That was only a battle, Schiavone!"

Rocco looked at the judge. "You think so? Maybe so . . . why not? But I still need to ascertain whether there were contacts between Cuntrera and Cutrì during his detention."

"Fine. Check it out. Ascertain to your heart's content. And smile for once! This is a huge success for us!"

"One more thing . . . I'd have liked to arrest Cremonesi myself. Showing up after the party is over doesn't sit well with me, not one little bit."

Baldi smiled. "If you like, he's in there. He's waiting for his lawyer, that Ferretti. Messina and I are going to start grilling him. Would you care to have a little chat with him? Be my guest. It's a favor I'm glad to do you in the name of our friendship."

"Are you saying that we're friends?"

"Yes, at least for today."

HE WALKED DOWNSTAIRS WITH BALDI, FOLLOWED A COUPLE of hallways he'd never seen before, and came up to a door where a carabiniere was standing guard. The police officer snapped to attention the minute he saw the judge. "Is my colleague Messina in there?" asked Baldi.

"No, Dottore. Just Cremonesi."

"All by himself?"

"Yes, but we left his handcuffs on."

Baldi opened the door and invited Rocco to go in. "I'll wait for you upstairs . . ."

In the room, there were just three chairs and a metal table. Cremonesi was sitting down, shirt rumpled and unbuttoned; he no longer had the same arrogant demeanor as the last time they'd met. Only his eyes were still sharp and jet-black. His square head, reminiscent of the darting head of a venomous serpent, had snapped suddenly toward the door, impatient and on edge. "Well, well, look who's here," he said. The chain to the handcuffs that bound him to the table clinked. Rocco took a couple steps toward him. Then he leaned against the wall. He didn't want to sit down at the same table with that man. He wanted to observe him from a distance. "How's it going, Schiavone?"

"I'm fine. I told you that I was going to screw you over again . . ."

"Let the cyclone tear through, and after the dust settles, everyone will have forgotten about me and I'll be out again in no time, footloose and fancy-free. Do you want to know a secret? Prisons are literally leaky as sieves. They won't be able to keep someone like me under lock and key." And he flashed a smile that highlighted the scar on his chin. "Do you have a cigarette?"

"I don't smoke."

"Why have you come to see me?"

"Do you have anything to do with the Cuntrera murder?"

"Again? Do you seriously think that I would bother lifting a finger for a microbe like Mimmo Cuntrera?"

"Who just happened to have documents in hand that nail you? You, that is, and your fine friends."

Cremonesi spat on the floor. "Bullshit! Like I told you, two years, three tops, and I'll be back out on the street."

"That's what you think, Cremonesi. But you see? That might be true for Turrini, for his wife, for the city commissioner, and even for Grange. They're members of the upper middle class, they have political connections, they're still members of the respectable citizenry. But you? Where are your friends from Rome and Milan? They don't count for shit anymore, otherwise you wouldn't have come all the way up here to make wine. You'd have stayed in your apartment over near the Colosseum, am I right? Nobody's got your back anymore, asshole. And you're going to pay every last cent for that fact." He stepped closer to the criminal. "Here at the prosecutor's office they're a little vicious, you know that? They'll kick your ass to ribbons. And believe me, you'll get old in prison."

"I'll get out and I'll come fuck your wife."

"But you have some kind of obsession, Cremonè!"

"You're pathetic, Schiavone."

"Keep on trying to piss me off, and maybe that way I'll put my hands on you, now that you're handcuffed, and you can see what you can do with that before the judge. But here's the thing, Cremonesi, you're going down. And you're staying behind bars this time. And even if you were ever to get back out, I swear to you, I'll make sure I kick your ass black and blue and then straight back into a cell. By now, you're at the center of my thoughts." He opened the door. "And trust me, that's not a place that you want to be. Because I literally have nothing else to do with my time!"

A TUMBLEDOWN LITTLE CHURCH ON THE STATE HIGHWAY, houses scattered, seemingly at random, a crossroads, and an old streamer hung up between two trees, advising the citizenry of Pitocco, a small village near Vico nel Lazio, in the province of Frosinone, that in July the Sagra degli Aborti would be held. The Abortion Festival.

Or at least that's what Flavio Buglioni thought he'd read on the rumpled, faded streamer.

The gas station attendant, a man with a gut that could easily accommodate the contents of an entire mini-fridge, explained that this wasn't the Sagra degli Aborti, luckily, but rather the Sagra degli Abboti, a type of tripe roulade that in July must have been a rare delicacy. A mistake that anyone could have made.

"I'm trying to find the house of the cousin of a friend of mine. My friend's name is Enzo Baiocchi. But the cousin is a lady, and I don't know if she has the same last name."

"Don't you even remember what her given name is? What was she baptized?" asked the gas station attendant, chewing on the toothpick that he kept wedged between his black incisors.

"No. All I know is that they told me to ask where the crazy woman lives!"

"Ahhhh," said the man. "I know who you mean. But I don't know if she's still alive, you know? It's been years and years since I saw her last!"

"And can you tell me where she lives?"

"You need to go uphill . . . that way, you see?" And he pointed to a dirt road that wound up through the fields. "You go up about five hundred yards . . . you'll find an intersection, take a right, another five hundred yards and you're there. If the house is even still there, it's probably falling apart, and there's a stench of cat piss that could kill you. Anyway, she's a strange old lady. No one ever talks to her, you know? So, you need any gas?"

THE HOUSE WAS STILL THERE. SINGLE STORY, UNPLASTERED, and the roof had given way in two places. Sticking up in the middle of the terra-cotta roof tiles was an off-kilter chimney. The windows were so heavily mended with duct tape that there was no need of curtains to protect the intimacy and privacy of the inhabitants, that is, assuming that there even were any (inhabitants) and that they even had any (intimacy and/or privacy). A low wall surrounded the property. The rusting body of a Fiat Ritmo rested on four cinder blocks. Weeds infested what had once been a garden and now covered an old stone fountain with a circular basin, now empty of water. Atop the fountain was perched a moldy cupid. Flavio got out of his car and put on his sunglasses. May had run riot. Whitish puffs of pollen wafted through the air, and the perfume of flowers mixed with rust was spreading in all directions, gently pushed by the wind.

"Anyone home?" he said as he pushed open the remnants of an iron gate that had been eroded by the passing years. Halfway, the gate ground to a halt, stopped by a mound of dirt, and Flavio just barely managed to squeeze sideways between the sharp-edged iron gate and make his way into the front yard. Long ago, beneath the weeds and the wildflowers, there must have been a pathway in rammed earth. A lizard twisted behind a stone. The ants were busy, marking the dirt with black lines.

"Hello? Anyone home?" Flavio arrived at the front door. He was peering around in search of some cat, any sign of the presence of the mistress of the house, but nothing met his eye. There wasn't even the stench of cat urine, or any old bowls with remnants of food or water. An old doorbell had popped out of its hole in the wall, dangling in precarious equilibrium at the end of a pair of red electric wires. He didn't feel safe touching it. He rapped sharply on the wood with his knuckles. The door shook, and flakes of old paint showered to the ground. He waited a few seconds, then knocked a second time. Harder, this time. No good. He decided to walk over to the nearby window. He placed his hands against the glass and peered in. A room with a dusty floor and cracked terra-cotta tiles. There was a green velvet armchair, an old smoke-blackened fireplace. On the walls, small picture frames or photographs had left shadows of their presence on the wallpaper that was peeling away here and there. Some crumpled papers. A dust-covered table with chunks of plaster littering it, plaster that had dropped straight down off the ceiling. The state of neglect and abandonment was unmistakable. He moved away from the pane of glass and went back to looking at the house as a whole. He decided to walk around it—maybe there would be some sign of life in the back. Taking long strides in order to avoid stepping on dandelions and underbrush, he noticed a small building with the door torn off its hinges. He went over to it. Inside were two rusty shovels, a deflated wheelbarrow tire, and a saw hanging on a nail. A veil of cobwebs covered a series of empty bottles standing on a shelf made of crumbling, rotten wood. On the back of the house there were two windows. One had the shutters nailed closed; the other had its glass smeared with bird droppings and a crack running right down the middle. He tried to peer in, but all he could make out was an old bathroom, consisting of a toilet black with mold and a small bathtub streaked with rust. All that was left was the window with the shutters nailed closed. But there was no way to see inside that window. He didn't notice the fact, but the nails that held the boards in place over the shutters were bright and brand-new.

On the other side of that window, in the silence of the abandoned house, a shadow sat observing Flavio's face. That shadow was silently smoking. Safe in the darkness, he knew that sooner or later the annoyance would turn and leave. He only had to wait there, like a spider in ambush. And if Flavio did try to enter the house, the 6.35 mm pistol that he held ready on his thighs would do its job once again. The shadow smiled at the thought that, if he so much as tugged on that trigger, the pistol would kill none other than the man who had sold it to him in the first place.

Flavio stepped away from the window. He looked around. The grass was crushed underfoot, but maybe that had been him. "Enzo!" he shouted. "Enzo, are you here? It's me, Flavio! I need to talk to you!"

There was no answer. He retraced his steps, with another circuit of the house. He slipped back out through the metal gate that stood half open and got in his car. He took one last look at that teetering ruin and took off.

Enzo Baiocchi crushed his cigarette under the heel of his shoe. He lay back on the old mattress that had belonged to his aunt, picked up the Peroni, and drained off the last of the beer in a single gulp. He hurled the bottle against the wall and it shattered into a thousand pieces.

"Welcome back, Rocco!"

"Ring the church bells! Let rivers of champagne run! Mark this date on all the calendars as a red-letter day!" shouted the deputy chief. "Caterina Rispoli has learned to call me by my first name!"

Caterina blushed and almost wished she could take those words back and stuff them in her mouth. "Heh . . . heh heh . . ." she managed to say.

"Well, Caterina, what are you doing in my office at lunchtime?"

"You have visitors waiting for you. A married couple . . ."

"A couple?"

"It's the Berguets. They just want to say hello and thank you."

"What the fuck? No! What is this? Did I get married to them?" Rocco shouted.

"Sshhttt," said Caterina, lifting her forefinger to her nose. "Hush, or they'll hear you."

"I don't want to see them. I can't stand them anymore! First of all the wife has problems with her husband, then there's the daughter, then there's the husband, who's flipped out completely . . . What do they take me for, some sort of psychological counselor? Let them go to the national health clinic! Tell them . . . tell them you couldn't find me, that I'm dead, that I've come down with some sort of contagious disease, invent whatever bullshit you can think of and get them out from underfoot!"

"I can't. They know that you're here!"

Rocco thought it over. "Then, if they won't believe you, let them in, and that way they can see with their own eyes that I'm not here!"

Caterina made a face. "But if I let them in, they'll see that you *are* here."

"They won't see anyone but Lupa, trust me! And after you send them away, come back into the office and stick your head out the window!"

Caterina nodded, baffled, and left the room. Moving quickly, Rocco opened the window, clambered over the sill, and found himself outside police headquarters, on the roof of the canopy over the front entrance. He squatted down. He waited. He took advantage of the passing time to scoop up a few roaches from long-ago joints. A minute went by. There was no sign of Caterina. "What the fuck are you doing?" he cursed her through clenched teeth. He waited a little longer. Perhaps the time had come to go back into the office. How long does it take a person to stick their head in and see that the deputy chief isn't in his office? he wondered.

As he was being tormented by these doubts, he heard someone leave police headquarters, right under the canopy on which he was hiding. It was none other than Signore and Signora Berguet! If they had chanced to turn around at that instant, they would have seen him perched, balanced precariously, atop the canopy over the front entrance. A passerby in fact did look up and spotted him in that strange position. Rocco gestured to him to mind his own business and keep on walking. The man laughed and walked away. Just as the Berguets were opening their car doors, Rocco's "Ode to Joy" started to ring. With a feline lunge, the deputy chief flattened himself, legs and arms splayed wide, onto the roof. Pietro Berguet had looked up toward the second-story window, his notice attracted by the cell phone's ringtone. In the meantime, Rocco managed to extract the bellowing electronic device. It was Baldi calling. He had no choice; he had to answer. "Yes, sir, Your Honor," he said in a choking voice.

"I'm calling about something important. Daniele Abela and Federico Tolotta must have caught on. They've disappeared."

"Oh, fucking . . . What about Amelia?"

"She's behind bars. Do you want to have a chat with her?"

"We'll see . . ."

"What are you doing? Your voice sounds strange . . . forced. Are you climbing the stairs?"

"No," he replied, his back plastered against the roof. "Everything's fine."

"I'll tell you something else. The fact that the two guards took to their heels as soon as they heard about the arrests of the Turrini–Cremonesi group tells us all we need to know about their guilt."

"That's for sure . . ."

"Take care of yourself, Schiavone!" Baldi ended the call without saying good-bye. Rocco put his phone back in his pocket. Leaning out the window, a yard above him, was Deputy Inspector Caterina Rispoli, looking down on him as he lay flat on the roof. "You're not a well man, Rocco. It might be best if you came back in before the police chief looks out his window."

"Yes. Might be best . . ." Rocco got up and climbed back over the windowsill, with the deputy inspector's assistance.

"What did the Berguets say?"

"They seemed disappointed. But they wanted to make sure I thanked you . . ."

"Fine. What time is it now?"

"One thirty."

"Shall we go get something to eat?"

"Actually, I ate lunch an hour ago!"

Rocco heaved a sigh. "This bad habit you people have up here of scheduling your meals as if you were in a hospital!"

"Here he is! Mr. Deputy Chief!" A shout echoed through the office. Lupa barked. It was D'Intino. He was carrying an enormous sheaf of paper. "All done!"

"What?"

"The list of the foreigners. Now we highlighted everything nice and clear. And we're done with the hotels, too. What should Deruta and I do?"

"What should you do? I told you, didn't I? You need to draw me up a list of all the guests of all the hotels who came from Rome. Okay?"

D'Intino's eyes opened wide. "All of them?"

"Don't you feel up to it? Would you rather I left this very important and grueling task to Caterina?"

D'Intino glared at the deputy inspector with hatred and, stung in his pride, almost snapped to attention. "I couldn't let that happen, Dotto'! We started the job, now we're going to finish it!" And he turned on his heel with a smart about-face and left the office.

"Don't you have any more useful work for them to do?" asked Caterina.

"No. Plus what do you know? It might turn out to be very useful!"

"You asked me for Amelia Abela's address in Aosta."

"That's right, the address where she lives, not the one where she receives clients."

Caterina looked at him, slightly bewildered. "What do you know about where she receives clients?"

"I'm a policeman, Caterì, and there are certain things that policemen just know."

"Then why don't you know where she lives and you have to ask me for it?"

Rocco threw both arms wide.

"Huh . . . anyway, Amelia Abela lives on Via Laurent Cerise, right behind the courthouse."

"I'm going to go take a look at her apartment."

AMELIA LIVED ON THE FOURTH FLOOR OF AN APARTMENT house on Via Laurent Cerise, right where the police chief had found a place for him to live, at least in theory. Rocco had already prepared his Swiss Army knife and his credit card to open the door, but a man in his early sixties came to his aid. He was the building's doorman, and at the sight of that badge and ID from police headquarters, he'd hurried to get the extra keys to the apartment. "She's a good girl," he'd told the deputy chief, unlocking the door, which had been triple-locked. "She works for a construction company . . . Why on earth do the police need to come take a look at where she lives?"

Rocco laid a hand on the man's shoulder. "Your name is Paolo, right?"

"Paolo Chinoux," the doorman proudly stated.

"Well, Signor Chinoux, I'm afraid that somebody's trying to get Amelia into trouble. And I'll need a few documents to get her off the hook."

Paolo shook his head. "Eh, I hear you. These days, with the

public works contracts and all these other stories we hear, you need to keep your eyes wide-open."

"That's for sure."

Schiavone entered the apartment. The first thing that struck him was the extremely modern furniture and decorations. The rather spacious living room was lit by two windows overlooking the street. All the furniture was upholstered in light-colored leather, the same shade as the walls. The scent of tuberose flowers dominated over all else. "You can go, Paolo. I'll alert you as soon as I'm done."

Signor Chinoux backed out of the apartment like an English butler, shutting the door behind him. The policeman gazed around the place with a sinking heart. There were dozens of places to look—who could say how long this was going to take? For starters, he checked to make sure there wasn't a safe installed in one of the walls. He looked behind the paintings, in the bedroom, in the built-in armoires. He checked the bathroom and the kitchen. He even checked all the wall switches, well aware that the latest models of safes were built to mimic in every detail those switch panels. The whole search took more than half an hour. He took off his loden overcoat, tossed it onto the sofa, and got ready to look in all the drawers. He started in the bedroom. And this time his lucky star gave him a hand. In the nightstand, next to a little jewelry box, he found a small picture album with a leather cover. The third picture put a smile of joy on his face. He slowly drew it out of its plastic holder and slid it into his pocket. That piece of evidence would be more than enough.

"All done, Signor Paolo," he said as he walked out the apartment building's front door.

"Did you find what you were looking for?"

"I sure did! Amelia is safe and sound!"

He was tempted to add, ". . . and locked up tight in a prison cell," but he decided that wouldn't help matters.

He sat waiting for Amelia in the visiting room in the Aosta prison, a room that Schiavone knew well. A damp patch of discoloration in every corner, a plastic chair, a flaking window up quite high, mold-green walls. He was starting to be heartily sick of prisons. He leaned back, with his legs stretched out, and didn't move when Amelia Abela entered the room. She was wearing a pink tracksuit with a Swarovski rabbit design on the front. Pink running shoes without laces, her hair loose, and her eyes highlighted with an application of eye shadow, also pink. "Well, well, we meet again," she said, without the shadow of a smile. She sat down. The scent of tuberose assailed Rocco's nostrils.

"How are you, Signorina Abela?"

The woman laughed. "So we're back on formal, official terms?"

"How are you, Amelia?"

"Quite shitty, thanks. Now then, if you don't mind, I'd just as soon make this a quick chat, I'm not very interested in spending time with you."

"Why?" asked Rocco, looking at her.

"Because you're not very pleasant company."

"No, what I was asking was, why did you get involved in the plot to eliminate Cuntrera?"

"I don't know what you're talking about."

"What a pain in the ass," Rocco huffed. "It's always the same old tune. Come on, Amelia, your brother is in Varallo prison, and he's been singing like a bird to the magistrates for the past hour and a half. All I want to know is why on earth you chose to get involved."

Amelia scrutinized Rocco before answering. "I don't believe you."

"My ass, you don't believe me." He pulled a cigarette out of his pack and lit it.

"So smoking is allowed in here?" the woman asked.

"It is for me. But not for you." And he took a long generous puff. "Don't make me drag out the old standby line of how, if you cooperate, they'll go easier on you, but the fact is: if you cooperate, they'll go easier on you. You didn't know Mimmo Cuntrera, so why did you drag your brother into it? For money, I'd have to guess . . . The people who paid you are behind bars just like you are, and it's only a matter of time before they talk. You see? Aside from Cremonesi, who's used to being in jail, they don't have the slightest idea. Doctors, bank directors, architects, half-assed politicians. Prison's going to have a bad effect on them all. All I can tell you is this: beat them to the punch. You could get off easy if you admit that all you did was put them in touch with your brother."

"Is my brother really in such bad shape?"

Uh-oh, missed the target, thought Rocco. "Your brother is screwed, and he's dragging you down with him. He says that he doesn't know why he was supposed to eliminate Cuntrera, he just obeyed orders that you gave him." Rocco dropped his cigarette on the floor and crushed it out.

"I don't believe it."

"Amè, do as you please. But you knew that that guy was named Carlo Cutrì, not Dodò, the whole time!"

"Who? Dodò? Who's that?"

"All right, then, let me show you these nice pictures that an eager young officer of mine took at the Ristorante Santalmasso a few days ago." He pulled an envelope out of his pocket. He chose the first photo and showed it to Amelia. "You see? It's you with Cremonesi, and right here, with his back to the camera, is old Dodò, who wasn't Turrini's stable boy, but actually Carlo Cutrì . . ."

"This photo doesn't prove a thing!" And she handed it back to the policeman.

"Which is why I brought this one, too!" And now he extracted from the same envelope a second photo that depicted Amelia and Carlo Cutrì, arms around each other and broad smiles on their faces. In the background, two horses were grazing in a meadow. "You recognize this picture? Look at the back!"

Amelia turned it over. On the back was written: "Winning Mood—May 2nd, 2012."

"Where did you get this?"

"At your house. Not where you receive your clients, the one on Via Laurent Cerise. It takes some nerve for you to live right around the corner from the courthouse. But given your current situation, it might prove convenient for your lawyer. You know what? Someone found me an apartment on that same street, but I turned it down."

"I had a hundred thousand euros riding on that horse, Winning Mood," Amelia said with a bitter smile. "He's a born champion, you know that?"

Rocco smiled. "You're up to your neck in shit, Amelia. Think it over. It's like in baseball. Do you know how baseball works?"

"No."

"If the batter makes it to base before the ball, then he's safe, but if the fielder catches the ball before he can slide to base, then the batter is out! It's the same thing with investigating magistrates. Get to base before they do. And you just might be safe." Rocco stood up, dragging the chair across the old cement floor. "You've got time to think it over. Take care of yourself!"

For dinner, they'd chosen the Enoteca Croix de Ville. Rocco and Alberto Fumagalli were sitting at their table, sipping a Fumin while waiting for dessert, two chocolate gateaus that made their mouths water at the very sight of them. The two men had mopped their plates clean, and in fact, Alberto had even ordered a second helping of chicken piccata.

"This is the first time we've eaten dinner together," said Alberto. "Are you feeling emotional?"

"'Disgusted' is the adjective I'd actually been thinking of." Then he raised his glass—"A toast to you, for having found Cuntrera's killer"—and they both drained their glasses in a single gulp. Alberto filled the glasses again. "And now let's drink to the death of the guy who broke into your apartment!" They drained their glasses again. "Any news on that?"

"Maybe something's starting to move, but the only thing I can be sure of is that the guy was in prison. Otherwise he would have struck sooner."

"Or maybe out of the country?"

"Or maybe out of the country."

A young woman brought the desserts. Alberto didn't even give her time to set down his plate before attacking the gateau. "It looks like you haven't eaten in a lifetime."

"Am I paying or not?" said the doctor through a mouthful of cake. "So, if you don't mind . . ."

The gateau melted in his mouth.

"Can you tell me something?" the medical examiner inquired. "Why do you look so sad?"

"Really? I do?"

"Yes, you do . . ."

"It happens to me all the time."

"But you look sadder than usual."

"It's hormonal, if you ask me. When I get to the end of a trudge through shit like this, it hits me hard."

"But you ought to be happy about it, actually. You caught them, you threw them into prison . . . Oh, well . . . just don't think about it and focus on the gateau."

"Anyway, I have a bad feeling."

"About what?"

"The murder in the prison. I have a feeling that things didn't go exactly as we think they did. It doesn't add up, I can't quite see that group of upright citizens as masterminding the murder of that poor wretch Cuntrera. I'm certain that there's something I'm missing."

"Sleep on it. Things will look clearer tomorrow morning."

"Now that we're far away from the morgue, the dead bodies, the blood, and all those other amenities, I have a confession to make."

Alberto stopped chewing and gave Rocco a level look. "You're a homosexual?"

"No. And even if I was, you're the last man I'd try to hook up with."

"I'd actually have given you some serious consideration . . ."

"All right, so are you interested in hearing this confession or not?"

"Go on!"

"You're an invaluable person. And I thank God that I found you here. Without you, things would have been much more difficult."

Alberto wiped his mouth, laid the napkin back on his knees, and took a sip of wine. Rocco followed suit. They sat in silence until the check came.

I ATE TOO MUCH. I CAN'T GET TO SLEEP. I OUGHT TO LEARN from Lupa. I get obsessed with staring at this light on the ceiling. Pink.

"After all, we're leaving here soon," I say. To no one. There's

nobody here. Just me and a sleeping dog. The pink goes from pale to dark, then purple. One two three. One two three.

You're not here. You're not coming back. Then you meant what you said. "Did you mean what you said?" My feet and my hands are cold.

"I read something about quanta. There are particles of the electron that only appear in reality when they collide. Then they disappear. Did you know that?"

Where do they disappear to? There's something they've never told us. Something that every once in a while appears here, in our world, but then, just as fast as it appeared, it goes away again, leaving no trace behind it. Not even a smell.

"Where are you?"

She's right to leave. On this side there are teeth, blood, and claws, Marina. They cut, they scratch, they make you bleed. Look at how my skin has been ruined. I look like I'm covered with tattoos.

But if I shut my eyes, I see her. With her back to me. Sitting on the beach. I call her name. She doesn't turn around. I call her name again. "Marina, will you answer me?" Her shoulders are shaking. She's laughing. Then, slowly, she turns around. But the sun blinds me and I can't seem to glimpse her face. She's raised a hand in front of her eyes, to block the light. She blows me a kiss.

FRIDAY

Italo, excuse me if I disturb you in my own office," Rocco said upon entering the room. The officer was stretched out on the sofa, holding some photographs in his hand. "Say, do you feel like adding another pain in the ass to the chart outside?"

"Sure, tell me which," he replied, sitting up.

"Intrusion upon other people's existential perimeter. I know that to you, it's an incomprehensible concept, but put it at the eighth level. No, wait, make it ninth."

"Intrusion upon . . . ?"

". . . other people's existential perimeter. You know what I'm talking about? Everyone has their own spaces, their personal times . . ."

"That's the same thing that Caterina says." Italo got up. He had a sad expression on his face. He actually scratched Lupa between the ears.

"Is that why you were here? To suffocate me with your love story?"

"No. I was here to tell you that the judge called. Daniele Abela has been arrested in Sanremo. He had twenty-five thousand euros in cash in his backpack."

"Was he planning to gamble them away?"

"Got me . . . but the other guy, Tolotta, not a sign of him yet."

"Well, where do you expect he's going to get away to?"

"I just happened to be looking at this photo . . ." And he held it up for Rocco to see. It was the picture of Amelia with her arm around Carlo Cutrì.

"What about it?"

"I've seen this girl before."

"On the Internet. She's an escort."

"But I don't look for that sort of thing on the Internet."

"What do you want from me, Italo? You must have met her just walking around Aosta. She's a good-looking girl, she struck your imagination. Or wait, no! Now that I think about it. Of course you've seen her before. The other night when we went to pay a call at the Turrini home, you remember?"

"Do you think I could forget it?"

"She was there. She came out of the house with all the other guests."

"You think?"

"I do. It's nine o'clock now, so if you don't mind, could you let me have the room?"

"What do you need to do?" Rocco was about to reply, but Italo beat him to it: "Your own fucking business. Understood, sorry . . ."

The officer left the room with his head low.

The young man needed a vacation, Rocco decided. He sprawled in his chair. The time had come. He pulled out the key and opened the locked drawer. He grabbed a joint and lit it. Before he even had a chance to exhale the first puff, the sound of the telephone clawed into his ears. He picked up the receiver. "Schiavone here . . ."

"Come upstairs!" It was the police chief.

"What's going on, Dottore?"

"I said come upstairs!"

HE FOUND COSTA SITTING AT HIS DESK. SERIOUS EXPRESSION on his face, which was gray in spite of the sunny day.

"Sit down!" And he pointed Rocco to the chair in front of his desk. Costa handed him a newspaper. "Read!"

Rocco opened it. On the page was a headline that hit him like a punch in the eye:

IS THIS HOW THEY SPEND TAXPAYERS' MONEY?

Under that headline, a photograph depicted Rocco hunkered down on the roof of the canopy over the front entrance to police headquarters. There followed an article, frothy and ironic, about the activity of the state police in the city, and of course the usual sharp asides about the Rue Piave case, still shrouded in the most absolute mystery. And, no surprise, the byline of Sandra Buccellato.

"I'm certain that you must have a million different explanations to offer me, Schiavone. But I only want one. The real one. What were you doing out there?"

"I was running away."

"From what, if I might ask?"

"From the Berguets, man and wife. They'd come in to thank

me. I've had to sit through three sessions of psychoanalysis with mother, father, and daughter. I'm sick and tired of them, I've got them pouring out of my eyes."

"And in order to avoid them, you climb out of the window of my police headquarters?"

"It was a hasty, reckless act, I recognize that, but dictated by desperation more than any other—"

Costa burst out laughing. "I swear to you, Schiavone, this goes right up there with the video clip of the De Rege brothers taking on the narcotics peddlers. I'm going to have it framed!"

Rocco didn't know whether he should laugh, too. One thing was certain: in that instant the entire city, including the prosecutor's office, was looking at that photo. Including, perhaps, Signore and Signora Berguet. "You look like a colossal ass, Schiavone. The kind of thing that might merit a transfer to the far end of the peninsula."

"I'll happily accept the offer!"

Suddenly, Costa stood up. "Instead, what I wanted was to congratulate you. You've done an excellent job. And don't worry, I can wrap these print-media journalists around my finger, I have a press conference at noon. This time, as you'll understand, I'm not going to invite you to attend. What is the official version of your exceedingly . . . feline, shall we say? . . . presence atop that canopy?"

"I was fixing a leak?"

"No."

"A safety check?"

"What are you, a fireman?"

"Why don't you give me a suggestion?"

"You were on the roof to get your wedding ring, which you'd carelessly dropped."

"My wedding ring?"

"That way we insist on the fact that you're a family man, that you care about maintaining a commitment, and we conjure up a romantic aura around your person."

"My wife is dead, Dottor Costa."

"That's a trivial detail."

"Not really, not to me . . ."

"I know that. But desperate times call for desperate measures . . . You know what these news vendors are like, don't you?"

"Speaking of which, do you know this Sandra Buccellato?"

Costa nodded like a wise old man. "Do you want the truth?"

"We're talking with our hands on our hearts, Dottore."

The police chief drew a deep breath. "She's my wife, or really, I should say, my ex-wife."

Rocco's jaw dropped in amazement. "Your ex-wife?"

"Right," the police chief admitted gravely.

"The woman who dumped you for an editor at *La Stampa* is a journalist now?"

"That's not all. She's even moved back here from Turin."

"I can't believe it."

"Believe it. And anyway, I'll get her in my line of sight one of these days. You know the saying? The world spins from east to west and sooner or later . . ."

"Is that a threat?"

"No, that's geography." And he smiled, baring his teeth.

"Do you realize that that woman has been attacking me in article after article for days now? And it's all your fault!"

"Schiavone, what are you talking about? If anything, I'm the one who ought to have it in for that bitch! She abandoned our conjugal roof, though perhaps I shouldn't make any mention of *roofs* today. Let's just say she dumped me from one day to the next! She just has a grudge and a running feud with the police force as a whole. And you are a member of that force. Even though, if you'll give me this point, that statement continues to ring very strange to my ear. On that, at least, I think we can agree?"

"I would say so."

"YES, THEY ALREADY SHOWED IT TO ME AT POLICE HEADquarters," said Rocco at the sight of the newspaper that Baldi, with a smile on his lips, had tossed on the desk in front of him. Lupa was scrupulously refraining from chewing on the imitation Bukhara. She lay there pensively, observing the window, her attention no doubt attracted by the curtain cords.

"I find it hilarious. The policeman on the roof! I swear to you that this is the first time I've ever seen anything of the sort!"

Baldi was in a good mood. The photo of his wife had magically reappeared on his desk. Offering tit for tat, or perhaps just to get an explanation once and for all of all those comings and goings, Rocco asked him straight up: "As long as we're talking about photographs, would you tell me why your wife's photo keeps vanishing from and reappearing on your desk?"

Baldi furrowed his brow. "My wife's photo? This right here? What are you talking about, Schiavone? It's always been here, it's never moved!"

Instead, Rocco raised his eyebrows skeptically. "Really?"

"Certainly. Why would I ever remove it? She's my wife!" But he didn't say it with total conviction. He seems to be reciting a script he'd memorized. "Now, let's talk about Cuntrera. Those people," he went on, referring to the band of white-collar criminals who had just been arrested, "deny any and all connection with the murder. The only one who isn't talking is Cutrì. He's involved up to his neck. Turrini and his wife claim they've never even met Cuntrera.

They're lying. The kidnapping of Chiara Berguet formed part of a very subtle plan, you know?"

"That part's clear to me. When they took her, they were operating on two levels. The grimy, obvious level of ransom, which is where Cutrì played the predominant role, and then the secondary level of discrediting the company."

"That's right. By suborning Berguet's right-hand man so that he could be shown to be a member of the gang that had kidnapped Chiara and undermine Edil.ber's credibility once and for all. And I believe that it constitutes a valid motive for eliminating Cuntrera."

"Why, because he could have revealed that understanding?"

"Exactly!" And Baldi slammed a fist down on the desk. "The kidnapping. The agreements that they had established. Clever, I say. What about that escort, Amelia, the guard's sister, anything new out of her?"

"Nothing. Obviously, she knows all about it. All it would take is to find out who gave the twenty-five thousand euros to her brother . . ."

"Difficult to do. We're monitoring the bank accounts, but do you know how hard it would be for Turrini to reach out to one of his Swiss corporations and withdraw that money to pay the killer?"

"Not hard at all."

"DOTTOR SCHIAVONE!" CATERINA RISPOLI'S VOICE ECHOED behind him.

"Are we back on a formal basis?"

Caterina lowered her voice: "No, but, I mean, in the middle of the hallway, maybe it would be better . . ."

"Tell me, what's up?"

"Two phone calls. Officer De Silvestri, Cristoforo Colombo police station, Rome."

Rocco hurried to his office, closely followed by the deputy inspector. "The officer said it was urgent. What's this about?"

Rocco dialed the number of his old police station hastily. Caterina didn't know whether to stay or leave the office. Rocco waved her to a chair.

"Cristoforo Colombo police station, who's caaaalling?"

"Officer De Silvestri please . . ."

"Who should I say?"

"Deputy Chief Schiavone!"

Background noise. Footsteps in hallways, bursts of static. A printer in the distance, then more footsteps.

"Dottore?" came the familiar voice of Alfredo De Silvestri.

"Alfrè, what's happening?"

"Do you remember that little research project you entrusted me with? The search for persons who might have escaped from prison, or else been recently released?"

"Of course I remember. By the way, I chanced upon a corpse. Or rather, they haven't found the corpse yet, but we know for sure the man is dead."

"Who?"

"Corrado Pizzuti. The one who was missing."

"Then I was right about that."

"All right, so tell me all about it!"

"A couple of weeks ago there was a prison escape. From the infirmary of Velletri prison. At the time, I didn't give it much thought. But then I looked back on it, connecting it back to Pizzuti . . ."

"Who is it?"

"Enzo Baiocchi!"

Rocco hung up the phone without saying good-bye to his old friend from Rome. He rummaged anxiously through D'Intino and Deruta's papers. All colored like so many rainbows, they looked like a class project done by a third-grade pupil. He found his officers' last note. Corrado Pizzuti had stayed at the Hotel Piedimonte, in Pont-Saint-Martin, on the evening of May 9!

He turned pale.

"Why didn't I read them before this, asshole that I am!" And he slapped his forehead with an open hand. Caterina watched him, the deputy chief's eyes were glistening. He blinked his eyes rapidly, as if an electric shock were darting through his body.

"Listen, Caterina, I'm going to have to be away for a while, I need to go to Rome and—"

"No!" the deputy inspector protested. "You've just driven all the way to Abruzzo and back, you have dark circles under your eyes. Do you think you can leave me here with the dog to stand guard over D'Intino and Deruta? You have Antonio for that. And Italo, too."

"Are you trying to keep me from—"

"I'm not trying to keep you from anything. I'm coming with you, and I'll do half of the driving. But only if you explain to me just what's going on."

"The murder at my house. We may have a name to go with it."

"All the more reason, I'm a cop, and I'm working on that case."

"Caterina, I—"

"This isn't a suggestion. It's an order!"

Rocco smiled. "And since when does a deputy inspector give orders to a deputy chief?"

"Since the deputy chief in question has started thinking like a teenager high on Ecstasy!"

"You can't come in uniform."

"I have a change of clothes in my office!" And she shot out the door.

Rocco ran to the desk. He took the keys to the car. "Lupa!"

The puppy came over to him. "Listen to me. Be a good girl with Caterina!" And he hurried out of the office.

THE VELLETRI HOUSE OF DETENTION STANDS ON AN ELEVATED plain not far from Cisterna di Latina, in the Agro Pontino, or Pontine Marshes. In the midst of that valley—once a marsh, since drained, originally inhabited by anopheles mosquitoes and butteri, or Italian cowboys, who challenged Buffalo Bill, but nowadays a stretch of countryside inhabited by Asian tiger mosquitoes and members of the Camorra who defy the Italian state—the prison looms high like a cement abscess.

Rocco knew the warden, and also a couple of guards. They conducted him to Pavilion C, the infirmary, where Enzo Baiocchi had made his escape sixteen nights earlier.

"He escaped from the ward by removing a bar from the window, and then in the courtyard he waited for the trash truck, he must have climbed onto it and made his escape . . ." said Francesco Selva, the prison warden, an extremely youthful-looking forty-year-old. "We searched his possessions. Nothing that could offer a clue. We went to talk to his daughter, who lives in Rome, on the Via Casilina, but she says she hasn't seen him or heard from him. Let's just say that she had a less-than-wonderful relationship with her father."

"Do you mind if I take a look around myself?"

"Absolutely, be my guest."

Selva took him down to the storeroom where they kept the convicts' possessions. "They've cut personnel to the bone, and the place has turned into a colander. Nothing's secure."

Rocco nodded.

"Staffing levels are down by at least forty percent. Brutal hours for poverty wages. You tell me how we're supposed to keep up . . ."

"They'll declare a nice fat amnesty and kick a bunch of prisoners out onto the street. Like always."

"Right. Can I tell you what I think?"

"Certainly, Francè."

"They ought to legalize soft drugs. Do you know how the prisons would empty out?"

"I couldn't agree with you more . . ."

They passed through two metal doors controlled from inside, and then, at last, a guard came toward them with a box. He entrusted it to the warden and then turned away. Francesco set it down on a metal table. "Okay, so this is the stuff that Baiocchi left us to remember him by."

The deputy chief opened it up. A couple of T-shirts, a silver bracelet. A porn mag, and inside it a holy card. Saint Franco Hermit. "Was he religious?"

"He used to pray."

"Strange place to hide a holy card, don't you think?"

The warden leafed through the magazine. After the third image of fellatio he tossed the magazine back into the box. "Yes, I'd say so."

"Saint Franco Hermit. Do you have an encyclopedia?"

"In the office."

"IT SAYS HERE THAT HE'S THE PATRON SAINT OF FRANCAVILLA al Mare, Chieti province. That adds up," said Rocco with the volume balanced on his knees, sitting in a green Naugahyde chair.

"What do you mean?" asked Selva from the desk where he was reading through the file of the now ex-inmate of his prison.

"Baiocchi was from Rome. Like his family, am I right?"

"You are right."

"So why would someone named Enzo keep a holy card of Saint Franco Hermit? Does your file tell you what his father's name was?"

Selva leafed through the pages. "His father's name was Giovanni, his mother's name was Concetta, a brother named Luigi, and a sister named Clara. No Franco, no Francis."

Rocco turned the pages of the encyclopedia. "In fact, a religious man named Enzo, which is short for Vincenzo, would have a Saint Vincent holy card, wouldn't he? Instead, Saint Franco Hermit. Who's not even a saint anyone's ever heard of."

"So why do you say that it adds up?"

Rocco shut the encyclopedia. "It's a message that he received from who knows who. He was trying to track down Corrado Pizzuti, obviously, and someone informed him where he could find him. So he's the one who killed him."

"Enzo Baiocchi killed . . . ?"

"He killed Corrado Pizzuti, a two-bit hoodlum. And he killed Adele Talamonti, a dear friend of mine." Rocco set the encyclopedia aside. "I have to catch this guy."

IT WAS A MAY NIGHT IN ROME, THE KIND THAT GRABS YOU BY the stomach and takes your breath away, when the scent of the linden trees finally overwhelms the smell of exhaust fumes, and the Tiber was no longer a slow ooze of slime moving lazily down to the sea but a ribbon of gold wrapped around a gift-wrapped present. The stars were all out, and so was the moon. From Furio's terrace overlooking the Tiber Island, you could see the line of traffic along the Lungotevere and the pedestrians slaloming between the cars stopped at the red light. A girl was leading a balloon along on a string tied to her wrist. Furio came out with a tray and, on it, four mojitos. "Here you are . . ." And he distributed the glasses to his friends, then sat down. He lit a cigarette and listened. Seba was looking Rocco in the eye, while Brizio had his legs stretched out and was toying with a nail clipper. The wind was tossing the sago palms in their terra-cotta vases.

"All right, Rocco, we're ready," said Seba.

"I found out who it was. And unlike what you and Brizio have done, I share the information I obtain."

Sebastiano sniffed. Brizio went on toying with the nail clipper.

"What can I tell you, Rocco? We figured out who had committed the armed robbery and—"

"I know everything. Luckily I have at least one friend who tells me things!"

Seba glared daggers at Furio, whose only response was to give him the finger.

"And what did you find out?"

"Enzo Baiocchi."

Brizio and Furio leapt in their chairs. Sebastiano instead remained impassive.

"He escaped from Velletri prison sixteen days or so ago. Then he killed Corrado Pizzuti."

"Corrado? Wasn't that the guy who was driving the car all those years ago?" asked Brizio.

"The very same."

Seba cracked his knuckles. "Did he do it to avenge his brother?"

"I'd say so," Rocco replied. "And Adele paid the price."

There was a long silence, a good solid ten seconds. Everyone was lost in thought.

"What are we going to do?"

"You promised me, Rocco. He's mine." And Sebastiano smiled, even though he had just uttered a threat. "I need to rip the heart out of his chest!" he added. "That's what he did to me, isn't it?"

Brizio nodded. Furio was looking at Rocco. He knew that the deputy chief wanted to be the first to lay his hands on the prey. And that he wasn't going to give him up so easily. "Do you have any idea where he might be hiding?"

"No. I know that he has a daughter . . . She lives on the Via Casilina," said Brizio.

"There's no way that rat is holed up there. That's the first place anyone would look for him. Where did he kill Pizzuti?"

"At Francavilla al Mare, Furio. A city in Abruzzo."

"No, I can sense that he's not in Rome."

"Why do you say that, Brì?"

"Because it would be risky for him here. Too risky. A tip, a rumor as faint as that western wind, and he'd be done for! No, he's holed up somewhere solid. Maybe he even went back up to Aosta, don't you think?"

Furio looked at Rocco. It seemed as if he were asking whether Rocco still had the pistol within easy reach at all times. Actually, though, the handgun at that moment was locked in a desk drawer in his office.

"That's true, he might head back up north. But now there's a difference. He's no longer a shadow. Now he has a first and last name!"

Sebastiano picked up his glass. He raised it. "To the death of Enzo Baiocchi, may he spit blood by the gallon!"

His three friends joined him in that toast.

"*Que reste-t-il de nos amours . . .*" Someone out in the street had just struck up an old French love song.

"These fucking tourists," said Brizio, wiping his mouth with his shirtsleeve.

SATURDAY

He hadn't been able to get a wink of sleep in his old apartment on Via Poerio. As he lay half awake, dreams and memories had piled up, along with sex fantasies and places he'd never been in his life but which he knew, strangely, like the back of his hand. It was all jumbled together in a tangled clump of brightly colored threads. It was pointless to try to sort them out; they were knotted together, and the best thing to do was to let his mind float free like a kite, allow himself to be possessed by this illogical sequence and watch it as if it were a film by a Czech director, without subtitles. He greeted the first faint rays of sunlight as manna from heaven, a vacuum cleaner that sucked away all those cobwebs, restoring a realistic view of the world. The bed, the furniture wrapped in plastic slipcovers, the walls of the room, Marina's paintings, the three framed photographs of her, the armoire. He took a shower and walked out onto the balcony. He looked at the plants, uncovered the lemon trees under their winter shrouds. Rome spread out beneath him, with its gleaming roofs that reflected the early shafts of sunlight. A few clouds appeared in the distance, toward the sea. The flowers wafted their perfume into the air, and dozens of insects were buzzing power dives to their petals, ready to suck the nectar and dirty their feet with pollen. Rocco looked at his reflection in the window, in boxer shorts and undershirt. He had the sensation that he was the only thing in black and white around there.

When he got back to Aosta police headquarters, after six hours in the car and with the taste of the cigar still in his mouth, Italo came toward him with an even more depressed look on his face. "Were you in Rome?" he asked him. Rocco nodded.

"Maybe it's not important. But since yesterday I've been thinking over and over about it, and I finally remembered."

"If you'd only tell me what the fuck you're talking about, then maybe I could join in."

"The escort, you know, the one in the photo."

"Amelia. Well?"

"I was right, I've seen her before. And it wasn't the night we broke into the Turrini property."

"Oh, no?"

"No. I saw her outside the Hotel Pavone, in Nus, a few days ago."

"Wait, didn't you tell me that the Hotel Pavone was a place for lovers having illicit trysts? I don't see anything strange about that."

"No, neither do I, but it's something I couldn't get out of my head, and finally I've nailed it down."

"Excellent, Italo. Good job!" And he slapped him on the back. He headed off toward his office. Then he froze with his hand on the doorknob. He turned around. Italo was heading toward the criminal-complaints office.

"Italo!" he called after him.

"What is it?"

"At the Hotel Pavone in Nus, you say?"

"That's right."

"But wasn't that with Pietro Berguet?"

"Exactly. You remember? I told you that his wife had been right when she said that her husband was stepping out on her."

Rocco nodded. "Where's Caterina?"

"Her?" Italo said contemptuously. "She was up in the police chief's office. Do you need to talk to her?"

"Yes, and right now!"

Rocco Schiavone and Deputy Inspector Caterina Rispoli got out of the car and started walking up Via Aubert.

"Let me understand . . . Lupa is at your apartment, right?"

"Right," Caterina replied sarcastically. "And I'll give her back to you when I'm good and ready!"

"Are you mad at me?"

"You bet I am! You took off and left me standing there like a complete fool. I was supposed to come with you to Rome! At least tell me who it is!"

"Not now. When you bring me back my dog."

"If you want her, you have to come get her. I'm not at your beck and call. I'm a police inspector, not a dog sitter!"

Rocco sped up his pace. "You really resort to some ignoble extortion."

"But at least I keep my word."

"Are you sure that this perfume store is well stocked?"

"It's the best one in the city, trust me. What did you say the perfume was called again?"

"Carnal Flower."

"Never heard of it . . ."

"INDUBITABLY, SIR, YOU HAVE EXCELLENT TASTE." THE woman behind the counter in the perfumery shop, slightly zaftig, dressed in an elegant knee-length navy-blue skirt-and-jacket ensemble, raised her finger to her lips accompanying the gesture with a complicit little smile. "I'll get it for you right away . . ." Swaying dizzyingly down the row of shelves, she pulled out a drawer in a briar-wood cabinet. The dozens of mirrors in the shop echoed the same image of Rocco in a rumpled corduroy suit and a pair of Clarks desert boots of an undefined blackish hue and the deputy inspector's uniform, which hung on her body with all the elegance of a burlap bag draped over a Bernini statue.

"It's an exclusive perfume for a special niche market . . . very, very commendable." The woman came back to the counter with a box in hand. Black and red. "It's a perfume by Frédéric Malle," she whispered, as if they were discussing a shipment of heroin to be peddled on the streets of the city.

"Forgive my ignorance, I don't know who that is," said Rocco. "Have you ever heard of him?"

"No," Caterina replied.

The shopkeeper's eyes opened wide. "He's the grandson of Serge Heftler-Louiche, one of the founders of the *maison de parfums* Christian Dior!" And as she shifted into a distinctly French pronunciation, she pursed her lips like a chicken butt.

"*Mon dieu!*" exclaimed Rocco.

"You see? Here, we're not talking about just some perfume, but about perfume *par excellence*. I don't have a tester, as you can imagine, this isn't some supermarket perfume." And she laughed at the very idea. "Would you care to sample?"

"May I?" asked the policeman.

"*Bien sûr!*" the woman practically shouted. She extracted the perfume bottle as if it were a holy relic, removed the top, and gestured for Caterina to extend her wrist. "Now be careful," she said, "I'm only going to spray a tiny bit. On your skin. Whatever you do, don't rub it!"

"No, no," said Caterina, intimidated.

"You know? Many women, interested in getting a strong whiff of the scent, make the mistake of rubbing perfume on their skin, and then forget about it! There's a radical change in scent. You have to give the essences enough time to settle into the dermis and interact with the skin. Let me have your wrist."

Slowly, Caterina extended her wrist toward the woman, looking at Rocco, who rolled his eyes elaborately. He'd already had his fill of that whole routine.

Psst! A quick spray and the scent filled the room.

"It's certainly very nice," said Rocco. "Tuberose?"

The woman smiled happily. "Yes," she said, closing her eyes as if confessing to who knows what sins. "Tuberose. The queen, the very symbol of the *haute parfumerie*! You have a sharp nose." Then she looked at Caterina. "And excellent taste, if you don't mind my saying so."

"Fine. Excellent. Caterì, do you like it?"

"I'd say . . . It's very nice indeed."

Rocco pulled out his wallet. "How much is it?"

"Listen, only because it's you—"

"Why just for me?"

"Because you have a good nose . . . it's one hundred seventy euros."

Rocco didn't bat an eye. Caterina intervened: "No, Dottore. What are you doing?"

"Allow me, Caterina . . . Do you take Visa?"

"*Mais bien sûr.*"

"*Ça va sans dire!*" And Rocco gave his credit card to the woman, who moved her bulk to the cash register.

"Why, no, Dottore . . . I can't accept."

"What are you doing? What am I going to do with it? It's a perfume for women . . ."

"You put me in an awkward position. Well, you could always give it to one of your—"

"You have the wrong idea about me, Caterina . . ." And he went over to the cash register to pay. "And I hereby order you to stop addressing me as 'sir,' even in public, and never to use the formal with me, otherwise I'll take it back." The shopkeeper ripped the receipt from the machine.

"Wait, you're . . . you're colleagues! I had assumed that between the two of you—"

"No, Signora, the young lady just arrested me and I've been trying to bribe her."

The perfume store clerk gazed in bewilderment at Caterina, who was in the meantime flashing a smile with every tooth in her mouth.

They went back to the car. They didn't say another word the whole way back. Caterina held the package with the perfume; Rocco smoked a cigarette. He had been transformed. His eyes had turned sad, glazed over, and the corners of his mouth twisted downward in a bitter frown. Even his hair seemed to have lost its body.

"Where . . . where are we going?"

"You're going back to the office. I'll take care of this on my own."

"Why have you gone all sad?"

"Because I'll never get used to reality, Caterina. The years go by, I see the filth over and over again, but I can never get used to it."

"What reality . . . What are you talking about?"

"Finding the truth, Caterì. That's my profession. That's what they pay me to do. Not much, but they do pay me. And every time I discover the truth, I wish I could close my eyes and pretend that it wasn't. But the facts speak loudly, my young friend, and they're unmistakable."

Caterina couldn't understand. She was looking at the deputy chief, and he had transformed right in front of her eyes.

"It's the shit, Deputy Inspector Rispoli. The shit that is constantly overflowing, and I can't stand the stench anymore. That's all."

THE SECRETARY HAD KNOCKED ON THE DOOR OF THE PRESIdent's office. She'd gone in. Then she'd reemerged with a bright smile on her face. "Please, Dottor Schiavone . . ." And Rocco went in.

Pietro Berguet stood up from his desk and walked toward him, arms thrown wide. "I owe you my thanks, Dottor Schiavone! Thanks to you and the prosecutor's office, my company—"

Rocco interrupted him with a brusque gesture, raising his hand flat in front of him. Pietro stopped halfway, as if he'd just been punched in the nose. The two men looked into each other's eyes.

"Why?" asked Rocco.

"Why am I thanking you?"

"No. Why did you do it?"

A timid smile appeared on Pietro's face as he held his breath. "I don't . . . I don't understand."

"Amelia Abela. The escort."

Pietro exhaled and relaxed. "Dottore, I know. But we're all men, and I wouldn't want you to think of me as a . . . a whoremonger, that's the word. It was a moment of weakness, I beg you to—"

"Pietro, I'm not here from the vice squad. I don't care either way who you go around screwing. I'm asking you why you were in cahoots with Amelia Abela and her brother."

"In cahoots about what?"

"About Mimmo Cuntrera, Berguet. You were the mastermind."

Those words landed with a glacial frost in the room. "The mastermind? I ask you, have you lost your mind?"

"Judge Baldi is reviewing your checking accounts. And recent transactions. He's pretty sure that somewhere in there we're going to find a withdrawal of at least twenty-five thousand euros, money that you gave Daniele Abela, plus something for his worthy colleague Tolotta. And a lavish tip to Amelia, too. Or am I wrong?"

"Dead wrong!"

Rocco pointed his finger at the desk. The perfume was still there, surrounded by its wrapping paper. "You don't give gifts worth a hundred seventy euros to an escort if you're contacting her for strictly professional considerations. That right there is a gift that you give to a woman you love, or someone to whom you owe a debt of gratitude. You want me to tell you the way I see it?"

Pietro Berguet's face had become a shard of gray slate.

"Maybe the first encounter was just a product of chance, or maybe not. The fact remains that you somehow learned about her family ties and the plan formed spontaneously in your mind. A clean and simple plan. A disreputable piece of shit like Cuntrera—how many different people wanted him dead? You wanted to take revenge for your daughter, and that's understandable. Only you overdid it."

Pietro burst into nervous laughter. "You're leveling a very serious accusation against me. And I believe that, at this point, our conversation is going to have to end here. From now on, we'll speak only in the presence of my lawyer!"

"Certainly, Dottor Berguet, of course. But you know something?

Make sure you have a good lawyer, because Amelia Abela is already talking with *her* lawyer. The young lady has everything to gain by giving us a hand. And you have everything to lose. That's not all, either. We've just arrested the brother with the swag. As for his worthy confederate Federico Tolotta, it's only a matter of time. Now, please accept a piece of advice from someone who knows the inside of this country's prisons very well. Two prison guards, two correctional officers, are not going to have an easy time behind bars. Whatever house of detention they might happen to wind up in. Let me just put it this way: in the interest of improving the treatment they can hope to receive from the courts, those two would be willing to sell out their mothers. So you understand, Dottor Berguet? You're up to your neck in shit."

"It's time to say good-bye, Dottor Schiavone."

"I hope you have a good day. One last thing, though. If you'd been satisfied to live your life instead of becoming a fucking out-of-control vigilante, today really would have been a wonderful day for you. Edil.ber would have won those contracts, everything would have gone back to normal, Chiara would have forgotten, and there would be a smile on your wife's lips again. You're just an idiot and a loser, Berguet. A miserable, small, insignificant man."

"I won't accept lectures on morality from you!"

"It wasn't a lecture on morality. It was a mere statement of fact."

"Get lost!"

LUPA JUMPED RIGHT AT HIM, MANAGING WITH AN EXAGGERATED leap to actually lick his face. Sitting on her Ikea sofa, Caterina observed that reunion with a serious expression.

"Did you miss me, little one? Have you already eaten your dinner?"

The panting of the dog and the chirping of the cuckoo clock marking the hour were the only sounds. There was a lovely scent of violets, and every corner of the little apartment had a story to tell. Books, photos hanging on the wall, two small African statuettes, and a collection of teacups.

"You have a nice place here. I understand . . . Italo would just clash with it."

"You're not getting off so easily . . ."

"Easily how?"

"The name!" said Caterina. She was still wearing her uniform. Rocco looked at her and she brushed back her hair. "Rocco, I want to know!"

The deputy chief went over to the window. "His name is Enzo Baiocchi. He's a bandit who escaped from the prison of Velletri."

"And why does he have it in for you?"

"It was July 7, 2007. My wife and I had gone out to get a gelato. I'd lost a bet, a silly trifle, a game we liked to play. On our way back, a car pulled up next to ours. Inside were two men. Corrado Pizzuti was driving, and Luigi Baiocchi, Enzo's brother, was in the passenger seat. I barely had time to turn around. Baiocchi had a pistol in his hand. He fired two shots. Instinctively I ducked. Marina didn't. She didn't duck. The first shot went right through her throat. The second hit her in the left temple. She didn't even have time to understand what . . ." His voice died in his throat. He shut his eyes. He bit his lip. Caterina had turned pale. She couldn't even move a finger, as she knit her hands together. Rocco resumed his story: ". . . what had happened to her. She was gone in a flutter of wings. One moment she was sitting next to me . . . A second later I was holding her head . . . and her blood was flowing down my hand. I was trying to close up the wound with my fingers."

He turned to look at the sky out the window. The colors were fading; he felt as if he were looking at an oil painting, vivid and luminous, that was slowly fading, being transformed into a faint, delicate, nuanced watercolor. Then a drop of water fell and the whole thing melted into a muddled, indistinct stain. In the end, night fell.

Caterina was behind him. She touched his arm. She looked up at Rocco's face. She dried his tears.

"I'm sorry . . . Forgive me."

"What have you done wrong? You're not to blame."

The woman stood up on tiptoes and gently pressed her lips against Rocco's. Her tears mixed with saliva. She grabbed his head, clasping tight the hair on the back of his neck. Their lips parted; their tongues met. Rocco wrapped his arms around her waist and pulled her close. Then they separated.

"No, we can't . . ." said Rocco in a low voice.

"No," said Caterina, looking down. "We can't . . ."

SUNDAY

It was a Sunday full of chores to get done. Rocco had taken possession of his new place on Via Croix de Ville. A lovely apartment, spacious and full of light. There were exposed beams on the ceiling and a wooden floor. It was nicely furnished with rustic antiques and a black lacquered Chinese armoire. The roomy bedroom had a window overlooking a small piazza. There were frescoes on the facade of the building across the street, and the balconies were full of flowers. If he avoided looking up, he didn't have to see the mountains, looming dark and ever present. It took him ten minutes to move, just enough time to bring Lupa, her new bed, and his clothing. That was all he had with him. He'd decided to leave his few books as a gift to the next occupant of his apartment on Rue Piave.

The deputy chief had done his best to distract himself by watching Serie A soccer matches, but a depressing tie score in a home game had killed any desire he might have felt to listen to the arguments of sports journalists on television. By now it had become clear to him that the eleven A.S. Roma team members in their red-and-yellow jerseys didn't so much have any problems in terms of technical skills, but rather a serious case of some mental pathology. More than one trainer seemed to have urgent need of psychiatric care.

No important news from Rome. Seba was on the trail of Enzo Baiocchi, but he seemed to have vanished into thin air. He'd literally demolecularized.

He thought about Caterina. It was a sweet thought, fresh and clean like the flowers that dotted the balconies on the buildings across the way. He would have liked to walk with her through those streets, stop for an espresso, fill his lungs with the May air. Maybe right at that moment she was looking out her window, just like him, thinking the same things. He looked over at the cell phone on the table in the living room, but his hands remained frozen in the pockets of his trousers. Because it was different with her. He couldn't behave the way he had with Nora, or with Anna. Caterina was a very different matter. Every time that he saw her, he had the impulse to hug her, to hold her tight and protect her from the bad things in the world. He got lost in that young woman's eyes.

Well? What are you afraid of?

Of a word. Of a simple word that he wasn't even capable of imagining. He felt as if he were being watched by the shadows, by that mist that wouldn't disperse from his mind and his home, from the years past that weighed like boulders on his shoulders and his eyes.

Go on, say it! It's not like it's all that hard.

All he had to do was say it out loud and everything would change. It would all become simple and straightforward.

I'm just an old man who's got some crazy idea into his head.

He stepped away from the window. Despite the fact that it was

Sunday, Maurizio Baldi had summoned him to the prosecutor's headquarters, and Rocco got ready to go to his office.

"ALL RIGHT, THIS IS THE WAY THINGS STAND RIGHT NOW. We've found withdrawals from Berguet's account for no less than fifty thousand euros, the president of Edil.ber is in Brignole and he's hiding behind a team of three lawyers. Federico Tolotta was found and arrested at his mother's house in Catanzaro, Daniele Abela has already made a full confession. Let's just say that the Cuntrera case is closed now."

Rocco nodded.

"Don't you have anything to tell me?"

"About what?"

"What happened in Rue Piave. Why did you go to Rome twice recently?"

"To investigate."

"And have you had any luck?"

"No," said Rocco. "I'm fumbling in the dark."

The judge gazed at him seriously. "I don't believe you."

"I'm sorry, but that's the way it is. I went and delved into the mud, but I couldn't find the snake."

"Do you feel safe here?"

"Safe enough."

"Whoever it was, they might come back, right?"

"You're right. But you see, now I know they might come back. And it's very unlikely that they'll catch me off guard this time."

"Shall I tell you how I see things?"

Rocco nodded and crossed his arms on his chest, ready to listen.

"You know perfectly well who it is. But you won't tell me. And you want to know why not? Because whoever it is that wants to kill you is interested in revenge for something from your past. Something that you did, something that you're keeping secret, something that"—and here the judge drew closer, lowering the volume of his voice—"it might be better to keep hidden, Schiavone. Tell me if I'm wrong."

Rocco did nothing but shrug his shoulders.

"You've been here since September. Nine months. And by now I know a lot about you. I haven't been sitting around twiddling my thumbs. We know the reason for your transfer, we know about your rather unorthodox methods. And we also know about your dubious friendships down in Rome. Sebastiano Carucci, Furio Lattanzi, and Brizio Marchetti. Three real pieces of work. You meet them in Rome, and not only in the past two days. No. You have ongoing relationships with them and you frequent them assiduously. In particular with Sebastiano Carucci, Adele Talamonti's boyfriend. And it's my belief that the four of you have uncovered something. Something that you have no intention of sharing with us." Baldi picked up a pen and started twirling it between his fingers. "Do I need to remind you that your first and primary allegiance is to the established institutions of this country? That your duty ought to be that of bringing a killer to justice? Or when something touches you directly and personally, do you forget that detail and act like an ordinary street thug, like one of your friends from Rome?"

"Are you done?"

"I could go on for hours."

"Why don't you judge my performance in terms of what I do. Not what you presume I'm doing. And if you don't like what you see, you can always file a complaint with the big bosses and get me transferred somewhere else. What do I know? To Sacile del Friuli or to the Gennargentu. Believe me. This city, you, these mountains, I won't miss any of it. Now if you're quite done lecturing me like a concerned head of household, I've got places to be."

"This hardening of attitude on your part tells me that I hit the bull's-eye."

"This hardening of attitude on my part is due to the fact that I don't like having my balls busted on a Sunday."

"Why, did you have anything better to do?" asked the judge.

"Look at me, Dottor Baldi. And look at yourself. It's a holiday, but the two of us are spending it in an office. Your wife's photograph has vanished from the desk once again, I lost my wife more than five years ago, we're two trains on dead tracks, and if they took this away from us"—he waved at the room around them—"we'd wind up in some old folk's home, sitting in rocking chairs staring at a blank wall. You and I are just dragging ourselves along out of inertia, Dottore. You cling to your work and your rules out of desperation, I hold on to those three sons of bitches I have for friends down in Rome. But I couldn't tell you if you're right, or I am."

"I keep my word when I give it."

"So do I." Rocco stood up. "And in any case, when I find out who did it, my intention is to put him behind bars."

"In Velletri prison?" Baldi asked with a smile.

"You see? You know more about it than I do."

"Why does Enzo Baiocchi have it in for you?"

"It's an old gripe."

"How old?"

"Let's say . . . dating back to 2007. A few years back."

Baldi picked up a sheet of paper that had been lying before him on his desk. "Two thousand seven? And yet here I read that you arrested Enzo Baiocchi only once, in 2003." He laid down the sheet of paper and leveled his eyes right at Schiavone's. "Did you just mix up the dates in a moment of distraction? Why should he want to make you pay for an arrest back in 2003? He was out on the streets for two more years before being remanded to prison once again in

Velletri. Help me understand . . . Is this a personal vendetta, or is Enzo Baiocchi making you pay for something else? More or less like our Pietro Berguet?"

"Find out for yourself!" said Rocco, and turned to leave the judge's office.

HE WAS SITTING AT THE USUAL REFRESHMENT STAND, NOW closed, in front of the Arch of Augustus, watching the few cars driving around it, as if it were a sort of merry-go-round. He was thinking back to Enzo Baiocchi and his brother, Luigi. Back to an August evening, hot as a pizza oven in a restaurant full of people, with sweat pasting his shirt to his skin. He had the taste of iron in his mouth, and his heart felt as if it had stopped beating, in an abandoned auto repair shop not far from the Rome beltway. Light poured in through windows filthy with dust and cobwebs. The car door wouldn't open; there were guns, shaking hands, the stench of piss and fear.

Fear.

Fear had become a person in flesh and blood, and was standing there, among them, to remind them that in any case they were people, made of blood and nerves. And memories that would torment him in the years to come, from morning until the depths of night, until the day finally came when he'd shut his eyes for the last time, forever and ever, abandoning body, brain, and regrets to the earth, to the worms, to the plants.

By now he had reached the banks of the river Dora. He noticed that the sun was out. He took the Ruger that Furio had given him. He threw it out into the river waters. The pistol disappeared, sucked down by a whirlpool. He switched off his cell phone, put his hands in his pockets, and turned around to head home.

ACKNOWLEDGMENTS

I want to thank in particular Laura, Giovanna, Francesco, Marco, and Valentina and everyone at the Sellerio publishing house, who work tirelessly beside me. And Cristina and Monica. A special thank-you to Toni and another to Fabrizio.

What follows is a list of Rocco's friends. The reason they are here is something that they and only they (and Cristina, it goes without saying) know: Carla Zamper, Antonella Imperiali, Antonella Poce, Vesna Draskovic, Miriam Caputo, Francesca Ghiglione, Monica Malpeli, Monica Dal Fante, Simona Donna Rumma, Danilo Fattorusso, Sonia Cremonese, Laura Corvatta, Barbara Corvatta, Annetta Cinque, Giulia Favero, Valentina Azzarone, Sara De Luca, Enrico Magli, Giuliana Di, Marita Lo Iacono.

—A. M.